Ghosts, Goblins, Murder, and Madness:
Twenty Tales of Halloween

Edited by
Rebecca Rowland

www.DarkInkBooks.com

First Published by *Dark Ink Books*, August 2018

www.AMInkPublishing.com

Dark Ink Books is a division of *AM Ink Publishing*. *Dark Ink* and *AM Ink* and its logos are trademarked by *AM Ink Publishing*.

for Kevin Bell,
and a Halloween as Shaggy and Daphne

"…all that the morn shall greet forlorn,
The ugliness and the pest
Of rows where thick rise the stones & brick,
Shall someday be with the rest,
And brood with the shades unblest."

-*Halloween in a Suburb* by H. P. Lovecraft

Contents

Asking for It
JR Pepper

It was amazing how it got worse and worse every year. Halloween became more and more drastic, heinous.

Sexy nurse.

Sexy witch.

Sexy police officer.

Sexy Barack Obama?

Good Lord.

It was great if these girls wanted to break out of their normal, everyday wardrobe. It was fine if they wanted to dress as a fantasy, so as long as it was *their* fantasy, not some teenage boy's late-night, basic cable porn fantasy.

Short skirts, heavy makeup, low-cut tops, knee-high stockings, crippling shoes… this was all well and good, but did they have to make the outfits from fabrics that were so damn cheap? None of these costumes were remotely warm, and almost all of them were see-through.

She absentmindedly held a hand to her face. When exactly did she grow to be so jaded? Was she growing that old? Every year the costume options for women got worse, more fetish than masquerade, but even she had to admit they did gather attention.

The men claimed that women in these costumes were "asking for it."

Asking for what, exactly?

She cast a glance across the space, observing the denizens of the bar. The girls to her left seemed determined to do as many shots of tequila as possible, for better or worse.

One of them, who had recently lost a boyfriend, had no problem drunkenly telling everyone in earshot while her friends drunkenly gave their support and ordered more shots. Silly girl, copious amounts of Mezcal were certainly not going to bring him back, nor would the tears that came afterwards. Meanwhile, the TV above the bar detailed the annual parade a few blocks away. It would not be long before the cascades of people leaving the parade route would fill up every bar and nightclub within a ten-block radius. She used her tongue to tease the olive from her drink, wrapping it around the little alcohol-infused fruit before sucking out its juices and devouring it. Savoring it.

It was not the best drink she'd ever had, but certainly not the worst one either.

She realized that the stupid holes in her fishnet stockings were stuck around her toes and pulling at her skin. *They may be fashion-forward, but they itch like hell*, she thought to herself.

The bar began to fill with various types of costumed idiots. They flooded in, already half drunk, loudly calling for shots or beers as they ripped off their masks of civility. This night used to mean something; Halloween used to be the night where the dead were freed to roam the Earth again. Jack-o'-lanterns, which were once left outside to scare away specters, are now decorated with cartoon characters. Hell, people used turnips back in the day. Whole families would wander the streets for soul-cakes; now, they purchase individual-size packets of raisins. Halloween costumes were supposed to scare away spirits. Nowadays, the only thing frightened away is the hemline on most costume dresses.

The bartender clearly could not be bothered with the Halloween festivities. She wore a simple pair of light-up devil horns. "Sorry, miss, but the bearded dude at the end of the bar said he'd like to buy you your next round. For the record, you are under no obligation to take it," the bartender said, breaking her reverie for a moment.

Well, that was certainly nice of her to add.

"No, that's quite alright. If he's paying, I'll take top shelf vodka this time." She smiled and winked at the bartender.

"Hell, I hear you," said the bartender, "but if you need me to get him to back off, let me know."

The offer made her chuckle to herself. She couldn't reassure the bartender that she wouldn't need any help, so she merely smiled politely. Her eyes turned to the bearded man at the opposite end of the bar. He wore a white shirt which was unbuttoned at the top and a hipster mustache.

Clearly, he couldn't be bothered with the Halloween festivities either. Perhaps he is an artist, or a writer? Maybe a poet…

Are there even poets anymore? Isn't everyone just a blogger now?

Either way, he was some kind of creative.

And those creative types made the most amazing evenings.

They were not the dashing suits she craved, but they were beyond nourishing. What they lacked in style, they made up for in passion. They had all the vigor of a teenager and reeked of lust. Men like that tended to be the best rush of adrenaline in the world, but unfortunately, they faded away just as quickly.

Ah, the best thing about these pseudo-Bohemian hipster types was that they adored her. They liked her traditional, flirtatious nature. They usually liked her better when she was pushy.

They liked when she dominated.

Then again, so did she.

After her new drink arrived, it wasn't long before the bearded man came over and began speaking to her: "Nice costume. I didn't realize doctors wore fishnets?"

He smiled while he spoke. She liked that.

"Yeah, I figured sexy doctor was a bit more progressive than sexy nurse," she quipped.

"Absolutely. I wager all the best hospital uniforms include fishnets and five-inch heels these days." He leaned onto the stool beside her as he spoke in an effort to isolate her from the rest of the bar.

He introduced himself and said his name was Patrick. He fumbled with his phone while he talked to her and explained that he "Ummm doesn't usually do this but…"

The damned phone. This entire generation with their fucking phones. It would be so easy, and so incredibly satisfying, to just "accidently" spill a drink on it. Patrick explained that he recently started work for a web developer. He mentioned that he was on call and apologized vaguely, though he never looked up from his phone's glaring screen.

She didn't care.

Frankly, Patrick seemed pretty nondescript. Hell, most men these days do.

Thick-glasses? Check.

Beard? Check.

Nautical tattoo even though he has never actually been on a boat? Double check.

She missed the suits. She missed the day when men smelled like men, not the gluten free, free trade, organic coffee from whatever gentrified coffee shack these people came from now.

He was still talking.

Why?

Why *the hell* was he still talking?

She placed her long hand on his and whispered something about him needing to take a break. He worked too hard, she told him. His bespectacled eyes followed her long fingers as they froze in a vain attempt to cover the scars on her arms.

Perfect.

It was clear she would have to change her approach. The dominating female would not work on this man. He was already too controlled by the electronic communications he so desperately clung too.

She would have to be the coquette.

She hated the coquette.

She would have to be the fantasy female, or what she liked to call "princess mode." She would have to become something that he could rescue. She fumbled out the words, "Oh, I'm so sorry about the scars, I used to ohh, um…"

"I'm sorry, I didn't mean to stare," he said.

He had clearly observed the deep scars that ran along each of her forearms.

Liar.

Looking down at her side, she fidgeted with her hands and blushed.

Blushed!!

It took every bit of her self-control not to laugh at the sorry state of herself, but it worked. He reached around her and pulled her close. He explained, "You don't have to talk about it, unless you want to. I completely understand."

So, that was his game. She realized she had been careless in her original approach. He preferred the self-destructive, manic-pixie "dream girl" type. How cliché.

"Maybe we should get out of here so I can hear you better?"

He put the phone away in his pocket. "Sure," he said, cocking his head with a grin.

Got him.

They leaned on each other, giggling as they walked out, until they passed a nearby corner. Suddenly, Patrick pushed her into it, placing his hands on the wall on both sides of her head. "I really like your costume, but don't you feel vulnerable and exposed dressed like that?"

She could smell the cheap whiskey from the happy hour "white trash special" on his breath as he spoke. It wasn't unpleasant, but it reminded her a bit of burnt leather. He continued, "You don't feel like some people might think you're asking for it?"

She could feel a deep-seated anger boiling beneath the surface of her skin as he spoke, but she forced herself to mask it. "Why would I?" She hated herself as she said it.

Patrick leaned in, held her chin in his right hand, and asked, "Can I kiss you?"

She hated that they asked now, but so many of them now thought women belonged to them, that they were owed something, or that they were entitled to a woman's attention. However, asking permission could mean that they were genuinely kind or concerned. It could mean that he was *actually* a nice guy who really cared—that maybe he was a good person. Or, it meant that they were trying to cover their asses, just in case they were taken to court later and are asked the question of "consent" was ever brought up.

She nodded and looked up at him with her big eyes. She slurred on words as if she was drunk, swaying a bit on purpose to gauge his reaction. He didn't seem too concerned.

He kissed her, lightly at first and then rough and rougher still. She felt his hand reach underneath her skirt.

No, no—clearly, he wasn't genuine.

She had been right from the beginning.

Playfully, she smacked his hand away and felt him grab her neck—hard—in response. "Do you like that?" he whispered in her ear. She could feel his words move through her earrings like a warm wind.

She gasped. Patrick had caught her by surprise; she always expected them to be a little less brazen. There was that anger again, boiling to the top.

She felt his hand moving up her leg again, and then she heard him scream.

With her left hand, she forcefully pulled on his unmanaged beard and reached to cover his gaping mouth. She couldn't let him scream again. She sighed, "Great, now I've got blood on my shoes. Hope you're happy."

Patrick finally had the presence of mind to look down as his cell phone dropped, shattering on the ground. There, among the shattered glass from his smartphone, were three of his fingers, severed and covered in a dense red slime on the filthy pavement.

"Good luck using that fucking phone now, asshole," she quipped. "God, I've been waiting for an excuse to use that one all night, can I just tell you?"

Her other hand reached down and grabbed him by his bleeding wrist and forcefully flung him away from her. Patrick fell hard against a nearby brick wall. He hadn't noticed it, but her nails had pierced deep into his flesh. They were long, pointed, black and— metallic?

Patrick thought to himself, *How the hell could I not have noticed that?*

She wiped the dripping blood from her nails on her arms, causing them to leave deep, open wounds amidst her already cavernous scars.

Hiking her skirt back up, she looked up to the starry sky above as the sounds of new wave music from the bar pulsated through the air. Crowds of costumed people walked through the streets in front of her. No one noticed Patrick bleeding on the ground; they were too lost in the revelry of the evening.

Sexy nurse.

Sexy pirate.

Sexy robot.

Maybe she would see another sexy Obama before the night was out.

When her gaze went down to meet Patrick's again, her eyes had changed. They were now deep yellow with slits from side to side. He looked into her cat-like eyes and felt a deep-seated fear fill his body. Patrick had forgotten all about the bleeding stubs that used to be his fingers when he felt something warm and wet on his cheek—her tongue. It was long and purple, and a thick slime covered his cheek as it massaged his face.

"Do you want me to stop, Patrick?" she asked.

But he had been asking for it. He had practically begged.

Tenants

George Plank

The key slipped effortlessly into the lock, and the sound of tumblers clicking into place soon followed. The doorknob turned quickly—with purpose. The elderly hand of the landlady pushed the door open for the young man who wore a very excited look on his face.

"And here's the apartment," said the woman. "I'm sorry—I'm terrible with names. Would you mind reminding me?"

"Grant. Charles Grant, but my friends call me Chuck."

"Well, Charles, I'm sure you'll like it here. Would you like the grand tour?"

Chuck nodded his head, and the two of them began exploring the expanse of the 300-square-foot studio apartment.

The landlady was highly energetic, despite appearing to be somewhere in her mid-eighties. Mrs. Gokiburi, a first-generation Asian-American immigrant, led the tour with her smile and cracked a few jokes over the coziness of the apartment. She had been married years ago, but after her husband died, she sold their house and bought several apartments. To this day, she is always highly recommended by her tenants, almost all of whom familiarly call her "Mrs. G."

Chuck laughed along with every joke that she lobbed at him. He needed to make a good first impression. He had lived in a few less-than-stellar apartments over the past few years, and after being evicted from his last place, he had been couch-surfing for the past two and a half weeks.

His hoodie was well worn even though it was only about a year old. As far as jackets go, it wasn't particularly heavy, so it was ideal for these late October days. The days were becoming shorter, and the early approach of night brought with it a chill that meant that summer was definitively over. Chuck saw his hoodie as his last defense against the cold before he would have to buy a new winter coat; he had been forced to give his old one up because living couch-to-couch afforded him no extra space.

It was by good fortune that he saw a listing for a small studio apartment in an independently run local newspaper to which he had forgotten he subscribed. He called the number in the classified ad, and Mrs. G gave him a specific time and place to meet her. Chuck thought to himself that she must have used the time before his arrival to tidy up the apartment because it was so clean—almost immaculate.

"How long has this place been available?"

"Not very long." Mrs. G said with a comforting smile. "My last tenant left rather abruptly."

Chuck was completely blown away by this. Between the cleanliness of the apartment and the low cost of rent, he couldn't imagine anyone wanting to leave, especially without warning.

Mrs. G must have sensed Chuck's unease because she added, "He never seemed to get along with my other tenants."

The tour concluded in the apartment's kitchen nook. It was a small space, but it offered enough room for some mobility while cooking—not that that was a selling point for Chuck: he could hardly make an oven pizza without burning the crust. The walls were lined with shelves that appeared to have once held a wide array of spices and other cooking essentials. Across from a gas range stove was a refrigerator;

though it was not, the clean whiteness of it made it appear to shine like new.

Just as the pair turned to leave the kitchen, Chuck's eyes were drawn downward by sudden movement. A small brown dot moved across the white tile of the floor directly in front of the doorframe. As if driven by instinct, Chuck's foot came down swift and hard on the roach. There was a loud crunch under the sole of Chuck's used sneakers.

Chuck lifted his shoe to reveal a sticky brown stain on the floor where the roach had once been. Mrs. G let out a large gasp and clutched her chest in surprise.

"Dear, I am so sorry that you had to see that. We've never had a problem with roaches in this building before." Mrs. G clasped her hands together and leaned forward a bit. Her posture and nervous smile gave Chuck the impression that she was bowing. She was clearly very embarrassed by the sight of a roach on her clean tile floor.

"It's alright, ma'am," he reassured her. "I saw a lot worse at my old apartment. It's nothing I haven't had to deal with before—and it's nothing that a few cans of aerosol pest control can't fix."

Chuck laughed quietly to himself all the way to her office. He also told her some of the horror stories from his previous apartments along the way and expressed how grateful he was to be in a place that was so well maintained.

In her office, Mrs. G told him that the rent was always due on the first day of the month. It was September 28th: he had three days to get his first payment to her. While not favorable, Chuck felt that this agreement was probably standard and so he agreed to the terms on the spot.

The next day, Chuck's rideshare arrived in front of the apartment complex and he took a good long look at the front of the building. From the outside, the apartment building was not much to look at; it was blocky and modular. Under each window was a small section of roofing that allowed rain to run off the building effectively, but what really caught Chuck's eye was the plastic skeleton hanging near the front door. The edge of the building's roof was also lined with what looked like orange and black tinsel. On his way into the building, Chuck walked past plastic tomb stones lining the miniscule front lawn. Plastic Halloween stickers and other spooky, decorative oddities clung to the hallway walls all the way up to his door.

Chuck unloaded all two of the boxes carrying his personal effects. He wasn't in any way a minimalist, he just didn't have all that much in the first place. Fortunately, Mrs. G allowed him to borrow a futon a former tenant had left behind. After living couch-to-couch it was nice to have something that resembled a bed at least part of the time. In his boxes were the standard faire of items: dishes, silverware, sheets, pillows, a couple of microwavable burritos—which had comprised the entirety of his diet for the last few weeks—and a few movies on DVD. He didn't own a television yet, but he intended to watch movies on his laptop for entertainment until he could have internet installed in his apartment.

He spent the rest of the day finding space for his few possessions. He unpacked and hung a print he had bought from a museum gift shop. It was the only piece of artwork that he owned, and against the clean but drab walls of the apartment, it looked incredibly out of place. The piece was glossy and colorful; while still very stirring, if you looked at it from certain angles, the glare from the sun or a rampant lightbulb would render the art itself unviewable. The walls, in contrast, were an off-white color and textured in such a way that they felt bumpy to the touch.

Chuck settled down for the night on his new futon. He was grateful that the futon's mattress did not smell too much like its previous owner. Over the past two or so weeks, he had been on futons and hide-a-beds that seemed to have retained every odor which had ever been in the same room as them. The lack of an odor did not stop Chuck from laying down a layer of aerosol disinfectant before applying his freshly laundered sheets. The futon was seated comfortably in the middle of the room. Thankfully, none of the windows faced directly east or were dead-on with any street lamps, so only residual light from the city at large dared to permeate his room.

Chuck drifted to sleep to the thought that he was finally getting his life together. He finally had a permanent address; tomorrow he had several interviews with businesses near his apartment, and he had some money saved away to tide him over until then. Things were finally looking up. He turned and looked to the now empty boxes near the edge of the room. He was certain that the next time he moved, he would need more than just those two boxes to move all his belongings.

Chuck could feel the tendrils of sleep closing in upon him. His eyes were getting heavy, so he let his head fall further into the pillow. The sounds of the night echoed from the window as the radiators hissed. Chuck felt these sounds meant that he was finally taking steps in the right direction. He was firmly on sleep's doorstep when the sounds were interrupted by a nearby skittering. Chuck's eyes opened wide for a moment but hearing nothing, he closed them again only to have his attention drawn away from his pillow by the sounds of something small scurrying and scuttling. The sound seemed to be coming from one of the empty boxes.

He listened for a moment to make sure that it was not his ears playing tricks on him. When the noise came again, he grabbed his phone and walked over to the boxes. He pointed his phone at the box and turned on the flashlight. The light shone into the first box, and then quickly the other. Nothing was found inside. Whatever might have been inside the box was now gone. Chuck turned the boxes upside-down and made his way back to the futon. Lying in the bed for what felt like hours, he waited and listened. A quick check of his phone told him that barely 20 minutes had passed. For the time being, he was satisfied. Again, he came close to sleep, but not before he heard the final creeping crawl of several small feet against cardboard.

Light poured through the window to illuminate the empty expanse of the apartment. The off-white seemed extra harsh in the morning light when paired with the grating tones of Chuck's alarm. It was the default tone that came with the phone, but it had proven time and time again to be more than capable of waking him up. He rose and paused for a moment in a dazed state as he remembered where the bathroom was in his new place.

He readied himself for the slew of interviews he had planned for today. He wasn't too excited about his prospects; he had next to no work experience, and they were for jobs where he had been paid under the table and off the books. He put on his best—and only—suit, brushed absolutely everything, and even put a few drops of cologne behind his ears. He would spare no expense in acquiring one of these positions today. His second alarm rang. He rushed towards the door, leaving the room in more or less the same condition, save for the fact that he had yet to adjust or re-make his futon.

Just before his hand was about to grab the doorknob, he heard something which reminded him of the sounds he had heard the night before. He turned his attention toward the upturned boxes on the other side of the room. He walked over to them and lifted them, one before the other, and flipped them over, not knowing what to expect. There was nothing inside nor underneath the boxes. Just then, he heard the sound of small feet again, this time, coming from just outside his window. He noticed a squirrel making its way across a section of slate roofing. Each step the squirrel took made a section of the roof shimmy, and the resulting sound emulated a kind of scuttling noise. Chuck breathed a sigh of relief, content to believe that last night was just part of his imagination. He turned the boxes back upright and made his way back to the door, closing it behind him.

The sound of Chuck's key turning the tumblers of the lock was the last thing to be heard in the apartment before the skittering of tiny feet in the boxes began again.

By the time Chuck returned to his apartment, it was the late in the evening. He returned with a smile, a couple of frozen pizzas, and a bottle of the cheapest liquor he had spotted in the store. While he didn't hear anything definite from any of the employers he had met today, several of them said that he had promise, potential, and "chutzpah." Chuck didn't know what chutzpah was, but it sure did sound promising. He was going to call today a victory, and hopefully they would be calling him soon.

He put the pizzas away in the freezer, poured himself a tall glass of the brown liquid—which Chuck realized was labeled bourbon—and fished a microwavable burrito out of the freezer.

In the kitchen, Chuck's head turned to the small brown spot he had created when he killed the roach during the tour. He grabbed a napkin and tried to wipe the stain clean. Despite his best efforts, the stain was too dried in to come up, even with a moistened napkin.

When the contents of the burrito had finished heating, he adjusted his futon into the sitting position. With a glass and plate in hand, he placed his laptop on his leg and inserted one of his favorite movies. It was a cheesy 80s movie that he had seen decades ago. On a good day, he could recite the entire script from memory. It was a comforting to him. Aided by the bourbon, he could take the time to become enveloped in the moment.

No lights were on in the apartment, and only a few of the streetlamps had flickered to life. Only the pulse of the light from his laptop illuminated the area around Chuck. He had a few more sips before setting the glass down on the flattest part of the futon. He stretched out, splaying both arms out along the top of the futon. He closed his eyes and listened to the sounds from the film.

He was plucked violently out of his relaxation by an unwelcome sensation: he felt something crawling on his right arm. He didn't even have the time to ponder how it got to the middle of his arm before he violently lurched, toppled his computer, and spilled the drink on his sheets. With a swift gesture of his left hand he brushed whatever it was away from him, and he heard it land with a *thud* elsewhere in the room.

He rushed over to the light switch and flipped it on. He scanned the room quickly but was unable to find the thing that startled him. He grabbed a towel and tried his best to salvage what he could of his bedsheets. For tonight, he would have to sleep on the mattress alone.

Chuck moved the damp coverings to the hamper for the night and decided that in the morning he would have to do laundry. He moved the plate and glass to the sink. If nothing else, he was going to clean the dishes tonight. Chuck wiped the plate with a damp cloth and moved it to the drying rack. He merely rinsed out the glass before setting to the side.

He let what little soapy water there was run down the drain before ringing out the dish cloth.

In the corner of his eye, Chuck saw a brown dot move in the sink. This one couldn't have been more than three centimeters in length, but its movements were definitely deliberate. This roach was distinct from the one he had stepped on during the tour. This one was a lighter brown in color, and close to the insect's rear was a large white section.

Egg sack or not, Chuck was not going to let this one get away. After the scare he had gotten before, he was ready to take out some of his aggression on this insect. His hand came down hard and fast on the roach. The roach had only a moment to run before its limbs crackled under the force of Chuck's hand. Chuck felt the crunch of its exterior shell and the soft release of its innards. Once more, there was a small brown stain where the roach had been. Using the sink's extendable hose, the swirling water in the drain carried the brown, white, and grey pieces down the drain.

The rest of the day passed by in mediocrity, and as the late hours of evening crept into the room, Chuck realized he had done nothing with the day. The employers he had met with had not yet called him back, and he realized the local laundromat was too far from his apartment for him to walk to clean his stained sheets. What he managed to accomplish was watching the entirety of his movie library in one sitting.

Chuck laid on the bare futon and waited—waited for sleep to take him again, waited for the urge to do anything at all—but what kept him awake was the anticipation of another visitor. He remembered the visitor from the night before. How the sensation of skittering had stirred him out of his sleep so suddenly. His hand instinctively went to the section of arm from which the sensation had come. The skin had become raised and he could feel small bumps all along his arm. He crooked his fingers and began to scratch.

The next morning's sun streaked through his windows and the brightness of the room stung Chuck's eyes. It didn't matter. He didn't get much sleep the last night. The light that shone through his windows revealed his legs and arms. There were red patches on every inch of his flesh. He had scratched himself raw in some places. He rose out of bed and put on his slippers. Maybe it had been the lack of sleep, or the constant scratching, but Chuck felt weaker this morning, and there was a definite soreness in his legs as he walked to the kitchen.

His head ached a little, and his vision was cloudy. As he staggered around the counter, he could still appreciate how he had yet to dirty the kitchen. It was just as pristine as ever with its clean countertops, and its white speckled floor—speckles that appeared to be moving the longer that Chuck admired the floor. He rubbed his eyes for a moment, and the fine speckles revealed themselves to be hundreds of tiny cockroaches. He was surprised for a moment, but his fear soon turned to anger. He rose his slippered foot and brought it down on a large cluster of the creatures. Chuck jumped into the middle of the kitchen and began stamping on anything that moved.

The roaches took notice this of the carnage and quickly scattered in different directions. Many ran towards the cabinets, but they quickly met the bottom of his slipper. Others made a bee-line for the underside of the refrigerator, or the oven, but almost all were squashed with the fervor of a man whose home had been invaded.

The casualties were many and scattered far across the expanse of the kitchen. Chuck stood there for a few minutes, breathing heavily. He collected himself before briskly exiting his apartment. He made his way down the hall and knocked loudly on the door of apartment 1A.

Before he could knock for a second time, he was met by a frantic Asian woman in her bathrobe and curlers. Mrs. Gokiburi didn't look tired despite the relatively early hour. Instead, she seemed like she had a million things going on at once. Chuck peered into her room for a second. He saw that she was boiling something in a large pot on her stove, she had her crockpot on high, and her TV was blaring some infomercial about non-stick cookware at full blast. She may have been a bit of a neat freak, but Mrs. G definitely had a flair for the kitsch. Her room was full of other Halloween themed tchotchkes. Every nook and cranny had another skull or pumpkin. Chuck hadn't noticed it when he first moved in, but her main window was covered in an elaborate spider web.

Mrs. G didn't seem to care about any of that. She looked at Chuck as if his issues were just another project for her to work on.

"What's wrong, dear?" Mrs. G's face wrinkled as she smiled widely.

"I'm sorry to bother you ma'am, but I seem to be having a bit of a bug issue."

"Bugs?!" Her smile disappeared just as quickly as it had appeared. Her head hung low, its creases made it look like her eyes had sunken completely into her skull, the way a snail recoils into its shell. Her shame was replaced with a sense of determination that Chuck had never before seen. She reached behind the door and retrieved an antique spray canister and swatter.

Chuck led the charge back to his apartment. With Mrs. G's help, he knew that the issue would be handled quickly. She'd see the scores of dead cockroaches on his kitchen floor, and then she would see to it herself that every last insect was eradicated once and for all.

He held open the door and Mrs. G advanced at full force. Chuck stood out in the hall, half expecting to hear a shriek from his neat-freak landlady, but nothing came. He entered to find Mrs. G in the middle of his kitchen with a flashlight. She looked at Chuck with an expression of confusion and exasperation. The area around her was completely white. There was no sign of any of the carnage from the morning's events. None of the exoskeletons were to be found.

Mrs. G looked under the fridge, the oven, and even within the cabinets: all the places that Chuck had seen them crawling towards. Even though she found nothing, she was very thorough. He told her about the one that he had caught on the lip of the sink. She looked the sink and countertop over, and again she found nothing. What she did find were the dishes that Chuck had washed yesterday; with one of her nails, she scratched at a dried-on food stain on his plate. Her look was short but disapproving and harsh.

She gave the room a once-over examination. While he was originally excited to have her in his place to do something about the issue, now every dart of her eyes brought with it more shame and embarrassment. She didn't say anything, but Chuck knew that she was less than thrilled about the unmade state of his bed and the empty boxes that he had yet to put away after his move. When she eventually left his apartment, he apologized profusely for tearing her away from what she was working on, but also silently for the mess that he had already let his room become. His door closed and seconds later, he heard hers do the same.

Chuck stared at sparkling white floor in the kitchen. Had he really encountered an insect horde this morning, or was his mind just playing tricks on him? His attention turned to the boxes which were still out in the open. The very least he could would be to fold them up and put them away for the time being.

He grabbed the edge of the cardboard structure. Remembering the sounds he had heard two nights ago, he peered inside the box, expecting perhaps to find the corpse of the thing that had crawled across his arm, but he knew that there would be nothing inside. If there was, Mrs. G would have found it in her very thorough search.

There was no tiny cadaver inside the case, but what was inside did take Chuck aback for a moment. On the bottom of the cardboard box was a large, discolored, wet spot. The stain seemed to expand outward from the middle of the box and creep its way to the edges. Chuck lifted the box to get a closer look at the stain, and before he could inspect the spot closer, he felt the sensation of several small somethings running across his feet. Thousands upon thousands of cockroaches emerged from the wet spot and skittered in every direction. Some made their ways to the walls and other sections of the floor. The few that had invaded his slippers were moving along every inch of his feet. He hurriedly took his slippers off and hurled them towards the wall. Dozens of roaches flew out like an explosion when it contacted the side of his apartment. He brushed off the ones that had begun crawling up his leg and stamped at the ones that were still at the center of the wet point.

When he felt even more crawling up his other leg, he dropped the box and headed straight for the door. In the hallway, he made sure that there were no others on his personage. Even without seeing them, he could still feel them crawling all over his body. Their tiny legs and antennae irritated his skin in ways he had not imagined were possible, and itching became more necessary than breathing. Chuck scratched hard at the already enflamed parts of his body. He more closely resembled a tomato than a man. His need to scratch superseded his pain tolerance. He scratched the back of his hand so hard that he broke skin, and a small amount of blood had seeped from the scrape.

He made his way—for the second time today—to his landlady's door. While visibly tired after the ordeal he had put her through earlier, she was still sympathetic for whatever he was going through. She recoiled heavily when she spotted the scrape. She had him wait out in the hallway while she made a phone call. Chuck heard her pick up the receiver, and a few minutes later she emerged.

"You know we can't keep meeting like this," she said, the hint of a forced joke in her voice. "Who knows what the neighbors might think."

Chuck laughed. Even though he was quite stirred after his ordeal, the last thing he wanted was to seem impolite. He could tell he was on thin ice with Mrs. G, and even though she was still cracking jokes, he knew that her patience with him was coming to an end.

"Besides," she added well after the moment had passed, "I do have *other* men in my life. Like the exterminator that will be paying us a visit this afternoon."

Chuck breathed a major sigh of relief and smiled. Maybe he could finally put all of this behind him.

He didn't dare reenter his room until the exterminator arrived. Every time he thought about even touching his door, he could feel himself itching from head to toe. He moved to a corner of the hallway for the moment. He checked his phone every five minutes for a new message, or maybe even a call from any of the employers whom he had met, but none came. It didn't matter. He was pulled away from his device every so often by a skittering sound that he felt was only getting louder and closer.

The final time his head rose to meet the skittering, he visibly jumped. Inches from his face was an enormous cockroach, and it had him cornered with nowhere to run.

"Is your name…" there was a pause as the roach seemed to collect its thoughts. "Is your name Chuck?"

"Uh. Yes?" Chuck almost dropped to the fetal position before he reassured himself that most cockroaches don't usually carry clipboards. The cockroach looked up and revealed himself to be a man, maybe thirty years old, with coke bottle glasses and a big smile on his face. His teeth were large and stained yellow and brown. His face was accented by a scraggly goatee. Chuck assumed that his hair was probably just as curly, though he couldn't know for sure because it was covered by the official Nexterminate uniform ballcap with a cockroach's face printed on it.

"Hiya. I'm Scott from Nexterminate. Mrs. G told us you have a bit of a roach problem." Scott outlined the basic Nexterminate package, which had already been paid for by Mrs. G, as the two of them walked from the front of the apartment to the Nexterminate truck. Scott grabbed a couple of canisters and other supplies and loaded them onto his white utility belt. He chatted briefly with his coworker, a teenager named Tucker, who seemed to be far less interested in making conversation than Scott. He was very young looking, and while it looked like Scott was preparing himself for battle, Tucker was intently playing on some kind of portable gaming system. Scott explained that although Tucker was not yet old enough to legally handle some of the more dangerous chemicals they had in their truck, Nexterminators were required to travel two per vehicle, and so since he was old enough to drive, the company hired him to drive the van.

Chuck opened the door to his apartment, expecting to see a large cluster swarming all around the room. But when he entered, there were none to be seen. Scott looked around the room and shouldered one of the canisters.

"Cozy place. Pay much for it?" Scott began pumping the canister and pointing a nozzle into various crevasses and cracks around the room. If anything was coming out, it was far too fine of a mist to be seen by the naked eye.

"N- no." Chuck scanned the room, stunned that he was unable to find any evidence of bugs at all. The only sign that there had been bugs at all was the light brown stain in the kitchen that Chuck had created when he stepped on the cockroach during his tour of the apartment.

"That's good. Mrs. G always gives a fair price. You know, we get called out to this here building maybe once every one or two years—but that woman is such a neat freak. We have never found a single bug in her apartment. Come to think of it, I don't think I've ever been in this particular apartment before. She must've just bought it or something. Hey, you lookin' for something there, friend?"

Chuck was suddenly made aware of the fact that he had been staring at the one brown stain on the floor the entire time Scott had been spraying the apartment. Scott had taken the canister off his shoulder and had now joined Chuck in staring at the brown spot.

"What happened there? Did you spill a little chili or something?"

"Ah, no. I stepped on a roach—or something—and that's what caused it."

Scott raised an eyebrow and slowly sank to the floor, all the while keeping an eye on Chuck. He turned and lowered his head, his nose not an inch away from the stain. He took a few whiffs and eyed the stain for a few seconds before rising to meet Chuck face-to-face.

"You said a roach left that stain?"

Chuck nodded.

"My friend, that was no ordinary roach. Have you ever heard of the elusive Scandinavian cockroach?"

Chuck shook his head.

"I didn't think so. The Vikings brought them over to America hundreds of years ago. These babies can live for years on the smallest amount of food and water. If you see one there's guaranteed to be hundreds, if not thousands, in the crawlspaces." He pointed to the empty canister that was leaning against the wall. "That stuff will take care of American cockroaches just fine, but against Scandinavian roaches, I may as well just be spraying water." He pulled a card out of his utility belt. "This is my personal extension. Call me if you see any more of those suckers."

Chuck took the card and watched as Scott gathered his things, made his way down the hallway, and walked out the door.

The room was quiet for what seemed like the first time since he had arrived. The hallways were dead silent, as everyone else had gone to work for the day. Even Mrs. G had left after paying the exterminator. Chuck held the card that Scott had given him tightly in his left hand. "Scandinavian cockroach," he said to himself. Somehow giving a name to his tormentor made it addressable. If it had a name, he could take care of it. Chuck closed his eyes for a moment before he was stirred by the sound of Scott slamming the truck's door and laughing loudly.

Chuck looked out of his open window and saw that the Nexterminate van was parked on the street directly below him. Neither of the two men looked up from what they were doing, so they were both completely unaware of his presence.

"Another good sale?" asked a voice which must have belonged to Tucker.

"Like you would not believe. So, I'm doing my spray routine, when I notice this nut-ball is staring at the floor. I finish up in the apartment and join him. He tells me he stepped on a roach a few days ago, and a stain had set into the floor, so naturally I went into my Scandinavian cockroach spiel and the sucker bought it hook, line, and sinker. Remember this, kiddo—you know what professionals call the Scandinavian cockroach?"

"Job security," Tucker said. He was clearly parroting something he had been told many times before. The pair pulled away, leaving Chuck alone at the window.

Bemused and betrayed, he closed the window and sat inside his apartment. He needed something to take his mind off what he had just heard, so he went to the freezer and pulled out a large pizza. At least he wouldn't have to worry about preparing meals for another day or two.

He turned the dial on the oven to 400 degrees before diverting his attention to the pizza on the counter. He peeled back the plastic and separated the cold food from the cardboard. Just as he was about to put it in the oven, he noticed a small brown speck crawling along the edge of the sink.

He put the pizza down and struck the spot with all the force he could muster. He took joy in this moment of violence. He didn't care that this specimen meant that the exterminators had cheated him and Mrs. G; he just cared about the swiftness of his hand and the satisfying crunch underneath. He raised his hand and watched as the antennae continued to move though separated of the body.

Chuck once again picked up the frozen pizza from the counter and swiveled towards the oven. Its dial was old and worn in places. This was entirely unnoticeable when he first entered the apartment, and he probably would not have noticed it now if it hadn't been turning backwards. From 400 degrees it rotated: 350…325… 300 degrees—Chuck leaned in to get a closer look, and a large horde of cockroaches began crawling out from behind the dial. Chuck stared at the oven in disbelief. Suddenly, he felt something crawling on his arm; thousands of medium-sized cockroaches were working their way down his arm from the pizza, the center of which appeared to be an entire colony of roaches eating their way out from the cold disk of dough. More roaches began pouring out from beneath the refrigerator, the oven—even from within the cracks in the walls!

He fled the kitchen and found himself in the living room of the apartment. The floor was dotted with more and more of the pests. Some had made their way from the kitchen into the living room by crawling along the wall. Chuck noticed that a few of them had made their way onto the art piece which hung on the wall. Chuck's hand struck the piece as he tried to exterminate as many of the roaches as he could; with each blow, he killed about five. Blow after blow, more of the roaches appeared on the piece and the walls. The piece was no longer glossy or shiny. If light struck it now, the painting would be scarcely visible underneath the layers of cockroach guts which coated it.

Tired, Chuck stumbled and found himself backed up against the futon. He was still desperately trying to swat away the few cockroaches which were clinging to his arms when he felt more of them crawling across his legs. He looked down to discover that his futon had unzipped slightly, and that more and more cockroaches were seeping out of it. The futon itself had begun convulsing as if there were some wild animal trapped inside of it that was desperately seeking to escape. Then, the zipper inched more and more open until the light seepage turned into a waterfall of insects.

Chuck ran towards the door to escape what his room had become. He placed his hand firmly on the knob and tried to turn it, but his best attempts were met in vain. He felt something scratching against his palm where his hand and the doorknob met. He removed his hand to find more roaches coming through the lock of the door. If he couldn't open the door, he was going to attempt to break it down. He braced himself and charged directly at the door.

As the full force of his body met the door, a shower of cockroaches rained down on top of him, landing on his head and in his hair. More of them came pouring out of every cranny of the apartment. The roaches had jammed the door, but Chuck knew he had to escape. He tried the windows, but again the roaches had jammed the locks tight.

The bumps that had made up the texture of the walls began to crack open, revealing more cockroaches. The floor no longer resembled a floor; it was now an undulating, twitching mass that held no definite shape. The scraping of feet on feet on feet, and the twitching of antennae, resonated deeply within the grains of the wood and produced a deep pulsating sound throughout the apartment.

Despite Chuck's attempts to swat them away, the roaches had found their way under his clothing. They were now crawling along nearly every inch of his flesh. His swatting turned to scratching, as he once again could no longer resist the incessant need to scratch that these insects created in him. Chuck spotted one of the larger roaches, one with a large white egg sack on its lower abdomen, making its way along his arm and down to the back of his hand. The roach seemed to walk directly along the trail of blood that Chuck's scratching had created when he broke skin. He watched in terror as the roach dove headfirst into his open wound. Chuck tried in vain to smash the roach, but wherever he made contact with his skin, he only managed to leave behind bruises that blossomed beneath the white and red streaks left from his consistent scratching. The roach in his arm made his flesh bubble up. He watched in horror as it moved freely under the skin of his arm.

There were suddenly two bumps: one that continued to move freely in his arm, and another that sat still perfectly still. Chuck lifted his hand and came down hard upon the stagnant mass. The lump flattened out, and for a moment he thought he had averted something terrible. After a second, however, movement came from where the lump had been. His skin ballooned a little at first, then hundreds of smaller flesh bubbles swarmed and scattered, tracing the veins and arteries of his arm.

Chuck screamed—in fear, in pain, in the hope that someone, *anyone* in the apartment building would hear him—but the wider he opened his mouth, the more roaches crawled inside. He tried to spit them out, but too many had already made their way down his throat. Even more entered through his nostrils. Soon, every orifice of his body was being invaded by insects.

The room became dark as a multitude of roaches blocked out the light that was coming from the window. Roaches had somehow found their ways into the light sockets and were shorting out the electricity. The roaches had knocked the art off the wall—what was left of the walls anyway—and the walls had been replaced by a pulsating brown mass. The multitude now resembled a single fleshy entity instead of millions-upon-millions of tiny insects. The ceilings had become saturated to the point that with every second that passed, hundreds of more roaches rained down from above.

Chuck was struggling to breathe. He could feel the roaches replacing his very being. He was still trying to swat and scratch them away, since it was all that he could do. He had scratched himself to the bone in some places. Flesh and sinew hung from his body, dripping into the waist-high pool of roaches. He could feel each one of them as they crawled outside—and *inside*—of his body. He could also feel them biting into him as he sank deeper and deeper under the wave of roaches. When only his face was left above the pool, he could no longer scream. His face contorted to the shape of abject terror, but he was incapable of mustering any sound. Roaches moved freely in and out of his mouth and nose as his eyes rolled back in his skull and his facial muscles relaxed at last.

The key slipped effortlessly into the lock, and the sound of tumblers clicking into place soon followed. The doorknob turned quickly—with purpose. The elderly hand that was clasped around it pushed the door open for the young man with a very excited look on his face.

"And here's the apartment. I'm sorry, but I'm terrible with names. Would you mind reminding me?"

"Thomas. Thomas Anderson."

"Well, Mr. Anderson, I hope the apartment is to your liking. Why don't you look around?"

The room was immaculately clean. The walls were well painted, and there was scarcely a mark indicating anything had ever hung upon them. The kitchen looked brand new. It seemed impossible that the floor could look so white, but somehow this kitchen was spared any blemish.

"So, why did the last guy leave?" Thomas was almost unwilling to believe someone would ever leave such a nice place.

"Oh, he didn't really say. I personally think he was a little antisocial. He was aggressive toward my other tenants from the very beginning." She paused for a moment to gather her thoughts and rummaged through a bag of goods from the corner store. "Now we do have to discuss the issue of payment. Usually, I collect rent on the first of the month, but I'm sure we can work something out." She pulled a pointy hat out of her shopping bag and put it on her head. "What, with it being Halloween and all."

Foul Treats
Jon Steffens

It was just after five in the afternoon on October 31 when Thomas Hutchinson pulled into the driveway of his single-story ranch-style brick home on Tucker Street after a not-entirely-horrible drive home from his marketing job, just in time to see his wife, Tara, and four-year-old son, Colton, placing a crooked-grinned jack-o'-lantern on the front porch of their home. Thomas climbed out of his Toyota and ran to meet his excited little boy who was already dressed in an adorable skeleton costume.

"Daaaaaddddddyyyyy!"

"You ready for your first real trick or treat, buddy?"

"Yes! Let's go noooowww! I want candy!"

"Give Daddy just a few minutes, then we'll go out until you're ready to come home. Sound good, champ?"

"I guess," the boy pouted.

"It'll be great, I promise," Thomas assured Colton, as he carried the sandy-haired ghoul into their three-bedroom, beige brick home with the painted grey marble trim. It had been transformed for the night into a suburban spook house with the carved pumpkin, a package of stretchy cobweb that was pulled apart and placed across the front window, a cardboard skeleton tacked to the front door, and few rubber spiders lying in wait on the porch.

"Hey babe, you sure you don't wanna come with us?" Thomas called to his wife of five years from the bedroom while he changed into a t-shirt and jeans.

"I'd love to, but somebody's got to hand out the candy to the neighborhood creeps," she answered. Her ponytail, grey yoga pants, and the night's first glass of merlot gave away that she'd be staying right here, thank you very much. "I *am* going to snap a few pictures of you guys before you leave, though. Okay?"

"Okay, but you'll miss the excitement of my Peter Lorre impression—the kids love it!"

The sarcasm wasn't lost on Tara. "I think I'll manage," she said drily. "What are you, eighty-five years old?"

"Some days I feel like it," responded Thomas.

After about forty-five minutes—more than little Colton would have liked—all the pictures were taken. His bright orange plastic pumpkin pail was eager to be filled with anything chocolate, fruit-flavored, sweet, or brightly colored. He and his dad were ready to venture into the quickly-darkening outdoors for a night of eerie adventure.

The pair started down the sidewalk, Thomas nearly as enlivened as little Colton, who had been warned twice already to "stop running."

"You boys be safe! And Colton, baby, have fun with Daddy!" Tara called from the doorway, already handing out treats to Halloween's first pint-sized creatures.

One of them, a dark-haired little girl of no more than six years was dressed as a witch, which Thomas liked—he felt it was respectful of his childhood's most sacred holiday. Though his interest in Halloween had waned throughout his teenage years and into his adulthood, now that his son was of proper trick-or-treating age, his appreciation of All Hallows Eve had been renewed.

The other child, a loud little boy roughly Colton's age, was dressed as some kind of robotic warrior, a flash of blue, red and silver.

The air was cool on Thomas's face as the sky grew a deep plum color and the sun dipped below the horizon. The leaves had yet to change, but he finally felt the oppressive Texas summer had well and truly ended. They approached their first destination: a house just two doors down from their own, but the first with its front-porch light serving as a beacon to the hordes of costumed candy-snatchers. The only decoration—a cartoonish, grinning plywood pumpkin— rested on a stake driven into yard near the bush-line.

"Alright, Colton, go do your thing! I'll be right here on the sidewalk."

The tiny skeleton hurried up the well-kept concrete path to the front door. After his son reached up and rang the bell, the door was promptly opened by a short, sweet-faced older woman with auburn hair and a slightly pudgy build. In her arms was a large orange plastic bowl with a ring of happy black bats circling its top. Its contents were a mountain of fun-sized Hershey bars: priceless treasures to a four-year-old.

"Trick or Treat!" Colton shouted just a little too loudly, his enthusiasm electric.

The woman smiled and deposited a handful of miniature candy bars into the boy's pumpkin pail and said, "You are too scary for me, little one! Here's some candy, please don't get me!"

Colton lifted his hands, made his best monster noise, then turned and scurried back to his father. Stopping halfway, he turned back to the woman and shouted, "Thank you!" just like his father had taught him.

"You get a good haul for your first house, little man?"

"I think so! Let's keep going!"

"You got it," Thomas answered, patting Colton on the head as they continued along their spooky path.

Thomas thought they'd have to call it an early night only six houses in, when a teenager in a gruesome clown costume proved he was no mere static prop. He lurched at

Colton, terrifying the little boy beyond reason. He turned and screamed into his father's legs, begging to be picked up, which Thomas immediately did. After what felt like an eternity of consoling his frightened son, he scolded the teenager.

"What the hell is wrong with you, kid? Take the damned mask off and show my boy you're just a person! I figured you'd have enough fucking sense not to scare a kid this small!"

"I'm sorry, man!" exclaimed the boy as he tore off his nightmarish latex mask. "Here, little guy, take as much candy as you want!" He held out the candy bowl to Colton, who calmed down momentarily and scooped up four handfuls of treats before his father told him it was enough.

"See, buddy? It's not a monster, just some dumb teenager."

"I *hate* clowns, daddy! Yuck!"

"Yeah, me too," Thomas muttered as they walked away.

The night was deep black now, though Thomas held a flashlight, and there were enough streetlights to illuminate the neighborhood. A group of five trick-or-treaters passed Thomas and Colton—older kids who were parentless, cutting through lawns and behaving obnoxiously—two of them wore no semblance of a costume, while the others just sported rubber monster masks and wore circles of black makeup around their eyes.

"You sure you want to keep going?"

"I sure do!" said Colton through his vinyl skull mask. "I'm not scared anymore!"

"That's my big man," said Thomas, with exaggerated depth in his voice.

The next half-hour or so went off without a hitch. They hit several houses on three different streets, most of which were sparsely decorated, though a few had elaborate fake graveyards, fog machines, and light shows. Thomas made sure to let the monsters haunting those yards know to take it easy on his young son. They all obliged, acting terrified of the tiny ghoul and doling-out generous amounts of candy, from peanut-butter cups and lollipops, to candy corn and that cheap orange-and-black taffy.

Colton asked his father to hold his mask after a couple more stops, complaining it was too hot. He pulled it off, and Thomas saw him yawn.

"Sure thing, buddy. You about ready to head home?"

"Just a couple more houses, Dad? Please?"

Dad? Who's that? This was the first time Colton had referred to his father as "Dad," and Thomas realized right then that he wasn't nearly ready to let go of being called "Daddy."

"We'll hit one or two more on the way, but we need to get home soon. Your mom is ordering pizza, and Daddy is starving!"

"Yes! Pepperoni is my favorite!" the little one blurted, his energy renewed as they walked.

Winding their way toward home, the pair took a right onto Juniper Drive. The air around them was crisp and cool, hitting Thomas with a wave of pleasant nostalgia. While father and son walked, searching for that final residence from which to collect the night's closing sweets, Thomas remembered Halloweens passed and dreamed of those to come, until Colton would find himself at an age where hanging with his father would be considered the polar opposite of fun. Thomas hoped that day was far in the future.

Thomas noticed there was only one porch light aglow on the entire street, about four houses away on the right. With none of the streetlamps on, and no moon visible in the black, overcast sky, the entire street was bathed in a thick coat of ominous darkness. The lone porch light was a welcoming beacon. Thomas felt the night's atmosphere instantly shift from innocent autumn fun to overbearingly sinister— threatening even. He looked down at his young son who didn't seem to notice. He just kept trucking in his serious pursuit of candy, smiling. Thomas mentally shook the feeling and promptly experienced a rush of giddy excitement. Halloween hadn't spooked him since he was a child; he welcomed the gooseflesh and shot of adrenaline. After all, isn't that what this mischievous, mysterious night was all about?

Father and son reached the last stop before home: 2213 Juniper Drive—a small ranch-style abode, nearly identical to their own, minus differing window placement and a forest-green trim.

As his four-year-old little boy scampered up the concrete path toward the house, Thomas observed that the street was entirely absent of people. No trick-or-treaters, no parents waiting in cars, no neighbors haunting their homes. The street was empty and silent save for he and his boy, and oppressively dark minus the one dingy bulb to the left of 2213's dark-green door. The street felt like a graveyard, and Thomas wondered where everyone was. It couldn't be later than seven-thirty, and he couldn't even *hear* anyone else— odd.

Colton reached for the doorbell, but about six inches before his little fingers would have pressed the button, the door silently opened inward, revealing what appeared to be complete, tar-thick darkness at first—until Thomas saw it.

Standing in the doorway, where before there was nothing but coal-black shadow, there was now a...*thing*. Thomas' brain was having difficulty accepting it as reality. His conscious mind wanted to dismiss the thing as an incredibly lifelike decoration or prop, but he knew—could feel—it was alive. It was knowing, thinking, ancient, and contemptible. It's very existence spit in the face of known reality. Its form seemed to shift and fluctuate in size from around four feet tall to nearly filling the entire doorway.

It had squat, impossibly bent legs, and an elongated torso that made it look like an upside-down triangle. Its arms, though muscled in a somewhat humanoid fashion, reached the floor. Where hands should be were two writhing, undulating appendages, bearing a simultaneous resemblance to the bodies of both slugs and snakes. It had no neck to speak of, but it had a large, misshapen head. The creature's face possessed a wide, flat nose with a sharp, downward point directly at the center. Thick, cracked lips were pulled back into an ugly, half-open grimace, revealing its long, yellow and brown needlelike teeth. Where its eyes should have been were four deep-set, hollow circular pits that were so dark they were like black holes in the vast, lonely reaches of space. Its flesh appeared bumpy and scaly in places, slick and smooth in others. The thing was colored dead fish-grey, though it wasn't static. The grey coloring was constantly shifting and swirling, like low-hanging clouds just before a tornado. Atop its bulbous head was thin, translucent hair that hung wet well below its unearthly visage.

The thing opened its maw as if to speak, but no sound burst forth. All surrounding air and sound felt as if it were drawn into that hideous, gaping mouth, when as quickly as the beast appeared, it reached out, wrapped its slithering appendages around Colton's head, and violently jerked him inside the house, enveloping him in the impermeable blackness within.

The door slammed shut, and the air returned—but Colton was gone.

Although Thomas felt rooted to the earth while the horror had been unfolding before him, as soon as the door was shut he screamed with all the air in his lungs and broke out into a run toward the house.

Thomas threw the green door open, plunging headfirst into the inky blackness inside. Whipping his flashlight from side to side and screaming "Colton!" repeatedly, he saw no sign of his son or the beast. The house was vacant—completely empty. He hurried from room to room, checking closets, beneath the bathroom sinks, anywhere he could see, screaming his son's name all the while. His voice was already growing hoarse from the strain, and his heart felt like it would beat through his chest. He ran into the kitchen, throwing open cabinets and the pantry door. Thomas banged his shin something fierce on the door frame leading to the garage; he barely noticed.

Feeling dread like he had never experienced in his life, tears began streaming down Thomas' face. Going through the side garage door and out into the backyard, Thomas still saw nothing. No pumpkin pail, no costume, no spilled candy, no giant goddamned goblin-thing—nothing. As he made his way to the small shed at the far corner of the yard, he began sweating profusely, his legs shaking.

Thomas Hutchinson wrenched the rickety wooden door open, flecks of old brown paint sticking to his sweaty palm. He shone the light inside, first seeing a strange, seemingly nonsensical sigil; it somewhat resembled a primitive spiral inside a rough, uneven trapezoid, and it was crudely painted on the back wall of the shed in what could only be fresh blood—the unmistakable metallic smell invaded his nostrils. When he veered the light to the floor, Thomas' world ended. There, he saw directly in the center of another rough, bloody spiral, crumpled in a vaguely fetal heap, was something that used to be Colton. Where he had hoped to see his smiling, laughing young son in a cartoonish skull-and-bones costume, was instead a small, frail child's skeleton, caked in wet gore and thoroughly stripped of all skin and tissue.

While his mind began to crack and fall to pieces at a feverish pace, something profane and terrible towered behind the man, studying him as gargantuan lizard-things studied their prey millennia ago. One wet, leathery tendril wrapped its way around his throat, and Thomas Hutchinson knew no more.

The Boatman's Rhyme
Neil May

As the classroom sat quietly, from the back of the middle row Teddy realized his Friday was dragging on. He had his All Hallows' Eve all planned out, and he was yearning to get on with it. Shuffling in his seat, he flicked his pencil against the hard top of the desk.

WHACK!

The sound reverberated about the room as some of his classmates looked directly at him. At the front desk, Mrs. Atwell looked up from her notes and peered at Teddy.

"Teddy, the test is not done," she said sternly. "I would appreciate it if you could concentrate on it and not disturb the entire class."

"Sorry, Mrs. Atwell," he replied, each word coated with sarcasm. "I'm just making sure everyone is awake."

She pointed at him with her finger and motioned for him to look back at his test. He smiled at her and looked down, muttering "Bitch" under his breath.

"I'm sorry. Was there something else?" Her tone now sounded harsh.

"No, ma'am. I was just coughing," said Teddy, lying through his teeth.

She watched him for a minute. With a shake of her head, she turned her attention back to the table and continued preparing a future lesson.

From the back of the class, Teddy peeked up to see if she was looking again, but her face was buried deep in her book. He looked to his left where Lily sat—his latest bullying victim. She felt his intense stare, but ignored it the best she could by shifting in her seat so that she could not see him.

"Hey," he whispered. "Wanna go make out after school?" His smile was awkward for a fifteen-year-old.

She glanced back at him with a look of pure disgust. Shaking her head "no," she turned back to her test.

"Mister Roth," the loud annoyed voice of Mrs. Atwell echoed through the classroom. "I have told you once and that should have been enough, but you seem to not pay attention. Do you need to go see the principal?"

"Sorry again, Mrs. Atwell, but I hate these goddamn tests." His retort was enough to make the majority of his classmates gasp.

Mrs. Atwell didn't reply. Instead, she stood up from her desk and walked down the center aisle to Teddy's desk at the back of the room. A stout woman in her fifties, with greying hair and an attitude that could stop a raging bull, she reached toward Teddy as he sat smugly in his chair and grabbed him by the ear. Teddy lurched upwards and followed her hand; he feared she would tear the ear off his head. A small squeak escaped him as she applied pressure to his now twisted ear. He stood a foot taller than her, but her will to move him was much greater than a small foot in height.

"I see we are at an impasse, Teddy," she said quietly. "I warned you once, and as you all know, in my class there is no second chance." She leaned in to his twisted ear and whispered, "I may look small, but I'm much more than meets the eye, Mr. Roth."

"Let go of my ear, you senile old biddy!" Teddy forced out, holding back the tears her painful hold invoked. He knew his bullying days would be over if he started crying, and that would not do. "I'll sue!" he shouted. The rest of the class sat shocked as she continued to hold his ear, twisting it a little bit more before releasing him from her grip.

Lily sat beside him and watched with slight glee on her face from seeing the class bully finally get what was coming to him. Teddy reacted to the release of his ear sourly, touched it gingerly, and rubbed his hand over it to soothe the burning sensation she had caused.

"Now, Mr. Roth, you can take yourself down to Mr. Canners' office and explain to him that you will not be attending the rest of my class due to your disrespectful attitude and inability to follow directions." As she turned, she said, "Everyone, back to your tests. You have twenty minutes left." Then she returned her desk and left Teddy to wallow in his embarrassment.

He grabbed his jacket from the back of his chair and pushed his test papers onto the floor. Smiling as if he had just won the lottery, he glanced at the back table which held the Halloween projects that were awaiting final grades. Each scene was created from the individual student's imagination of what Halloween *really* meant to them personally. The small scenes were made from Styrofoam, different household materials, and the many hours his classmates put in for their fall grade.

Teddy turned, setting his eyes on these projects as he walked along the back of the room. Before leaving, he grabbed one that resembled the Charlie Brown Halloween special and threw it to the floor. It exploded on impact, the tiny Charlie and Snoopy characters flying in different directions as other small pieces hit a boy who was seated in the back row.

As Teddy continued out the door, Mrs. Atwell rose from her desk once again. Without looking back, Teddy moved quickly down the hallway and into the boy's bathroom. As the door closed he could hear feet shuffle past, which he assumed belonged to Mrs. Atwell as she hunted for him. He put up his middle finger to the door and walked into the stall area. It was a small bathroom with only one toilet and two urinals. He moved past the urinals to the toilet and went inside the stall.

The lock slammed home as Teddy reached into the pocket of his jacket and pulled out a pack of cigarettes. He sat on the toilet and began reading the back of the stall door: "Mrs. At-hell is the Devil!! She will take your soul!!" It was signed "C.T. '82," a former classmate, a.k.a. Cam Throut, the previous bully of Cafton High School. Teddy snickered at the statement on the back of the door and thought back to Cam, remembering that he disappeared a year back. Most people thought he moved, but Teddy always wondered if Mrs. Atwell "took his soul" as the graffiti stated.

He retrieved the lighter from his jacket pocket, flicked a cigarette out of the package, and lit it, pulling in a big first drag. The smoke hit his lungs hard, the pair ablaze with the relief he craved. He held the smoke in for a moment before letting it out slowly; its haze lingered around his face. A second after releasing the smoke, the door to the bathroom opened and footsteps entered. He quickly dropped the cigarette into the toilet and flushed it away, swiping his hand in front of his face, determined to rid the smell from the room.

"Theodore Roth!" a stern voice boomed from the other side of the door. "Come out of that stall and talk to me."

Teddy knew right away it was the Principal, Mr. Canners. Dreading the confrontation, he unlocked the door and exited the stall. Mr. Canners stood by the only sink in the room wearing his standard well-used black suit. His large frame took up most of the counter as he waited impatiently for Teddy to emerge. As Teddy came out he saw himself in the mirror, he noticed that his jean jacket looked worn from the years of wearing it and almost nothing else. Underneath, his black shirt blasted the metal band *Death*, with its artwork that was sickening to anyone who saw it. The rest of him was also shabby, from his greasy brown hair to the baggy jeans that sat a little low on his waist.

"It seems you just refuse to get along with Mrs. Atwell," said Mr. Canners with a small amount of concern in his voice. "Would you like to explain to me why you're behaving this way?" His bald head gleamed in the fluorescent light.

Teddy faced him and said, "I just don't like her."

"That's it?" Mr. Canners asked. He rubbed his bald head with his hand. "Listen, just because you don't like someone doesn't mean you can be a disruption in their class. You have to understand that she is there to teach you, but you are constantly interrupting or talking. I want you to come to my office." He turned and headed for the door. Teddy didn't move, but he knew that Mr. Canners was no ordinary Principal. He wouldn't tolerate the disrespect that Teddy was showing Mrs. Atwell. A large man, Mr. Canners still believed in using the strap to discipline kids.

The principal opened the door and Teddy followed him out of the bathroom. Mr. Canners quickly headed back to his office with Teddy trying to keep up with him in tow—Mr. Canners was a man who didn't wait for anyone and one who expected you to keep up with his fast footsteps. They entered his office, and Mr. Canners sat behind the desk while Teddy followed him into the office before taking a seat in the chair directly in front of the oversized desk.

The Principal opened a drawer, pulled out a pad of paper, and threw it on the desk. Reaching over to his pen holder, he withdrew one and tossed it on top.

"Ok, Theodore," he said, "I want you to write me an essay on *why* you act like you hate everyone—single-spaced, two thousand words."

Teddy's mouth dropped as Mr. Canners finished his sentence. "That's not fair!" he tried to explain.

Unwavering, Mr. Canners stared directly at him. "You have the remainder of the day to complete this. You can use the mini table here in my office beside you." He pointed to the table and chair that stood alone in the corner of the room facing out the window.

"Mr. Canners?" a voice called through the door. "Mr. Sherwin needs to see you in the gym."

"Ok, Lydia. I'm on my way," he called back. As he stood, he glared at Teddy once more. "I will be back in a little bit, and I expect a wonderful tale of *why* you are the way you are." He strode out the room quickly, slamming the door behind him.

Teddy knew he wasn't going to write some stupid essay. He noticed the window; it was open and big enough for him to squeeze through. Without hesitation, he walked to the window, moved the table a little, and removed the screen from the window. Luckily for him, the Principal's office was on the first floor so the drop to the ground was minimal. Off like a fox he ran, across the field and away from the school. His Hallows' Eve plans had now changed, and it appeared that an unfair principal and a nasty old teacher were now on the agenda for a serving of eggs.

***

He sat in the treehouse he and his dad had built years ago and counted the eggs he had stolen from the fridge. "Ten eggs," he muttered to himself. "Good enough for some evil doing on Satan's night." He smiled a devilish grin. The sun was about to quickly disappear from the sky. Darkness grasped the receding light, a reminder for him to get everything ready. He picked up the cardboard holder and placed it gently into the black backpack on the floor beside him. He set it gently inside next to some paint cans, which were already in there, and secured the top by zipping it shut.

"Teddy!" called a voice from below him.

"Ya?!" he called back, sitting in the middle of the floor, unmoving.

"Get down here for supper!" his mother bellowed from the patio.

"I'm busy! I'll eat later," he replied half-heartedly.

"Don't stay up there too long," she yelled back, "or your food will get cold!"

"Okay, Ma!" he said, and he heard the patio doors close shut.

Time to go and make some stupid teachers pay. Grabbing his backpack, he headed out.

He wrenched up the trap door and whisked himself down the six nailed-in pieces of wood that served as his steps before exiting the back yard through the gate and into the alley. He looked at his watch: 6:30 PM. He did some quick calculations in his head to determine when to return home so that his mother wouldn't suspect too much. A few years ago, Teddy ran the paper route in his small town, so he had precise knowledge of the target houses very well. It would be about an hour—tops—to complete his rampage of hate against both Mr. Canners and Mrs. Atwell.

His bike was waiting for him as he entered the alley. He grabbed it and jumped on; he was off, and revenge was already tasting sweet. Striding hard, he rode fast to Mr. Canners' house first, which was only two blocks away. Darkness had consumed the town, and the street lamps were lit to show the way, and he seemed to cast shadows out from the lights as he sped under them. Within minutes, he entered the cul-de-sac where the Principal's house sat.

The street was quiet; presumably, everybody was sitting down for dinner which created the perfect conditions for him to launch the egg flurry. Mr. Canners' house sat in darkness except for a couple of lights shining through the windows. Shadows caressed their panes. The front of his house had a bay window which was a shining beacon for Teddy to hit. As some of the light flooded out of the bay window, Teddy could see Mr. Canners inside with his wife, rustling around the dining room; he wore the same gaudy black suit from earlier, and she was dressed like a fifties housewife.

Teddy sneered at them from the street, dropped his bike off at the next house's front yard, and slinked back over to the Canners' place. A shrub which sat in the middle of their yard would be the perfect cover for unleashing his egg mania. He came in low, stopped and crouched by the shrub, pulled his backpack off, and removed four eggs from the container. He slid his bag back on and waited for his chance. The figures inside were now sitting down for supper, and the street was still devoid of human life—perfect for anonymous throwing.

Standing up from behind the bush, he threw the eggs one after another, hitting the bay window with all four.

WHAM! WHAM! WHAM! WHAM!

They exploded in rapid succession against the pane, tossing egg guts and shells across the window and siding. Teddy smiled wondrously as the eggs shattered; knowing that Mr. Canners would have to clean up that mess made him extremely happy.

The figures in the window jumped from their seats with one running to the door. Mr. Canners burst through the door like a madman, looking for what had just made that loud noise. Coming down the steps to the front lawn, he looked to the window and saw the mess that now littered it. "Son of a…"

he started to say, but then he heard something off behind him on the street; a black figure on a bike was riding away rapidly.

"You son of a bitch!" he yelled furiously. "I'll find out who you are, you little shit!"

The bike rider responded by flashing a middle finger at him and laughing heartily before disappearing around corner.

Teddy felt glorious as he sped from the scene. His pulse raced as adrenaline flowed through his body at an impossible pace. Smiling wildly, he headed for the second victim on his list, Mrs. Atwell. He quickly looked at his watch: 6:50 PM. *Good*, he thought, *about half an hour to destroy her house.*

Pushing hard, he managed to reach her house in ten minutes. Sweat mounted on his forehead and leaked into his eyes. Not caring, he wiped it away and dropped off his bike just before he reached her house. The street was quite busy, so he would have to move in close to bring the damage to the house. Her house was an old Victorian which stood in the middle of the lot. The driveway passed along the right side of the house and led to a detached garage in the rear. Both sides of her property were covered with large trees that secluded the house from the others in the neighborhood. Her front lawn was covered in air-filled Halloween decorations; they were gaudy, but they did the trick for Halloween's candy night.

As Teddy moved in, he noticed that no lights were on in the house, though the blow-up decorations smiled their ugly grins back at him, greeting his presence as they swayed slightly in the dark air. He headed down the driveway towards the rear of the house, his head flip-flopping side to side in search of anyone watching him. Passing the back of the house, he headed for the garage and peered inside the door window— no car.

Excellent, he thought, *she must not be home*! Looking back and forth once more, he went towards the house and up the couple steps leading up to the back door. He reached in, grabbed the knob, and turned it slowly. The latch clicked as he turned the knob, removing itself from its home, and the door opened.

Unbelieving of his luck, Teddy wiped his head once again and passed through the entry into Mrs. Atwell's home. His hatred for her was high—as she had embarrassed him in front of the whole class—and now he was in the lion's den and ready for desecration. He entered the kitchen area from the back door, moving slowly. He stopped at the table and dropped his backpack. He unzipped it and retrieved the spray cans from inside. He listened carefully after he removed the cans, but there was no sound in the house: it was dead quiet.

The kitchen was extraordinarily clean, and the cupboards looked like they were original with their gold-laced handles and vintage doors.

"This is for being a bitch," he said and pointed both cans at the cabinets. Plunging the triggers, he let the paint loose upon the cabinets. Creating lines all over the cabinets, he made sure he got every single one. His conscience felt pretty good about what he had just done, and he walked out of the kitchen and down the hallway.

As he walked, he saw pictures of Mrs. Atwell and her family scattered along the wall.

"I think these pictures need some updating," he said with a sadistic grin. Plunging the cans' triggers once more, he covered the pictures with black and orange paint. He released the plungers and continued into the living room.

Upon entering the room, he immediately noticed what was probably the oldest piece of wood he had ever seen atop the fireplace mantle. It was shaped like an oar but wasn't straight due to the few crooked spots along the length of it. It was framed in a glass case with a small gold plaque which was locked at the top. The blackened stain on the wood mesmerized Teddy as he walked towards it, wondering what he should do with it. As he came to it, he placed both cans on a small table before spreading his arms out wide. He hadn't realized how big it was; his arms couldn't reach either end while standing at its middle.

He stared at it a little closer and saw that the wood appeared to be moving. He shook his head and rubbed his eyes. He inched his head nearer to the glass and gazed back upon the darkened wood; the rings of the large oar were moving in a shimmery style. They faded back and forth along the length of it, as if electricity were running rampant through the old piece of wood.

"Get away from that," a stubborn voice said from behind him.

Teddy turned slowly from the glass case and found himself face-to-face with Mrs. Atwell. "Well, I thought you weren't going to be home for a while. Guess I was wrong," he said.

"Teddy, get away from that case right now," she said again from the entrance of the hallway, unflinching. "I don't care about the paint in my kitchen and all over my pictures, but that art behind you is off limits. It's a family heirloom and priceless to me."

"Why would I do that? That is one nice piece of wood you got there," he remarked sarcastically back at her.

"You have no idea what or who you are dealing with—this isn't class anymore and you have entered my home." She moved a step closer to him. "You see, I love this time of year. Hallows' Eve is very special to me and my family."

Teddy stepped away from her advancements and remarked, as if he hadn't even heard a word she had said, "What do you think you can do to me now? You going to take my soul like you did Cam's?" he taunted. "I think I'm going to take this piece of wood from you and break it, just because you thought you could embarrass me in front of everyone."

"Teddy, you don't know what you're playing with. Cam thought the same thing a year ago. Now he isn't here and my brother gave him a fantastic ride to his new home." A slight smile crossed her face. "There are things in this world not meant for some people, and that oar is not meant to be out of that glass case or touched by human hands. Have you ever heard of the Boatman's Rhyme?" she asked cautiously.

"What the hell is that?" he said, confused. "I'm not here to learn or to have a history lesson about Cam's whereabouts. I'm here to teach you a lesson." Upon saying this, he turned to the glass case, reached up, grabbed an end, and pulled the oar off its stand.

"NO!!" she screamed as the glass case crashed down, exploding into a million little shards.

Teddy blocked his face from the glass fragments as they flew around the room. He reached down and picked up the oar—immediately he felt the immense energy that flowed through it. Mrs. Atwell charged him, screaming incoherently. She grabbed onto the oar and struggled to take it away from Teddy, but he wasn't giving it up that easily. He whipped the oar back and forth, sending her flying onto the couch.

"Teddy," she pleaded from the couch. "Oh my, Teddy! You have done the worst thing possible by touching my precious oar. Give it back to me and I'll reconsider your fate. This is your last chance, Teddy."

"I like this oar. Think I'm gonna keep it as a memento of you pleading with me." He grasped the oar hard, feeling its energy flow through him.

"You were warned, Teddy." She stood from the couch, shaking uncontrollably. Her body began roiling with convulsions, saliva flowing from her mouth.

Teddy backed away from her, heading towards the hallway, with his eyes locked on the indescribable scene which was unfolding. Her appearance grew darker and more sinister as she convulsed in the center of the room.; her eyes had rolled back into her head, and her hair fell from her scalp.

Teddy had seen enough. He ran from the living room, down the hall, and out the back door of the house all while still holding onto the dark oar. As he ran onto the driveway, the windows on the lower level of the house blew out with a shriek from within that penetrated the outside world. Each of the Halloween decorations imploded instantly as he passed them on his way down the driveway. His fear topped his adrenaline, so he dropped the oar in the middle of the driveway and ran for his life. Rounding the outside of the trees, he grabbed his bike and took off as fast as he could.

As he strode away from the crazy house, his legs ached the faster he pedaled. Darkness chased him as he headed home. Something colder than the dead of winter and darker than the depths of Hell followed him every step of the way.

He rode up to his house quickly and jumped off his bike in the front lawn. It rolled away from him and struck a prop skeleton. Darkness closed in on him, cold and unforgiving, as he pushed through the ache of his legs to the front door. The door opened from the inside and his mother appeared in the entrance. "Teddy, what the hell?" she screamed up at him as he pushed past her as fast as he could and raced up to his room, slamming the bedroom door.

As Teddy's mother was about to close the front door, a figure emerged from the darkness—it was Mrs. Atwell.

"Oh, hi. I didn't see you there, Mrs. Atwell. What brings you here?" Teddy's mother asked.

"It seems that your son left his backpack at school, and I thought I'd drop it off for him," she replied, handing the bag to her. Teddy's mother reached for the bag, and when she touched it she felt something solid. Her heart stopped from a simple touch and she fell to the floor instantly. Mrs. Atwell stepped over Teddy's lifeless mother and headed up the stairs towards his room.

Teddy cowered in his bed with the covers over his head, as the pain in his lungs and legs continued to ache from the bike ride home. A knock came at the door. Teddy froze in fear as the knock resonated throughout his room.

"Teddy! Let me in, Teddy," a voice yearned.

Teddy knew right away that it wasn't his mother, and since his father had died a couple of years earlier, he knew this voice must belong to Mrs. Atwell.

He rolled from his hiding spot and peered at the door. From this new view, he saw the door handle jiggling from someone trying to get in from the outside. Suddenly, the door handle stopped jiggling and the door itself began to vibrate continuously. Then, a dark mass resembling an arm entered the room *through* the door. Teddy's eyes widened as the arm turned into a larger black mass which also passed straight through the door. He covered his head and closed his eyes.

The door stopped vibrating as suddenly as it started. He lay curled up under the blankets, eyes still closed for what felt like an eternity. Eventually, he opened his eyes and pulled back the blanket to see.

A small plaque lay on the bed beside his face. He grasped it with one hand and read it:

Dark of the water
The oar cuts the still
The boatman steering
Souls pay for free will
Touch of the oar
A human hand
The brother of the boatman
Takes the remaining sand

As he finished reading the final line of the Boatman's Rhyme, his fear level shattered his soul and his mind fell into the abyss of chaos. His eyes focused on the entity standing at the foot of his bed—it was black and foreboding and held the oar in one skeleton hand. With a slam of the oar onto the floor, the side of the oar opened and a scythe blade flung out of its body and snapped into position at the top of the oar. The metal blade curved away from the wood in a deadly arc.

"You were warned about the rhyme, but again you just didn't listen," an all-too-familiar voice echoed throughout the bedroom. "So it's time for your sand."

Moving swiftly, the dark figure shifted to Teddy's side, where he sat frozen with terror. His eyes met the face of his tormentor, but only two hollow eye sockets gazed back.

As it reached out with its skeletal hand, Teddy felt the touch of Death.

Gate Night
Nick Manzolillo

Over and over, Clark Turner told himself that it wasn't *really* dark outside. The stars were little lanterns, guiding him. The moon, having slipped into a crescent sliver, wasn't needed. Despite the desolate expanse of rolling hills and windswept planes along his ranch, he had to remind himself that he wasn't alone out there. Somewhere, either creeping through the shadows on the far borders of his land or walking along the dirt road that lead to civilization, mischief was coming. The night before Halloween was in full bloom.

Clark had no idea whether the vandal was a single man or a whole thrill-seeking pack of them. For the past two years, on this very night, the gates to his ranch and cattle pen had been left open. Both times, after long days with his wife and sons spent gathering all the cattle they could find, several of the beasts had remained missing. The year before, one had been found drowned in a river a few miles off. While the beast could have easily slipped in after attempting a drink, nothing made Clark want to go back to a time where interfering with a man's property was a hang-able offense more than the thought of the vermin who trespassed onto his land to get their rocks off by drowning a defenseless heifer.

Some of Clark's cattle were for meat, and he'd always worried that some far-left vegan would cause him a headache, but there had been no indications that such a culprit was responsible. Regardless, Clark's gates were always left open the night before Halloween, and he told himself he was going to catch whoever did it this year.

His wife, Michelle, begrudgingly kept an eye on the front gate from their porch. While she wasn't thrilled with the idea of being alone, at least she got to hold the rifle which could fire a brutal number of rounds per minute. She also left the porch lights on, with a lit jack-o'-lantern on either side of her chair, "Just so they're aware I know what time of year it is," as she put it.

Clark's oldest son, Shawn, was away in school a few states away, while his youngest, Tom, was supposed to be helping him secure the grounds. The boy was worse than his brother, though, and was always lost in his head. He was spacey, often wandering away from the ranch on his own to read a book somewhere or stare up at the clouds or the night sky. Clark didn't mean to be hard on the boy, and he said that out loud as much as he silently regretted it, but dealing with that kid was frustrating. Tom had a habit of talking back whenever he was asked do chores, and when he did help out with them, he'd often rush the job, creating more work for Clark—like when it came time to reinforce the fences with chicken wire.

Tom had been in his room last year reading comics during the time of the vandalism, and while Clark didn't honestly suspect his son, he was relieved to see the boy passive and out of trouble. There were nights when Tom would leave his room at all hours of the night, wandering through the nightscape like one of the coyotes that always howled in the distance.

Sam, who had given Clark plenty of trouble when he was younger, had turned friendly after moving out for college. He had been eager to tell Clark all about how the night before Halloween was commonly referred to as "Cabbage," "Mischief," or "Devil's Night." As Sam put it, it was "the trick before the treat" in regards to Halloween.

As the boy went on, he told Clark that what was happening to him actually had a name, too, though it was less common. "*Gate Night* describes it perfectly, yeah? No more, no less. You're not the only one, but it really seems like you don't hear much about it these days. If you were in Scotland or Ireland with the real Celtic, All Hallows' Eve traditionalists, that'd be one thing—but where we live? As far as we live from town? I can't see why they'd choose us over tagging some local graveyard."

As far as Clark was concerned, there was no point in celebrating a holiday that, as he saw it, boiled down to community when you lived in "the middle of nowhere," as Sam called it. Even though Clark's family didn't get trick-or-treaters, he had plenty of candy from the town's general store poured into in a bowl in his kitchen. Come the actual Halloween night, all the bastards damaging his livelihood had to do was knock on his door and he'd treat them to their heart's content.

Whatever excuse the vandals had, thousands of dollars of damage and the aches and pains of a day spent tracking down the escaped cattle wasn't exactly *harmless*. It was criminal, but the cops in Clark's jurisdiction didn't want to wait around for an entire night for a "pre-emptive" crime any more than he did. He told them that if he caught anyone on his land, on this night of all nights, there was going to be hell to pay. And with a wry grin and a tip of his hat, the sheriff told him, "Well, that's your right then, isn't it? Just don't shoot anybody, Clark." Clark took that to mean don't shoot anybody with bullets: he packed rock salt into his shotgun an hour before sunset.

He didn't often stray far into his property after sunset; there were too many holes in the grass and no destination was worth the effort. If he shut off his house's exterior lights, the stars were as rich and vast and beautiful as they come. He didn't need to stray much further from his porch to enjoy them, or to roll up a blanket and lay beside Michelle like he used to when the fires of their passion burned brighter and the boys were younger or nonexistent at all.

Propping along a post at least thirty yards from the actual gate, Clark slung his gun across his lap and un-crunched a bag of pumpkin seeds that Michelle had toasted and seasoned with garlic salt. He needed something to wash the bitter taste of black coffee out of his mouth, and also, apparently, the seeds were really good for your prostate: he figured he could use that.

Feeling around the perimeter of the fence, Clark discovered chunks of what must have been a broken pumpkin. Every year, his buddy Phil Zachs, who lived closer to town and had a pumpkin field and corn maze, gave him a trunk full of pumpkins in exchange for the fair prices Clark gave him for meat. Tom had probably been the one to smash it. At the end of every season he'd take the rotting pumpkins to the far end of the property and use them for target practice. It used to be a tradition for both Clark and Tom to do it together, but last year Tom had done it without waiting for him. He figured that this year maybe the boy got even more impatient.

Worse than Sam or any teenager Clark had known, Tom was selfish in a way he couldn't understand. And when you're a parent, you can't just brush that attribute aside and accept is as the way things are. Clark figured he was somehow responsible for this behavior, yet fixing it seemed like more of a mystery than he would be capable of solving.

The hours drew on and Clark's adrenaline began to wane. His imagination ran wild with what he'd do to the vandals, but that could only sustain him for so long—it wasn't like thinking of a warm meal waiting for you after a hard day's work. Soon, all of Clark's well practiced insults and threats about the "business end" of his shotgun melted away into weariness. He then imagined himself rather politely saying, "Just go on back the way you came, and you're lucky I'm not talking with my trigger finger, you hear?" This would have been the end of it, if the night moved along like he was expecting it to.

Then he heard the voices from *within* his property.

There were cackles on the wind—the voices were more like creaking floorboards on Clark's porch than anything else—but he clearly heard the words "treat" and "full" strung along with some level of coherence. He sighed as he rose to his knees and peered over the top of the fence. When you spent enough time alone with animals, especially noisy cattle, pigs, and chicken, you'd eventually here a real word or two that was just your brain searching for meaning like a radio trying to pick up a signal. Humanoid shadows moved in the distance, and between them trudged cows that moved faster than Clark himself could ever hustle them. He arched his rifle and sucked in a deep breath that he was ready to explode all over these vandals who must have hopped over the fence from some other corner of his property, despite the barbed wire. He stopped when he saw the tall figure in between and looming above the cattle.

Realistically, it was six-foot-something feet tall, but the shadows caused it to grow. Its arms were long and its neck a thin, scraggily stem that fluffed into a round head consumed by wispy strands of silken hair. The arms stretched the length of the cattle—shepherding them, moving them along with precision. There were at least four smaller shadows, and, on top of only having about two rounds of rock salt in his gun, Clark was feeling outnumbered. *Who are they?* he thought. They chattered among one another, but they didn't giggle like children let loose on Mischief Night. There was a single metallic ringing sound from the gate a few feet away from Clark, so he crouched low into the grass and pressed his stomach to the ground.

The chittering procession of cattle thieves passed through the gate and across the dirt path leading to the road. It was only when he could breathe with confidence that they couldn't hear him that Clark realized he couldn't just let them leave. Running home to call the sheriff wouldn't do, he'd lose sight of them—even though the main road didn't have any detours for a few miles yet, they could still disappear if they went into the grazing fields on the opposite side of the road.

Hunched over his shotgun, Clark followed. The chilly autumn air caused his lungs to ache and burn. Free from his property, the procession picked up the pace. For what felt like miles, Clark studied the cattle thieves, and the more he studied that big, tall thing, the more he decided it wasn't like any man he had ever heard of before. He figured that it could be that the thieves were the sort of rural country folk that depended on the stolen meat to get them through the winter. The idea that they were stealing to populate some down-on-its-luck farm wasn't logical; no farmer would risk losing everything over a couple of meat cows with another farmer's brand on their flank. Either the thieves were desperate or looking for trouble, and Clark couldn't determine which was worse. At the very least, none of them appeared to be armed with weapons—but that big tall thing? Even if Clark had actual bullets, he wouldn't want to risk it not going down with the first two pumps of his gun.

The thieves only followed the main road for about ten minutes before branching off into the neighboring field that bordered a forest. Clark was extra cautious about following them into the woods, but he figured more trees meant he had more places to hide. It had gotten to the point that he didn't know what he was going to do anymore. He wouldn't be able to lead the cattle back to his property in the dark single-handed. All he could do was watch and learn and try to figure out who the thieves were. He smelled smoke in the October wind before he saw the first tell-tale signs of fire flickering up ahead.

The last time Clark had paid mind to the Native Americans who used to roam the land—and whose artifacts he occasionally dug up—was when Tom had to do some project for school. What Clark saw in the clearing ahead kind of reminded him of them, at first, until the thought of associating the things in front of him with any sort of man became a petty fantasy.

The fire was a fallen star, a pit of flame that burned like a scorned god. Opposite the flames, and blackening, was a misshapen and tumorous pumpkin that was as wide and as tall as the front end of Clark's truck. Dancing in front of the flames like true fanatics paying homage to their false altar were little people who wore animal skins and sported bone necklaces and bracelets so white they reflected the glamor of the flames. Their chins were pointed and their ears were thin little pikes. They were goblins, or elves, or fairies if Clark had ever seen one, and there was nothing charming or beautiful about them. He had thought the ugliest thing in the world was death and the depravity that men can do to one another, but the creatures before him had that beat. They thrived in the rot, and they wielded a mercilessness that ran unparalleled to the worst acts in mankind's history. They were evil, truer than the biblical definition: all this Clark felt in his chest like the opposite of an epiphany.

The tall thing that Clark had seen was covered in matted fur like that of a sheepdog left in the rain, and it had nubs which reminded Clark of horns on its massive, Neanderthal skull. It was something that Clark believed would never have left the woods before tonight. An apex predator, it seemed void of everything Clark had ever known. Civilization was a fairytale to the tall beast, and to further prove Clark's suspicions, it wrapped its long fingers ending in jagged black nails around one of the four cattle's necks and dragged it to the middle of the small dancing people. The cow, at first somehow lulled by those savage monsters, began to bleat in panic before the tall, hairy creature dug those black fingernails into its stomach.

As the beast squirmed in its death throes, the tall thing presented the entrails to the dancing crowd. Tongue clicking chitters went up from the crowd. "Treat!" their voices came and went like a rising and falling wave, and then they swarmed on the entrails to begin their feast.

Then the—devils?—took their heads off.

It took Clark a moment to register what he was seeing. The gore from the cattle, the fire: it was all a distraction. But the hungry little people were putting their hands on either side of their necks and pulling up as if to remove a mask; their heads popped off, but their chittering sounds and the echoes of "Treat!" continued uninterrupted. They held their heads up, bone necklaces dangling from their neck stump, as they toasted to the night sky before popping their skulls back on and digging into their meal.

Clark had seen enough. He had mistaken his seemingly justified frustration with being robbed. He had pulled at a thread that unspooled the fabric of the world, and by doing so, he would never be comfortable again. It was only when one of the creatures' faces, instead of its head, was knocked off that Clark realized that he couldn't run away—not if he didn't want to lose a *son* along with the cattle.

Tom lay sprawled on his ass behind the feasting savage things; his mask, a crude wood carving that only vaguely resembled the little monsters around him, was on his lap. He fumbled with it for a moment, bringing it to his face but it slipped from his fingers. One of the devils turned from the cow entrails, craning its neck and sniffing at the air. When it set its eyes on the defenseless boy, it pounced. Several other devils pulled away from the feast and circled Tom.

"Trick?" one called.

"Treat!" another responded.

At that point, Clark had raised his gun and charged forward.

When he was twenty feet away, he fired at the closest devil. While rock salt was good for knocking a man on his backside, when his hit the thing, it began to smoke and sizzle worse than the timber in that great inferno of a fire. Letting loose a bloodcurdling howl of pain, the devil's chest collapsed in on itself as it split in half, both ends going still before they touched the grass. Tom's mask was back on. "Dad!" he called, scrambling toward Clark. The feasting creatures all turned from their meal, and the power of their combined eyes became a weight that caused Clark's breath to catch in his lungs. The devils ignored Tom and began running towards Clark, who aimed and fired the barest scattershot of rock salt, causing the closest devils to squeal and burn. Their afflicted body parts melted into gore.

Tom reached his father's side, and the boy pulled of his mask and held it to Clark's face. Instantly, Clark felt the devil's attention shift to Tom like the unstoppable minute hand moving on a grandfather clock. The idea of masks and treats and mischief all collided, and in the briefest of moments that he had to make his decision, Clark understood. A lonely boy had discovered something on the outskirts of society that made an education from a liberal arts college in California pale in comparison. Devils are easily tricked. Clark tore off his mask and pressed it to Tom's face, pushing him away as the monsters converged. Jagged fingers dug into Clark's chest, and the tall hairy king of the forest lumbered forward through its legion, a dumb grin slowly unfurling across its lips.

From the outskirts of the devil's hollow watched a stray creature with a false face running free from the congregation. Clark was able to follow Tom's plight until he disappeared into the darkness at the edge of the fire's light—he had plenty of time to watch, as the devils ate him slowly.

Tom never did forgive himself. Before he had joined the little people in the hollow, he had told his mother to go to bed and that he would guard the porch. He had then blown out each of the jack-o'-lanterns before smashing them. Breaking tradition was what brought the little people to you, like leaving a deer carcass robbed of its choice meat for these scavengers.

When Tom returned home, after the tragedy in the hollow, he carved new pumpkins and relit them. When no flake of skin, stray piece of bone, or other trace of Clark showed up, Tom remained at home with his mother as she nursed her broken and lonely heart. He threw himself into the always available work around the farm. He also burned the collection of masks he had made, including the one he had been sent from some contest he saw in the back of a comic book.

Fun had teeth, and Wonder did not know the difference between black and white.

When next October came, Tom carved all the pumpkins Phil Zachs gave him and his mother before setting them around the farm's perimeter. At each gate, he presented a bowl of pumpkin innards along with a few pieces of candy—

it didn't compare to a whole cow, but come Halloween morning, the gates had remained closed.

Devils were a silly sort, and their ways made sense to none. Picking up the picked-clean bowls and disposing of the pumpkins on the first of November, Tom made due with the thrill these fleeting, half-forgotten traditions gave him. To want for anything more was childish.

Dear Dead Jenny
Ian McDowell

It was Halloween 1972 and Jenny Locklear was dead and I'd never find another girl like her. I guess she was my first girlfriend, although I hadn't gotten around to calling her that when a car hit her while she was walking home alone in the rain, her Bride of Frankenstein wig slipping off her head and makeup running down her face. Maybe she was crying. If so, that also makes me her boyfriend. You have to be that to make a girl cry, unless you hit her or do something else dumbass mean when you're both kids. I never did, even when I was little—she hit back too hard.

What made her special, other than she's the only dead person I ever knew other than Mom? Mom went into the hospital the summer between the first and second grade and never came out, and I don't remember the next two years. But I remembered every one of the 364 days since my dad told me that Jenny had been found in the ditch along Raintree Road, the four dark lanes that separated her neighborhood from mine.

I'd known her since kindergarten. A little scabby monkey girl with tangled brown hair and black eyes. She threw dirt clods really hard and—because of her older brothers—was nobody to tussle with. Not just because they'd kick your butt or maybe stab you—at least we all thought they would, them being part Lumbee, as their last name would tell you if you were from this part of North Carolina, where all the Lumbee are either Locklears or Oxendines—her brothers were as dark as a Sugar Daddy, the Lumbee in Fayetteville supposedly being as much what we then called colored—or sometimes the "N-word," as the Indians they claimed to be—

71

not that you told them that unless you wanted a stomping. She was a lighter caramel, though darker than her blonde and dough-colored mom.

The dirt clod fights ended when Jenny lobbed one into my left eye so hard I fell down crying—although I was later happy to get a patch like a pirate. Mom drew a skull and crossbones on it, and let me wear it longer than I needed to— then she got sick and died and I don't remember Jenny, or much else, except being sad—until it was the fourth grade, and I wasn't so sad anymore, and Jenny had somehow become my best friend. She later told me she jumped on the Robinson twins when they were making me eat one of those big green hornworms—but I don't remember that. She said they would make me chew instead of just swallowing, like the time I gulped down a fat wiggly tadpole on a dare. According to her, mustard-colored goo squirted out my mouth right before she hit David Robinson with a softball bat. I wish I could remember her hitting him, but I'm glad I don't recall what the caterpillar tasted like.

The first time I remember her doing best friend stuff was when she borrowed a stack of my monster magazines. I'd been reading them ever since Tony, this grownup who did plays with my father at the Fayetteville Little Theater and wanted to be a professional makeup man, lent me a copy of with a cool painting of a snarling werewolf on the cover. Big scary letters said it was "The Werewolf of London," but Tony explained that the magazine had goofed, and it was actually the one from a movie—which bugged me when I saw it later because I didn't think werewolves should talk.

I guess Tony, who would come over to our house to run lines with my dad when I was younger, and whom I started regularly visiting once I was old enough to go to his place on my own, was the first monster movie fan I knew. I soon became one, too. A few other kids my age had some of the Aurora monster models, but I was the only one who had them all, even the Old Witch and the Bride of Frankenstein. Many of us watched monster movies on *Dialing for Dollars* in the afternoon or *Sunrise Theater* on Saturdays, but I was the only one whose father let him stay up late on Saturday nights for *Shock Theater* with Dr. Paul Bearer. By the fifth grade, my dad was buying me *Famous Monsters of Filmland* and by the sixth, *Castle of Frankenstein*—which wasn't really meant for kids, but he didn't know that. I was always afraid he'd look inside that magazine, because sometimes the pictures had tits in them, but he never did.

The important thing is that Jenny liked monsters just as much as me. She never got the models, but she played with mine, bringing over her Barbies and making them look like the Frankenstein Monster or the Mummy was carrying or strangling them. She was the only kid I knew who called him "The Frankenstein Monster" instead of just "Frankenstein." Girls weren't supposed to like this stuff. Girls weren't supposed to like comic books, either, but she read them—and I don't mean the romance ones. Unlike my male friends, she called the big green guy that Bruce Banner turned into the Hulk, not Huck—like Tom Sawyer's buddy on the raft. She didn't care for Spider-Man, and I didn't like Wonder Woman—even when they changed her to look like Mrs. Peel on our favorite program *The Avengers*—but we read them together, sitting back to back under the big oak tree in my yard, or side by side on the couch with our feet next to each other's heads. We even loved the ads—she said she'd heard the submarine was just a big cardboard box, but surely the live squirrel monkey wasn't a gyp.

She came over to watch *Star Trek* and, of course, *The Avengers*—we were sad when Mrs. Peel left and didn't like

Tara King. Her folks wouldn't let her come over for late night movies, but we watched plenty of afternoon ones. We would race to get home from school in time for *The Attack of the Giant Leeches* or *Gigantis the Fire Monster*, although these were never as good as the Karloff and Lugosi stuff on Shock Theater. Dad dropped us off at Christopher Lee and Peter Cushing matinees downtown, and by the seventh grade we were getting a lot of "Jim and Jenny, sitting in tree, K-I-S-S-I-N-G," but all we ever did was wrestle. Her brothers acted like they almost liked me, and after that neither one of us had to worry about anyone giving us grief.

At the other end of my neighborhood were some old houses that had been divided up into apartments. That's where Tony the makeup guy lived—although I knew him before she did, and I was the one that asked him to show her his stuff. Tony had been in Vietnam, where Dad said he'd been a combat photographer. I heard he kept a scrapbook of photos of real wounds and dead guys, but he wouldn't show it to me and changed the subject whenever I asked him. What he would let me—and then later Jenny—do was read his amazing collection of monster magazines and books. Some were older than me. He also had a couple of those really expensive Don Post masks that were advertised in the back of *Famous Monsters*, and some he'd made himself that were just as good—with real hair and everything. He worked in a costume rental place for a living when he wasn't acting or doing makeup at the Fayetteville Little Theater. I'd known him since I could remember stuff again. Dad had really thrown himself into the theater after Mom's death and while I never acted, he would take me with him and I'd hang out backstage where everybody called each other by first names no matter their age; Tony was the first grownup I ever did that with.

In the seventh grade, Jenny and I decided it would be the last time we'd ask Tony to make us up to go trick-or-treating together, since next year we'd be thirteen and that was too old for it—if not for Devil's Night pranks—and anyway, Tony kept talking about going off to do professional makeup for movies, and we knew he soon would. He agreed to make Jenny up as the Bride of Frankenstein and me as the Monster. He said he'd send a photograph of us in to *Famous Monsters*—they were always running photos of kids in monster makeup, some really good.

Halloween afternoon, we went over to Tony's and I sat on his busted-up porch and read his magazines while he made Jenny up as the Bride. He painted her face and neck and arms really pale with green highlights and used something called collodion—which puckered her skin up—to make that scar on her neck. He'd already made the wig with the lightning bolts in it, saying it was only the second time he'd ever worked with that much hair, the first being when he made the mask for the ape suit in *Cabaret*—the costume was rented but he'd hated the mask that came with it, and made something that looked more like *Planet of the Apes*. He said the hair was real and that it might have come from a dead person, but when Jenny got grossed out he laughed and said "no, women sold their hair all the time" and Jenny said, "yeah, we'd read *The Gift of the Magi* in school," and the way she smiled at him bugged me. Tony was my hero, and like the uncle I never had, but he was a handsome guy—dark and Italian and muscular—but for some reason it bothered me to see him touching Jenny, even though he was twice her age and wasn't doing anything creepy—and of course he had to touch her to make her up. But I suddenly didn't like, it and that's why I took his magazines out on the porch.

Jenny finally came out and she looked amazing—maybe not as great as the Jack Pierce makeup for the Bride in the movie, but at least as good as anything you'd see on a comedy show or commercial—he'd wrapped bandages around her arms, and he'd found a long white dress somewhere. She stared at me with those dark eyes and she knew that I was jealous of Tony, and she knew that I knew it. "You're beautiful," I said, my face burning as the words came out.

She stared at me hard and then she kissed me—and time just stopped. I couldn't hear the cicadas, or the lawn sprinkler, or cars going by, or the Moody Blues eight-track Tony was playing on his stereo inside—just my heart beating.

She finally drew back. "Did you like that?"

I did. I did so much. But somehow, I couldn't say it. I was too afraid to say anything.

It was getting dark and Tony's porch light had come on. Tony was still inside, getting his makeup chair ready for me.

"Jimmy, did you like it?" Jenny asked again.

I looked away, then down at the issue of *Castle of Frankenstein* I'd been reading. On the cover, a Doctor Frankenstein who was supposed to be Peter Cushing—but looked more like a white Greg Morris from *Mission Impossible*—and a Boris Karloff Monster were threatening a blonde in a mini skirt with really big tits popping out of her top.

"What's the matter? You don't like that I don't have those?" she asked, nodding at the magazine cover.

I mumbled something about wanting to kiss her again and told myself I should just grab her and do it like they did in movies, but I was too afraid.

"Nobody has boobs like that," she said.

I tried to make a joke: "I dunno, Natalie Johnson's are pretty big."

She stopped smiling and her black eyes suddenly looked like holes in her green-white face. "Why don't you go trick-or-treating with her, then!"

Yeah, like that would happen—Natalie was already dating an eighth-grade jock.

I knew I needed to say something, but I couldn't think of what. My chance to kiss her back had passed. She stepped down off the porch. "Get Tony to give you a ride home. I'm walking, don't follow me." This wasn't unusual; kids walked everywhere back then, even after dark.

The cicadas had stopped and I could hear something hitting the leaves. "It's raining," I said. "At least let me see if Tony has an umbrella."

"Screw that," she said. "Screw that *and* you."

"Well screw you right back!" I shouted after her.

She began to run—why didn't I run after her?

The sky got darker and the rain started to fall harder. I watched the rain fall and waited for Tony, but he didn't come out. I went back inside.

He was smoking a joint. "Be ready in a few minutes, man."

I didn't know what to say about Jenny. "You don't need to make me up, just let me borrow that mask you made of Karloff as the Monster."

"It will be kind of big on you. And it will look weird—you in a mask and her in makeup. Where *is* Jenny?"

"She went home," I mumbled.

He finished the joint. "You guys had a fight." He didn't say it as a question. "I guess that had to happen."

He put the rubber headpiece he'd made for me back on the plaster cast he'd made of the top of my head and got the mask from its display atop his bookcase. He was very proud of it and had never lent it to me before. "You know she's special, right?"

What, did he think I was stupid? "She's the only girl I know who's into this stuff."

"That's not what makes her special, Jim. You better treat her right. If it was your fault, tell her you're sorry. If it was hers, apologize anyway."

"Nights in White Satin" started up again on the eight-track.

Tony took me home and I called Jenny's house. Her dad said she wasn't there. Later, I found out she'd been hit in the early evening, but nobody saw her lying there in the muddy ditch for hours. Maybe she was already there when we drove past. Maybe, if we'd seen her, we could have gotten her to the hospital in time. But no, they later said she'd died right away. I hope that's true. The only thing worse than the thought of her lying there dead would be her lying there dying.

But I didn't know that yet. I called her again, and again her father said she hadn't come home yet. Then he started asking me angry questions and yelling. My dad got on the phone, yelled back, and hung up. I didn't dress up as the Karloff Frankenstein. Dad and I sat on the couch and watched something with Dennis Weaver on the CBS Sunday Night Movie. I don't remember what it was. Well, he watched, and I pretended to watch, and he put his arm around me for the first time in a while. Then he made himself a gin and tonic and drank it and made another one, as he always did on nights he wasn't at the Little Theater. And then he fell asleep, snoring, his face red and his glasses down on his nose, his head nodding back into the wall paneling with a dull *thump thump thump*. Something else he always did on nights he was at home. I moved from the couch to the armchair.

Eventually, Shock Theater came on. They showed movies all night on Halloween, but the first was *The Mummy*—which is pretty boring once Boris Karloff stops being a real mummy and is just an old guy. I fell asleep.

Shock Theater was playing *Captive Wild Woman* when the cops knocked on the door. Apparently, Mr. Locklear had told them I was the last one to see Jenny. They'd found her by then. Dad came to the door and spoke to them outside, where he apparently convinced them they didn't need to talk to me that night, although they'd want a statement the following day. Then he came inside and told me what had happened.

"That's not true," I said. "You're joking." He said he wished he was and hugged me hard, and then I was crying. I don't know if I'd stopped by the time I went to bed.

I dreamed Jenny and I were standing out on the street in the autumn leaves she loved. In the dream, it must have been earlier in the evening, because all down the street the jack-o'-lanterns were still lit, although there were no trick-or-treaters. Jenny kissed me, and I touched her neck where Tony had made the scar. Instead of collodion and greasepaint, I felt real stitches. Her eyes were so black—more like holes. They popped open and blood flowed out and down her white neck and white dress, turning both red.

I woke up and sobbed for a long time in the dark.

They never found out who hit her.

I didn't go back to school for two weeks. Dad dropped out of the play he was in and stayed home with me at night. He tried not to drink until I went to bed. For dinner, he cooked steaks and burgers or brought home pizza, no more macaroni or spam or TV dinners, but I didn't care. When I finally went back to school, Leonard, Jenny's older brother who was in the ninth grade—while we called ninth graders

"Freshman," they were still in junior high and didn't go off to the high school until the next year—grabbed me and shoved me into a row of lockers and was going to hit me, but then he started crying and hugged me before letting me go and walking away very fast.

He wasn't the only one to hug me. Natalie Johnson did too, and when she did I could feel her boobs against my chest. I closed my eyes and saw Jenny standing there looking like she wanted to throw a dirt clod at me, so I pulled away. Natalie's eighth-grade jock boyfriend Mitch glared and cracked his knuckles, but you don't hit a kid whose girlfriend just died.

I remembered my mom dying, and I remembered it being two years later and me not so sad anymore. Why couldn't everything jump ahead like that now, with me in the ninth grade and starting to think about other girls? Why hadn't I grabbed Jenny and kissed her? Why hadn't I done so long before that afternoon? So many *whys*—those were my thoughts every night and most days.

We didn't get much snow that winter, but a lot of freezing rain. Spring took its time, but summer got really hot. I didn't do much on my summer break, mostly staying in my room—although one time I walked in the woods and carved her and my initials on a tree. Once or twice, I prayed for her and for me. I hadn't been brought up religious. Dad later told me that he'd studied for the seminary but quit when he realized he didn't believe in God, that he was just in love with what he called the "theater of the pulpit." Mom had been a Quaker, who Baptists don't consider to be real Christians, and she never sent me to Sunday school. I didn't even go to her funeral, as Dad thought I couldn't deal with it—I did go to Jenny's, but never visited her grave after that. Whatever was in the ground, that wasn't her.

The week before she died, she'd given me a green stone the light shown through. It looked like nothing so much as the bottom of a Seven-Up bottle. She said her grandma had given it to her, and that it was a Wish Stone, and that if I put it in my pillow and made a wish at night, the wish would come true when I woke up. I thought it was silly when she told me that, but now I sometimes picked it up off my night stand and felt its smoothness—but I didn't make a wish because I already knew how I'd feel when I woke up and it hadn't happened.

At least, I didn't make one until the next Halloween.

It was now the eighth grade and I was thirteen. Not that I could have stood to go trick-or-treating even if I was still twelve, having done it with Jenny since the fourth grade or maybe earlier. I didn't even want to help Dad carve a pumpkin or decorate our porch, so he did it by himself. I looked at it and thought even harder of Jenny and ran upstairs.

I had a little black and white TV in my room. Channel 11, one of two I could get with the bent antenna, was rerunning *The Night Stalker*. Not the show that came later, when I was in high school, the first TV movie with the vampire. I watched it thinking Jenny would have liked it a lot.

Dad knocked on my door: "Jim, you can't go on like this. She wouldn't want you to—it's been a year."

I told him to go away. After a while he did, and I could hear Johnny Carson on the big TV that was plugged into the stereo downstairs. Dad was hard of hearing; he hadn't worn his earplugs when he was in the artillery in Korea.

I eventually switched to Channel Eight and Shock Theater. I used to love the host, Dr. Paul Bearer, but his jokes now seemed so corny. The first movie was *The Raven*. Unlike the poem, which I'd memorized to impress Jenny, there was no lost Lenore in it—but soon it was a midnight dreary.

I looked over at my night table where the Wish Stone flickered green in the light from the TV. I picked it up and put it in my pillow. *Come back Jenny. Even if just for tonight, so I can say I'm sorry, and kiss you again.* Dr. Paul Bearer must have been doing a Poe thing, because after *The Raven* was *The Black Cat.* I fell asleep before Lugosi started skinning Karloff and the weird looking castle blew up.

My door opened, and Jenny came in. Her eyes were more like holes than ever. She was so pale. The blood on her wasn't makeup.

I woke up. Someone was knocking at the front door. I went downstairs and saw Dad snoring on the couch. There was a big orange bowl on the coffee table, and judging by how much candy was still in it, not many trick-or-treaters had come by. Surely none were still out this late—so, who was knocking?

I walked to the door and opened it. Jenny stood there. She wore her Bride of Frankenstein wig, but it wasn't crooked now. There was no blood or mud on her white dress nor her bandaged arms. She was pale, but it was the pale of makeup, and the porch light was bright enough that I could see caramel-colored skin at the hollow of her throat.

"Hi, Jimmy." Her voice was that of a live person. She sounded embarrassed. "Trick or Treat." She smiled that smile that I realized—just then—meant everything to me and had for years. "I'm not much of a treat, but I swear this isn't a trick."

My face was wet. I knew I wasn't dreaming. I knew that she was dead. I knew that she was really standing there.

"Are you a ghost?"

She knew she was dead, too. "Yeah, I guess. I'm not all messed up, like the kid the monkey's paw brought back. I feel alive. But I know I'm dead—just not right now."

I didn't say anything.

"Aren't you going to hug me?"

I did. She was cold, but not too cold.

"I still don't have big boobs. I guess I never will."

"I'm sorry," I finally said. That sounded stupid, like I was sorry about her boobs.

But she knew what I really meant. "No, I'm sorry. I'm the one who got mad and ran away."

"I'm the one who was too dumb to kiss you again—or before. We knew each other for so long, and I never kissed you before."

"You can kiss me now."

I did. Either her lips weren't as cold as her body, or she was getting warmer. She rubbed one of her bandages on my mouth, then showed me the black lipstick on it. "Let's go trick-or-treating."

I just wanted to hold her again. "This late?"

"Just one house. There's something I've got to do, then we can come back here and I can be with you for the rest of the night."

I wondered if she meant sex. That was scary. Not because she was dead, but because sex was scary.

She seemed to know what I was thinking. "Just hold me for a long time. Until I'm dead again."

In the living room, I heard Dad grunt and roll over on the couch. I shut the door behind me, not caring that I didn't have a jacket.

We walked down the street holding hands. Hers was colder than her lips but got warmer as I held it. Unlike the road where she died, my street was well lit. In the buzzing glow of the street lamps she looked black and white, like the real Bride of Frankenstein. Tony hadn't given her Frankenstein shoes so she was wearing Keds under her dress, but her wig made her seem taller than me. She kicked at dry leaves, sending them skittering down the pavement. I didn't care where we were going and was happy.

She laughed to see someone had toilet-papered the Robinson's house. "Remember what we did after Mrs. Robinson called me a red nigger?" I remembered, because it had happened a couple of years after she'd rescued me from the twins. The Robinson boys were bullies, and their mom was so big and mean they must have gotten it from her instead of their dad, a meek little guy with a head like a light bulb. Two summers ago, I'd taken my life-size model skull and a veal chop from the fridge and she shredded the meat with scissors and mixed it with Elmer's Glue All. We spread it on the skull and she got an old cheap black wig from a previous Halloween and glued that on too. Then we climbed our old oak tree and nailed chicken wire over the skull on a thick limb, so no varmint could get it. Once it smelled awful and was full of maggots, we took it down and left it in the Robinson's garden. Mrs. Robinson found it, crawling with flies, when she came out to water her roses. She nearly had a heart attack. The cops took it away and couldn't figure out it was a fake until it was back in the morgue. Dad knew I'd done it and grounded me for two months, but he still let Jenny come over and hang out with me. She thought it was the funniest thing ever.

She still did, and as she laughed, her hand gripped mine very tightly. We turned onto Sagebrush Lane, which ended in a traffic circle. At the bottom of it was Reverend Jackson's house. I'd never gone to his church, but I didn't like him—I knew from the paper and the TV news that he was always trying to get books taken out of the school library, and he'd tried to organize a protest when the Fayetteville Little Theater did *Cabaret*. For some reason, you never heard him say anything about the nightclubs and strip joints and porno theaters on the 400 block of Hay Street in downtown, where all the soldiers from Fort Bragg went on the weekends.

Jenny led me to his door—of course there wasn't a jack-o'-lantern. Reverend Jackson didn't like Halloween. Any kids who trick-or-treated here got a lecture about Satan.

Jenny rang the doorbell. I was nervous and didn't understand why we were there. I wanted to spend time with her, not with some angry grownup who'd yell at us and might call my dad.

She had to ring six times before he came to the door in a big fluffy nightgown. He smelled more of booze than my dad ever did.

"You damn kids shouldn't be out this late. You shouldn't be trick or treating at all," he mumbled groggily.

"You shouldn't cuss. Or drink and drive," said Jenny quietly.

He stared at her and his expression changed into something scarier than any monster makeup. I think that was him knowing before he knew.

"What?" he asked.

"You shouldn't have hit me and not stopped."

Whatever else his expression was, it wasn't surprise. couldn't stand to look at his face, so I looked at hers. Her eyes grew very black and I saw that they really were holes. Her mouth spread wide, no lips, just teeth. She was thinner. She let go of my hand before hers became mostly bone.

"Jesus save me," he whimpered.

"No," she said.

He fell to his knees and started blubbering. I hoped I hadn't made noises like that when I cried. "I should have stopped—when I heard about you, I—I should have turned myself in."

"Yes," she said.

"I still can. I will. I swear to *Jesus* I will."

She tapped his bald spot with her bony hand and he yelped liked a dog. "If you don't, I'll be back."

"I know," he said very softly.

She reached for my hand, hers living flesh again, and started to lead me away.

"Wait," he said. "Were you in Heaven?"

She stopped. "No."

"Were you in Hell? I know that's where I'm going."

She shook her head. "I wasn't anywhere."

"You can't say that," he whimpered. "There has to be a Heaven and a Hell. How could you come back if there's not? There *has* to be a Hell. I *have* to go there."

Jenny didn't say anything. We walked away, leaving him shaking and blubbering on his knees. Next door, a light came on.

Jenny's hand was colder than before, but it still felt like a hand, not bones.

"So, that's why you came back," I finally said.

We kept walking, the leaves all crunchy underfoot. She squeezed closer and put her arm around me, and I put mine around her. She felt warm again.

"No. I came back for you, not him. But this way everybody will know he did it. When they have somebody to blame, nobody will be mad at you anymore."

Even with her father yelling at me on the phone that night and her brother starting to threaten me, I hadn't notice people being mad—but I guess they had been. "I shouldn't have let you walk home in the dark."

Her arm around me squeezed tighter. "Never say that again. Or think it. I command you as a girl *and* as a ghost, and you know better than to disobey either."

Back home, I opened the door quietly. I could hear static and Dad's snoring from the living room. The stairs didn't have any carpet, so I took off my shoes. Jenny's footsteps didn't make a sound.

In my room with the door shut, she took off her wig and shook out her hair, all dark brown and curly. Then she took off her gown. Underneath, she wore a tank top and shorts. In the dim light, her arms and legs and the place where her throat met her chest were darker than her normal caramel color, her face makeup paler. She lay down with me and we kissed a lot. Her makeup started coming off, some on me and some on the sheets. I kissed her collodion scar, which had started to break apart. I rubbed my tongue over it until it was wet and then picked off some of the flakes. She sighed deeply and nuzzled my neck.

I didn't try to get to second base, much less further— even though if I'd ever wanted anyone to be my first time, it would have been her.

"Girls must like you now," she said softly. "We like sad boys when they have something to really be sad about. I did, when you were little and so sad. I wanted to take all that sadness out of you."

"Maybe you did," I said. "I'm not sad *now*."

"You can date anyone you want *now*. Even Natalie Johnson."

"I don't want to date Natalie Johnson."

"Realllyyy?" she asked, teasingly drawing out the word. "They really are quite big."

"Dammit, Jenny!"

She laughed. "See, I can still make you mad."

"I'm sorry." How many times had I said that tonight?

"Don't be. My teasing means I love you."

"I love you," I whispered. "You're the only one I want to date."

"Can't do that, Jimbo," she said, looking older than me even though she was still twelve and I was now thirteen. "I mean, not unless you dig my body up like a perv—and that's *not* dating. I can't come back again."

"But—but you told Reverend Jackson you would if he didn't turn himself in?"

She smiled the saddest smile I'd ever seen. "Ghosts can lie, too. All I know is that I really can't come back after tonight, not to him or to you, but I won't need to."

"I'll need you to."

She started crying then. "You won't, not any more. But we'll have this. That's enough, even if you don't think so." I used my shirt to wipe her face, leaving a dark patch of skin. "I'll visit your grave every day," I said through my own tears, feeling guilty I'd not done so since her funeral.

"That's sweet, but why? I won't know it. After sunrise I won't know anything ever again."

"You won't know you love me?"

"I know you love me right now. That's enough. When you wake up I'll be gone, and I'll never be back. Cry then if you want, but when you're done, don't cry anymore—at least, not for me. Promise?"

We said some other things, but after a while I made that promise. I've even kept it.

We talked some more, and I held her tight. We watched some of *Son of Frankenstein*—it's not as good as the first two, but it felt right. Eventually, I slept a bit. I don't know if she did.

I woke up to light shining in the window and Dad knocking on my door.

Of course I was alone.

Of course I cried.

Dad came in and squeezed my shoulder and said, "I'm going to make breakfast. Please come down and sit with me."

After a while, I got up. There was makeup on my t-shirt, but it was the same one I'd worn a year and a day ago—when she kissed me when she was still alive—and the makeup smear was small and looked old. There wasn't any on the bed sheets. I changed and went downstairs. Upon smelling bacon frying, I was surprised to find I was hungry. Dad squeezed fresh orange juice and made coffee for himself. He started to talk about counseling, and how it could really help, but I just shook my head. "Maybe I needed that before, but now I don't."

He stared into my eyes for a long time, but eventually he looked relieved.

After eating some bacon and drinking some orange juice, I started to talk about her. He listened without saying anything and I didn't cry—and haven't since. But sometimes, in late October when the wind sends lipstick-colored leaves dancing down the street and the skinny bare tree limbs shake like Jenny waving her arms, I think I hear her calling my name.

Alone on Halloween
Michael Gore

The jack-o'-lantern had started to rot prematurely. Nick rolled it onto his side with the edge of his dirty sneaker, and a slow-motion squishing sound softly emanated from the jagged mouth of the sad pumpkin. He shook his head with slight shame, but also as if inspecting it, in the same way a detective in one of those cop shows did when they hunched over a dead body. "People always carve them too early," Nick said out loud, to no one but himself, again taking up the role of a detective, his hands in his hoodie pockets. "Day before, day before Halloween, if you want them fresh." This line was mumbled more than spoken out loud. With more slight movement of the shoe, he applied pressure to the triangle shaped eye and mashed the face into a pile of orange mush. Somehow, the fact that he had done it gently made it almost all right that he had just ruined some innocent child's pumpkin. It was on the curb of the street though, so he rationalized with himself that it was probably being thrown out anyway.

Shaking the pulpy mess off his shoe, Nick kept on his walk. It was warm, warmer than most Cabbage Nights—or at least that is what they called it in his hometown. His new town didn't have a name for it, no one even seemed to know the traditions that took place on what Nick used to think was the most fun night of the year—the night before Halloween. What he did last year on that night, well, that was why he was in a new town, one that didn't have such traditions. His mother thought, maybe it would be "good for him" to get away and have a fresh start. After all, everything that happened last year—the destruction, the uproar in the town and the eventual ban of trick or treating that next night—was one-hundred percent his fault. There they would never treat him fairly again.

Leaves crunching under his feet, some of them sticking to the drying orange muck, he thought about how long ago that year now felt. It felt like another life time ago. Hell, the six months he had been living in the middle-of-ass-nowhere already felt like six years. And it wasn't just time and distance, he felt like a different person now. Looking back over the past year and thinking of that awful night that was supposed to be "fun as fuck," he couldn't believe how stupid he had been. Thankfully no one in *this* town knew him as "Oh, that kid" when people mentioned his name. Now, he was just the "new kid who doesn't talk much." While he would have had no problem meeting new people and making friends in this new town, he didn't see the point. Nick was sixteen and a senior, so making friends for half a year before they all went off to school seemed pointless. Besides, most of them had been together since preschool and had formed bonds he couldn't even imagine. Keeping his "head down and grades up" was his motto—get through the year, graduate, and start a new life in college.

That's why the walk tonight seemed so… lonely. Though traumatic, last year he had been surrounded by six friends he had known since preschool. Friends he could trust with his life—or so he thought—until the night they all pointed fingers at him when the handcuffs came out. Part of him realized that is why he didn't even want friends this year: if old ones would turn on him in a second, what would new ones do? The walk, which he had already taken about a hundred times since moving into the new house, was simple and nice, but with purpose. While the ultimate goal was to get to the 7-11 for an energy drink and few Slim Jims, Nick found himself using it as an excuse to get out of the house and enjoy the street. He already had his license, but his mother said he could not have a car until he turned seventeen and showed enough responsibility; thankfully, it was only a few months away. Regardless, Nick thought he would still take the walk. While he didn't believe in "hippie crap," there was some sort of Zen in the fourteen-minute walk to, and fourteen-minute walk back from, the store that put him at ease, especially in the fall weather, with the crunchy leaves making satisfying sounds under his feet. However, he would never admit this to anyone and would defend to his death that the walk was solely for the Slim Jims.

After two lefts, a right, and then a long straight stretch, Nick arrived at the dingy old convenience store and walked through the automatic doors. A cold burst of air hit him—for some reason they still had the air conditioning on, causing the store to be ten degrees colder than outside. The sudden cold made Nick hesitate with confusion for a second, but he quickly righted himself and headed straight for the cooler where they kept the thirty-two ounce, overly caffeinated drink to which he had become so addicted. Opening the cooler, he paid no attention to the pumpkin decals that adorned the glass; they had already been there for a month. What he did notice was that the inside of the cooler was warmer than the store. He shook his head in frustration but grabbed two blue cans anyway.

Three steps before the cash register, he grabbed two Slim Jims—the monster-sized ones—and a Twix. Throwing all his stuff on the counter, he pulled the crumbled money out of his pocket. He had the exact change ready, tax included, and put it on the counter to await his cheap plastic bag. The indistinguishable foreign man behind the counter just nodded and accepted the money without looking—he knew Nick and his routine, and the fact that he always gave the exact amount. As he cracked open a can and walked towards the door, Nick looked up and saw a bright orange flyer with a ring of Inkjet ghosts making up its border.

Nick stopped, took a sip of his acidic caffeine drink, and read it:

Alone on Halloween?
Don't be a ghoul,
Come out you fool!
Get the scare of your life,
Even if you're old enough to have a wife.
Treats for all,
Even if you don't survive the fall!

345 Wentworth Ave – Starts at Dusk

Make Sure to Vote for Ruben's House as
"Scariest House" this year!

It was a cheesy poster, but something about it intrigued Nick. He pulled out his phone and took a photo of the flyer before starting his walk home. The entire way, he tried not to think about last year's events, but seeing the Halloween decorations, the flyer, and the countless pumpkins lining the way forced him go over what happened again and again—not that he hadn't already done so a million times over the past year. He knew the anniversary would be hard, but he hoped that a new town would help ease the memories. It didn't.

When Nick got home, he knew he had just missed his mother because there were pumpkins on the steps which weren't there before and her car was not in the driveway. He looked at the three round, squat, but almost perfect pumpkins without showing emotion, then went inside to read her note. She *always* left a note, rather than just texting; she said it was more personal. Inside, on the fridge like always, was the large hot pink sticky. He read it quickly, same old story: had to rush off to second job, frozen dinners in freezer or pizza money in drawer, don't go to bed too late, clean up, blah, blah. The only difference in this note was that she asked him to carve the pumpkins for her, "all three please, with different faces on each." It was the last thing he wanted to do, but after last year, there wasn't a single thing he didn't do when she asked. He had been the prefect son since November 1st of last year.

One by one he brought the pumpkins in, cleaned them off with wet paper towels, and then set them down on a spread of newspaper. On the television in the kitchen, he popped on AMC to watch their horror movie line up; thankfully, Kane Hodder was on the screen wearing the classic hockey mask and gutting people left and right—those movies always made him happy. Nick always loved Halloween; love was probably an understatement. And yet, last year, he didn't even get to see a single minute of his favorite holiday because he was in jail of the courthouse while the little kids of Bethwick cried about not being allowed to go trick-or-treating. That day, Nick knew what it felt like to be a real monster.

Pulling out the flimsy orange saw-like device that came with the pumpkin carving kit, Nick looked at it and sighed. The thing was three inches long and could easily be bent by a strong wind, yet it did a hell of a job carving through the orange flesh. After holding the tiny blade to the pumpkin to start carving an eye, Nick suddenly stopped, pulled away the saw, and slid the miniature teeth across his left wrist. It stung and left a red line, but only one tiny droplet of blood— not even enough for a sugar test oozed from his skin. He stared at it, then dropped the mini-saw on the counter. He had never done anything like that in his life, and it scared him. His doctors asked him countless times if he was depressed, if he ever harmed himself, if he had suicidal thoughts, and he honestly told them "no" every time. So, what the fuck *was* that?

He returned his focus to the screen; seeing the giant machete in the killer's hand, Nick was suddenly happy that he did not attempt to cut the pumpkin with a real knife. With a big breath, he gently cleaned his wrist, decided it did not need a bandage, and then started to carve the pumpkins again. By the time the last pumpkin was done, the incident seemed to be a fluke that was already in the past. After putting them outside and hoping there would be no Cabbage Night vandals like himself, he went back in and rinsed all of the pumpkin seeds he had set aside. His mother didn't ask him to do this, but he knew she loved roasted seeds, so he washed them all off, spread them on a sheet pan, covered them in oil and sea salt, and set them in the oven to cook.

Twenty minutes later, after flipping the seeds once, they were done. Using oven mitts, he grabbed the big cookie sheet with both hands and turned towards the counter where he had a trivet waiting—but just before he could set it down, both of his arms involuntarily pulled the tray against his chest. The red-hot lip of the pan hit his shirt with a searing, popping sound followed by the smell of burning. The heat burned its way through the shirt almost instantly and seared his flesh. This was no quick tap-and-move; the lip of the pan stuck deep and hard into his ribs for a solid ten seconds until the pan itself started to cool from Nick's body heat. Amazingly, he never dropped it nor pulled it away. When the burning stopped he simply set it on the counter, took off his glove, and shut the oven door.

When the oven door shut, his screams began. Peeling off his shirt, he raced into the bathroom to see a long fifteen-inch red, black, and brown line which ran an inch thick across his chest. It was bubbled in parts, and other parts oozed and a few tufts of burnt gray t-shirt material stuck to his skin. Turning on the water, he quickly tried to splash his chest but it was too late to do anything. Jumping in the shower, he turned the water to ice cold and stood under the spray screaming and crying.

An hour later, with taped together ice packs laid across his chest, he knew the burns needed medical attention, but he could not—and would not—put his mother through any sort of traumatic incident, not again, especially on the anniversary. So, he was going to have to live with it for a while. Antibacterial ointment and bandages were going to have to do for now.

With bandages and a new t-shirt uncomfortably on, Nick went to the kitchen to bag up the seeds. The pan itself was going to have to be thrown away, since Nick just couldn't stomach trying to scrape-off his own flesh to salvage a ten-dollar cookie sheet. With some painful effort, he concealed it at the bottom of the recycling bin along with the burnt t-shirt. With everything done, he skipped dinner and went to bed just as the sun started to dip down behind the horizon—the same time he put on his mask last year.

Lying in bed, Nick felt uneasy in a way he never had before. Part of him felt like he was losing his mind, and the other part just didn't know what the hell was going on. The rational part was trying to tell himself that his mind was just processing last year's events in some messed up way. Subconsciously, he thought he was punishing himself. Hell, he got off with only community service due to his young age, a lawyer that was so expensive his mother went broke, and his having no past record—even though *two people died.* Maybe the guilt he thought he had handled was actually suppressed, as his countless court ordered therapists suggested. After endlessly talking to himself in his head, this was the best solution: the date was bringing up suppressed guilt and he was subconsciously punishing himself. All he had to do was go to sleep, and by tomorrow, the date would have passed and he could start over. Nick also tried to trick his brain by telling it that he would now have a permeant, massive scar on his chest forever that would recognize and pay tribute to his sins. He didn't think it would work, but he'd try anything to get to get some sleep—which only came after four Tylenol PM.

Nick woke with a start from a nightmare that consisted of pumpkins attacking him, lots of fog, and running knives. It only seemed silly after his screams died down and he realized what the dream had been about. Regardless how childish it was, he was still covered in sweat and his body was sore from tensing. As he calmed, searing pain shot across his chest and quickly reminded him about his self-mutilation from the night before. Puss had oozed through the bandages and dried, sealing his shirt to his skin with a layer of crunchy browns, blacks, and reds. It took almost half an hour to pull the shirt and bandages off. The sight of the wound made him nauseous and reconfirmed that he should have gone to the hospital—and probably still should.

After an excruciatingly painful shower, more ointment, bandages, and a fresh shirt, Nick went into the kitchen to find a bowl next to a box of cereal and another hot pink sticky note. He wasn't surprised to read that his mom had to leave early, again, to go to her first job of the day. It also went on with almost the exact same wording as the day before: "Sorry I missed you, have a great day at school honey. Let's catch up this weekend." The only thing that differed this time was a line asking him to hand out candy tonight. And when he ran out, he was to shut off the lights. Nick hated that buying more than two small bags of candy was now a luxury his mother couldn't afford. Yet again, he was ruining some kid's Halloween.

Snapping on the television, he poured himself some Frankenstein-themed cereal and enjoyed the irony of eating it on the only day the cereal was relevant. He watched on the screen before him as morning show hosts jumped around in asinine costumes that weren't meant to scare but instead get an "awwww" from the crowd. Nick shook his hand with slight anger but he pushed it away. It was these same angry thoughts that had started the whole situation last year—a simple conversation about the origins of Halloween and why it was *supposed* to be scary. That dressing up as cute princesses and superheroes made no sense at all. That rabbit hole of a conversation is what lead to his "idea" to scare the shit out his town. He just never thought it would work so well.

Pouring his second bowl he suddenly found himself standing, though he didn't remember getting up nor understood why he did. Then, with the speed of a falling cinder block, Nick slammed his head down into his cereal bowl. Thankfully, with a split-second thought, he turned his head slightly so that the left side of his face took the brunt force. The rim of the hard, red ceramic bowl dug into his flesh and then exploded, sending cereal, pink milk, and shards of red flying in every direction. Lifting his head back up, Nick knew without a doubt that there was going to be pieces of the bowl stuck in his scalp and cheek. As calmly as he could, he went to the bathroom and looked in the mirror. Sure enough, there were several marshmallows, a few cute pink pieces of cereal, and half a dozen chunks of the bowl protruding from the sides of his face. He removed the cereal first, then pulled out the shards one-by-one. The entire time he acted like he was doing nothing but gently pulling lint off his face.

Twenty minutes later, after washing his face and treating the wounds, which thankfully were not deep, he had realized he had missed the bus—but he didn't care. There was no way he could go to school and risk doing something like that in front of a teacher: he'd end up in the looney bin before lunch. He had to stay home, and he had to make sure he couldn't harm himself again.

Nick desperately wanted his mom, but he just couldn't do that too her. He couldn't make her leave work—and worse, he couldn't make her worry about him, not again. The trial last year almost killed her. She was so devastated her hair went half gray, she started taking anxiety medication, and she saw a therapist twice a week. While she claimed she was fine on a consistent basis, he could tell his mother was only holding herself together by a thread. Nick did not want to be the one to cut that last thread, especially since he was already the one who unraveled the others.

An hour later, Nick had devised a contraption to keep himself safe. It wasn't anything complicated or fool proof, but it should protect him enough from any other major impulses—at least he hoped. It involved several pillows, two oven mitts, and two old blue jump-ropes he found in a storage box. With his hands in the gloves, the pillows all around him, his legs tied shut, and one hand tied to a bedpost, he figured one padded hand couldn't do much damage. Beforehand, he had been wise enough to put some food and drinks next to the bed as well as the ever-important pee bottle. And that is how Nick sat for the next six hours, doing nothing but snacking and watching *Halloween 1, 2* and *4* all in a row. Having seen the movies ten times each, if not more, it was insanely boring, but at least it felt like Halloween.

When three o'clock came around—the time he would normally be home from school after the bus dropped him off and he got his normal snack at the store—he dared untying himself as there hadn't been a single incident. Besides, he needed to stretch. To be safe, he kept the oven mitts on for the next hour as he cautiously moved around the house as if waiting for someone to attack him. At four o'clock, when still nothing had happened, and he saw the first of the very little children start to go door to door, he slipped off the gloves and put on his orange pumpkin t-shirt and got the bowl of candy ready.

Over the next two hours he dutifully answered the door, put on a happy smile, and gave out candy while complimenting the costumes. Princess after princess, superhero after superhero, the occasional fireman or cop, and a few cartoon characters he didn't recognize came one after another. Not a single monster, goblin, troll, or serial killer in the bunch. It depressed him, but he was happy to not have harmed himself—especially not in front of a child. Mostly, he was just happy he was getting to have somewhat of a Halloween this year.

As the last candy was handed out, well before seven when the older, more demanding kids would be coming, Nick sighed and shut off all the outdoor lights and most of the indoor ones. Sitting in his room, with just the television on and hearing the laughter from the hoards outside, Nick felt a deep depression wash over him. Guilt, self-loathing, and anger over the events of last year started to bounce around in his head like sharp daggers, each one sticking in causing a ripple of pain that wouldn't leave. Slowly, the desire to hurt himself crept into his brain. The other times, he felt nothing before this happened. This time, he knew *something* was going to happen. Jumping out of bed, he took deep breaths and paced back and forth.

He needed fresh air.

Less than twenty second later, Nick was outside and walking his normal path towards the store. He didn't even know if he wanted to go to the store, or where he was going, but it seemed to be the most natural path. Unlike normal days, where he was usually alone on the streets, tonight there were countless children and adults walking in every direction, causing him to zig and zag constantly. Regardless, breathing the air and looking at costumes was helping him calm down and keep his mind off the past. Slowing his pace, he started to relax and take in the beauty of Halloween. It truly was the only day of the year you could see so many people out on the streets after dark. And while it was meant to scare away the demons trying to creep into our world, hearing the laughter and excitement of the crowd did make Nick smile.

Leisurely strolling, watching the kids and teens run from house to house, he simply people-watched and enjoy the seasonally warm air. Slowly but surely, his mind settled, and he was enjoying the night. As a few teens walked by him, he heard them talk about the "kick ass haunted house." It was then that he recalled the cheesy flyer he saw in the store the other day. Pulling out his phone, he looked at the photo he had taken, noted the street and pulled up his map—it was only a seven-minute walk. As he headed directly there, he realized this town *was* pretty cool. His old town didn't have any sort of contests for "best Halloween decorations" or "scariest house." Hell, his old town was so stuffy, the city board once made a family remove a hanging skeleton from the yard because it was declared "too disturbing" for locals. At least this town was supporting Halloween—maybe this place was going to be just fine after all.

Turning down Wentworth Avenue, Nick was shocked to see it was even crazier than his and the last few streets he walked down. Almost every single house on the block was decorated with purple and orange lights; some lawns had bubbling cauldrons, others had entire displays set up on their yard, and not a single home had the lights off. Almost every resident was sitting outside in lawn chairs, some by fires, having a hell of a time handing out candy to everyone. Nick even noticed that most of the houses had *cases* of candy to ensure they did not run out. As he walked, looking at the house numbers, Nick realized he was smiling—it was probably the most real smile he had in a year. Then, he came upon number 345 and noticed the line of teens and adults waiting to go through the homemade haunted house. Nick excitedly joined the back of the line.

Looking ahead to the front of the line, he noticed a little green light flicker that told the next group when to walk through the black tarp tunnel which ran along the side of the house to the back yard. Nick couldn't believe the amount of work put into something that was free and just for locals. It gave him hope that there were others out there like him, people that truly loved and believed in the holiday. In front of him he noticed a group of three teens; he recognized them from school but didn't know their names. One girl was clearly with her boyfriend—as they couldn't keep their hands off each other—but the third was alone and seemed to feel awkward being the third wheel. Nick tried not to pay attention to her, but she kept looking back and smiling at him. After three more groups walked through, she turned and talked to him.

"You're that new kid, right?"

Nick smiled and nodded. He quickly stuck his hand out and told her his name. When he heard her name was Laurie, Nick laughed out loud, which got a strange reaction from her. "Your name, it's the same as the main character in the *Halloween* movies—I can't believe I'm meeting a Laurie *on* Halloween." The girl laughed shyly and said her mom actually named her after the character because she wanted her child to be a "survivor." Nick's heart skipped a beat hearing this. As the line moved forward, Nick was introduced to the other two kids who didn't seem to care much about meeting him, but mostly he talked to Laurie, who eventually asked if he would go through the house with her. He agreed without hesitation, and the smile she gave back to him melted everything away and made him realize things would be alright in life.

It was their turn to walk inside a few moments later; Laurie got close to Nick and he felt his heart start racing. The tunnel was darker than he thought it would be, and he actually got a bit creeped-out as the fog machine pumped smoke in, making it hard to see. The first few jump scares, mostly animatronic spiders and monsters bought at the seasonal Halloween shop, were effective but not by any means terrifying. The best part about them was that they made Laurie jump and grab Nick's arm. The light touch of her hands on his arms radiated through his entire body. The touch was subtle, but to Nick and his deflated heart, it felt like a giant fireworks display was being set off inside of him.

As the tunnel curved around the back of the house, it apparently had a huge jump scare that sent the other couple scurrying forward. There was enough separation between them that whatever had scared them was now resetting and getting ready to jump out at Nick and Laurie next. She grabbed tight to Nick's arm, preparing for the jolt as they took another step forward. A giant scarecrow jumped out from behind a black tarp, almost making contact with Nick's face. The noise and movement were so sudden that Laurie jumped away, losing her grip on Nick and running towards her friends who were laughing and standing at the far end of the tunnel. Nick on the other hand, didn't move—for the face he saw staring back from the scarecrow was his own.

It wasn't *really* his own, but he saw himself behind the rubbery, toothy grin of the macabre scarecrow. It was the same mask *he* had worn last Cabbage Night. Suddenly, all the warm fuzzy fun he was having drained from his body. There were all sorts of noises around him—yelling, screaming, laughing, haunted music, and canned cackles—but all Nick could hear was the sickening rip of flesh from last year.

As the scarecrow slowly moved away from his face to reset, Nick shook his head and tried to tell himself it was just a coincidence. Nick wanted that warm elation again; he wanted to fight the past and have a new life in this town, maybe with Laurie. Turning to find her, he saw the door at the end of the long black tunnel shut—her friends must have pulled her with them.

Racing to the door, he saw a red light on telling him to "Wait, *or Else.*" He ignored it and tried the door; it didn't open. Hearing the piston hiss behind him, sending the scarecrow launching up at the next group, he knew he couldn't stop himself—he shouldered the door and burst into the room. It was obviously a garage, but the owner had done a hell of a job setting it up to look like some sort of Satanic ritual, with a man dressed as a cult leader in red robes standing in front of a rubbery dead body that was laying across an altar. Nick let out a small laugh, not because he thought it was stupid, but because he was happy and excited about how cool the room looked. Regardless, he didn't want to lose Laurie, so he started to jog across the room towards the exit. Something caught his foot—he only saw a glimpse of, but it looked to be an enormous red demon's hand. Since he had been jogging, the sudden removal of his foot to the Styrofoam claw sent him flying, face first, into the hard concrete.

As his nose shattered into over two-dozen tiny pieces, Nick saw a brilliant flash of light. When his two front teeth tore through his upper lip, he saw darkness. In the darkness, he saw the face of the man and the poor girl who died last year. He always thought of them that way, *the man* and *the girl*, as giving them names made it too real. They were playing together, happy and content in the fall leaves. The image made Nick happy. He tried to smile, but the teeth protruding through his lip would not allow any sort of facial expressions to be made. In a hazy state, he felt hands on his body and rolling him over. He tried to open his eyes, but the pain and blood pooling around them did not allow that either. All he could do was mumble.

A bright light shone in his eyes—he could see the brightness through his bruising lids, and he heard an adult talking to him—but he could still see the man and the girl playing and he didn't to let go of that image. Then the hands released him and he was alone again. In his vision, he saw the little girl jump into the leaf pile and disappear, but when she jumped back out of them, she was bloody, and her face torn just like his was now. The image shocked him back into consciousness. Opening his eyes just a tiny sliver, he saw a man—the man he saw when he entered the room, dressed in a cult leader's robe—fixing the door he had just broke. Two seconds later, the man was picking him up. Nick thought of Laurie and wondered if she was waiting outside and if she would ever talk to him again, with his broken nose and split lip.

Then, the man placed him, with a lot of pulling and struggling, onto the alter—this confused Nick, as he didn't know why the man wouldn't have just let him lay there until the ambulance came. The table was uncomfortable, and his head dangled backwards, sending blood dripping down his throat. Nick tried to speak again, but there was too much blood choking him.

"It's the judges—sorry kid, but I'm not losing to my brother again *this* year." Through blurry eyes, Nick could see a hidden monitor on the floor by the man's feet; three people with clipboards where coming down the tunnel. Then, Nick watched the man pick up a very realistic looking knife as he heard the buzz of the door. The man started to speak loudly—some Latin sounding chant—and raised the knife high above Nick.

In the moment before knife came down, Nick realized that everything in the past year had been leading up to this. That no matter how good he was, no matter what he did, it was his destiny to die. Fate couldn't let him live; he needed to be punished for what he had done, it just wanted him to suffer for a year before finally taking his life. Now, just like his horrible tricks had turned wrong, he was not about to meet his demise at the hands of another person who was taking things just a bit *too* far. As the knife plunged into his chest, slicing through his burns, he heard gasps from the judges and one of them exclaim, "how realistic!"

With his last breath Nick whispered, "I'm sorry." Then he tried to smile, because he knew his death would become the stuff of legends. It would be a tale that kids would forever tell each other on Halloween.

Home
Lewis Crane

Part I: A Heart That Roams

A cool wind whistled across the barren streets; the rustle of the fallen leaves the sole, echoing, sound to break the eerie silence of the sunlight soaked afternoon. The time was October and, thus, all traces of leaves had been plucked from the trees, leaving little wooden skeletons to sway harmoniously with the gentle tune of the autumn breeze. The silence was typical, both of this time of year and the fact it was a Sunday, a day where families basked in the leisure of God's restful day after their periodic sermon at church. It was a chance for old friends to catch up, a chance for children to talk outside of the mundane constrictions of school, and a chance for the community to come together with a single and unified goal: an unbroken harmony between the families of this small town. Church was important for every family, and heavy ridicule was given to those who failed to understand its significance. The town lay especially still at this time of year, as people braced for the celebrations of the town's founding on October 31st. The day was spent in celebration of the community and of the future of its life, and the night would commemorate those who had passed in the name of bringing the town and its community to life. The inhabitants embodied this celebration as a sign of the town's survival throughout the changing tides of time, and as the system that the town had thrived upon for generations.

The town existed as almost a family unto itself, with the same bloodlines occupying the same houses for generations. Everyone knew each other, and most members of these families could recite from memory every occupied house and significant family name within the town. They could recite the importance of the Harpers, who ran the florist on Regal Street, and the elderly couple who ran the antique shop, Mary and Benjamin Stork. Families and businesses that had lived for generations—the town almost existed within its own realm of unchanging reality. A never-ending familiarity that gave the town an almost fairytale-like demeanor that appeared unbroken by its own reality. All knowledge of the world around the town existed merely as gossip among the ladies and gentlemen who had spent the last 40 years following a similar pattern to that of their parents before them, and their parents before them, and so on so forth. The local paper, the sole paper advertised in Mr. Brighton's newsagents, gave little real gossip to which one could sink their teeth into. Instead, it existed as a platform for the hollow gratification of the church committee, the mayoral office, and any other mildly exciting charitable event that arose within the town square, which then drifted from the minds of the people as new acts of charity rose and the old ones fell. Bake sales and swap meets constituted exciting weekend events, and delinquency, if there was any, disappeared from the streets and minds as quickly as it appeared. From the eyes of a city dweller—the ones who struggled endlessly with the pencil pushing and suited corruption of the concrete goliath of city life—it was almost as peaceful as an undisturbed slumber.

The inhabitants of the town did not care for the city folk who passed through or, at the disapproval of the locals, decided to settle down in this quiet town and disturb the tranquil system it had maintained throughout its history. The introduction of a new family always brought whispers amongst the townspeople, the judgmental eyes and hushed mumbling almost deafening in their lack of subtlety. The women in the square would watch the new inhabitants like ravenous vultures, eyes gleaming with distrust and borderline hatred for their existence within this realm. The one story that had echoed throughout the town—and by this point had been recited and repeated to the point that anyone who sought gossip had heard the tale in some form an almost nauseating number of times—had been the tale of a couple who had moved from Chicago with the supposed intention of refocusing both their careers and mending their slowly fragmenting relationship. Of course, the reliability of this aspect of the tale had been thrown into question by the nature of the frequency of its retelling. The aspect of the tale that remained consistent within the various retellings was how the couple were seemingly driven out of the town. Sunday had come around, much like it had always, and church was the intention on everyone's mind.

Almost everyone.

The couple were branded as heathens for their lack of faith and were subsequently driven from the town after weeks of endless harassment and vandalism; the makeshift cross which burned on their front porch still rots there this very day. The house had remained empty since the ordeal, and no mention of the couple—or the violent harassment they had endured—had appeared in the local paper. They had disappeared as quickly as they had arrived, and now existed as a mere folklore. Some children, for either reasons of boredom or belief of their status as heathens, claim that if you were to approach the house today, you could still hear the echoes of their fearful sobbing. No one ever dared try to prove it. With their disappearance, the town had continued as it always had, and the system the town had known so well continued on. It was a system the town had grown to love, as they knew that the town loved them also.

As the militant swaying of the naked trees continued, the eerie silence was broken by the loud creak of an oak door opening and banging against the side of the front porch, revealing a sole figure standing in the doorway. The figure shielded its eyes from the sharp sunlight of the brisk Sunday afternoon and clutched closer that which it held within its other hand as not to drop it. The sun revealed eyes of tranquil blue and an expression that displayed the unique innocence of childhood. The sunlight unveiled a boy of sixteen, wearing a baggy hoodie and pajama pants—which only served to make him look younger. He held a tinfoil-covered bowl under his arm like a small space saucer, like the ones he had heard about from one of the city children he had met in his classroom. The boy stood, reeling from the accidental force of which the door had swung open, and the silence was once again broken by another, equally as violent sound: that of a bellowing voice.

"Bradley! Haven't I told you a thousand times to be gentle with that damn door?" roared the voice of Bradley's father from the comfort of his living room recliner. Bradley's racket had disturbed his Sunday tradition of an afternoon nap.

Bradley yelped out a sheepish apology and scuttled out of the house, carefully and patiently closing the door behind him as to not anger Father further. Bradley had been tasked with delivering the tinfoiled goods to their peculiar neighbor, Mr. Riddley. This had, much like his father's snoozing, become a Sunday tradition for Bradley, as every Sunday he had been given various morsels and leftovers of their afternoon banquet to be given to Mr. Riddley. The thought of walking around always succeeded in generating a sense of crippling dread within Bradley—it began when he was thirteen.

He marched along the street, as he had done every other Sunday, up to the putrid green door of number twenty-four, Ashvale Lane. The paint of the door had peeled and chipped in several places, revealing the slowly rotting neglect beneath, and the knocker had rusted to be unrecognizable from the shimmering iron that once greeted every guest of the once proud household. Bradley rapped his knuckle upon the door, fearful that too much force in his knocks would collapse the withered door all together and waited what felt like an eternity before the startling clicks of the first and second lock that prohibited entry to any outsider. The door had always remained double-locked after Mr. Riddley's incident. The door swung open, revealing a disheveled corpse-like body of an elderly man—his hair thinning, teeth jagged, a neglectful beard hung upon his wrinkled chin and a posture that twisted his body into an almost inhuman hunchback. He was a man who kept to himself these days, only leaving the safety of his residence in dire circumstances like in times when the rations he bought from Mr. Brighton's store had run dry.

Mr. Riddley regarded Bradley with a row of crooked teeth that attempted a warming smile; Bradley was none too warmed by his demonic expression. Bradley responded by attempting a sincere smile and held out the culinary offering to the being that stood before him. The bowl was taken from him instantaneously and there was a long moment of rustling before Mr. Riddley popped up again from behind the tinfoil. The expression on his face another attempt to show his sincere gratitude, despite the appearing more like a rabid wolfman who would rather feast upon Bradley himself. The silence was broken by a gruff voice which spoke no louder than a whisper.

"Thank you, Bradley," he muttered. "These little Sunday deliveries are really the only luxury I have any more since…" There was a momentary pause before he concluded his point. "…since Martha left."

The story of Martha—and what once had been Jonathan Riddley—was one that Bradley had known very well from what had been told by his mother. Martha had always been headstrong and remarkably stubborn when it came to the quarrels with her husband. They had always bickered, some nights it led to Jonathan's removal from the premises and into the recliner that was now occupied by Bradley's father, but it always seemed these arguments would end as quickly as they started, and thus it never became newsworthy within the town—until the town's 350th anniversary on October 31st, 2000. The night of the intended festivities, the couple's arguing become violent. There was damage to the front room window, which was later covered by a row of wooden planks hastily nailed to the outside of the frame, and by morning Jonathan had found his house ransacked, his car stolen, and the most crushing revelation—that his wife was gone. A hollow apology note was the last remnant of her existence within his life besides the ring that still hung upon his withered finger. Ever since the day of her absence, Jonathan had waited for her to return but he knew deep within his heart and mind that she would never come back. What argument brought her to leave the life she had lived for so many years? Nobody knew.

Bradley looked back at the skeletal face of Mr. Riddley, who had already started picking small morsels of turkey from the carcass that had been presented to him and felt it right to leave without any awkwardness.

"It's quite alright, Mr. Riddley," Bradley chimed in as Mr. Riddley continued his picking at his reheatable feast. "You're a friend of our family, and we wouldn't like you to be without something nice *once in a while*." Bradley punctuated this with a glowing grin which masked his rational fear of the ruffled beast which stood before him.

Bradley turned and began to leave, but his progress back to the safety of his house was halted by a final barking question from the feasting werewolf.

"One last thing, my boy," he crowed with keen interest. "Just heard some whispers yesterday in Brighton's that the house those devil-worshipping bastards from the big city were livin' in has been sold." He chuckled in bewilderment and concluded, "after they got ran out, I wouldn't think anybody was gutsy enough to move into a house that Satanists lived in." He continued to chuckle like a ravenous hyena that had found its next victim and regarded Bradley's leave with a wave of his crooked fingers.

Bradley did not stop to wave back.

All that filled his mind now was the laughter of Mr. Riddley and the thought that the house—that his classmates had sworn was haunted—which had now had new victims to feast upon. He went to bed without so much as a word of goodnight to his parents and pondered silently the kind of monsters that would move into a place like that—a place that had the haunting history that this one had. Bradley fell asleep thinking of the house that lay empty for so long, and of the ceaseless cries that are said to echo throughout its hallways.

Part II: Thy Kingdom Come

Bradley was awoken by a soft rapping at his bedroom door; it reminded him of his visit yesterday to the residence of Mr. Riddley the previous evening. Unlike that visit there was no clicking of locks, and when the door slowly swung open, the face that appeared was not that of the skeletal monster which Bradley feared but the calm, warm face of his loving mother, a glass of orange juice clutched in her tender grasp.

Her smile eased Bradley, who had been troubled since the mention of the new people. He sat up to greet his smiling mother with an equally cheerful expression. She had always been the voice of comfort in his life, and always acted as the perfect counterbalance to the stubborn and serious nature of his father. Bradley loved and respected both his parents equally yet acknowledged them as being two very different people in his life; his mother had always been caring and reassuring, but where his father lacked in compassion he made up for in wisdom.

Bradley sat up and wished his mother good morning before gulping down the contents of the glass, rising out of bed, and heading through to the small bathroom that adjoined his room. He caught himself in the mirror—his tired eyes and now glum expression matching his realization of the fact it was now a Monday. He stared at his reflection in the mirror for a long while, taking in the figure that blinked back at him in perfect motion. The dread of a Monday at school began to sink in, as Bradley realized another weekend had seeped through his fingers like water. He thought of Martha—in a sense, he envied her sought of freedom from the life she was expected to lead. Bradley could not ponder what is—or what it could be—as there was more immediate matters to attend to in the kitchen.

He dressed himself in the uniform that lay neglected on his floor since the previous Friday evening and made his way through to the kitchen. Warm toast sat waiting for him, but Bradley felt no desire to eat now, as thoughts began to fill his mind of the day ahead. School was something of a mundanity to Bradley. He neither liked nor disliked it but saw it as an obligation that had been forced upon him without his consent—similar to how the Sunday visits to Mr. Riddley were also thrust upon him without so much as a word of agreement.

His mind drifted once again, back to the words of the former Jonathan Riddley and of the old house; that infernal house that wept in the night. He felt his arms raise into goosebumps and a chill replace the heat of the kitchen. He visibly shivered before forcing the thoughts out of his mind and back to his dire Monday predicament of school. Bradley mulled over his now ice-cold toast, thinking of all the things he could be accomplishing if not bound to the seven-hour burden that was his education, before being a voice cut through his silent pondering. It was the heavy and familiar voice of his father.

"Something wrong, Bradley?" he asked with a calm sincerity. "She's called you three times to eat up or you'll be late for school, and now you're sitting here staring into space?"

Bradley looked up at his father, his arms folded as he waited for an excuse as to why he had ignored his mother's call. All the thoughts that had plagued his mind disappeared in a flash as the reality of his impatient father came into focus.

"I'm sorry, Dad," Bradley mumbled distantly. "I was just thinking of something Mr. Riddley had said about the haunted house." Bradley noted the foolishness of the statement when said it aloud and couldn't help but smirk.

His father noticed the mood of Bradley's face changed, and his expression softened considerably into a smirk of his own.

"You don't honestly believe, at your age, all that trash about the place being haunted by that horrible couple that moved here?" his father asked with a chuckle. His face suddenly dropped again into a frown and he put an arm around Bradley. "You need to understand, however, that they were bad people, Bradley—you understand that, don't you?"

Bradley nodded in response.

"They didn't belong here and, quite frankly, people like them are the kinds that give a community like ours a bad name." Bradley noted that his father's tone had become deadly serious and his eyes shone with calculated anger.

"I understand, Dad." Bradley noted the fire in his father's eyes had left, and his calm demeanor had returned with the sound of his son's voice. "I just hope these new people aren't as crazy as they were."

Their conversation was ended by the sound of clacking footsteps as Bradley's mother entered the room, an impatient look written across her face. Bradley shot up to avoid any further delay and embraced his father goodbye before bracing himself for the Monday ahead.

Bradley arrived at the school grounds and watched momentarily as hordes of similarly dressed students, all of different shapes and sizes, flood towards the front door of the school like a swarm of bees to their hive. He gave his mother the obligatory goodbye kiss—which he hoped none of his classmates ever saw, at risk of looking foolish—and joined the ranks of the marching students entering the building. His first class was English with Mrs. Lucille, and Bradley cursed himself at his foolishness to not have read the material that she had lined up for today's lesson. He entered the classroom marked "A24: English," which stood at the end of a long corridor with various numbered doors lined in a row on either side. He sat in silence, listening to the loud rumbling of chatter and noise as people entered and took their respective seats around him. The room fell to silence with Mrs. Lucille's entry. All eyes fell to her, and she met every one of their gazes, a stern determination in her eyes that only worried the underprepared Bradley further. She cleared her throat and began the lesson for the day.

"Good morning," she said without lowering her gaze, "I hope everyone has read through the text I gave you last week on *The Island of Dr. Moreau*?"

Bradley felt his face grow warm. He had glanced over Wells' supposed "classic" and had hated every word that it told. He acknowledged how Wells looked to tear down the boundaries that that formed human society and civility, and the idea made him shiver—surely nothing was more important than community? How could the world function without a system? The portrayal of the half-human monstrosities within the story as creatures of sympathy also left a sickly feeling in his mind. They were monsters, after all— no different from the ones that the people had driven from the haunted house—like the one which was now inhabited by a new breed of monsters, no doubt. Bradley was driven from his thoughts by the mention of his name; Mrs. Lucille was staring straight at him. He looked up, met her gaze, and simply shrugged to avoid whatever question she may have asked. Her stern expression hardened into a look of impatience with his response; she let out a great sigh and repeated the question.

"Bradley, Bradley, Bradley…" she muttered defeatedly. "Have you prepared so little for this lesson that you can't even hazard a guess as to what Wells was trying to say with this story?" She punctuated her frustration in the question by slamming her book down on the desk in front of her.

Bradley found himself unable to speak. The hot, burning feeling he felt before had risen to the point of being almost painful—a feeling only magnified by the burning gaze of Mrs. Lucille, as she waited for any form of a response from him. Her efforts had failed, and she returned to a seated position to begin a lecture on thematic analysis; Bradley slumped and looked down at his desk in embarrassment.

Mrs. Lucille continued to drone on about the interchangeable nature of society and how man and beast were not unlike one another; Bradley mentally scoffed at the idea. He had been raised to understand that humans had superiority over animals, a control of themselves unlike that of the beasts that roamed in the wilderness and jungles of the world. Bradley just couldn't believe in Wells' ideas, and his mind drifted back to Martha Riddley, the one who escaped civility for her own selfish gain. He thought of Mr. Riddley, a shambling corpse of a man whose life had been ruined by her desires, and of the heathen couple who were nothing but a complication to the happiness the town had spent generations establishing. Bradley's father had told them they were selfish, much like this new family were surely selfish all the same—they were city folk after all, and Bradley had been told many stories of the cut-throat backstabbery of city life. He already stood as an outcast in the small town, his quiet demeanor and thoughtfulness misinterpreted as awkwardness by his fellow classmates. The few friends he possessed were similarly ridiculed and rarely spoke to him outside of the school environment.

Mrs. Lucille's passionate ramblings were cut short by the loud crackle of the intercom which sat above the door through which she entered.

The slightly muffled voice of the principal followed shortly after: "This is a brief announcement—could Bradley Brons please report to my office, post haste." The Principal's voice echoed throughout the corridors and through the mind of Bradley as he realized he had potentially dodged the soaring bullet that was Mrs. Lucille's piercing glare and contorted expression of anger. He leaped out of his seat at the request of his presence, shoved his various booklets and notes into his bag, and scurried out of the room towards the principal's office as the cold, displeased look of Mrs. Lucille followed him like a singular spotlight over a stage actor. He did not attempt to meet her blinding gaze and felt the gust of wind from the door as he slammed it behind him.

The principal's office was unlike any other room found within the admittedly claustrophobic structure of the school grounds; it's winding corridors and rows of doors much akin to that of a prison—of course, Bradley hoped to never see the inside of a real prison, and thus kept this analogy based solely upon stories he had been told and his own bleak sense of imagination; school was enough of a prison to satisfy his curiosity. His footsteps echoed with every thumping step; the eerie silence between each step lasting a small eternity as he progressed closer and closer towards the man who beckoned him. Bradley could see the office in the distance, its black exterior and polished brass handle separating it from the rows of light brown doors that surrounded it. On it, in letters of similarly polished gold and on a frame of murky gray, were written the words "Head Office." He felt his hand reach out for the handle, its brass shimmering in the dim light as if hot enough to scald any curious souls looking to uncover its secrets, and felt his grip tighten over it. He could hear a soft rattling sound and immediately realized the hand which held the glimmering doorknob was trembling with fear. Bradley grew ever fearful of what punishment faced him behind the blackened gate that led to the abyss. His fear was heightened by what appeared to be a shadowy figure, an unmoving darkness that stared at the petrified Bradley through the blurry glass of the office doors window panel. Bradley steadied his grasp, held his breath, and turned the handle until a startling click could be heard from the door latch. The door swung open in eerie silence as he stood looking into a dimly lit room with a large desk straight ahead.

Bradley realized his breath in a gasping pant and his met eyes with the sole humanoid figure in a black suit jacket, his spectacles reflecting the solitary light that swayed hypnotically from the ceiling, and who upon meeting the gaze of Bradley, contorted his face into a leathery grin that brandished a row of unnaturally white teeth. They had never met face to face, but Bradley knew this man very well from his preacher-like assemblies and the stories of his chastising towards kids of trouble. He recognized the thick-rimmed spectacles and the sharply ironed gray suit, he recalled the reptilian-like wrinkles upon his face and the teeth that matched in brightness that of bones picked clean by ravenous vultures—he was standing face to face and eyes locked with Principal Reinhart.

Their eye contact remained unbroken for several moments until Reinhart removed the glinting spectacles that shielded his dull, green eyes that now gazed at Bradley's fearful expression. His smile shrunk back into a look of concentration and he beckoned Bradley to the chair that sat across from him. Bradley obliged without a word of protest and shuffled his way into the hard, wooden chair—his gaze never dropping from that of Reinhart.

The venomous smirk re-emerged across the face of the principal as he cleared his throat.

"Bradley Brons, I presume?" The tone ruling the question rhetorical. "Could I interest you in anything to drink while we have our little chat?"

Bradley did not trust anything this serpent had to offer and refused with a timid shake of his head, a response that brought Principal Reinhart into a devious chuckle as he continued with the one-sided conversation.

"Relax, my boy," he insisted. "I just wanted to ask if you could do me—" He paused for a moment and finally hissed out, "—a favor." He clasped his leathery hands together on the desk and waited persistently for a response.

Bradley's face receded into a scowl of curiosity mixed with distrust—but in the end, his curiosity became the victor. "Why do you need a favor from *me* of all people?" he asked, puzzled. "What could I offer to someone like you?" His tone became more hostile with each word uttered.

He was dealing with the school equivalent of the devil in his mind; a devil that he sadly knew had control over him, given his status. Bradley despised how little he was regarded by those older than him or seen as having a superior role to him in society, and found that as much as it sickened him to compliment the man behind all of his educational belittlement, the asking of a favor from him to be one both flattering and refreshing from the norm. The burning sensation of his anger receded slightly as he considered the beneficial nature of the situation. After all, the head of the entire school was requesting a favor from *him* of all people. He eased slightly but did not drop his suspicion of the suited deceiver who had wormed somewhat through his suspicious mindset. Principal Reinhart unclasped his hands, leaned back in his black leather chair, and began to reveal the answers which Bradley desired.

"I've been watching you closely for longer than you might think, Bradley." His dull eyes now gleamed brightly in the dimness of the gloomy office and his voice lowered to that of a phlegmatic hiss. "You stick out to me as someone who doesn't quite fit in, and I can see by the look in your eyes that you would agree with me." His smirk returned more venomous than before as he continued. "We have a new student, one who joined just this morning, and I need you to take care of him—maybe teach him about how things work around here?" He punctuated that last statement with another leathery smile that revealed his freakishly perfect set of teeth.

Bradley pondered over his words for a moment, fixating his glare upon the brown, wooden surface of Principal Reinhart's desk. He was determined to question his authority to the bitter end—they say to never put your trust in a snake.

"And what benefit would that have for me?" Bradley barked before realizing the error in his tone.

Reinhart's face grew stern; his serpentine smirk shrunk back into an impatient frown and the eyes that glinted interest now shone with a deep irritation from Bradley's defiance. His tone remained calm, but Bradley could sense a more concentrated coldness in Reinhart's words. He was no longer *asking* for Bradley's favor.

"I wouldn't squander this opportunity, Master Brons," he sneered at Bradley. "You just might learn something about each other—and more importantly—about yourself." His expressions had changed multiple times during this meeting, but Bradley's curiosity of the proposal had shone through when a smirk appeared for a moment upon his face. Reinhart's expression was now fixed in the position of the same venomous grin that Bradley had seen upon his entry to the office. Bradley had said nothing before Principal Reinhart pressed the button of the intercom, leaned towards the microphone, and called upon a name that Bradley had never heard before.

The door swung open after several minutes of tense silence between the two, and what stood in the doorway was a face of fear; a face which appeared younger than Bradley's. What Bradley saw, illuminated by the dull light of the single-bulbed office, was a 13-year-old boy with anxiety and fear written across his face as his wetting eyes stared at the two figures at the desk. His uniform hung loosely upon his flimsy frame, the bagginess of it only highlighting his young demeanor. Reinhart's predatory smirk widened and he beckoned the quiet boy towards the desk with a wave of his reptilian fingertips. The boy shuffled towards Reinhart, a fly towards the spider's web, and stopped short right beside the seated Bradley. They made eye contact as the young boy began to tremble slightly at the interested looks of the two. Reinhart reached out a wrinkled claw and clasped it upon the boy's shoulder—a soft yelp was heard as this was done.

Again, Reinhart looked at Bradley.

"This is our new student, Master Brons," Reinhart declared in a tone louder than the calculating mumbles he had been speaking in beforehand, which startled both boys at once. "Bradley, meet Julius Preston!" The two boys regarded each other with a glance, and Bradley attempted a sincere smile to mask the fear they both felt towards Reinhart; the look was not returned by Julius.

Reinhart released his vulture's grip from the small shoulder of Julius and dismissed the two boys from his office. "I expect the two of you to be useful to each other," he said. "I wish for the two of you to become closer than brothers." He demonstrated this idea by clasping his hands together as a symbol of unity.

The two boys nodded and began to leave the room. Julius left first and, as Bradley was about to finally leave the chilling presence of Principal Reinhart, he heard his name called by the daemon one final time. "I expect you to take care of him, Master Brons," he cooed at Bradley. "You will thank me for this one day," and he brandished his shimmering teeth once more before Bradley closed the office door and hoped to never view the face of Reinhart again for as long as humanly possible. The slam of the door echoed through the stillness of the corridor and Bradley could feel a chill run up his body. His thoughts and fears dissipated with the radiance of someone watching him, and he turned to see Julius staring up at him, whose fear turned to relief in the absence of Reinhart even though his shoulder now ached from his claw-like grip.

The two stared at each other for a long while in the gloomy corridor—both outsiders in their own right and neither wanting to make the first move—until Bradley thought it his role as the eldest of the two to break the silence.

"So, it seems I'm in charge of you—somewhat." He relished these words; the idea of having control over someone else was both bizarre and oddly exhilarating for Bradley. The words rolled off his tongue like sin—they had an undeniable sickening quality to Bradley, and he felt himself grow disgusted by this selfish desire. It reminded him too much of Reinhart, and his own manipulation of Bradley into this very situation he now found himself in. A wave of sympathy washed over Bradley as the pale face of Julius stared up at him, waiting for Bradley to guide him in the right direction.

Julius shifted slightly and spoke for the first time since their meeting. His voice had the squeaky and high-pitched tones of a boy just beginning the drastic change of puberty. "I usually don't have much in common with other boys—especially ones that are older than me—but I could see both of us were pretty scared of Mr. Reinhart." He attempted a laugh that came out shaky and fearful.

Bradley returned the motion with a soft chuckle of his own and chimed back, "Yeah, he is quite an intimidating guy." He paused before adding: "Oh, and it's *Principal* Reinhart—if he ever catches you not calling him *principal*, he can get a hell of a lot scarier from what I've heard."

The two shared a smile of agreement; their friendship began with their mutual fear of Reinhart, and soon, they would connect over their mutual hatred of him too. Bradley suggested they head for lunch to continue their discussion, and Julius followed Bradley obediently back up the darkened corridor, looking back at the abyssal black of Principal Reinhart's office door.

The two spent the afternoon together eagerly questioning one another about their various differences. For Bradley, it was the intrigue of the city life that drew his interest, and how Julius had come to be here now. Hearing of the abundance of traffic that lined the city streets, and of the lights that forever shone bright, had an appeal to the thoughtful mind of Bradley; if anything, it highlighted the mundaneness of his existence and of the town he was forced to live in. He had always longed for more—his envy of Julius grew with every question he threw at him, his imagination creating the picture of grandeur that was the bustling metropolis of the city and he yearned to be there in the paradise his mind had concocted from the words of Julius. They continued to talk about their differences in upbringing; they trusted each other with their answers, and a mutual confidence grew amongst the two as their questionings became more personal. The conversation shifted gravely upon Bradley's question of where Julius was living in the town.

"Well, my parents wanted to leave Seattle—so my Dad could ease up on how much work he was doing—and they found a house for sale that had been on the market for quite a while, apparently." He attempted to recite the street name, but eventually gave up when his attempts at recalling the name just elicited shrugs from Bradley. He continued: "Anyway, I also wasn't doing too well in school, so they thought about moving me here and—at the request of my mom—agreed to have someone here to help me fit in a bit more." The idea of friendship caused the lonely mind of Julius to gleam with hopefulness.

Bradley felt flattered by the notion and said nothing of his own status as an outcast, as not to upset the thoughts of

Julius—after all, as Reinhart had said, he was to take care of Julius. The ringing of the school bell startled the two out of their conversation and Bradley led Julius to his class before departing.

Bradley found every moment of his afternoon class—which was a dull slog into the theorem of Pythagoras—extremely lonely, having returned to his status of solitude amongst those of the same age group. He looked around the room and saw faces that were hostile, uncaring, or indifferent to his existence and it made him yearn for the bright-eyed and conversational Julius. He watched the clock hypnotically, every tick pounding in his head as if a legion was patrolling along his mind, and he became impatient of how slow the time was passing. He sat, doodling nonsensical shapes and thoughts in his notebook, until finally he heard the harsh ring of freedom. Bradley was the first to pack up and leave the classroom, without another word or glance to the classmates who regarded him so little. He hurried towards the class where he led Julius to earlier and found him waiting patiently for his arrival; a smile appeared upon his face as he noticed Bradley approach. Bradley offered to walk Julius home from school, and he nodded his approval at the offer; Julius was the one leading Bradley this time.

They walked in a silence that neither found overly awkward—until a suspicious object caught the attention of Julius, who raised an eyebrow as he darted a confused look at Bradley. The object of peculiarity that caught his attention was a tall, gray structure of painted cardboard with various crafted turrets and a drawbridge that folded into the front of the structure by two rope mechanisms; Bradley identified it as a medieval castle. The explanation of it did little to ease the look of confusion on Julius's face, and they moved closer toward the ominous structure. They got within touching distance of the structure before an elderly gentleman appeared from behind the structure. He sported paint-splattered overalls and a head of white hair that also appeared to somehow have traces of paint laced throughout it.

"Don't even think about touching that, boy!" he barked at Julius. "I didn't spend all afternoon in this damn autumn chill just to see a messy handprint in my beautiful creation."

Bradley recognized the gentleman as Father Bellum, the town preacher, and noticed the unusual hostility in the face of Bellum as he berated Julius for his curiosity. Bradley interrupted this irritated belittlement of Julius, and the Father's angered tone lightened slightly upon his notice of Bradley.

"I urge you, Young Bradley, to please tell this hooligan to keep away from my castle." He showcased his pride in the expertly crafted cardboard with a confident wave of his hand. "I want it to be perfect for the parade and celebration of the town's founding tomorrow afternoon, and I will not be answering questions about any fingerprints on my work."

Bradley nodded obediently to the Father's request, and led Julius away before he angered him further—Father Bellum knew Bradley's parents personally from his Sunday service, and Bradley had no desire for his parents to find out about Father Bellum's irritation.

Julius halted at a street corner whose name Bradley could not recall and assured him that he could walk the rest of the way. Julius pointed towards his destination with his finger, and Bradley felt his blood turn to ice as he witnessed which building Julius was pointing to—it was the house of the outsiders, the house that wept in the night—it was the house of the heathens from Chicago. Bradley felt the world fall still as the house stared at him from across the street. Julius did not notice his fear and bid him farewell before walking towards the house.

Bradley stood frozen in fear with his eyes fixated upon the house. His fear mixed with hysteria as he pondered the irony of the situation—the monsters he had imagined turned out to be the very person he trusted most. Bradley felt his hand reach out towards the departing Julius, his brain screaming for him to save his friend from the house, but his mouth made no noise and he felt his hand lower as Julius waved a final goodbye before closing the front door behind him. Bradley turned and began walking back towards his own house; he swore he could hear something more than a whistle in the cold October wind—something like a soft, chilling, and fearful moan.

Bradley arrived home, his thoughts blank as he marched frantically away from the house of nightmares and sat across from his father in the kitchen; a newspaper shrouding his face as the front pages showed the same mundane headlines about the tragic death of Mrs. Denburn, who had lived in the town for what felt like eternity before passing at the age of ninety-four, according to the front page. His father heard the creak of the chair across from him and lowered his paper, noticing immediately the troubled look on Bradley's face.

"Hey Bradley," he attempted to no response. "You're looking a bit down—did something happen at school today?"

Bradley looked at his father and quietly mumbled

"Could I have a friend 'round for dinner tomorrow?" His voice trembled with every word: "He's new and a bit scared of people." His words petered out as his father began to speak again.

"I know about them, Bradley," he said sternly. "Principal Reinhart phoned this morning to let us know about the situation." His tone seemed almost cold to Bradley.

The conversation fizzled out between the two and he retired to his room and eventually succumb to slumber, leaving a mostly untouched meal cooked by his mother.

Bradley awoke to find himself no longer within the confines of his comfortable bed but lying upon a floor of polished brass. He lifted himself up slowly—a soft aching and an overwhelming confusion bringing him to a stir—and glanced around to find an endless black abyss. He surveyed his surroundings further but found nothing except what imprisoned him—that being a circular wall of glass which showed a view of eternal darkness on all sides. Bradley attempted to shout and found his words noiseless in this peculiar prison. He panicked, ran at sprinting speed towards the glass and began pounding violently upon the walls of his prison; damage to the structure of the glass was non-existent as it only released a deafening bang with every clubbing blow of Bradley's fists.

His frantic bashing slowed gradually as Bradley noticed another, more consistent sound that distracted him from his panic; it was the sound of a low hiss—he swung around to find grains of sand, white as bone, pouring in from above at a rapid rate and spreading across the floor of the brass prison as it filled the chamber. His panic reignited, and Bradley's frantic bashing became a terrified flail as he tried everything he could to escape the rising sand that was filling the chamber. He cried out for help but found no-one to answer his cries as the sand seemed to consume his body, leg-by-leg and arm-by-arm, until Bradley's head was barely above its depths. It was then that he saw a gargantuan figure skulking out from the darkness, its grey suit and clasped leathery hands were the only visible parts of its being. It spoke to Bradley in an ominous whisper as the sand continued to ingest him.

"Join us, Bradley," the voice whispered, "or be lost to the sands of time." The whisper turned to a ghostly cackle as the sand began to shroud Bradley's vision.

Bradley struggled against the consuming sand, his wriggling and flailing achieving little but rendering him breathless, and the sand began to mask his vision as the last of his being sunk into the sandy tomb. With his last moments of sight, Bradley caught one final image of the goliath creature—it was a flash of shimmering white. Bradley saw rows of teeth, white as clean picked bones, appear across the face of the creature and Bradley let out a horrifying scream before he was consumed completely.

The world fell black and all sound dissipated.

Bradley awoke with a gasp and shot up in bed to find himself in a darkened room—

his own bedroom. He felt his heavy breathing and his heart beating rapidly as he came to terms with nightmare he had just experienced. He felt his forehead. Hs hair was plastered to his forehead from the cold sweat that had formed. He slumped back into bed. He thought of what he had seen—of the encompassing sand, of the glass prison, and especially of the suited monster that had watched him from the darkness before devouring him. The words rattled in his head; the demand of "join us" chilling him with every chanting whisper. Bradley found himself sobbing lightly before falling back into a deep and dreamless slumber.

Part III: Never Finds Home

Bradley sat at school the next morning in a deeper daze than usual. Thoughts rushed through his head of what that gargantuan, suited specter had whispered to him in his dreams—or what he *hoped* were just his dreams. He tried to rip the ghostly voice from his mind but, try as he might, its hissing proclamation slithered through his mind; every whispered syllable slicing at his concentration like a knife across skin, smooth as silk. The ticking of the classroom clock did little to ease the voices. Constantly pounding against his mind all the time, the voices almost recited in motion with every thundering tick of the clock. He was eager to see Julius, but not for the reasons of joy that he felt the previous day— but because he felt an unshakable fear of which his attempt to point out the absurdity did not ease. The chanting voices fell silent with the startling ringing of the bell, and Bradley leapt up to locate Julius.

He found Julius sitting alone on the corridor floor, his knees tucked to his chest and an apple clutched in his hand; he regarded the approaching Bradley with a glowing smile.

"Hey Bradley," he said cheerfully. "Thanks again for walking me…"

His words trailed off into silence as Bradley lay a heavy hand upon his shoulder.

"I would like for you to come to my house for dinner tonight," Bradley mumbled in a passionless tone. "It is a special day today."

Julius had little time to think of what Bradley meant by that before he felt the grip of Bradley release from his shoulder, and Bradley gave Julius an address and time to arrive for the evening. Julius nodded without hesitation before Bradley skulked off dreamily down and corridor and disappeared around the corner.

Julius sat and pondered what he meant by "special day" and it occurred to him of what today was—his face lit up as he thought of ghosts, jack-o'-lanterns, and hordes of children roaming the streets dressed as the various ghosts and ghouls of fiction. Julius could not contain his excitement at the idea of sharing this Halloween with his new best friend. He spent the rest of the day in plotting, imagining all of the blood-soaked costumes and face painted faces that he would see; he had always watched from his bedroom window when he was younger, and now he would get his chance to live it. He would have until six o'clock, two hours after the end of school, to get himself ready for what could be the happiest night of his young life. He spent the day impatiently waiting for the bell to signify the end of the day, and when the bell finally chimed he ran out without waiting for Bradley; he did not want to ruin the surprise of what his costume would be.

Bradley sat in silence on the sofa next to his father's recliner, occupied by his lounging father who was waiting eagerly for his meal. Bradley glanced over, his mind racing with questions for his father, and sound himself remain silent as his father rustled with the day's newspaper. The headline titled "A glorious day as town celebrates another regal year" and a large picture was plastered under the capitalized headline. Bradley could make out Father Bellum in the image, standing atop his cardboard tower with several others, all with crowns on their heads and smiles as wide as the castle itself. Bradley remembered back to the hostility of Father Bellum the previous day and shuddered at how Julius had been treated by the irritated preacher. He turned from the celebratory headline to the clock that hung from the wall; it emitted a high-pitched bong as it struck six o'clock. Bradley began to regret this decision; his palms grew sweaty as he realized that he had led Julius into a dire situation, and he felt his legs begin to tremble when there was a soft knock at the front door. Bradley sat, frozen in fear and hoping that Julius had the sense to escape. His father folded his paper and headed toward the door; Bradley felt his heart stop as the door swung open.

The door swung open and Julius stood in the glow of the autumn moonlight, covered by a plain white sheet, his eyes peered out of holes he had cut for himself so that he could see through it. Clutched in his right hand was a small wooden box painted orange to resemble a pumpkin. Julius felt his excitement bursting out of him at the sight of someone admiring his costume.

"Happy Halloween!" he proclaimed excitedly and held out his makeshift pumpkin.

Bradley's father stared at the shrouded figure and his face began to contort; it was overcome by a glistering shade of red, and his eyes bulged, and his breathing became labored as his outrage at Julius began to consume his entire being. He was moments away from slamming the door when Bradley appeared behind beside him and nervously invited Julius in, despite the disgusted glances from his disapproving father. He stormed off to take his place at the head of the dinner table.

Bradley led Julius to the bathroom before slamming and locking the door behind him.

"Julius, you have to take that off right now or my dad will kill both of us!" Bradley shouted fearfully. "What made you think that was alright to wear *that* on a day when we are supposed to be remembering the glory of the dead?" Bradley's tone had become scolding, and Julius felt himself whimpering at his friend's disapproval. "You are never allowed to celebrate Halloween—it is strictly forbidden as a sinful holiday here, and it's disrespectful to the dead," Bradley recited from memory from one of Father Bellum's Sunday sermons.

"I—I just wanted to surprise you for Halloween," he mumbled disappointedly, removing the white shroud that covered him to reveal eyes wet with tears.

Bradley felt his heart sink as the despair written across his little friend's face became clear in the harsh brightness of the bathroom; his eyes puffy and face red with embarrassment at having angered his sole companion. He took a deep breath and put a lighter hand on Julius's shoulder. A smile was written across his face at his friend's attempt, but in the back of his mind Bradley felt a sickening fear of what Julius was. For the first time since they had met, Bradley acknowledged how their differences could be hurtful. He wiped the tears from Julius's eyes and smartened him up before the two returned to the kitchen, where Bradley's father sat in deafening silence. His eyes followed Julius as Bradley led him to his seat across the table.

Julius felt judgmental eyes fixated upon him and looked up to see eyes of fiery hatred in the man who sat across from him. All together the room hung in tense silence until there was a loud bang as the oven door was shut and Bradley's mother presented a succulent roast beef that was placed between Julius and Bradley's father. Steam twisted and twirled off the meat like nimble dancers and distracted his father's attention momentarily from Julius, who sat in silence looking at Bradley for approval.

The meal was eaten in silence, a soft and periodic chewing from the four who sat in silence was the only sound to break the endless hush. Bradley's father had maintained his unbroken gaze upon the terrified Julius, and Bradley had sat in fearful silence of his father's underlying anger; both boys once again shared in a sense of terror. Julius found the silence unbearable and frequently glanced over to Bradley for any kind of guidance to break it; Bradley was frozen in fear at the disgust that was written across his father's normally stoic face. Julius was overcome with the desire to break the awkwardness of the silence and the sourness of his initial arrival and made an attempt at conversation.

"Bradley was asking me about what it was like in Seattle," he followed with an awkward giggle. "It's funny just to see just how different—"

But his speech was cut off by a violent clatter as Bradley's father slammed his cutlery down, the fire in his eyes had ignited an ever-brighter rage, and his voice raised to that of a ferocious scream.

"You are just like every other city boy who thinks he can just waltz into this town and call it home!" he screamed at Julius, his face had turned a dark crimson and he was shaking with fury. "This town was not built for people like you." He pointed an accusative finger at the shaking Julius. "It's people like you—like those bastards who came from Chicago—that will be the death of this town and everything it stands for."

He began slamming his fist down onto the table, causing cutlery to shake and glasses to be tipped over and their contents to seep across the table. Bradley attempted to calm his father down and only managed to ignite his bloodlust for Julius, who could no longer hold back his fearful tears at the monster that was viciously barking at him. He continued slamming, pointing, and screaming at the petrified Julius.

"We are the lifeblood of this town and I will not have you lead my son astray with your city ideas. This town, this community, this life—is all he needs, and we don't need someone like you to destroy all of that!

Bradley had gotten up from his seat and had grabbed his psychotic father by the arm. He was pleading for him to cease this verbal onslaught on his friend. Bradley's mother had sat silently, her head leaning down as if staring at the floor, and Bradley felt a panic return at his mother's ignorance to the situation. He screamed at his father to stop, shaking his arm violently to snap him out of the hatred that filled his being like venom—and found the rage within his father beginning to dissipate as he became aware of the inconsolable fear that lay within his son's eyes.

He slumped to a seated position, his face glistening with sweat and his breath heavy from the intensity of his malice, and simply stared wide-eyed at the broken Julius, his face streaming with tears and his entire body trembling with agonized terror. Bradley's father leaned on the table once more, the various pieces of tableware and food items strewn chaotically across it, and mumbled coldly to the quivering Julius:

"Get out."

The words bashed like hammers in the sudden silence of the room. "Get out and never return." He pointed one final, outstretched finger towards the door he had entered through. Bradley shot up and led his bewildered friend towards, and then out onto the front porch of the house.

The cool air felt cold against the wet patches of Julius's face and his fear prevented him from shedding any more tears. Bradley thought it right and took his frightened friend in an embrace; the two stood in trembling silence as Bradley felt the shaking of Julius in his arms. A two-bid farewell, and Julius ran home without stopping to look back at the nightmarish house with its ghoulish monster who had banished him. Bradley re-entered the house to his father standing in the hallway, his face showed regret and remorse.

"Bradley, I was just doing what I had to," his father began.

Bradley put out a hand as a sign for him to hush and fought tears as he spoke. "He was my only friend, Dad." The tears were forming around his eyes as he fought the urge to cry. "What do I have now that you've done this to him— and to me?!" He felt his voice rising to an angered shout that mimicked the display he had witnessed that evening.

"You don't understand," his father responded in a hushed tone, "that boy is dangerous for you."

"If he is *so dangerous* then why was I trusted with him by Principal Reinhart—why did you allow me to lead somebody that you thought was a danger to me?!" Bradley's tone had turned to a bark of confusion and anger at his father.

"You will understand in time, son," his father mumbled, and he walked back into the kitchen to deal with the earlier destruction.

Bradley stormed off to his room, slamming the door behind him, and laying down with a debilitating mixture of confusion, anger and fatigue all rushing throughout his body and mind. He felt his eyes grow heavy as the adrenaline of his anger began to disappear; he was too weak from the evening to fight off the oppressive grasp of slumber and he felt the world fall dark as his eyes shut. He awoke, no longer lying down, but in a standing position in a rusted, metallic room that was shrouded in darkness. Squinting, Bradley could make up a seated figure on the other side of the room and called out to them to no response. Bradley was uneasy in this rusted hell but felt himself drawn to the humanoid figure, who sat slumped in the chair as if slouching. Bradley walked towards the creature, his feet clanging metallically on the rusted iron floor. He was startled still by brightness of a single spotlight which swung like a pendulum from the ceiling and illuminated a single spot on the floor. Bradley followed the beam of light downward and spotted a peculiar item which lay isolated on the floor—the shimmer of a blade caught the eye of Bradley. Bradley was looking down upon a knife, but not unlike that which was kept in a knife block in the corner of his kitchen. The hypnotic glow of the knife made Bradley reach down for it curiously. He felt his grip tighten around the dark, wooden handle of the knife and he lifted it up to inspect it. *What is a knife doing here?* he pondered, before coming to terms with how absurd that was for a first question. He heard the creature release a guttural moan from the chair; its groan echoed throughout the iron chamber and startled Bradley. He felt the urge to turn and run from the being, but Bradley knew that the knife would keep him safe from whatever monster lay ahead. He pressed on cautiously with the knife pointed out at arm's length in front of him.

Bradley walked within reach of the form and noticed that its arms were bound behind it; the being seemingly unable to struggle against its restraints. Bradley whispered to it and its response caused his stomach to wretch and a shiver to run throughout his body. The being lifted its head to speak, and Bradley heard a familiar voice that weakly called his name. Sitting bound to the chair was a badly beaten Julius. Bradley felt tears well up in his eyes as he witnessed his struggling and beaten friend, the panic now visible in his eyes. He reached for his friend and felt himself freeze as his mind began to fill with a chilling and familiar voice—it was the beast that had haunted his dreams.

"Join us!" Its serpentine hiss cut through Bradley's mind and he began to shiver. The knife still clutched tightly in his grasp, the whispered voice was soon joined by many more of different pitches and tones; all chanting the same demand in unison: "Join us! Join us!"

Bradley trembled in fear as the chanting grew louder and louder, echoing through his mind and seemingly filling the room. He looked back at Julius, who lay petrified in the chair, and felt himself drawn to the control he had over the boy; this was the control he had yearned for all of his life. The voices continued as he marched closer to Julius; the voices of

Mr. Riddley, Father Bellum, and Principal Reinhart all chanting along with every labored step. Bradley clutched the knife in his hand and felt himself hypnotized by the familiar voices of those he had grown up with—is this who he truly was? He felt the knife rise weightlessly in his hand towards Julius, who began to scream for Bradley to stop. Bradley heard none of Julius's cries as the voices grew louder and more feverish with every movement of the blade. Bradley attempted to fight the desire that filled his mind and forced himself to look upon the panicked face of his friend—he saw the fear in the eyes of Julius and eased his grip on the knife. The voices began to quiet as he took in Julius's fear, as he forced himself to talk despite the agony.

"B—Bradl—" but his speech was cut off as the blade ran effortlessly across the young boy's throat, bringing his words to a panicked gurgle. The body slumped forward in the chair and was completely motionless as Bradley stepped back from the lifeless corpse of Julius, the bloodied blade still clutched in his hand.

Bradley felt forms appear behind him, and a single hand lay upon his shoulder; it was the hand of his father. Bradley turned, still reeling from the horror of his brutality, and felt sickened by the smile that was written across his father's face. His father chuckled, and his words echoed through the metallic chamber: "May he be forever lost to the sands of time."

Bradley dropped the bloodied knife, and as it fell to the floor with a resounding clang, his father's smiling face disappeared into a shroud of darkness.

Bradley awoke in a panic; however, unlike the previous nightmare, he showed no signs of sweating. He jumped up and headed through to the kitchen to ease the traumatic fear of his nightmare. He was surprised to find that the house was not in complete darkness, but a solitary reading lamp glowed soothingly in the darkness. A rustling of paper could be heard as a page was turned. Bradley snuck through to find his father in his lounge chair, a book in his hands and a pipe hung loosely from his lips. He looked up with a smile that showed pride for his son, closed his book with a thud and regarded the pipe that hung from his mouth. He took a deep puff before looking back at the fearful face of Bradley and whispering in a hushed tone, "We will always be there for you." He put his hand on Bradley's shoulder.

Bradley did not scream, did not run, or even attempt to kill his father. He slumped to the floor with tears in his eyes and realized that his friend was gone forever—Bradley had joined them.

That was the last time the name Julius was ever uttered in the town.

Part IV- Epilogue

Julius was never seen or heard from again. His parents' desperate pleas to the local authorities proved fruitless, and the local paper continued its standard, routine headlines. There was never any mention of a missing boy. Eventually, Julius's parents left the town in despair, the unknown fate of their son tainting the town for them forever. The house would remain empty until another outsider attempted to settle down and, inevitably, would be devoured by the town itself. The town continued life as if Julius's family had never existed, and Bradley found himself falling back into the standard routine he had grown accustomed to.

Bradley never spoke to anyone of Julius; his silence was a mixture of his traumatic grief and remorse for his own actions, and he fell back into his standard role as an outsider. His parent's never spoke of that evening again, and it was treated as if Bradley had hallucinated the entire ordeal—an outcome Bradley could only lie to himself was the case despite the reality. Bradley would think back to Martha Ridley, the one who escaped, and pondered how things could have been different if it was him who had run off to the city—the fantasy brought little reassurance. Bradley spent his days wandering the town, every freshly laundered sheet blowing in the wind was a reminder that Bradley had chosen his destiny. He had chosen the town—he had chosen to join them.

The Bathroom Mirror

Kenneth Stephenson

Mirrors have always given me the creeps. I always felt that something was on the other side of them—little did I know that I was right all along.

I was moving from a small rural area in central Pennsylvania to the big city of San Francisco just under two weeks before Halloween. My new job promised to be fulfilling and challenging. I looked forward to the move with some trepidation as I have never been in a city larger than Harrisburg in my life. I was moving to one of the largest and most diverse cities in the country, if not the world. I was more than a little intimidated by the sheer size and complexity of the metropolis I was about to find myself in. Though I had put most of my stuff into a storage locker, I did box-up a few things and shipped them to my new office building—essentials like bedding and electronics that I didn't need to replace. I was ready to take the next step in this thing called life, and it was October 19th when I boarded the plane that would transport me there.

My new position was made possible by the recent and mysterious departure of the person I was replacing. I never really cared all that much about these things until I heard that the person I was replacing had vanished without a trace and had yet to be found either dead or alive—simply gone. I found this out the day before I left for California.

The company was a Fortune 500 type and gave me an offer I couldn't refuse. They offered to put me up in corporate housing until I could get on my feet and find a suitable apartment. I accepted this kindness eagerly; I knew that the small one-bedroom apartment was near work and hoped it would be near some local hot spots as well. During my orientation I was told that I would receive the keys and directions to the new housing. My first night in Cali was spent in a posh hotel that the company put me up in. I lay in my bed staring at the ceiling for a long time thinking about the great life I would have here and the things that I would see and do. I couldn't wait to start my new life here in the big city.

My first day at the new office was filled with meet and greets, paperwork, guided tours, and lots of smiling faces and back patting. The last stop on my first day was housekeeping; this is where I received my keys and directions to the new temporary apartment. I was told that I was able to stay there for up to six months here, and then I would have to find my own housing. I thought to myself it would be relatively easy to find something and should be able to save enough money in six months to furnish and equip my new place, knowing apartments here are expensive—like *really* expensive. I was told that there was a binder on the kitchen table with all of the needed information and passcodes and passwords for the Wi-Fi, security system, Netflix, Hulu and the like. I thought to myself, *This place sounds pretty sweet—maybe I can just stay here forever.*

I arrived at my new temporary housing early in the afternoon, as my new boss told me to go and get settled. As I walked into the apartment a strange feeling came over me like I wasn't alone. *Stop being so stupid*, I said to myself and sat my backpack down on the kitchen chair. I strolled around the apartment—smallish living room just off the kitchen, short hallway bathroom to the right, and finally the nice sized bedroom fully equipped with crisp new sheets and blankets. I walked into bathroom and was taken aback by one thing that immediately made me feel uncomfortable, a large ornate full-length mirror—I mean this thing was OLD, or at least it looked old. It was hauntingly beautiful, with black wrought iron patterns on each of the four corners. I thought it odd to have such a thing in a bathroom and inspected it more closely. The glass looked *deep*—I can't describe it any other way. It felt warm to the touch, but I just thought that since it was black it was holding the heat better. I snapped a few pictures of it on my phone and sent them to my friends back in PA. I knew that the responses would be "get rid of that thing" or "it's a portal to hell" or some other nonsense. I was sure I would laugh at some of their crazy responses.

The apartment was equipped with smart technology and had automated lights and lots of other fancy things like powered blinds and motion-sensing light switches. I messed around with some of the gadgets, like the powered blinds and mood lighting that could change colors, then set about connecting my laptop and phone to the Wi-Fi. I did a quick Google Maps search of things to do near me and found that this area was indeed nearly in the center of what promised to be a fun and exciting time.

I took a more careful tour of the place once I had settled down a bit. The place was spotless—the maid really did her job well, I could find not a speck of dust or dirt anywhere. I would have to tell the head housekeeper about the stellar job that she had done on the place. I got to busying myself in getting some of my things put away in the dresser drawers and putting my few personal items away. The boxes I had sent from Pennsylvania were still stored in the office building; I would get them when I found an apartment. After a bit of work related stuff, like filling-out some paperwork and the like, I took some time to flip through the channels and chill for a bit before heading off to bed.

My first night was uneventful and I slept soundly knowing that the apartment was equipped with a state of the art alarm system. Sometime in the middle of the night, around 3AM, I woke to use the bathroom and walked into the good-sized lavatory.

I had almost forgotten about that weird mirror in the corner. I finished and washed my hands and glanced at my reflection, and I thought I saw something black and slender right behind my reflection. My heart skipped a beat and I looked behind me.

Nothing.

I chalked it up to shadows or some other trick from the light coming from my bedroom. I thought no more of it and went back to bed.

At work the next day, I was in the break room chatting with my new co-workers and was surprised to hear that the person who I was replacing had only been with the company for twelve days before disappearing. The company was on the rise and had no real time to let my position be vacant too long, so they posted the job on the internet and that's where I found them. In fact, the very apartment I was currently staying in was the one where he had stayed, too. I thought that this was a bit creepy, but I was told they searched the apartment and found no signs of foul play or anything. The police told the HR person that the guy just *vanished*, most likely before he even returned home from work. The investigation was still open but had gone mostly cold since they had not found any clues.

When I got home that evening I found that the bathroom light was on, and I walked into the room knowing that the lights turned off within thirty seconds if no motion was detected. *Odd*, I thought, *I just got home and hadn't come anywhere near the bathroom—so why is the light on? Maybe the motion sensor is faulty or something.* I turned off the light manually and went about fixing myself dinner. After I ate, I went for a short walk around the area looking for things to do for the upcoming weekend. I arrived home about two hours later, feeling confident that I had made the right decision to move here. There were so many new things to do and see, and I couldn't wait for the weekend to come so I could go out and explore the area more. I thought that buying a bike would be a good idea, since it would be easier to get around town without having to worry about a parking space and I had passed a bike shop during my short walk around my area of town. I would eventually have to get a car but since the place that I was in was so close to my office building, I figured it could wait until I found a permanent place before having to worry about getting wheels.

As I was getting ready to go to bed, I brushed my teeth using the little vanity mirror in the bathroom. I could see the bigger mirror's reflection in the smaller mirror of the vanity— and there it was again, the black shape just behind my right shoulder. I spun around just in time to see the shape recede into the mirror. I blinked several times—this had to be some kind of optical illusion, a shadow. It must have been a trick of the light, or too much beer with dinner—something *explainable*, something not otherworldly, because that kind of stuff isn't real, right?

The next several nights were unremarkable, though the bathroom light turned on and off at points throughout the evenings, and I promised to myself that I would have to tell the housekeeping service at work to get the switch checked out for me whenever it happened. In the meantime, I would try to get in and out of that bathroom as quickly as possible because the place gave me the creeps—more specifically that mirror gave me the creeps. One of the nights I actually tried to move it out of the room, but it was either too heavy or fastened to the floor and I couldn't budge it. I thought, *They must have needed two guys to move it into the room.*

The tenth night I stayed in the apartment, as I was getting out of the shower and toweling myself off, the lights in the bathroom flickered and went out for several seconds. They came back on about five seconds later. I had avoided looking at that creepy mirror in the corner ever since the last time I saw that weird trick of the light. I decided to hang a towel over most of its length; it didn't cover it entirely, but it did the job.

That Friday, which was the twelfth day I was to be in my apartment, I went to the housekeeping department as I was on my way out of the building, hurrying to get home to shower and change so that I could meet up with a couple of coworkers for some of the parties that were going on tonight—as today was Halloween—and I told them about the light switch and asked them to check it out. In passing, I asked them why they would put such a weird mirror in the bathroom. The guy behind the desk looked at me oddly and said, "What mirror? We didn't install a second mirror in that apartment," and went back to his Sudoku puzzle.

That evening after I got home from work, I was hurriedly getting ready to go out for the Halloween festivities and gathering clothes to do a quick load laundry for tomorrow when I absentmindedly grabbed the towel covering the mirror. Half thinking something was going to jump out at me, I hurried to put it back. *You are being so stupid*, I silently scolded myself, and threw the towel into the laundry basket.

I turned and began to walk out of the room when I saw in the reflection of the vanity two black arms shooting out of the mirror. They grasped my shoulders and pulled me backwards into the blackness.

I am now trapped by the entity that has dominion over this place. I know that I will never leave here, but I do have company—lots of company—and they all have stories to go along with mine. I never showed up to celebrate Halloween with my new-found friends. I never showed up to work on Monday or the day after either; another investigation was opened. The company waited for the allotted time and then reposted the job opening on the internet. A month or so later, the new tenant of the place opened the apartment door for the first time. As she was taking the grand tour of the place, she walked through the bathroom—where the light was already on—and thought to herself, *what a weird place to put such a mirror.* We watched her stare into our realm and wished we could warn her somehow to get out of the apartment, but It has us under control.

We can never leave.

Small Bites
Rebecca Rowland

Isabel Juergens had been small for her age; that is, until this past summer, when her toffee-tan skin had soaked up so many hours of running and swimming and sunshine that she gained a full two inches and thirty pounds on her athletic, 8-year-old frame. Her family called her Belly, not only as a reference to her given name but as a tongue-in-cheek homage to the slightly rounded pooch that always seemed to peek out from under t-shirts and tank tops, no matter how hard she pulled at them. She was what her mom called "long-waisted," whatever that meant, and in the past year, Dylan, her mother's only sibling, had taken to calling her Lucky Star after a music video that prominently featured the tummy of some forgotten female vocalist with a badly bleached hairdo.

Dylan, Uncle D, was a nostalgia junkie, a sworn bachelor with a soft spot for pop songs, television shows, and action figures from his childhood in the 1970's and 80's. The year previous, he paid top dollar for front row tickets to Night Ranger when they toured the Northeast, and he was quick to point out to anyone who doubted it that Van Halen and *Van Hagar*, as he called it, were "vastly different rock bands." He could not eat Life cereal without thinking of Mikey, and with the birth of eBay, had started a collection that seemed never to be complete of yuppie-era collectibles many considered *kitschy*. Erica, Belly's mother, called them something else; although Belly didn't know exactly what the word was, Erica merely told her it rhymed with "tap." When Uncle D visited the house, he always shared his newest acquisitions with Belly, and his niece could not help but imagine him clicking and soft-shoeing his way up the steps every time.

It was on the third Saturday in October that Uncle D brought her the doll. Belly remembered this clearly, as it was a rainy, leafy autumn day and she had been disappointed that they could not decorate the outside of the house for Halloween, since Erica had feared she'd be electrocuted plugging in the net of orange string lights she'd drape along the front bushes every year. Belly didn't know if her own myriad of fears—clowns, spiders, fire, spontaneous combustion: if it grimaced, crawled, crackled, or appeared out of nowhere, chances are, Belly cowered from it—were learned from watching her mother's reactions or had magically jumped into her body and proliferated, like the flu germs she had learned about in school that year.

About once a month, like someone who had contracted a strange illness, Erica would retire to her bedroom or into the dark recesses of the shade-drawn living room, curl up into a ball, and stare out into space for days on end. Belly learned quickly how to fend for herself, although after a solid month of marshmallow fluff sandwiches, she'd decided the white sugary concoction was the most disgusting thing one could possibly eat. Each time, after a short while, Uncle D would appear, bringing groceries and fresh air, and Belly and her sister Renata, two years her junior, would be whisked away to the movies, or the mall, or a playscape-adjacent fast food joint for flat hamburgers and soggy fries. By the time they returned, the windows would be open and bright and their mother would be showered and smiling: the sad, moldy parent discarded and replaced with a fresh, sparkling doppelgänger. The girls never asked questions; they were simply happy to have a caregiver again.

Dylan, on the other hand, was at the end of his rope. "Erica, Jesus: why can't you just *take medication*? You know how you get. Why do you do this time and again?" he had pleaded with his sister just the week previous.

"You don't know how it makes me feel," was her pat response. "I feel slow, and tired, and... well, stupid. What do you think feels worse: having a panic attack that lasts all of five minutes, or being in a stupor for 24 hours a day?"

"When's the last time you talked to your doctor about it?" Dylan asked.

"Doctor? What are you, nuts?" Erica replied. "I get my pills on the down low from a guy down the street. 'You think I want depression, or anxiety, or—God forbid—incidences of *psychosis* logged in my medical file? Do you know what that would do to my premiums?"

Erica worked for one of the big insurance firms down in Hartford. She had graduated magna cum laude from UCONN with a degree in finance, studied for her certification dutifully, taken the series of qualifying exams, and before the ripe old age of twenty-nine, had climbed the corporate ladder to senior underwriter. She could list the top ten pre-existing conditions most likely to affect policy rates in the order of severity of influence off the top of her head, and out of sheer paranoia that she'd log a white coat blood pressure spike on a yearly exam, was known to pop a beta-blocker she'd borrowed from a friend an hour before a visit with any medical professional, even her daughters'. When the battles with anxiety began to gang up on her, the panic speeding up in frequency and intensity like a roller coaster car on a downward dive, she'd throw a sprinkling of Xanax at the back of her throat, chase it with a bottle of Poland Springs, and wait in the dark for the effect to close in on her like an eclipse. When it seemed safe to venture out into the world again, she'd swallow a couple of the Adderall the mother of one of Renata's friends sold to her, and lickety-split, she was right as rain.

Belly was finally at that age where she understood her mother's carnival tricks weren't normal, and they weren't fitting of an upstanding parent, but she also knew in the scheme of things, she had it relatively good. Billy McMillan's father was an on-again, off-again drunk, and a mean one at that, and she had witnessed Mr. McMillan putting his hands around Mrs. McMillan's throat more often than she'd like. If Carrie Lewis was bad, her father "got the belt"; Carrie wouldn't elaborate on that, and Belly didn't ask. And no one—*no one*— wanted to sleep over Deenie Butler's house: the feeling of Deenie's mother's boyfriend's eyes as they slid greasily from her shoulder to the bony angle that jutted out just above the top of her thigh gave Belly a sick feeling in the pit of her stomach, like she had eaten something rancid out of the garbage can. Deenie's house was the one house Belly would be skipping this year while trick-or-treating. No, no one was ever brutalized or sexualized or terrorized at the Juergens house; they were just neglected every once in a while, and hey, in the long run, what was the real harm of a fluff sandwich here and there?

And so, it was that as Belly sat pouting on the padded seat of the big picture window, watching the big puddles pitter-patter with raindrops and the dried oak leaves pirouette alongside like competitive skaters at the city rink, Dylan's big and boxy Kia SUV tottered into the driveway. Belly had been preoccupying herself with ideas for a costume for trick-or-treating all morning. Last year, Erica had purchased a pair of pink tights with silver sparkles to complete a princess ensemble, but her eldest daughter had been too short to wear them at the time: they had bagged terribly in the knees and ankles, making her look like a shimmery, malnourished Shar-Pei. *Maybe they'll fit this year*, thought Belly. She was taller, after all. She was making a mental search of her dresser drawers and closet floor, trying to locate the misplaced stockings, when her uncle's truck appeared. Seeing it, she put the costume out of her mind and was renewed with unexpected joy.

Renata, who had propped herself up in the oversized rocker nearby, clapped her hands with excitement and alternately kicked up her feet. Her legs were so short, so they did not bend over the edge but stuck out like two thick tree branches. She coughed two, then three times without attempting to lift her hand and cover her mouth, but Belly was too happy to scold her about it.

In the kitchen, Erica was busy peeling an eggplant for the baked parmesan she planned to make for dinner that night. "Well, hello to you too, D," she said, as her brother sailed past her without a word to see his nieces.

"How are my two favorite girls?" Dylan said, kicking off his loafers and half walking, half sliding across the shiny hardwood floor in his greying sports socks. He shook off the faded brown windbreaker and draped it over the back of the wingback chair, then collapsed onto the couch, folding his legs into a pretzel in front of his body like he always did. "*Indian-style*, that's what they used to call this pose," Uncle D told Belly once. When she asked him why they didn't call it that any more, he told her, "It's racist, I think," and she did not inquire further.

Uncle D carried with him a bright yellow plastic bag about 14 inches high. It read *Tower Records* in big red letters on the side and was a recycled carry-all for everything from his lunch to a pair of sneakers to change into after work if he planned on walking home. Belly and Renata had seen this bag a million times, or maybe they had seen the million Tower Records bags their uncle had been hoarding for decades. This time, the bag had taken on an oblong shape, surrounding its contents and straining to contain it in some places. Whatever the booty, it was larger than the Transformers robot with the deep scratch on its back he had brought to show them last weekend, and taller than the sandy-haired Cabbage Patch kid with the worn face and tattered gingham dress he had shared in early August.

"You're not going to believe what I got," Uncle D said, his eyes wild and his grin wide. He patted the cushion on the couch next to him. "Come sit next to me."

Belly sprang to the couch in an instant; Renata had a bit of trouble climbing out of the deep pocket of chair she had nestled in, but after a few kicks and an eventual last resort flip onto her stomach and push backwards, her tiny body was able to free herself from its grasp and she padded over to the couch next to her sister.

Dylan shifted back and forth and turned his body so that it was facing his nieces, his toes pointing toward their eyebrows. He put both arms behind his back and with them, the bag. "Okay, now, this is super cool," he prepared them. "Are you ready?"

They nodded their heads furiously. They were ready.

He pulled his right arm back around to his chest. His hand clutched a stuffed animal; no: it was a stuffed doll. A doll made out of cotton canvas, one big piece of fabric cut and sewn into a human-like shape. But the sight of this doll made Belly draw back in horror.

"It's the Hamburglar!" announced Dylan, his smile expanding so that it practically swallowed his whole face. "From our favorite hamburger place!" He squeezed the doll's torso with his free hand, seeming to tickle it. "When I was a kid, they had this whole story-land thing where these characters lived. There was a guy made out of french fries, and even a mayor of the town where they all lived." He paused for a moment to think. "Yeah: his name was Mayor McCheese: isn't that a riot?!"

Dylan began to laugh hysterically, not seeming to notice that his nieces' reaction to the doll was anything but joyful. In fact, Belly could not take her eyes off of the doll, but in the way you wouldn't take your eyes off of a growling, salivating dog. The Hamburglar was dressed like some sort of Depression-era escaped convict: his shirt and pants were black and white striped. He sported bright yellow shoes and a black, Zorro-like mask from which beady, black eyes peered out suspiciously. Incongruously, around his neck was a bright orange business suit tie, but it had been fastened hastily, as the back flap was longer than the front flap and hung sloppily in full view. He wore a strange, mariner-like black hat pulled down over his ears, but overall, it wasn't his clothing that made Belly instantly uneasy.

It was his teeth.

"Please... please don't bite me," Belly heard herself say to the doll in a flat, hollow voice. She didn't know why she had said it, but she knew as soon as the plea tumbled out of her mouth that she meant it. Earnestly. Desperately.

The Hamburglar, with his black-ringed eyes and nose like the top of a witch's hat, stared back at her silently. Two sharp, triangular teeth jutted out from his upper lip. It was clear that they weren't visible because he was opening his mouth or sneering. They were visible because they were too big for his mouth, like a vampire whose fangs had grown together in a grotesque dental nightmare. And to top it off, the Hamburglar seemed to be...smiling.

Belly forced herself look away, but before her eyes had shifted, she saw it. The doll opened and closed his mouth ever so slightly three times—*sssclick sssclick sssclick*—like a cat gnawing on a chicken bone. She even thought she could hear a soft, metallic clicking sound coming from his head, like two spoons striking. She stared at the doll, silently willing it to move again.

It did not.

Had she imagined it? She looked at her sister to gauge if she, too, had seen the toothy monster move. Renata's eyes were wide as saucers, and she was pressing her open palm to her sternum, her mouth agape and forming an O as she sucked in air with what appeared to be great difficulty. A thick, mucous-y wheezing sound spat from her mouth, and when she attempted to cough, nothing but a dry, crackling noise like walking on hay came out.

"Oh my god, Renny—hold on, sweetheart, hold on," Dylan said quickly, leaping to his feet and throwing the doll in his abandoned place on the couch. He ran toward the kitchen. Belly kept her eyes on the doll, which now buried its face in the cushion, and put her hand on her sister's back, rubbing wide circles to try to calm her down.

Erica rushed into the room alongside her brother, shaking a small red canister. She placed the inhaler up to Renata's mouth and with her other hand, smoothed her daughter's hair from her forehead. "It's okay, baby. Okay, deep breath," she instructed and pressed the administration button. The inhaler emitted a quick *whoosh*, like a snippet of the sound a plane going by overhead would make, as Renata sucked in the medication and held her breath for as long as she could.

When the urgency of the asthma attack had passed, Erica placed her arm around her younger daughter and hugged her tight. Dylan ruffled her hair and made a joke about vintage toys always leaving him "breathless as well." Belly stared at the McDonald's trademark insignia stitched across the doll's back.

She could have sworn she saw the back move up and down.

Whether by accident or on purpose, Dylan left the Hamburglar behind when he returned to his apartment that afternoon. As soon as his truck was out of sight, Belly grabbed the doll gingerly by its yellow foot and shoved its canvas body into the back of the linen closet.

That night, Belly laid in her bed, staring at the pitted texture of the ceiling, trying to make out its topographical map through the night's darkness. She could see the shadow of a spindly cobweb dancing just inches from where the ceiling met the yellow wall of the room she shared with Renata. Once, she had asked Uncle D where cobwebs came from.

"Where do spider webs come from?" he asked her back.

"Spiders!" Belly shouted, then clasped her hands over her face tight, convinced that even speaking of the vile creatures would lure them out of their crevices and into her hair and mouth.

Dylan flashed a sly grin. "Well, then it stands to reason that cobwebs come from *cobs*!" He laughed uproariously at his terrible pun, but Belly was confused. What were cobs? She imagined them as shiny black beetles with sharp antennae like sewing needles, poking her eyelids, their tiny bug teeth gnawing at her skin while she slept. Hordes of cobs, swarming her body until she appeared to be wearing a suit of undulating black, wet scales.

Belly flipped onto her side and pulled the thick comforter up to her neck. She could hear the slow rhythm of delicate snoring that was usual when her sister had drifted into the heaviest cycle of sleep floating up and away from the twin bed against the opposite wall. Belly, however, could not sleep.

The clock on her dresser against the wall closest to the door beamed the sole light into the room. Red digital numbers screamed 2:35.

2:36.

2:37.

Belly closed her eyes and watched the poltergeists of numbers float lazily up and to the right of her field of vision. When she opened her eyes again, barely thirty minutes had passed.

3:05.

She let her eyes waltz along the dim outline of the top of her dresser, willing her sight to adjust to the darkness. After a minute, she could see the Wonder Woman piggy bank where she had stuffed every coin and dollar she found or earned; this year, she had lost four teeth (three naturally, and one when she emerged from what she had believed was a particularly graceful dive and ran headlong into a cannonballing neighbor boy's elbow—that last bicuspid had earned her triple the payment from the Tooth Fairy, although she was not sure why.) A short while longer, she could see the jewelry box that opened to reveal a tiny ballerina twirling slowly to a song by some guy named Elton John: a birthday present from Uncle D, of course. And next to the jewelry box...

Wait, what?

It couldn't be.

Belly felt her throat dry and close. Next to her jewelry box was the doll: the Hamburglar, standing, slightly leaning, with its back against the wall, a confident but casual pose, its stripes seeming to glow below the triangle teeth. Its eyes, round and black and empty, looked like those of the rabbits Belly sometimes saw creeping around their backyard in the summer at dusk. She squeezed her eyes closed, making tiny silver and blue stars shoot behind her lids. There was silence in the room: even her sister's breathing had calmed and quieted. Then,

ssssclick... ssssclick... ssssclick...

Belly inhaled a deep breath as quietly as she could. If the doll believed she was sleeping, maybe it would go away. Maybe it would leave her alone.

ssssclick... ssssclick... SSSCLICK...

It was closer. It was moving closer. Belly wanted to move; she wanted to pull the covers over her face to protect it from whatever the doll planned to do when he reached her pillow. And then, Renata coughed.

It was a quick, stuttering cough, one that she hadn't willed to happen but was purely instinctual and reactionary, her body still cocooned in the deepest clouds of sleep. Immediately following the sound, Belly thought she felt the tiniest gust of wind caress her cheek, and she strained to hear what would happen next, but almost immediately wished she could shut her ears as tightly as she had shut her eyes.

The next noise was different: a moist, sucking sound, coming from the opposite wall, then: *ssssclick ssssclick ssssclick*. The teeth mashing was definitely away from her now, but in between sickening clicks was an unnerving sound like someone trying to breathe through a wide, wet straw. It sounded like the doll was... drooling... yes, *drooling* as it opened and closed its mouth.

Belly felt her legs turn to cement. She could not move, could not scream, could not open her eyes. *Go away go away go away go away*, she pleaded with her mind, willing the doll to be anywhere but right there in her butter-yellow bedroom with her and her sister.

Renata.

Belly could no longer hear her sister snoring. Instead, she heard a strange noise, like someone clicking their tongue loudly, the sound she thought glue should make when she put a finger into a blob of it and pulled it back. A tacky, wet sound. Then, a muffled, choking noise. It was her sister. It was Renata. It sounded like someone had stuffed her throat with handfuls of wadded-up Saran Wrap. There was a muffled scream.

Belly tried to open her eyes. She really, truly did, but she couldn't seem to move her muscles. It was like Belly had taken one step back behind Belly: a second Belly, watching from the sidelines, in the safety zone. A puddle of warm wetness spread from her crotch to her thighs, like she was sitting in a warm tub with her panties still on. She breathed in deep, like she was preparing to dive and touch the filter at the bottom of the pool. She held her breath, held it for what seemed like forever, until the darkness behind her eyes turned deep red, then indigo, and finally, black.

The next morning began like a starter pistol shot at a racetrack. Erica was yelling, no, *screaming* for Belly to *Jesus oh God oh God oh God what happened?! What happened to you?!* fetch her cellphone from the charging stand on the microwave in the kitchen. Belly sprang from her bed, not even bothering to glance at her mother, who was bent over Renata's bed, shaking. The worn, padded soles of Belly's footed pajamas, the plastic footpads mostly erased like dark fabric stains that had been left to fester before laundering, slipped and skidded on the floors, making Belly run like a goofy dog in an old Saturday morning cartoon. Once in the kitchen, she grabbed the white smartphone and turned to return to the bedroom, but she forgot to disconnect it from its tether and was yanked backwards after taking two steps. Once she was free, she skated back to her mother, her brain finally catching up with her body and putting the pieces together. Renata. Choking sound. *sssclick sssclick sssclick.* The doll—The DOLL!

Erica snatched the phone from Belly's hand and began to tap it furiously, her hand trembling. "Yes, yes hello. My daughter is a patient of Dr. Wen's." Pause. "What? Well, what time does the main desk open?" Pause. "Can you page the doctor? Isn't that what an answering service is for?" Belly could see the worry on her mother's face; usually it was the signal to stock up on peanut butter and bread and prepare for auto-pilot mode, but today it was something else: it wasn't anxiety, it was terror.

Belly craned her head to see past her mother's curved body, but she could not see around Erica's hip. She could hear her sister breathing, Renata's wheezy everyday breathing, slow and steadily rising like smoke from the direction of the bed.

"Listen! My daughter woke up with—with *wounds* all over her chest and neck." Pause. "No, no, no—wounds, like cuts. Pricks. No, not pricks. Bigger than pricks." She put her free hand on her own forehead, looked down at her younger daughter lying in bed, and cleared her throat. "They look like tiny fucking stab wounds, okay? I've never seen anything like this before. And she feels feverish... should I just go to the hospital?"

Belly walked closer to her sister, tip-toeing as if trying not to startle a wild animal. Her mom was right. From the space just under Renata's tiny jawline, down to the edge of her shoulder and scattered across her chest and throat, were pin-pricks. Not scattered, exactly: each wound had a matching partner less than an inch away. Twin lacerations dotting her café au lait skin, at least fifty pairs. Some were just surface nicks; others had drawn real blood that had dripped out onto her nightgown and dried brown. Most were perfectly round, but others... others were teardrop-shaped, then long and deep, like whatever had made the wound had sunk deep into her flesh and torn down, trying to pull its victim to the ground.

Renata was crying. Big, glass-like tears streamed down her cheeks noiselessly. Belly crept cautiously onto the mattress next to her sister and put her arm around her protectively, then felt instantly guilty. Where was her protection last night?

"Belly," her sister said weakly. "It bit me. It bit me." Her eyes were wide again, as wide as they had been on the sofa the day before. Belly could smell the stale yellow stench of dried urine. It was only then that she realized it was coming from her own pajamas.

The Hamburglar was nowhere in sight.

The following week, Belly pulled out object after dust-bunnied object from under her bed, looking for her pink tights. A ratty grey zippered sweatshirt she'd outgrown. The Cabbage Patch kid from the summertime, its peach face streaked with a layer of fine dirt. A blue sneaker whose mate was suspiciously absent. No tights. She *had* to have the pink tights with the silver sparkles for her costume, and Halloween was only a day away.

Belly wandered down the hallway noiselessly in her bare feet, unconcerned at how black the bottoms were getting. No one had swept, vacuumed, or mopped the house in weeks. She paused only momentarily at the door to the living room. Her mother was asleep on the couch, her mouth agape and her throat purring with the faintest of snores. She would be comatose for the weekend. Belly was on bachelor time again.

Renata was sitting alone at the kitchen table, wearing a V-neck t-shirt and drinking the world's largest glass of strawberry milk. An open canister of Quik and a silver spoon awash with pink sat on the kitchen counter. Belly replaced the top on the container, slid the spoon into the dishwasher, and stretched her arms to open the cabinet above. She assessed the contents: a slightly crushed box of Frosted Flakes, a box of Triscuits, a jar of store brand tomato sauce, and two unopened boxes of frosted blueberry Pop-Tarts.

"Do you know if Uncle D is coming over today?" she asked, more to the wall than to Renata, who was staring blankly at the table and tracing the side of her glass absent-mindedly. Belly could see the dark brown scabs that drizzled her sister's neck and chest like decorative icing on the danishes her mother sometimes bought at the supermarket for breakfast. Belly had not seen the doll since that night. She had even searched their bedroom for it (in broad daylight, holding Uncle D's old baseball bat, of course) but found nothing. Somehow, its disappearance made its existence all the scarier, like a centipede that had wiggled its way into a crevice of the floor, making her wonder in which shoe or hat it would resurface to slither across her unsuspecting skin.

"Hey, do you know where my pink sparkle tights are?" Belly asked.

Renata said nothing, only winced slightly as she shrugged her shoulders and chugged down the remainder of her milk. Belly watched her tiny Adam's apple dance up and down beneath a pair of deep gashes. They reminded Belly of the fork marks her mom made on the edges of a pie crust before she put it in the oven.

Belly closed the cabinet, opened the door to the basement, and felt along the wall for the switch just inside. Brightness flickered once, twice, then dimmed to bathe the room below in light.

She hadn't checked the laundry room.

Belly padded down the creaky wooden stairs, holding the railing tight in her right hand. Two years ago, Uncle D had renovated their basement, adding a faux wood floating floor, a white dropped ceiling, and grey paneling. There had been talk of Dylan moving in with Erica and the girls when his sister had been at her sickest, but it was only talk. Erica went back to work, the beige pull-out couch gathered dust and sat unused pushed up against one of the grey panels, and the recessed lighting continued to strobe each time they washed clothes or retrieved a box of frozen hamburgers from the chest freezer.

The washing machine and its matching dryer were located under a rectangular window at the far end of the room. Belly walked over to them, scanning the area for any sign of pink or glittering fabric. There was a mound of dirty clothes piled on the washer. Belly began to pull out pieces from the heap, tossing jeans and socks here and there, looking for her tights.

And then she heard it: a strange clicking sound coming from the ceiling.

Belly looked above her. There was nothing but white pressboard tiles sandwiched between white rails. She was not tall enough to see out of the window, but the sound was coming from above. Maybe someone was rapping on the pane?

The sound came again. It was faint, as if muffled by one of the winter scarves her mom made her wear to school each January.

sssclick... sssclick... sssclick...

Belly pushed her body forward onto the washing machine and balancing on her tummy, wrestled her legs up and underneath her torso. Once she could twist her feet and grip the cool metal shell with her toes, she pushed down with her palms so that she was squatting, then standing on top of the washer. From here she could look out of the window, and the hair on the top of her head brushed the ceiling lightly.

No one was outside of the window. There was nothing that Belly could see that could have made the noise. She must have been hearing things, but

sssclick... sssclick... sssclick...

here it was again, louder this time. It was coming from right above her head. Belly placed her palms on the nearest ceiling tile, her wrists making right angles. Gently and ever so slowly, she pushed the tile upward, revealing a small slice of darkness. She held her breath and waited a moment, but nothing happened.

Belly loosened her hold on the tile and relaxed her arms, and the tile began to fall back into its frame, when in the last sliver of empty, dark space there appeared wet eyes framed by a black mask, staring down at her. In a panic, Belly thrusted the tile forward in an attempt to push the Hamburglar back and deeper into the recess of the ceiling. Instead, the sudden motion jarred the doll free from its hiding place and it toppled downward toward the washing machine. To Belly's horror, it landed face down on her left foot, near the bottom of her leg.

Sssslluuuuuurrrrrpppppp

SSSCLICK SSSCLICK SSSCLICK

Belly felt the sharp pain sear her ankle. She shook her leg violently, kicking the cycle knob of the washing machine in the process. The doll had clamped its teeth into her flesh. No: clamping wasn't the word—that's not what it was doing. It was *gnawing*. Its razor teeth sank in and out of her flesh like an industrial sewing machine.

Belly screamed. A sound she had never heard before shot out of her lungs, through her throat, and out of her mouth: a high-pitched primal wail. In an act of pure survival, she wrapped both of her hands around the doll's neck and pulled upwards as hard as she could. As its face tore free from her leg, she felt both a sickening rip and the sensation of a piece of her outside shell severing from the muscle and bone with which it had been entwined. Riding on the wave of Belly's forceful tug, the doll sailed upwards, pulling Belly with it, and the two fell in a heap on the scattered dirty clothing on the ground.

Belly's first instinct was to run. Her second instinct was to bury her face in the dirty jeans and t-shirts surrounding her. However, she understood something as clearly as she knew her mom would never stop riding her revolving door in and out of the dark living room. She knew if she did not kill it, if she did not destroy the doll, it would return time and time again to torture them for eternity. But how? It was made of canvas. It was one, smooth piece of fabric. There was nothing to maim, nothing to remove, and nothing to disassemble.

And so, Belly did the only thing she could think of.

She grabbed the Hamburglar by the scruff of its neck, like a momma cat scolding her kitten, and pulled it back towards her. Keeping its face turned away from hers, she took a deep breath (*think: dive to the bottom of the pool, touch the drain, hold it hold it hold it*), opened her mouth, and closed her teeth around the back of the doll as hard as she could. Then she pulled the doll forward with its canvas shell still firmly clenched in her jaw. She opened and closed her mouth, tearing at the fabric over and over, pulling it this way and that, even shaking her head until she felt it give a bit. She chewed harder and pulled more desperately, with as much force as she could muster, and then she felt it break away. The fabric tore. The Hamburglar's whole back was ripped, and white, foamy stuffing peeked out.

But Belly didn't stop there. She bit and ripped, bit and tore. She mashed the doll's masked face into her mouth, tugged at the orange tie with her molars, and caught the edge of the front fabric behind her front teeth, pulling and slashing it further, chewing and tearing until there was nothing left of the Hamburglar but scraps of black and white, sopping wet with her saliva, and piles of yellowed filling. When there was no piece left large enough for her to bite, she wiped the wetness from her lips with the back of her arm, trudged back up the stairs, and shut off the light behind her.

Belly grabbed Erica's phone from the charging port on the microwave, found Dylan's number in her mother's contacts, and hit the phone button. She pressed the phone against her ear and walked into the bathroom. Just a year earlier, she would have had to use the step stool to see herself in the mirror. Now she could stand on her toes and see her reflection. Her chin and neck were covered in dark red goo. When she opened her mouth, she discovered that most of the blood was coming from her own gums: she had lost two more teeth that afternoon. More surprisingly, though, she had chipped one of her two front teeth. A large chunk had broken off of it, creating a sharp, jagged fang shaped like an upside-down triangle.

"Uncle D?" she said in a small voice.

"Yes, my Lucky Star?" Dylan answered back. She could feel his smile through the receiver. "Do you need me to bring anything this afternoon? I'll be there before dinnertime. Should I pick up a pizza?"

Belly thought for a minute. "Yeah, that sounds good. And would you help me with my costume? I can't find the right pieces, so I think I want to go as something else." She turned her head sideways and examined her profile.

"Of course, darlin'. What do you need? I'll swing by the party store on my way."

She turned back towards the mirror, rolled her tongue along the bottom of her chipped tooth, and was surprised by how sharp it was. "Oh, Uncle D, I ruined your Hamburglar doll. It's all... messed up now," she said, hoping Dylan wouldn't ask for elaboration. "I'm sorry."

"Oh, don't worry about it. It's just a doll," he said. "Now what would you like to be for trick-or-treating tomorrow?"

Belly smiled at herself, digging her jagged tooth into her bottom lip. She gave her uncle a list of supplies: a black and white striped shirt and pants, a black mask, and an orange tie. She clicked her teeth together *sssclick sssclick sssclick* and realized: she was going to stop at Deenie Butler's house this year after all.

The Hermit of Singer's Creek

J. Tonzelli

On many Halloweens past, when we were kids, my older brother would terrify me with stories of a hermit who lived in a shack miles into the vast woods that bordered our small town. According to the stories, one could find the shack by entering those woods where Sycamore Street bisected Little Gunpowder Road and walking dead ahead a few miles to Singer's Creek, which you then followed to the west. In doing this, the brave and the curious would run right smack into the hermit's so-called home—and the alleged horrors that adorned it. As far as anyone knew, this hermit had no friends or family, no tax records or other official paperwork on file with the county, not even a name—no history or identity. Outside of being the town myth, there was nothing that suggested he actually existed.

To me, the lack of those connections was reassuring. Because any of those characteristics would have suggested he were even minuscule bit real. Or human.

And the lurid details of his monstrosities didn't leave much room for humanity.

"No one knows how long he's lived out there," my brother's stories began. "The hermit of Singer's Creek has *always* been a legend, even when the oldest members of the town were kids. Some folks believe he's 150 years old. They say he was never a child—that he'd never actually been born—but instead, somehow, had come into being."

On these Halloween nights, I'd gawk through the campfire with terrified eyes as my brother told me the hermit lore, which was filled with acts of grave desecration, strange experimentation, post-mortem mutilation, black magic, and necrophilia. Every year he told the same story, anchored by the same grisly details, but every year the fear I experienced always felt different, as if I were hearing the ghastly tale with different ears or processing it with a different mind. I chalked this up to a new year of experiences in the world, a slow maturation, and a steady understanding of what *real* horror was—but if I'm being honest, it's that every year he pushed me incrementally closer toward believing it.

According to the legend, those who dared look upon the hermit's shack of Singer's Creek would witness something culled from their nightmares: dead bodies, whole or in pieces, hollowed and hung from rusty hooks; grimy buckets filled with the coagulated fluids that dripped from mutilated human remains; severed limbs crudely attached to each other with barbed wire, iron fasteners, fishing line, or industrial adhesives; reams of flesh stretched across the ground like picnic blankets, their corners staked into the hard earth to dry like cracked leather under the sun; and slivers of bone protruding from piles of large timbers and broken branches for a prepared bonfire that had yet to blaze.

They say the hermit chose that spot for his shack so he could nightly wash his bloody hands in the flowing creek. They say, as a result, its muddy banks have been permanently dyed Petunia pink over the many years he's lived there. They say, even miles downstream, nothing living can be fished from the water, for everything beneath the surface has long since choked on blood.

These claims were reported to the sheriff, who was quick to dismiss them, calling them "fantastically silly" and likening them to "the stuff of EC Comics." But some folks accused him of being too afraid to investigate the hermit and his house of horrors for himself. "He's just a weird old man," he often replied when challenged. "Just leave him be and knock off all this morbid talk." But the sheriff's refusal only fueled the stories, which grew more grotesque with each person who retold them.

My brother always grinned deviously through the legend's finale, which was the part he knew unnerved me the most: a reminder that the old hermit's shack may have been far out in the woods, but it was also less than five miles from our own front doors. He'd lived out there for 150 years, and he'd live out there for 150 more. He'd be living out there when we buried our family, our friends and neighbors, and ourselves. He'd be living out in those woods sharpening femur bones into spears and plucking teeth from severed heads for his gravel walkway, as he waited for our desiccated bodies to lower into the earth for his inevitable harvesting.

"What do you think he'll turn *you* into?" my brother would ask. "After he digs up your coffin in the middle of the night? After he ties a length of rope around the back of your neck and under your armpits, and drags you all the way to his shack? Maybe your leg bone will be a torch to light his bloody workshop. Or maybe he'll skin your fingers and toes for his wind chimes, which he'll hang outside to catch the October winds. Or maybe he'll... *heh heh*... plan something *very* special for you. Maybe he'll keep you whole, while *you* keep him company on those cold winter nights."

"Gross, shut up!" I would bellow, kicking dirt at him through the campfire, desperate to mask my utter fear with amused boyhood disgust. And he would take a swig from his beer or a puff from his cigarette and he'd laugh at me in that way only an older brother can, with the knowledge that he could terrify me with little effort.

In spite of the dark, and my fear, and it being Halloween— the night when *anything* could be real— it was

175

all safe. Yes, his stories were foul, and yes, it was dark and we were in the woods, but he was with me. We were together. And if something monstrous manifested in that dark—flung itself at me with madness and murder in its eyes—my brother would step into its path. He would die for me. He'd never said anything as dramatic and silly-sounding as that, but he didn't have to. A brother knows. So, I let him tell his yarns about the hermit of Singer's Creek. I let his words wrap around my spine like frigid, twisting hands. I let his words infect my head like slimy worms burrowing six feet underground. Because it was Halloween and we were kids and we were safe. It was all safe. It was all make-believe. Of *course* I knew this. But at my young and impressionable age, my brother was a hero to me, and anything he told me was gospel—even if just a fraction, and even on Halloween.

I admired him more than he ever knew.

He was the all-American cool kid that many of my friends and I aspired to be. He was handsome, having received all the best features of my mother and father—unlike me, who instead received an awkward hodgepodge. With his depthless knowledge of sports and cars and rock 'n roll bands, and his revolving-door cache of pretty girlfriends, I'd never known anyone cooler. I remember the day he casually waltzed into our house wearing that famous grin, and once my parents were nowhere in sight, he rolled up his sleeve to reveal the brand-new tattoo on his arm of a black-hooded skeleton with pentagram eyes whipping a chain seemingly right at me.

"Are you nuts?" I demanded. "Mom and Dad are going to kill you!"

And he shrugged, sliding his sleeve back down. "They'll get over it. You only live once, right?"

I was in awe of him. I was envious of the way he seemed indomitable. He didn't fear punishment or judgement, didn't disappear inside himself around the other kids at school like I did. He was born into confidence, yet somehow humbled. I like to believe he was fearless—even in the moments leading up to his death—because our heroes are paramount to us, as my brother was to me. It's irrational, I know, but it's important that I believe this fearlessness existed beyond my romanticized view of him. The last thing anyone should ever be forced to experience upon their death is the fear that it causes, but for most of us, that's inevitable. I like to think that my brother defied inevitability and brought that fearlessness with him into the blackness. A large part of me died on the day he did. It was a motorcycle accident that claimed his life, but the anguish and heartbreak it left behind has forever marred mine. I lost my best friend.

I grew up, married, and gave the world two sons, all in the same town where I spent my youth. In a Halloween tradition I tried to keep alive—and in a strange way, also keep my brother's memory alive—I retold my own kids his story of the Singer's Creek hermit. But I could never recite it as effectively, never with that same amount of sick glee peppered with that convincing believability of which only he was capable. While my sons were only ever amused by the story, writing it off as typical Halloween cabaret, the act of retelling it filled me with a melancholy which I did my best to hide.

On one of these Halloween nights, and after having a bit too much to drink, I wandered out of my pitch-black and slumbering house and began an unexpected walk to the woods. The warm burning in my gut and my blurred combination of sadness and nostalgia had overpowered my common sense. I was determined to find the exact location of the hermit's shack, temporarily forgetting that it didn't exist.

I followed Sycamore Street to its end, catching the final remnants of Halloween night in the form of swaying witch and skeleton cutouts on front doors, and the last few jack-o'-lanterns still emitting tiny candlelight. Party streamers and crepe paper danced like willow leaves in the cool wind. Half empty bowls of candy sat on porch steps and wicker chairs. The town was quiet and serene; the houses' many occupants had long retired for the night. The only sign of life was the occasional blue glow of a television behind a drawn curtain—no doubt someone nodding off during the final flick of the all-night horror-thon.

Everyone was asleep—everyone but me. I was out in the middle of the night, away from my warm bed in the house I shared with my family, in pursuit of something that wasn't real. I thought of a line from a very old horror film whose title I couldn't remember—one that might've been playing on someone's television at that very moment.

"Spirits surround us on every side. They have driven me from hearth and home, from wife and child..."

I passed beneath the blinking traffic light of Little Gunpowder Road and stepped into the woods without trepidation. It was just a Halloween escapade, after all. Just a quick journey down memory lane before putting Halloween back in the box, and that box back in the crawlspace for another year. Nothing out there except bittersweet memories and maybe some tears.

The walk through the woods was pleasant, if a bit cold, and light from the half-moon illuminated my path, substituting the need for the flashlight I'd foolishly forgotten to bring. With each step, the cries of unseen nocturnal critters surrounding me in the dark invaded my brandy-fueled brain, and the realization of how silly or even dangerous my late-night walk might prove started to gnaw on my insides like a marauding horde of ravenous rodents. But I forged ahead and soon came across Singer's Creek, the steady trickling which alerted me that the location of the shack—*if* it existed—would be a couple miles further down its muddy clay banks.

I followed the creek, my eyes wafting back and forth between my graceless steps and the swirling dark and gnarled autumn trees. The repetition of the crunching beneath my feet and the trickling of the creek lulled me into a trance, and I was soon overtaken by the memories of youthful nights spent in those woods.

"You know what they say about Halloween night, don't you?" my brother had once asked me, as I watched him shovel a lump of cold dirt onto the campfire, dousing the flames and laying to rest another October.

"I think so?" I mustered. Halloween, to me, had seemed pretty straightforward—wear costumes, get candy— but something in the way he'd asked led me to suspect otherwise. "What do they say?" I surrendered.

"That on Halloween night," he began, "the world of the living and the world of the dead converge. On Halloween night, awful things can walk down the very streets we live on, and creep into our bedrooms and nightmares. It's the one night of the year—"

"—when *anything* can be real," I finished. It was something I remembered hearing once, forgotten until that very moment.

He grinned that grin of his and grabbed his knapsack from the ground, telling me, "Let's get home before we see a monster for *real.*"

I was suddenly broken free of this trance by nearly stumbling headfirst into a gully camouflaged by a blanket of fallen leaves. It was then, under the moonlight, and through the trees, I could barely make out what looked like the jutting roof of a brooding structure.

A shack.

It was ensconced in the blackest darkness I'll ever remember, in spite of the brilliant torches that dotted each of its corners and which threw off wavy orange pumpkin light. The shack had been assembled using obviously found materials, mainly errant scraps of plywood, corrugated metal, sections of fencing either wood or plastic, road signs, and mini billboards, all of which offered it a patchwork look. But every single piece had been methodically placed. Nothing was hastily cut or nailed or glued or tied down. Every piece had a purpose. The shack did *not*, at all, reflect a construction by someone unhinged and without the capabilities for an analytical mind— *not* by someone inhuman, but by someone human enough to embrace the complexities of mathematical precision and the obsessive madness that came with it.

I took a breath, held it, and crept a little closer, opening up my view of the shack a bit more. I could see it had windows, a chimney, and an off-the-warehouse-floor front door. Likely because of my presence, I saw distant movement disturb the night's hazy stillness as a man-shaped thing stepped backward into the shadow of the shack's mouth-like entrance. It was too dark to see his features; at first, I couldn't even determine if he was facing toward me or away. I heard a sick, wet, and ragged cough, and saw a small orange light appear, which floated momentarily in front of the hermit's face before extinguishing. The wind pulsed and I caught the smell of rancid cigarette smoke. Soon after, everything went impossibly quiet, as if the entire world were a carnival carousel shutting down for the season. The chattering of the animals ceased; the many swaying tree branches above and around me became still. The only sound to be heard was my own heart, which beat so furiously I could feel blood pumping behind my eyes. Foolishly, I became afraid that the man by the shack would hear the chaos in my chest and follow it like a beacon to find me in the dark.

I heard a sharp sound, and another small light appeared. It sank slowly to the ground and momentarily disappeared before roaring back to life as a face built of amber light. Hovering just above the weeds, the face had eyes, a nose, a mouth, and an array of foreign shapes, all of which were so intricately designed that I knew they must've had a purpose.

It was a jack-o'-lantern.

Although I already found myself existing in a situation that couldn't have existed, and which I couldn't believe, the sheer idea that I was seeing such a typical and *normal* Halloween ornament so far into the woods, so late into the night, carefully rendered by a fictional monster, was nearly the last straw for my sanity. My mind shut down; it had reached its peak for trying to process the irrational. I remember thinking that I wanted to laugh, but that I shouldn't because the man by the shack would know I was there, but that didn't matter because the man by the shack had *always* known I was there—had known the second I stepped into the woods—had knelt behind the brush and listened as my brother told me campfire stories about him over thirty years ago—had known that he and I would cross paths this Halloween night long before I was ever born, before he ever *was*.

Soft, guttural, and unhinged laughter littered the night air.

I had dared not laugh, so the man by the shack laughed for me.

It was then, in that awful and artificial serenity, when I heard something crawling rapidly toward me, snapping twigs and trouncing dead leaves. Though I repeatedly told myself it was only a raccoon or a possum, my body went ice cold. I stood stock-still, afraid to disturb anything around me. The frantic scurrying stopped, and in the wake of its silence I heard another heinous laugh.

It was coming from the man by the shack.

The wind picked up again, storm-like and sudden, and it carried the resuming scurrying sounds all around me. That world's carousel wasn't done spinning after all; its brief rest now made it supercharged, maniacally making up for lost time. The wind blew stronger, the animals screamed louder, the air hung heavier, and the moon ripped and pulled at my heart as it did the morning tide. And when the low-crawling thing I'd been hearing finally burst through the brush and revealed itself to me, I turned and ran. Blindly and clumsily, I ran without stopping, unable to cease the abrupt and fever-dreamlike image of my long-dead brother laughing at me through a roaring campfire—only instead of his voice, it was the terrible, perverted laughter of the hermit in the dark.

I dodged fallen logs and half-hidden rocks as I tore disjointedly through the darkness like a shot fired from a broken gun, pushing myself off tree trunks and swatting away branches, attempting to follow no particular direction except *away*.

As I ran, the mainstay details of my brother's stories echoed around me in the Halloween darkness. They bounced off the northern hardwoods strung with dead and dying leaves, the pine needles that undulated against the wind, the sudden biting cold. They haunted me in sickening surround-sound, as if the entire forest had been ambiently prepared for this night. My brother's words, in a voice that sounded like his and mine and perhaps that of the man by the shack, assaulted me from every direction.

"...dead bodies, whole or in pieces, hollowed and hung from rusty hooks..."

I hurtled into the night, which slowly darkened as the moon retreated behind October clouds. My footsteps were hurried and clumsy, but even through my panicked yelping and breathy gasps and the crackling of dead leaves beneath me, I could still hear that awful thing scuttling across the forest floor in steady pursuit. At the heights of my terror, I even convinced myself the thing were *growling* at me, but I knew—*knew*—that couldn't be true. Even if the thing's existence were possible, *no way* was it growling at me. *No way* that could be.

And all this time the impossible thing pursued me, so did our overlain voices.

"...reams of flesh stretched across the ground, their corners staked into the hard earth..."

My head was pounding, and my stomach was boiling, threatening to surrender its contents across my half-buttoned autumn jacket. I ran with preternatural speed toward the dull glow of the not-far-off street lights hovering in the distance.

Toward civilization. Toward safety.

"...severed limbs crudely attached with barbed wire, iron fasteners, fishing line..."

I stumbled out of the woods and onto Little Gunpowder Road. I passed by the same witch and skeleton cutouts, now docile and still, and the same jack-o'-lanterns, whose candlelight had finally succumbed. No windows housed the comforting blue glow of a television: of ongoing life, of everyday normalcy. Everything was dark. The whole world was dark. In that moment, no one knew me. No one could help me. I was the last man on earth, and I was going to die on the street in front of their houses, either from total fear or from the mutant impossibility that was in steady pursuit.

"They say, on Halloween night...anything can be real."

Finally making it to my house, I crashed through my front door and slammed it behind me. After throwing a series of paranoid glances out every window—expecting to see my unnatural pursuer scurrying across the driveway or getting ready to ram itself against the door—I saw nothing at all, and finally collapsed against the wall and let the sobbing begin.

I remember urging myself to forget what had nearly pounced on me in those dark woods. I remember forcing myself to believe that an overactive imagination and too much brandy had birthed this awful Halloween-inspired hallucination. Except for my heavy gasping, the house was quiet. There was no pounding at the door. There was no impossible thing outside.

Darkness there, as Poe had written, *and nothing more.*

No way had there been a structure out in the middle of the woods, in the same spot my brother's stories had claimed. No way had there been the shape of a man taunting me in the dark — a man who, if the legends were true, was two hundred years old. No way had I heard the sound of something stalking me in the darkness before it lunged at me and crawled around at my feet like a primordial spider. No way had it been a dismembered arm with an extra hand crudely nailed to its rancid, rotten stump.

And no way, etched into that arm with artistic precision, was there a faded tattoo of a black-hooded skeleton with pentagram eyes whipping a chain seemingly right at me.

Three Spirits
Daniel Loubier

Edmund Weezer was once a kind man. A thoughtful, gentle man. A man who always put the needs and interests of others before his own. Edmund lived and loved with passion and purpose, and he shared that same spirit with many close friends and loved ones, but none more closely than with his fiancé, Marley.

Edmund wasn't looking for love when Marley came along, but she stole his heart and never gave it back. He adored her sophisticated perspective on life and her playful, light-hearted demeanor, while she fell for his strength and charm, and his boundless, childlike energy.

She loved him deeply and admired him for his many wonderful qualities. Edmund loved her, too, and he cherished her every waking moment until she died.

It was cancer that took her so unforgivably. Marley had fought with vigor and grace for two-and-a-half years, and Edmund fought by her side. It wasn't until the last couple weeks that they both accepted the end was coming, but it wasn't until after she'd gone that Edmund changed.

In the weeks and months following her death, he'd become a shut-in. He only left home to go to work, and always returned immediately following the end of his shift. He routinely declined invitations to dinner and drinks with coworkers and friends. He rarely spoke with his family, and only when they showed up at his door—Edmund never answered his phone during this time. He even resorted to having his groceries delivered to his home lest he risk crossing paths and being forced to converse with somebody who knew him.

After a long time living in solitude and having excommunicated himself from society, Edmund finally emerged from his self-imposed catatonia. That was when things became much worse.

He once took a drive to the beach near his house. He rolled the windows down and closed his eyes as the salty air played through his messy, wake-up hair. He sped recklessly through residential areas, scaring children playing hopscotch on the sidewalk, angering parents tending their yards and frustrating cyclists who lost their balance when the car came dangerously close to them.

He got upset with his long-time barber for making him wait an extra five minutes while a two-year old boy received his first haircut. Incensed, Edmund tore the register away from the counter and threw it across the waiting area. Luckily no injuries were sustained, but the small child refused to return for subsequent haircuts.

Edmund, never one to initiate physical conflict in the past, now got into bar fights often. He shouted obscenities in public places and was generally rude to service workers. He once knocked out a restaurant patron for claiming Ren would make a much better house pet than Stimpy.

He had never felt this alive for so many *wrong* reasons.

Edmund's coworkers noticed the change immediately. They were happy to see *any* change in his attitude at first; Edmund hadn't been so conversational or "present" for years, but now he was giving attention to everyone with whom he interacted. His coworkers quickly realized, however, that this was not the same Edmund from before. This person was not full of life and love. He was full of something far uglier.

Edmund would let doors shut without holding them for the person behind him. He would smile bitterly at people from inside the elevator while the doors closed in front of them. He went out of his way, routinely, to embarrass peers during important meetings and presentations. He was no longer encouraging or supportive. He became brutally and unfairly critical of every idea proposed by his coworkers. He so frequently snapped at clients over the phone, he seemed to make a game out of how hard he could slam the phone back into its cradle.

His best friend, Sam, had been the first to approach him about his behavior.

"Everything all right?" Sam had asked. "You seem a bit…off."

"How am I *off*?" Edmund barked defensively. "Everybody I know wants me to cheer up, speak up, and stop moping around! Jesus," he held his arms out wide, "what else do I have to do to get you people off my back?"

Sam and Edmund had been friends for years, long before Marley came along. He felt fortunate for having gotten to know Edmund back when he was everything anyone could possibly want in a best friend: reliable, trustworthy, compassionate, sincere—Sam's only regret was that he hadn't been able to meet Edmund sooner in life.

He was the first one to visit Edmund after Marley passed away.

The house was neat, nothing was out of place, and that was exactly as he always saw Edmund's home. The thing that felt different was the emptiness; because, although Edmund continued to maintain a neat, clean living space, it felt neglected all the same. It felt sterile. Unlived-in. There was a quietness to the home which Sam had never felt before. A silence that subdued all the joy that had once radiated from his friend.

"If there's anything I can do…" Sam had told him. "If you need to spend a night or two at my place?"

"I'm fine here," Edmund said. His voice was distant.

"Right, I get it—that's cool." Sam's words came quickly and awkwardly. "It's just—I'm worried about you."

"Don't worry," Edmund said flatly. "I'll be fine."

And Sam left it at that.

He continued to try to engage Edmund over the next year, inviting him to social gatherings, sporting events or simply a beer at the local pub. Edmund would always decline. Sam would purposely try to "run into" Edmund at the office and force conversation, but Edmund always had an excuse.

"Sorry, Sam, I'm late for a meeting…"

"I'm on my way to a Doctor appointment…"

"Actually, I have to run to my car…"

After many unsuccessful attempts to connect with his friend, Sam stopped trying to initiate contact with Edmund. He vowed to himself not to disconnect from Edmund for good, but instead to keep a watchful eye over his friend from afar. Edmund wanted space, and while Sam was reluctant to do so, he decided to give his friend as much space as he needed. He wasn't abandoning him, only giving him time to grieve.

It came as a shock the day Edmund showed up to work acting like a man who was trying to get himself fired.

"Follow me," Sam hissed. "I need to show you something."

Sam started down the hallway, ignoring the eyes of his co-workers. He never once looked back and only trusted that Edmund would follow.

When he arrived at an empty conference room, he stepped inside and waited. He tapped his fingers impatiently on the top of a long table in the center of the room, took several deep breaths, and stared through the open door as he waited for Edmund.

Thirty seconds later, Sam's head and eyes fell to the floor. Edmund wasn't coming. The best and closest friend he'd ever known was gone. Instead there was a shell that resembled the friend he once knew, but inside was—

"What?"

Sam looked up and saw Edmund standing there. "You came?" he said. It was as much a question as it was a statement of Sam's shock.

"Well," Edmund said, "you told me to follow you—so here I am. What is it?"

"No," Sam said. "It's just…we haven't talked in so long and usually when I—"

Edmund began to turn toward the door. "Listen, I have a lot to do, so if you don't mind…"

"What the hell happened to you, man?" Sam walked past Edmund and pushed the door closed. "Three years!"

"Hmm," Edmund said. "Is that how long it's been?"

"Stop being an asshole," said Sam.

"Okay, well, when your fiancé dies tragically, you be sure to let me know your secret to bouncing back."

"That's not fair," Sam said, his finger in Edmund's face. "I've been trying to reach you for three years, goddammit! You won't let me in. You won't let *anybody* in. You just kept pushing people out with your silence."

Edmund waved his hands, mocking Sam's claims. "Good, good—get it all out. How much more you got? Three years' worth, right?"

Sam grabbed Edmund by the front of his shirt and shoved him into the wall of the conference room. Edmund's eyes went wide; he clearly hadn't expected a physical confrontation.

"*Listen to me!*" Sam shouted, unafraid of who in the surrounding rooms and halls might hear him. "I loved Marley, too! Maybe not as much as you, but she was a dear friend to me!" He then backed away and let him go. "You both were."

He let the word *were* echo in Edmund's head a few extra seconds, hoping the impact would be as great as he intended.

"She was the *best* thing that ever happened to you!" Sam added. "And the shittiest part? You were already pretty awesome even before she came along."

"Gee, thanks," Edmund said, still unimpressed by Sam's efforts. "Are we done here? Can I go?"

Sam balled his fists. He'd never considered striking his friend before, but the urge swelled inside him. "Don't you get it?" he asked. "This is not the guy Marley fell for." He eyed Edmund up and down with disgust. "You are *nothing* like the person she loved."

"Good to know," Edmund said, his eyes lacked all emotion.

Sam paced along the table in the center of the conference room until he reached the opposite wall. He then turned and faced Edmund from a distance. "If she met you like this, like you are now," he said, "she would have wanted *nothing* to do with you."

Edmund's eyes danced around and there was a moment when Sam thought he detected some self-reflection, as if maybe Edmund agreed with what Sam had just said. It was an insensitive thing to say, and Sam knew it, but it was no less correct.

"Mmm," Edmund said. "Probably best, then."

His tone was no longer defensive or aggressive, but rather sounded like that of a person who had finally accepted a hard truth. Sam wondered if his words might finally be getting through.

"Yeah, probably," Sam kept on. "God knows she could have done better than this. And the saddest part is, she *did* do better than this."

Edmund stared back at his friend and said nothing.

"*You* were better than this," Sam said. "You were everybody's best friend. And I get it—you lost your soulmate. I can't imagine what that does to a person." Edmund nodded, but it was mostly an empty gesture. "You're better than this, Eddie." Sam was now fighting back the familiar burn in his throat that happened every time his emotions were about to erupt. "And Marley would tell you the same thing."

As he stared across the room at this friend, Sam could see Edmund's eyes were starting to redden, too. Had he finally broken through a three-year barrier? Was his friend's tough exterior finally starting to weaken? He wanted to believe this was the case, but he also knew it would likely take more than a five-minute conversation to erase years of hurt and suffering.

"Well," Edmund said, "when I speak to Marley in my dreams tonight, I'll be sure to ask her what she thinks."

"Right," Sam said. "Make sure you do." He walked back around the table, but turned once more to Edmund as he opened the door: "I'm sure she'd be furious with me if I gave up on you, just like you've given up on everyone else."

Sam left the room but Edmund stayed, his head lowered and his eyes to the table.

***

Edmund raised a bottle to his lips and took a drink. The beer was sour, and it puckered his mouth just as any good sour beer should do. And when he swallowed, the flavor stayed true through the finish. He smiled.

"Damn…"

John Carpenter's classic, *Halloween*, played on the TV and Edmund turned out all the lights in the house.

It had long been a tradition of his to watch the movie that introduced the world to Michael Myers every year around this time. He'd maintained the tradition even in the years following Marley's passing. It was one of her favorites, too.

There was a time in his life when Edmund celebrated Halloween bigger and bolder than anyone else.

When he was young, he would dress up and trick-or-treat with all his friends. But as he grew older, he preferred to hand out candy. He loved seeing the different costumes as, one-by-one and group-after-group, kids and their adult companions would greet him at his door. He marveled at the imaginations of the truly original costumes and vowed to do something original and memorable with his treat-giving practices.

As a teenager, he made more elaborate haunts in his parents' yard. With the blessing of his parents, he designed a simple haunted house "tunnel" out of tarps, cardboard boxes and props. Visitors would enter through his front door, make their way through a tunnel that snaked through the living room and kitchen, and eventually exit through the garage. The neighborhood kids loved it. He would keep track of how long it took for people to make it through each year, hoping for a longer, more thorough experience each fall.

He carried on this tradition when he bought his first home. And when he met Marley, he was ecstatic to learn that she celebrated Halloween with the same enthusiasm.

When she died, that enthusiasm passed along with her.

And even though he no longer had the energy or desire to participate in Halloween and he no longer handed out candy—though he still made the effort of watching their favorite movie each year. It was the one thing they shared that he could still do quietly and privately to honor her memory.

The missed call indicator blinked on his phone; it had been a few hours since Sam called. There was also a new voicemail to which Edmund had no interest in listening.

He replayed the conversation from earlier.

The nerve of that asshole, trying to tell me what to do!

He glanced at his phone again and sighed. Finally, he picked it up and listened to his friend's message:

"*Hey, Eddie, it's uh…it's Sam. Um…look, I'm not sorry about what I said earlier, but I* am *happy to have any kind of conversation with you. With my friend. It's uh… it's good to talk to you again.*" Edmund rolled his eyes as Sam's voice continued in the message. "*Anyway, I'm not sure why I'm doing this… I know you won't come… but it's Halloween tomorrow and we're having a party at our house. Lots of costumes and decorations. I know you and Marley always enjoyed Halloween so…just figured I'd put it out there. Pretty sure you still know where I live. That's about it, man. Hope to see you tomorrow night.*"

Edmund knew even before he finished listening to Sam's message that he wouldn't be attending.

"Give it a rest, Sam," he said out loud before finishing another beer.

He set down the empty bottle next to several others on an end table and tried to stand up. He stumbled forward and then backward again. The seat caught him in the back of the knees and he fell into the recliner.

"Okay, fine," Edmund said groggily. "We'll do things your way."

He laid back, refocused his eyes as he watched Myers attack a semi-nude girl in an empty house, and got comfortable.

Five minutes later, Edmund was asleep.

***

His eyes fluttered open and Edmund awoke in a dark room. The TV was off, likely due to the built-in automatic shut-off feature, and the house was completely silent. Not even the low-level purr of the refrigerator could be heard in the kitchen. The clock in the living room wasn't illuminated, either. It was as if the power was out.

Edmund leaned forward in the recliner. He stared through the sheer curtains that hung in front of the large picture window in the living room. His road was deserted, but the streetlamps were on. The porch light on the house across the street also shone brightly. Surely his neighborhood had power. Why was his the only one affected?

He rose unsteadily, and his head ached—the early onset of a hangover quite recognizable—and he headed toward the door to the basement.

That's when he saw Marley.

"*What the hell!*" he screamed. Edmund stumbled backward and into the recliner and fell awkwardly on his side.

"Don't be scared, Edmund," she said.

He scrambled into a seated position but continued to back away as she approached him. "*Who the...why...what is—*"

Marley placed a finger softly against her lips.

"Shh...it's okay, sweetie. I'm here."

Edmund backed into the sofa and was now trapped. "Huh?! *How* is this—this isn't real! This isn't happening!"

"Edmund, my dear," she said. Her voice sounded strangely hollow and ethereal. "It's okay. I know this must be hard for you, but you must calm yourself."

Edmund's chest heaved rapidly in and out. His dead fiancé stood before him. She wore a white gown that gathered around her body as if she were floating in water. Despite her appearance, Edmund felt no comfort.

He looked around quickly, as if to reassess his surroundings and to verify he was still, in fact, in his house.

"This must be a dream!" he panicked. "Come on, Edmund. Wake up!" He slapped himself in the face and punched himself in the arm.

"Please don't hurt yourself," Marley said. "I assure you this is real, and this is no dream. I needed to come see you."

"This is insane," he argued.

"It is not," Marley said. "Edmund, you had a disagreement with Sam today. Did you not?"

Edmund finally stopped shaking. He stared at her and cocked his head to the side in disbelief.

"How do you… what the hell is going on?"

"I need you to listen to me," she said. "What I am about to tell you is very important."

Edmund remained on the floor and braced himself.

"You are no longer you, Edmund," Marley said. "You have become that which you despised, and even that is difficult to admit because you were not someone who looked down upon anyone or anything."

"I—I don't understand, Marley. Why are you here, *how* is this happening?"

"I wish I could provide you with answers, but I am only here to give you a message."

Edmund shook his head. "Wh-wh-what about?"

"You are going to be visited, Edmund."

His body went cold. "Visited?"

Marley nodded slowly. "Three others will come to you. They will be like me, except—" her eyes looked away from him and there was something ominous in her visage, "—*not* like me."

"What do you mean?" Edmund asked. He reached out for her but felt nothing; his hand passed through her completely. "*Who's* coming? *Please*, Marley, please tell me who!"

"That is all I can say," she told him. "I must go now."

At this Edmund rose to his feet. "Wait!" he insisted. He reached for her again and she remained still, seemingly unconcerned by his inability to touch her. "Why can't I hold you?"

"It is not for me to understand either, Edmund."

A feeling of scorn suddenly overwhelmed him. "Are you even *her*?" he asked. "Or is my subconscious doing this? Huh? Is this all a bunch of bullshit of my own doing?"

She offered a kind smile. "Sweet Edmund, I assure you I am the woman to whom you proposed marriage."

His breath caught in his throat and his eyes started to burn.

"I will always be her," she continued. "And I will love you forever—but I am no longer part of this world. That is why the others must *save* you."

Tears started to spill over his cheeks and his lips. "Save me?" he asked. "What does that mean?"

"You will soon find out," she said. "But now I must go."

"NO!" he begged her. "You can't go—I need to be with you longer! Please!"

"I no longer suffer," she said. "It is okay for you to let me go."

"I don't want to let you go!"

"You can," she said, "and you must. But please, Edmund—" she raised a hand to his cheek and this time he felt her, "—please know that I will *always* be with you."

Her hand was warm and the warmth filled his face and then his neck and his shoulders. Soon he felt it surge through his body and into his legs. He stared into her eyes and they filled with light. The light spread into the room until it was too bright to see the furniture and the walls. He could just barely see the outline of her body until everything was white.

Then he could see no more.

***

The white light faded and it was dark again. Edmund's eyes adjusted slowly, and to his surprise he found himself outside. He stood alone on a sidewalk in a quiet neighborhood. It looked vaguely familiar but he could not yet determine why.

Up ahead there was a house with lights on. There were cars in the driveway and he heard the faint hum of music and chatter from within.

He looked around to find his car, but it was nowhere.

He was also no longer alone.

A figure appeared in front of the house with the gathering. The person wore a white sheet with holes cut out for the eyes—a classic ghost costume—and it dawned on Edmund that it *was* still Halloween. The figure raised a sheeted arm and waved in his direction.

Edmund looked around, confused, and saw there was nobody else outside. The figure in costume was signaling to him. Edmund obliged reluctantly and walked toward the individual.

As he approached he could hear what sounded like a word being chanted. The nearer Edmund got, the clearer the word became. He could also tell the voice was male.

"*Ehhhd-muuund... Ehhhd-muuund... Ehhhd-muuund...*"

The man in the ghost costume moved his arms under the sheet in dramatic fashion. He was taller than Edmund, who wasn't considered short at six-feet two-inches, and Edmund wondered who it was that knew him by name. He didn't know anyone as tall as the man in the costume.

"Do I know you?" Edmund asked. He was still about ten feet away from the ghost.

"Come to meee, Deadmund."

It was the first time Edmund heard clearly that the person was referring to him as "Deadmund," and not by his actual name.

"Wait a minute," he said. "Are you calling me *Dead*mund?"

"Why, yesss, I aaammm."

"Uh, why?" he asked with annoyance. "I'm not dead."

Suddenly the ghost let his arms fall at his sides and his shoulders stooped forward. "Well, no—not physically dead," the ghost said, having completely dropped character. "Just dead on the inside. You know, uncaring, unfeeling—a loner."

"Huh?" Edmund uttered.

The ghost doubled over and let out a long, wheezy laugh. Edmund could hear the man slapping his knee under the sheet.

"I'm sorry! Oh, that was good! Sorry, just a little after-life humor. It'll make sense in about…six decades." The ghost looked Edmund up and down and he said, "Maybe a little sooner." The ghost laughed again.

"Yeah, right," Edmund said nonplussed. "Look, I'm glad you're having a good time, but I really need to go—"

"To this party?" the ghost interrupted with enthusiasm. "You're damn right you do!"

"I think I'm all set," Edmund said.

The ghost closed the void between them, his body now only an inch away from Edmund's. "*You will enter the party*," the ghost said, and this time his tone was flat. Edmund looked up and it was as if the ghost had grown even taller, he now towered over Edmund by at least a foot. His eyes, which had been dark from a distance and should have been revealed given their current proximity, remained a deep black. It was the first time Edmund felt truly uneasy about their interaction.

He cleared his throat—mostly because when he tried to respond, he could form no words—and nodded toward the house.

"This house?" Edmund asked, as if it were anything but obvious.

The ghost nodded.

"Right," Edmund said, realizing that further argument would certainly increase the level of danger. "Sounds good." He turned and began to approach the house. A scarecrow stood up from the mulch bed on one side of the front steps. On the other, a floating ghoul with glowing red eyes hung from the edge of the roof. "Who did you say lives here?"

"I didn't say anything about that, Deadmund."

Edmund rolled his eyes. He was certain the face of the man in the ghost costume wore a smirk at this moment, and he chose not to correct him. "Ha, I get it now," Edmund said instead.

The ghost said nothing.

"I like it," Edmund continued, even though a cold fear had already grabbed hold of him tightly and burrowed in the pit of his stomach.

The inside of the house was filled with decorations. Spider webs, orange lights, candy and pumpkins were in every room. The stereo played the 1962 Bobby Pickett hit, "Monster Mash," and everybody was in costume; there were vampires, sexy nurses, superheroes, and police officers. One person was even dressed in a half-dog/half-alien outfit. When Edmund saw this costume mash-up, he immediately recognized the wearer.

"Oh my god! I know what this is!" he shouted. "Oh, thank god! I remember this! This is a dream!" Then another realization struck him. "Wait—can they see me?"

The ghost shook his head slowly.

"Whew… okay, good. Why am I here, anyway? What is—"

The door opened behind them, and a man and a woman entered. They were dressed as Raggedy Ann and Andy. Edmund recognized them, too, but his breath caught in his throat and he couldn't help but stare at the woman dressed as Ann.

"Marley…" he exhaled. She looked stunning, even in the silly red wig and white apron. "I—I absolutely remember this."

The couple moved into the house, and the ghost shoved Edmund forward. They followed Marley and his former self as they headed toward the man in the dog-alien costume.

"Eddie! Marley!" the dog-alien said when he spotted the raggedy couple. "You made it!"

Costumed Edmund gave the man a hug. "Of course, Sam. We wouldn't miss one of your father's legendary Halloween parties!"

Sam laughed. "Oh man, he's going to love that you said that. Have you guys seen him yet?"

"No," Edmund said. "We just got here."

"Oh, well he's around here somewhere. Come on, follow me."

Sam took the couple further into the house while the ghost and Edmund followed behind. Along the way, Edmund recognized more faces, faces of those with whom he worked and saw often at the office.

Edmund's first job had been an entry-level position with a small accounting firm. At the time, Sam's father, Tim Hain, was a mid-level manager working at the firm. When Edmund was hired, he worked directly under Sam's father. It wasn't long before Mr. Hain realized Edmund was turning himself into a highly valued company asset, and as Mr. Hain rose up the corporate ladder he made every effort to bring Edmund along with him.

He was successful in doing so every time.

Eventually, Mr. Hain convinced Sam to also get a job with the firm and it was through their work relationship that Edmund and Sam became close friends.

Edmund and the ghost arrived inside Mr. Hain's large galley kitchen where many guests sipped wine and beer and munched on delicious-looking appetizers of all kinds.

Tim Hain stood against one of the counters talking with a guest. He was wearing a Van Helsing costume, complete with a long dark coat and fedora and a crossbow prop strapped to his back. When his eyes met Raggedy Edmund's, he recognized him immediately.

"Eddie!" he exclaimed. He excused himself from his guest and rushed to shake Edmund's hand. "So good of you to come, man! And you brought a lovely woman!" In a softer yet very mocking tone, he then said, "Nothing Sam does regularly, you know."

The three of them laughed while Tim elbowed his son in the ribs.

"Thanks, Dad," Sam said with a sheepish grin.

"Good to see you, Mr. Hain," Edmund began. "I'd like to introduce you to my girlfriend, Marley."

The older Hain took her hand gently. "Pleasure to meet you, Marley. Eddie is a close friend of our family, and a good man."

To this, Marley quipped: "Good? Yes. *Man*? Not so much…"

Mr. Hain laughed loudly at the unexpected dig toward Edmund. "You are welcome in my home *ANY* time, Marley!" Then to Edmund he said, "I like her, Eddie. You did good!"

"Thank you, sir," Edmund said.

"And Marley," Mr. Hain added. "Please do us all a favor and remind Eddie that life isn't *only* about work, hmm?"

"Well, it's easy around this time of year," Marley said, "but I'll do my best to keep an eye on him."

"Thank *God*!" he replied with mock relief. "I understand that new job of his is keeping him very busy."

"That it is," she said.

"Mmhmm… well, Eddie, the door is always open if you wish to come back."

"I appreciate that, sir," Edmund said. "By the way, you may find it interesting to know that Marley is an even bigger fan of Halloween than I am."

Mr. Hain's eyes became large and he took an overly emphasized step backward. "No! That's not possible."

"It's true," Edmund continued. "You should see our— uh—my house. It looks like a morgue, graveyard, and funhouse all in one."

Edmund smiled remembering this moment. He watched as Raggedy Edmund cast a sidelong glance at Marley. Her reaction indicated she also heard him nearly say "our house," but backpedaled just in time. Mr. Hain had noticed it too, but fortunately the old man didn't take advantage of Edmund's slip-up.

"Well," said Mr. Hain, "that makes sense. 'Tis my and Eddie's favorite time of year, after all. Anyway, I'm going to see a few guests—you all enjoy yourselves. Let me know if you need anything."

Mr. Hain walked away and Sam stood in front of the couple. It was obvious that even Sam was aware of Edmund's faux pas as he fidgeted awkwardly, no doubt trying to think of his own escape plan.

"You guys need drinks!" Sam finally blurted out. "I know what you drink, Eddie. Marley—can I get you wine?"

"Nah, I'll have the same thing Edmund is having."

"Awesome! Two virgin daiquiris right away!"

The three of them chuckled.

Sam winked and said, "I'll be right back."

After Sam slipped away, Marley turned to face Edmund. Her eyes narrowed coyly and her lips shifted into a half-grin on one side of her face.

"Don't," Edmund said through a smile of his own.

"Awh, Eddie," she teased him. "Whose house is it again?"

Edmund laughed and sighed at the same time. "I know," he said, "I know…"

She shushed him, placed her hands on his rose-colored face, and kissed him. Then she stared into his eyes.

"I liked it," she said.

"I know it hasn't been very long—" Edmund started.

"But it's real," Marley finished. "This is *very* real, Edmund. And I'm not going anywhere. I'm here forever."

Edmund and the ghost stood in the doorway to the kitchen, watching the happy couple. The ghost nudged Edmund.

"Looks like you weren't always dead inside."

"You didn't know her," Edmund said. "She was… magical."

"I can tell," the ghost said.

"When she died," Edmund continued, "the magic died too."

"And you don't know how to make your own magic?" the ghost suggested.

"I didn't say that," Edmund said defensively.

"No, you didn't," the ghost agreed. "But it's obvious. It's also obvious you won't let anyone help—you know, if you were less of an *asshole*, you might still have some friends."

Edmund's pulse began to turn into a rage that melted the fear he once felt toward this stranger in the ghost costume. It burned hot and before he said another word, he turned to face his antagonist.

But the ghost was gone.

And the house was empty. When he looked back, he no longer saw himself with Marley all those years ago. They were all gone. The scene had vanished entirely.

***

At work the following day, Edmund sat quietly in his office and worked on several filings for one of his accounts.

The memory of the previous night's dream remained a fresh yet tangled mess of confusion. It had been so wonderful to see Marley again. He hadn't dreamt of her in years. He'd envisioned her face many times since her death, but never as vividly or as lifelike. It was like she had been alive again, and he'd briefly felt the magic one more time.

The ghost and its flippant demeanor, however, seemed to make no sense at all. Marley had indicated he would be visited by others, but why a cheesy ghost? What relevance did that have to the dream itself—or to Marley? Edmund, having lost focus on his client's endeavors hours ago, tried to wrap his mind around what it all meant.

"Hey."

Edmund looked up and saw Sam standing in the doorway.

"Oh… hey." His voice was tired but he was unfazed by Sam's presence. "What's up?"

Much like Edmund, Sam eventually outgrew his role at his father's company. He longed for something more fulfilling—and better paying—so when an opportunity opened up with Edmund's employer, Edmund gave him a strong referral and Sam interviewed quickly. It wasn't long before he was hired and placed on a team working directly with Edmund.

"Not much," Sam said as he walked casually and uninvited into Edmund's office. "You busy?"

"Yeah."

"Nice," Sam said, as if it mattered nothing at all. "You get my voicemail last night?"

"Yeah, I got it," said Edmund, and he started tapping at the keys on his computer. "Listen, I have to—"

"I'm surprised you don't have any Halloween decorations in your office," Sam said as he looked around.

"Thought for sure you'd have some cool lights up or something."

Edmund rolled his eyes. "Yeah, I… I kinda don't do that anymore. Would you—"

"What *do* you do anymore, Eddie?"

Edmund sighed. "What do you want, Sam?"

"Becky says hi, by the way, and she misses you—said she hopes you can come by tonight."

Becky was Sam's wife and Edmund knew her well. Sam and she began dating before Marley died, and then married a few years later. Edmund had been invited to the wedding, but as with every post-Marley event, he made an excuse as to why he couldn't attend. He still felt badly about it, though. Becky was a good woman—very good for Sam—and deep-down, Edmund was happy for them both. As much as he had no interest in attending their party, he wasn't about to make any personal attacks at either of them.

"Yeah, well… we'll see," Edmund said.

Sam scoffed. "Right. Is that a real 'we'll see,' or is that a 'we'll see how long I can go without answering until end of work tomorrow when I can go home and not have to talk to Sam about this again'?"

Edmund groaned and didn't hide his annoyance. Sam was clearly prepared for an argument and Edmund wasn't about to disappoint.

"What do you want from me, man? I'm busy."

"You're always busy," Sam grumbled. "Either you're busy with work or with your car or an appointment somewhere. That's a lot of *busy* in three years, Eddie."

Edmund raised his hands with indifference. "You got me. We done here?"

"You know what," Sam said, his tongue laced with disgust, "most people would be thrilled to have a friend who cares as much as I do!"

"You're right," Edmund said. "You should find those people and invite them to your party."

Sam's jaw hung open and he stared back in disbelief. Even Edmund knew it was a harsh thing to say. He'd been many things over the past few years, but he hadn't been overtly callous to Sam, only passively.

"Screw this," Sam said. "I'm done with you."

Edmund said nothing and only watched Sam storm out of his office. There was a fleeting moment when he wanted to call out to him, to ask Sam to come back and talk it out, but the desire to do so left him quickly, and he sat at his desk and continued his client's paperwork.

***

It was hours later and the daylight had gone. Edmund kept himself buried under his work as the five-o'clockers left for the day. He watched the rush from his periphery, and only when he noticed the exodus was over did he close his laptop.

Lingering guilt from the exchange with Sam conflicted him, and as he left his office he decided to stop at Sam's desk. He hadn't done so in a long time and it felt awkward now, but he felt it was best to try to smooth things over.

It's best for our working relationship, Edmund told himself.

When he arrived at Sam's desk, he was gone. There were very few people left in the office, but he always knew Sam to be a harder worker than most, often staying late to spend additional time on his assignments.

Edmund got the attention of a young woman who sat across from Sam. She seemed shocked and even a bit scared that he acknowledged her.

"Hi, um…"

"Claire," she offered.

"Right. Hi. Claire, do you know if Sam is still around?"

She squinted while she thought. "I think he left about a half hour ago."

"Oh," Edmund said. "He usually works late."

"Yeah… I don't want to sound like I'm trying to spread gossip—" she looked around and lowered her head before she finished, "—but he seemed really upset about something right before he left."

"I see," Edmund said. There was a pit in his stomach, and he wished he had called Sam back to his office earlier in the day, but it quickly faded again. "Okay," he said to her, "thanks."

***

Edmund sat in front of the TV, in the same chair in which he sat the night before, drinking the same beer he drank then. The third game of the World Series was on but he wasn't watching.

It was Halloween night.

In years past he would have been preparing for either trick-or-treaters, or for a party of his own, but tonight his mind bounced wildly around a number of different things: if he would have another bizarre dream this night; what seeing Marley meant, if anything; and confusion about why he would care about Sam's feelings after having cast his friend from his life years ago.

Why *had* he dismissed Sam? Marley's death had crushed Edmund, for certain, but Sam had been his friend for much longer.

Edmund remembered needing time to find himself after she died, and in doing so, he pushed away everyone who mattered to him and everyone to whom he mattered.

It was difficult in the beginning. He didn't *want* to shut himself away, but he also didn't want to have to see the same sad faces whose voices offered the same empty condolences day after day. Every time was a constant reminder of what he had lost. So, he locked himself away—mostly emotionally, but also quite physically—and decided not to come out until he was ready.

After a while, being locked away was easy. He never had to explain himself to anyone, never had to answer questions about anything, never had to make eye contact or small talk. It was so easy.

Miserable, but easy.

A loud *crack* interrupted his thoughts and his eyes found the game again. The Red Sox were beating the Cardinals three-to-two in the seventh inning. He smiled on the inside.

Then he realized the game was in the middle of the inning, and the sound he heard hadn't been the crack of a bat.

That sound had come from outside.

The hell?

He heard it again, this time by the window in the kitchen. It was unseasonably warm and he had left a couple windows open on the first floor; he deduced without a doubt that something—or someone—was stirring outside.

He grabbed a hammer from a toolbox in the hallway closet and raced to the back door. He slipped outside quietly, his heart pounding with an irregular rhythm, and tip-toed around the house. He crept along stealthily until he decided it would be best to try to surprise who or whatever was out there, and he broke into a sprint.

Trepidation turned into confidence and a growl began to form in his throat. It grew into a terrible yell and as he approached the spot below the kitchen window, he let out a *Braveheart* shout.

There was nobody.

He waited; perhaps there was someone here, but they were merely hiding? He checked his watch and saw it was still a bit too early for trick-or-treaters.

"If there's anyone out here," he said, "I *have* a weapon."

He stayed a while longer until he was satisfied there was nobody outside trying to force entry into his home.

Probably just an animal, he thought.

Edmund retraced his steps to the back door and re-entered his house. He made sure to engage the deadbolt and then headed toward the hallway.

A man stood there.

"Jesus!"

The man reached for Edmund with one arm, while the other arm fell limp at his side. His clothes were old and tattered and he moved with an awkward shuffle.

"What do you want?" Edmund shouted, wielding the hammer high above his head.

The strange man opened his mouth as if to speak, but instead of words a horrible, scratching sound came out. It sounded like a garbage disposal on full, trying to destroy a metal can.

"The hell is wrong with you!" Edmund cried. "Get the hell out of here or I *will* hurt you!"

But the man kept coming, slow and determined. Edmund reached into his pocket for his cellphone and realized he had left it in his coat pocket, which hung in the closet just past the stranger in his hallway.

The man was now only a couple feet away. His face lacked color and his eyes were sunken. His head lolled unsteadily on his neck and his mouth remained open, emitting that same awful sound.

As the man trapped him at the end of the hallway, Edmund did the only thing he could think of. He turned the hammer so that the claw was forward and he swung hard at the man's outstretched hand. The claw severed the man's hand at the wrist and it flew to the floor and skidded down the hall.

"*Oww!*" the man shouted. "What the hell was that for?" His voice suddenly seemed to work fine.

"I'll do it again!" Edmund threatened. "I swear!"

The man turned and bent over slowly toward his severed hand. "What the hell is the matter with you, Deadmund?"

Edmund lowered the hammer and cocked his head to the side; the absurd moniker gave him pause. It was the same name the ghost had called him the previous night.

"Wait—what did you just call me?"

The strange man collected his hand and straightened. "You know," he began, "it's like a play on words with your name. You're not *actually* dead, but you sort of are—you know, like on in the ins—"

"Yeah, yeah, yeah," Edmund said, cutting him short. "I get it, but why are *you* calling me that? Do you and that—guy—in the ghost costume know each other?"

The man let out a hearty, wheeze-and-cough-filled laugh. As he did, something dark fell from his mouth. It crawled away once it hit the floor.

"The *guy* in the *ghost costume!*" the man said between laughs. "That's too funny. Yeah, that's Larry. He doesn't like to give his name. Likes to be all—" he raised his one good hand and gave it a shake, "—*mysterious!*"

"I see," Edmund said thoroughly confused. "So, wait… that was *not* a dream last night?"

"Oh, no," the man said. "This is all real. Didn't Marley tell you we were coming?"

Edmund thought back to her visit. She told him he would be visited by three people and that they were going to save him, whatever that meant. He was certain *all* of it had been a dream, but, clearly there was something odd happening in his life—maybe this newcomer could explain what was going on?

"So, what's this all about?" Edmund asked.

"Oh, gosh," said the man. "Where are my manners? Name's Chad. Harvard, Eighty-Three." He offered to shake Edmund's hand and realized it was no longer attached. "Oops. Uh… could I bother you for some duct tape?"

***

Chad and Edmund walked a long time. Edmund offered to drive, but Chad insisted they travel on foot. It wasn't long before Chad's slow, shambling pace made Edmund wish they had simply driven to wherever it was they were going.

He was mesmerized by Chad's uneasy gait; his shoulders bobbed and his waist bucked back and forth as he walked.

"This is the fastest you go?" Edmund asked.

"Gimme a break," Chad said. "What do you expect? I'm a zombie."

Edmund sighed. "Now it makes sense."

"What makes sense?"

"You know, the whole—*this*." He gestured toward Chad with an up and down motion of his hand.

"Hey man, don't judge me. All right?"

"You're right," Edmund said. "Sorry." He realized immediately that it had been years since he apologized to anyone, and wondered what had compelled him to do so now. This person was a complete stranger; what made him so special as to warrant any kind of leniency? Edmund ignored this for the moment and changed the subject. "So where are we headed, anyway?"

"Right here," Chad said.

Edmund stopped abruptly and looked straight ahead. They stood at an intersection, on the other side of which was a large building. A sign out front read DICKENS MEMORIAL CANCER CENTER.

"A hospital?" Edmund asked. "You took me to a hospital?"

Chad left the question unanswered and only said, "Let's go inside."

They crossed the road and entered the hospital through a revolving door. There was a bank of elevators inside the lobby and Chad led Edmund toward the one with the open door.

"Follow me," Chad said.

"Where are we going?" Edmund asked. Chad had been very forthright and conversational up to now; his sudden lack of any explanation as to their endeavor only increased Edmund's concern.

Inside the elevator, Chad pushed the button for the seventh floor and the doors closed. Edmund's concern grew into fear. Who was he going to see in this place? Marley died from cancer here—was he going to see her? He had never been able to erase the final images of her withering body from his memory—nor did he ever wish to—but to actually *see* her in that sickly and frail state again was not something for which he was prepared.

Ding.

The elevator doors opened. "Follow me," Chad said, and they entered the hall.

The slow, rhythmic sounds of beeping and of air ventilators expanding and contracting filled his ears. The lights were low, as could be expected for this time of night, but there was something ominous about this floor. Edmund couldn't help but feel like this was where the near-death patients were kept. And with that, he turned his head and saw a priest standing in a patient's room.

He stood with a man and a woman, who were no doubt loved ones of whoever remained unseen and hospitalized in the room with them. Edmund watched briefly as the priest's lips moved—he was too far away to hear what was said—and he made several motions with his rosary beads. The man and woman held each other and wept. Edmund, feeling guilty for watching this long, finally looked away. He took a deep breath, steadied himself, and continued to follow Chad.

"Here we are," Chad said as he stood in the doorway to one of the rooms.

"Who's in there?" Edmund said.

"Please," Chad insisted. "Enter."

"I need you to tell me. Is it…is it Marley?"

The zombie said nothing more and only nodded toward the room, which did nothing to assuage Edmund's fears of what he might find inside.

Edmund's index finger tapped rapidly at his side as he debated whether to enter or not.

Please don't be in there…

Several of the many images of Marley lying in the hospital bed played in his head. Some were of when she was first diagnosed and when she still looked like herself, others were of when she was close to the end, her body emaciated and ravaged by the cancer. Edmund still told her only the sweetest things about her appearance, even though they both knew how unwell she looked and how their future was not to be.

Ultimately Edmund decided if he *did* see Marley, even in her most dire state, he told himself it would still be better than having never seen her again.

The room was very much like the one Marley had been in when she was going through treatment—private, cozy, a television mounted in the far corner of the room. The local news played, but the sound was low so as not to disturb other patients on the floor. A curtain was drawn around the bed and Edmund could hear voices. Neither sounded like a woman's, and Edmund felt a wave of relief. It wasn't Marley.

He looked back at Chad who remained just outside the room and waited. Edmund, realizing he would not be seen just as he wasn't seen by anyone in the memory of the party, pulled back the curtain.

Tim Hain laid in the bed. He was fully conscious, but weak. Sam stood next to the bed and held his father's hand. His eyes were filled with tears and his voice trembled as he spoke.

"I'm sorry, Dad."

"What?" the elder Hain said. "Nonsense—what do you have to be sorry about?" His voice was tired and frail.

"I just…" Sam choked up and couldn't finish.

Tim reached with his free hand and covered Sam's. "You've been with me through the entire journey. Maybe if I was younger I might have stood a fighter's chance."

Edmund's jaw dropped. "Is this really happening?" he asked Chad.

The zombie nodded.

"H-how?" Edmund asked. "*When*? Why didn't Sam tell me?"

"When would you have preferred him to tell you?" Chad asked. "You haven't made yourself available in a very long time, Edmund."

"That's bullshit," Edmund said. "I know we haven't been close lately, but he could have shared *this*. He *should* have shared this with me. Tim Hain was like a second father to me!"

Chad continued. "Perhaps you should have spent more time inquiring about your friend's life and his family— *your* extended family—rather than removing yourself from it."

Edmund shook his head. "No. No, this is different. This isn't fair."

"Well," the zombie said, "you should know very well about the unfairness of life."

To this, Edmund wanted badly to respond, but he realized there was nothing untrue about the zombie's words. He humbly swallowed any response he might have offered and returned his attention to Sam and his father.

"I'm old, Sam," said Tim. "And although I hoped for a different outcome, I prepared myself long ago for this one."

"I know," Sam said, his voice barely audible.

"And what about you?" his father asked. Sam's eyebrows furrowed; he seemed confused by the question. "How have you prepared?"

"What do you mean?" Sam asked.

"I know you, Sam," Tim said. "You're not a loner. I know you've got Becky, but you've always been one to take comfort in the company of your friends."

Sam nodded.

"Speaking of, where has Edmund been?"

Edmund's blood went ice cold. Mr. Hain hadn't referred to him by his birth name in years.

"Oh, Eddie?" Sam asked. "Yeah, he uh…"

Edmund suddenly felt very self-aware. He dreaded what Sam was about to tell Mr. Hain. Surely Sam was not about to report anything pleasant with regard to Edmund's behavior as of late—but what if Mr. Hain already knew? What if his opinion of Edmund had already soured long ago?

"He's been really busy with his new job," Sam said. "He's been traveling all over the country."

What? Edmund thought. That didn't make any sense. He wasn't traveling anywhere. Why would Sam lie?

"Ah, I see," Mr. Hain said. Then he added with a chuckle, "You tell him I could have paid him the same—and kept him home more often!"

"He knows," Sam said, forcing a smile. "But he likes the travel. *And* he's been asking about you; he said he wanted to talk to you on the phone the next time I was here, but I told him I wasn't sure when that would be."

"Ah," Mr. Hain nodded. "Well, give him my best. He's a good man. Always has been. Shame what happened to his— what was her name?"

"Marley," Sam said.

"Of course." His father smiled wistfully. "Such a shame—she was a lovely woman. Made him a better man, too."

"Can't argue with you there," Sam said with a noticeable hint of resentment.

Mr. Hain's expression turned to one of concern. "Something wrong?"

Here it comes, Edmund thought. But to his surprise, Sam again said nothing to disparage his former best friend.

"Oh, ha, you know… just remembering her sense of humor is all."

The old man nodded and his face relaxed again. "She sure kept our Eddie on his toes, huh?"

"Yeah," Sam said. He raised his head and stared out into some distant memory. "It's really too bad she's not still here."

Mr. Hain squeezed his son's hand and Sam's face fell and their eyes met again. The elder Hain offered a knowing smile. "Then you'd still have *him*, too."

Sam laughed softly in spite of himself. "Yeah," he said. "Something like that."

"Edmund," Chad said. "It's time to go."

"Wait, no!" Edmund protested.

"We must," the zombie said, and he grabbed Edmund's wrist. The light in the room suddenly burned bright white and Edmund could no longer see. When the light faded, Edmund saw the figures of many people.

He was no longer in Tim Hain's hospital room.

"What the hell—where are we?"

"You are exactly where you need to be," Chad said; and Edmund knew.

He stood in the living room of Sam's home. There were many guests, each one in costume. They snacked and drank and laughed over delightful conversation and amongst Halloween-themed decorations. Sam's wife, Becky, was an artist with jack-o'-lanterns and her talent was on full display. She made everything from evil cats and pirates, to vampires and celebrity faces. And they weren't just good, they were exemplary.

Edmund walked through a doorway, underneath a set of dangling bat lights, and through the wispy threads of a faux cobweb. Chad walked behind him.

"So," Edmund began. His body felt weak, shaken by what he had just seen. "Mr. Hain… he—he's really gonna…" He couldn't bring himself to say the word.

"Die?" Chad sighed. "Yes. Or at least it certainly looks that way."

"I don't—I don't know what to say."

"What else *is* there to say?" Chad asked.

"What do you mean?" Edmund asked dubiously. "My best friend's dad is dying! He was there for me when Marley died, how could I not be there for him when his father is almost gone?!"

"Edmund," Chad began to explain, "you spent a lot of time internalizing your grief. Like *a lot* of time."

"So what?"

"So, everybody grieves in different ways. You, like many, have grieved a long time. There's nothing wrong with that. But you also became mean, bitter, standoffish—"

"That is horseshit! Okay, the love of my life died and I—"

"You need to try seeing the world with you in it, as an observer, and not *only* through the narrow lens of your own eyes. You still have the power to change things."

Edmund tried to wrap his mind around this. Sure, he had pushed people away, but that was how he mourned. After all, everybody mourns differently, just as the zombie said. Why should *he* be criticized for how he chose to honor his true love?

She would have understood…

Wouldn't she?

Edmund heard the sound of a man crying and walked in that direction.

"I'll wait here," Chad said.

Confused, Edmund asked, "Why?"

"I think you deserve to take this on your own," Chad said. There was something not quite sinister, but altogether cryptic about what the zombie told him.

"What does that mean?" Edmund asked. "Hey— where am I going?"

The zombie grinned. "Take a left at the jack-o'-lantern that looks like Clooney."

Edmund walked by himself until he found the pumpkin with a face that looked like Danny Ocean, Seth Gecko and, quite possibly, the *worst* Batman ever. He then entered a small sitting room. Sam was there. He sat in a chair while his wife, Becky, stood next to him and rubbed his back and shoulders. Sam was clearly distraught, and Edmund had already made an assumption as to why.

"This *sucks*," Sam said through tears. He took a long sip of a golden-brown liquid from his glass and then slammed it on the end-table next to him.

"Please, baby," Becky said gently. "I don't want you to break a glass and cut yourself."

"Who gives a shit?" he asked bitterly. "Cuts heal, glasses can be replaced. Cancer doesn't and people can't."

She kneeled in front of him and rested a hand on his leg.

"Hon, I know this is hard, but your father loves you so much. He wouldn't want to see you like this."

"That's fine," Sam said. "I was okay when he saw me earlier—now it's my time to get pissed about my dad dying."

He smashed the glass against the table again and this time it broke. The bottom skidded out and onto the floor, and the walls of the glass shattered in his hand. Surprisingly, he wasn't bleeding.

"Look at that!" he shouted. "How fucking lucky am I?!"

"Babe," she tried to calm him, but to no avail.

Sam stood abruptly from the chair and moped toward a window. There were children outside trick-or-treating. The doorbell rang every couple of minutes, and the masked and made-up faces of the neighborhood kids shouted the time-honored greeting with great cheer.

Sam scoffed. "It had to be on Halloween—of all the days for my dad to pass away. What a *great* memory."

"Babe, please stop…"

"I'm serious!" he said. "This used to be my dad's favorite holiday. How the hell am I supposed to remember it now?"

"You can still remember it well, Sam. It hurts now, but one day, you'll—"

"No," he stopped her. "This day is only going to represent one thing now." He whirled and his eyes looked frantically around the room. "I need a new glass." He paced around and searched for another one. "And where's the bottle? Screw it—I'll just drink from the bottle, dammit! Shit—it's not in here. Can you get it for me, please?"

Becky seemed determined not to let his drinking continue.

"Have you talked to anyone, Sam?"

"*What*? Like who, my mom? Forget it. She's a mess. Takes everything I got just to act like a rock around her. No, I can't talk to her about this yet—probably not ever." He continued to look behind a candle. Then behind a lighted cat in a hair-raised pose.

"Okay." Her eyes danced around and Edmund could tell she was very uncomfortable. "What about Eddie?"

Sam stopped. He stared at her with squinted eyes. Edmund couldn't tell if it was because Sam was in fact trying to remember if he *had* called Edmund, or if he was merely curious as to why she would even ask.

"*Of course* I called Eddie," he said. "Why wouldn't I call him?"

"Okay, good," she said with much relief in her voice. "And what did he say?"

"I left a voicemail. Just like every time I call him. It's why I invited him here tonight. I figured of all the people in the world, on *this* of all nights, *he* would be the one to know exactly what I'm going through."

"I'm sorry, baby." She approached Sam with her arms outstretched and tried to hold him. "Maybe if you just tell him that—"

Sam batted away her hands. "Tell him what? Huh? What the hell difference would it make?!"

Becky finally had no response.

"The guy isn't even a person anymore! He's a... a fucking empty tomb where there used to be the greatest man I ever knew, after my father! And now look—they're both gone!"

"Honey... you don't mean that."

"Of course I mean that! My dad's dead, and Edmund died *years* ago..." Sam froze in the middle of the room. His eyes widened, as if he had stumbled into some incredible realization. "That's it."

"What?" Becky asked. She turned her head away slightly, as if bracing with trepidation. Even Edmund was puzzled by what Sam had discovered.

"Son of a bitch figured it out."

"Figured what out?" she asked.

Sam smiled, but it was anything but a happy expression.

"I'll just seal myself up."

"No…" Becky said. She sounded defeated.

"Yep. Lost my best friend years ago. Now I lost my dad. I still have you—but you're not going anywhere—so I'll just shut down inside too."

Becky straightened, her face full of shock. "Sam!"

No! Edmund thought.

Sam shook his head as if to clear his thoughts. "Where *the hell* is that bottle?"

He moved quickly toward the door. Becky tried to get in his way, but he shoved her to the side.

No, no, no!

Edmund reached for him as well, before remembering he could not interact with people in these visions.

"Sam, no! You're better than that!"

Chad finally reappeared but offered no guidance.

"Where the hell is he going?" Edmund asked.

Chad shrugged his shoulders. Then he turned and left the room.

"Hey!" Edmund shouted. "Get back here! What is going on? How do I fix this?" He began to chase the zombie. "This can't happen, not to Sam!"

When Edmund exited the room, Chad was gone.

The inside of the house vanished and Edmund now stood in the middle of a darkened street. The neighborhood was quiet. The hour was unknown, but nobody was trick-or-treating and Edmund assumed it was very late. To his left, Sam's house was completely dark.

"Chad!" Edmund called out, but there was no response. "What is happening!"

The vision was over and he was alone. Chad had left, but Edmund was still there, which was strange. He had woken up after the previous visitor left. Why hadn't this vision ended?

Something moved in the middle of the road ahead, just at the edge of his sight. A cloaked figure walked slowly toward him.

"Chad?" Edmund asked more quietly. "Is that you? Did you change? Listen man, I don't know what the hell is—"

The figure removed the hood and a woman's face appeared.

"Oh. Who are you?" Edmund asked. "Where's Chad?"

"I don't know Chad," she said, and continued to approach him.

"Well, where's Sam? What happened to him? Is Mr. Hain all right? Did he… die?"

The woman offered no insight into the whereabouts of Sam, his father, or of Edmund's previous guide.

"My name is Jasmine," she said. Her voice was silky and mysterious. "I am a witch."

"Hi. Uh, I'm—"

"I know who you are, Edmund," she said. "I am here to show you what is to come."

"I don't understand," Edmund said. "You mean… what's to come of Mr. Hain? Of Sam? I don't—"

She suddenly stood next to him and took his hand. Edmund's feet shook and skipped along the asphalt.

She placed a finger over her lips. "Shhh. I will show you."

Jasmine snapped her fingers and the environment changed immediately. Edmund stood with her in a large room filled with people, chairs, and large floral arrangements. Everyone he saw was dressed nicely. Most men wore either suits or collared shirts with ties and slacks; women wore pantsuits, dresses, or pants with blouses. Many people spoke casually in low voices. Some laughed, some cried. It was then Edmund realized he was at a funeral.

"Oh no," he said.

"Yes," Jasmine agreed. "This is a very sad time."

"Mr. Hain…" Edmund spun on his heel and saw a casket at the front of the room. It was closed, as is the case when a body isn't suitable for viewing, and he began to envision how badly Tim Hain's body had deteriorated before he died. He shuddered at the thought. He then told himself it may have been the family's choice not to show the body. "I never said goodbye," he lamented, and he moved slowly forward.

"You haven't said much of anything in recent years, Edmund."

He ignored her comment; Edmund felt only sadness. He was hardly defensive over anyone's judgment.

"I must warn you," Jasmine continued. "You may not like what you see inside."

He looked back with confusion, but ultimately did not break his stride as he pushed through the crowd.

He was surprised he didn't recognize more faces. Then again, Tim Hain was a well-known and widely respected man in the community. It was very likely Edmund was not familiar with most of the man's friends.

He stood at the end of the line and waited out of respect to others. He knew they couldn't see him, but that didn't change the fact that a man for whom he had great respect lay dead. And although Edmund hadn't made any effort to acknowledge social graces over the past three years, that wouldn't be the case today; he would honor Tim Hain in every way he could.

He clasped his hands together and stared at the floor and moved forward as the line progressed. Jasmine stood next to him.

"Where the hell did you come from?" he asked. "I thought you were back there?"

"I am your guide," she said. "And as I said before, I am here to show you what is *to come.*"

"I think it's pretty obvious at this point," Edmund said.

"Perhaps…"

"What, is Mr. Hain going to reach out of his casket and strangle me?" Then, to nobody in particular he said: "I guess I deserve that much."

The witch smirked. "You are not that fortunate."

"Yeah, well, as soon as this is over, and I see Sam at work tomorrow, I'll be sure to give him shit for not telling me."

"Do you truly believe it would be wise to do so?"

"Why not?" he asked. "The guy should have said something."

"But you have not been there for him," Jasmine said.

"Been there for him *how*? What has he gone through?

"I think I should be asking you that question."

Edmund's face twisted. He could not believe this woman—this witch—had the nerve to challenge him in this way. *Of course* he knew his friend. After all, they—

Edmund replayed as many memories as he could, from the day Marley died until this moment. He saw Sam standing outside his house, knocking on the door to no answer. He saw hundreds of text messages and phone calls that went ignored. There were countless times Sam attempted to engage Edmund at work, through conversation or email. All this time he assumed Sam had been trying to intrude upon Edmund's grief, and only now did he consider an alternative motive.

"How long has Sam's father been sick?" he asked the witch.

"Tim Hain was diagnosed with stage four leukemia two years ago."

Edmund's heart sank and his head felt light. His breathing became rapid and he tried to suppress the nausea that suddenly filled his stomach.

"Wh—why…" he stammered.

"Why, indeed," Jasmine said.

Edmund was now at the front of the line. He looked at the top of the lid and just then, the witch's warning played in his head: *You may not like what you see inside.*

She must have known all along that he would look inside. After all, none of the funeral-goers could see him; he was invisible. Opening the casket would be harmless.

When he did, it was like staring into a mirror. Except the eyes were closed. And the hair was much neater. And he was wearing a suit. And his hands were folded. And Edmund was dead.

"I—I don't…" Edmund started to back away. "Is that…*me*?"

"It is you," Jasmine said, and her voice sounded tired as if she'd been waiting endlessly for Edmund to figure it out. "Please, it is time to sit."

"Am I… *dead*?"

Her eyes shot up in a moment of consideration. "Mmm… in a manner of speaking, yes."

She took Edmund by the arm and guided him away from the dead version of himself.

"Wait!" Edmund said. "I don't understand…"

"You will," said the witch.

They sat at the front, off to the side and away from everyone else. A tall man wearing a plain black suit walked toward the middle of the room and stood in front of the casket.

"On behalf of the Cratchit Funeral Home, I just want to thank everyone for coming, and we would like to extend our condolences to everyone here. At this time, the family invites anyone who wishes to say a few words about the deceased to come forward."

Edmund looked around the room. Several visitors shifted uneasily in their seats. Some heads turned as if looking to see if anyone was going to offer a eulogy of some sort.

Edmund slumped forward, his jaw dropped open. "Nobody?" he asked, his voice weak and pitiful.

"What did you expect, Edmund?" Jasmine asked. "Who are your friends? What would they have to say about you now?"

"I guess…" His mind wandered and he thought of his interactions with people in recent years. He realized he was a fool for thinking there were any of genuine value. But even now, with nobody coming to acknowledge his passing, the tears that collected at his feet fell with every bit of remorse stored within his heart. "Not much," he said.

"This is the future that lays ahead of you," Jasmine warned.

He shook his head and caught a tear with his hand. "It can't be."

"But it is."

Just then, Edmund caught movement in the crowd.

"Wait!" Edmund said.

A man walked between the rows of chairs and toward the front of the room. Edmund didn't recognize him, but a smile began to form on his lips at the mere idea that even a stranger was about to say something about him.

"Thank you, sir," the funeral director said.

The man wore a tan suit and wiped his palms nervously against his slacks. His eyes were moist as he looked out into the audience.

"I couldn't believe it when I found out," he began. "I mean, what can I say? This guy was one of the good ones, ya know?"

Several heads nodded in agreement and Edmund started to feel relief.

"Now that he's gone," the man continued, "I'm kinda lost. He uh... he helped me a lot. He was always there whenever I needed some advice or just a little company."

Edmund was puzzled. He appreciated the kind words, but he couldn't remember how he knew this man. He certainly didn't remember ever having any conversations with him.

"I'm really going to miss Rick," the man began to say. "And to Rick's family, I just want to say—"

The funeral director approached and held up a hand. "Excuse me, sir, I'm sorry—did you say *Rick*?"

"Yeah," the man sobbed. "Such a great person."

"Sir," the funeral director said, "I'm so sorry, I think there's been a mistake—this memorial is for Edmund Weezer."

"Huh?" the man said. He turned to look at the casket and expressed confusion. "I thought this was for Rick Hodges?"

"Ah," the director said. "I believe the Hodges memorial is happening at the funeral house a few blocks east of here."

Edmund could not believe what was happening. Was this a joke?

"Oh, wow," the unknown man said. He dabbed a finger at both eyes. "Uh… okay then." He looked out to the crowd of people and offered curtly, "I'm very sorry for your loss."

The man lowered his head, embarrassed, and walked back through the crowd. Many people turned in their chairs, each sharing the same look of confusion. There were whispers:

"Did he say Rick Hodges?"

"Who's this Edmund person?"

"Is it rude if we leave?"

"Well, this has taken a turn," Jasmine said, her voice a clear indication she was not surprised at all.

This can't be happening, Edmund thought, and he buried his face in his hands.

A man and woman seated together stood awkwardly, and then quickly made their way to the door. A few others saw this and did the same. Then an entire row followed them out. Soon the whole room was on their feet and shuffling toward the exit. Edmund watched everyone bunch together, as if nobody wanted to be the one to walk out last.

Jasmine placed a hand on Edmund's shoulder. "My, my…you certainly know how to clear out a room."

He raised his head. His eyes and cheeks were red and raw. "You think this is funny?"

"Well, no, not necessarily. I wouldn't say there's anything funny about this at all."

"An entire room left when they found out they were at the wrong funeral!"

The witch nodded in agreement.

"There's *nobody* here for me!" Edmund emoted.

"Well, that's not true," she said. "I'm here for you."

"Oh, yeah, that's right. You've been such a good friend to me. Who are you again?"

She dismissed his sarcasm and said, "And look, *they're* here for you, too."

Jasmine was correct. Three people remained: his mother, his father, and Sam. His heart was heavy as the only people to attend *his* memorial approached the casket. His parents' presence didn't surprise him—but Sam's did.

"After everything I've put him through," said Edmund. "He still came."

"He loves you," Jasmine said. "You're like a brother to him. When you deserted him, he didn't understand; he *wanted* to understand, but you wouldn't let him. You still don't let him, and yet he won't stop caring about you."

Edmund ran the back of his hand across his eyes as the tears blurred his vision.

"He's much better than me," he said.

"Sam's who he is in large part *because* of you."

Edmund looked at her strangely. "How so?"

"You met him at a time in his life when he was lost. Not quite as lost as you are now, but… lacking direction. His father took a great liking to you and when he saw who you were, he knew you would be a great influence on his son."

"This was all his father's doing," Edmund said.

"That's right," Jasmine said. "Edmund Weezer and Sam Hain, two peas in a pod."

Edmund finally laughed at this.

"What happens now?" he asked.

"Well, it looks like there aren't enough pallbearers, so your parents have asked the funeral home people to help get your body to the hearse."

"Wait, what?" He watched six men lift the casket—three on either side—and carried it from the room. Sam and his parents followed them. "No, wait! I'm not ready yet!"

Jasmine sighed. "There's barely any time left, Edmund. You might as well go in peace."

He leapt from his seat and ran to the casket.

"No! I don't want to die like this!"

He grabbed the end of the wooden box and pulled hard, but the pallbearers were strong and undeterred by his attempts.

"It will be okay," Jasmine said. "You will see them all soon. They will join you and Marley eventually."

He dug his feet into the floor, leaned backward, and pulled with every bit of strength but it still wasn't enough.

"Not... like... this! I'm sorry!"

***

Edmund gasped and his hands gripped the arms of the recliner.

He was completely alone. Sam, his mother, his father, and the pallbearers were gone.

His eyes took in the objects of his living room—the TV, the coffee table, and the lamp in the front window.

I'm not dead!

Through his sheer curtains, he could see people walking up and down the sidewalk.; they were in costume.

Oh my god, it's still Halloween!

He jumped out of the chair and whipped his head in every direction looking for his coat.

The closet!

A knock came at the door as he yanked his coat from the hanger. He stuffed his arms into each sleeve as he hurried to the door. He opened it and several costumed children shouted, "Trick or treat!"

"Hey!" Edmund shouted back, a smile curving his lips. "I, uh…" He hadn't bought candy for Halloween in the three years since Marley died, but he always kept a small assortment of random candies for whenever he had a craving for something sweet. "Hold on one second!"

He raced to the kitchen where he kept his snacks. There was a small bag of bite-sized chocolate bars in a small cabinet. There wasn't nearly enough for the entire night, but it would work for the few kids at his door.

"Here you go!" he said, dumping the bag of candy into a small bowl and extended it to the trick-or-treaters. "Just take one, please—I don't have a lot left."

"Thank you!" the kids said, as they dug for their favorite variety. When they were gone, Edmund wrote a note: "PLEASE BE PRUDENT" and taped it to the side of the bowl.

After he left the bowl on the top step, he ran to his car and started the engine.

He thought of Marley as he put the car into gear.

Thanks, Mar. I don't know where I've been these last three years, but thanks for finding me, and for bringing me back.

He checked the time on the dashboard. The clock showed 7:32 PM—there was plenty of time to get where he needed to go.

Edmund pressed the accelerator and left his driveway with a renewed enthusiasm for life and friendship.

***

Fifteen minutes later, Edmund pulled onto Sam's street. His driveway was full and many visitors had parked along the street. He drove past a few parked cars until he found an open spot three houses away from Sam's.

The significance of what he was about to do suddenly weighed down on him. He felt happy and inspired at first, but now he felt scared. Many co-workers and friends were likely to be here. They would all see him grovel to have his friend back. They would see him at his most vulnerable.

What if Sam rejected Edmund's friendship? It had been a long time—too long—since he had been a decent friend to Sam, and it was possible Sam had already decided to move on. Edmund considered this as he shut off the ignition.

He tempered his expectations as he exited his car.

A few children in costume had just left Sam's house and they ran down the front path, their bags bouncing with the weight of their hauls. Edmund sped-up to a trot and timed his arrival a few seconds after the door closed.

The storm door was full glass and he could see far into the house. Sam's guests looked happy and festive. Edmund heard music and laughter coming from inside and wondered whether coming over was the wrong thing to do. Would he ruin the mood? Would the rest of them accept his apology as he hoped Sam would?

Just then Becky appeared. She was about to close the entry door when she saw Edmund standing on the top step.

Her face was frozen at first, but then her eyes softened and a tiny smile began to form. She opened the storm door.

"Hi," she said.

"Hi, uh…"

"Wait here," she said. "I'll go get Sam."

Edmund only smiled back and nodded.

Becky left momentarily and Edmund stared into the house as he waited. Several people passed within his view, one of which was Claire, the co-worker who sat across from Sam.

Her eyes were unable to disguise her shock at seeing Edmund standing outside the door, and he offered a gentle wave. She returned it, and then disappeared quickly into the house, no doubt informing other guests about the potential drama about to unfold.

Edmund could now hear Sam's voice. It was obvious Becky was keeping Edmund's presence and identity a secret.

"…don't understand," he could hear Sam say, "…just tell me who…"

"Oh, stop it," Becky insisted. "Just come see."

Edmund steeled himself as their footsteps sounded closer. Nerves and clarity collided at once, and only then he considered that he might have rehearsed what he wanted to say on the drive over. He hadn't, and he now realized he didn't know where to begin.

Sam stood there. "Oh…" he said.

Edmund was disappointed when his friend expressed no excitement or even interest in his arrival.

"What, uh… what's up?" Sam asked. The words came out disjointed, as if it wasn't what he wanted to ask, but couldn't think of anything else given his utter confusion over Edmund's presence.

Edmund couldn't do much better.

"Uh… you invited me, so… here I am?" It was his best attempt to explain his visit while simultaneously asking, *am I still invited*?

"I'll leave you two be," Becky said, and she started to duck behind Sam.

"No, wait!" Edmund said. Becky stopped. Her eyebrows arched and she stared at him. "Stay," he said. "I want to talk to both of you."

Sam's visage now revealed a guarded interest in what Edmund had to say; Becky stood by his side.

"I should probably start by saying I'm sorry," Edmund said. "Because I am."

He paused, hoping Sam would say something in return, but there was no response.

Edmund cleared his throat. "I realize '*sorry*' doesn't make up for three years of being an asshole to your best friend."

"No," Sam replied coolly. "It really doesn't."

"Sam—" Becky started, but Edmund cut her off.

"It's okay. I deserve that. I know I deserve that," he sighed. "Look, I know I was a different person before Marley. I was a *good* person. Then, when she came along, she saw everything that was good in me and just—" his eyes searched for the right word, "—*enhanced* all that. I thought I was doing just fine before I met her, but I had no idea. She helped me grow, she made me a better person. This may sound funny, but—I kinda felt superhuman.

"Then when I lost her," Edmund continued, "I lost every bit of who I was." His throat contracted as his emotions swelled. "I no longer knew how to be the person I was. You guys tried for years to help me, but I couldn't see that, and I rejected it. I trapped myself inside my own grief, which eventually turned into resentment and bitterness."

His eyes fell to the ground and he tried to think of a better or alternative way of describing what he felt, but ultimately determined he had expressed everything he needed to say.

"Yeah," Edmund affirmed. "That's…that's about it. I checked out, man. I was gone. Lost. And I'm sorry."

He took a moment to watch their reaction and saw pity in their eyes, which was better than what he saw in Sam a few minutes ago. He took a long breath and composed himself enough to continue.

"I can't undo the last three years," Edmund said. "I can't even give them back to you guys, and I'll always regret that."

At this point Edmund could no longer contain his emotions. His eyes filled and the tears flowed over his cheeks. He tucked a hand into his sleeve and wiped away the moisture.

"But I *can* give you all the years moving forward," he continued. "I promise you that. I'll make it up to you guys—prove to you that I'm not an asshole, and that I can be the friend you remember."

Becky cried and wore an appreciative smile, but Sam's expression hadn't changed.

"Selfishly," Edmund said, "I want my friends back. I *need* them. And I only hope it's not too late to make that happen." As an afterthought he added, "I guess if it takes three years to get you guys back, that's fair."

Edmund had borne his soul and he waited to hear Sam's reaction.

To see it.

To *feel* it.

As Sam stood across from him, Edmund saw that his best friend from years back appeared unimpressed. His silence demanded more from Edmund, but there was no more. Edmund had said everything he could think of, he was simply too late. The friendship was gone, and there was nothing he could say to get it back.

After nearly a minute of uncomfortable silence, Edmund took his leave.

"That's about it," he said. "I guess... see you later?" He turned and walked down the steps.

"That's all?" Sam asked.

Edmund stopped and looked up at him. He wished he'd known some magic words to set everything right.

Edmund shook his head and said, "Hardly."

Sam nodded. "You should probably sit down then… have a beer in my house and tell us more."

It was as if Edmund had been holding all the world's air in his lungs when he finally exhaled with relief. The emptiness inside his heart filled with warmth and he smiled. "I'd like that."

Sam extended his hand and Edmund walked back up the steps to shake it.

"Missed you, buddy," Sam said.

"Yeah," Edmund agreed. "I've missed me, too."

Becky gave Edmund a warm hug and the three of them went inside.

Across the street stood a witch, a zombie, a man wearing a white sheet, and a pale, ghostly-looking woman. They had been quietly watching the interaction in front of Sam Hain's house for some time.

The witch was the first to speak.

"I give it five minutes before he says something that gets him kicked out."

"Nah," said the zombie. "You don't know him like I do." Then he turned to offer his hand. "I'm Chad, by the way. Harvard, Eighty-Three." The witch eyed his waxy, decayed hand with disdain. She snapped her fingers and it fell from his wrist and landed on the sidewalk. "Shit…"

"Here," said the ghost, "let me get that for you." The sheet began to rise as if the ghost was shimmying out of the fabric.

"Oh, thanks pal," Chad said. "I really apprec—"

The sheet pulled away and there was nobody. Chad stared at the ground and watched his dead hand rise from the asphalt and float upward until it was in front of his face.

"Oh..." Chad said. "Right."

"Edmund is going to be just fine," said Marley. "I wish I could see his reaction when he sees Sam's father, alive and well at the party."

"I still don't know how you managed to pull that off," Jasmine said. "The hospital, the cancer ward..."

Chad inched closer to the witch and grinned suggestively. "You should see what *else* I can pull off."

The witch stared at him slackly. "Uh, you're disgusting and *no thanks.*"

"You love it," he said, and blew her a kiss.

"Okay, I'm leaving," Jasmine said.

Chad and the ghost turned to follow her, but Marley lingered a bit longer. She watched Sam and Edmund through the kitchen window. Becky sat with them, too. The three of them laughed and drank together, and Marley was happy they'd found each other again.

She missed Edmund and longed to be with him, but his happiness in life was most important to her. Because although life had ended for her, Marley's love for Edmund had not, and would never. She would be with him again one day—but his time to join her would come much later.

Then she left and caught up with the others.

"Hey," Chad said. "We should totally do this again, like around Christmas!"

"Terrible idea," the ghost said. "It would never work."

"Really?" Chad asked.

"I'm busy that night," Jasmine said.

"Well maybe we could get a few others to do it," Chad suggested.

"Just stop," said the ghost.

"Oh, fine!" said Chad. "*Bah humbug*, man."

Not This Girl

Michel Sabourin

Stupid girl, she thought. She'd seen enough of these movies to know you *never* go upstairs. Never box yourself in where there's nowhere else to go. But, she had panicked and went left in the hallway instead of out the door. Stupid. Unlucky. Probably dead soon.

She pushed away just enough of the panic to stop for one second and think of the next steps a little more carefully. She paused, panting at the top of the stairs. Options. Options. Options. Let's see. Three bedrooms, two bathrooms, the attic door, or the back staircase—and no time.

She could hear his curses and screams from the kitchen still. Shit. She did it. She really fucking did it. She cut the bastard. He hadn't seen the knife she snuck into her hand at the last second, the one she had dropped just before the doorbell rang and decided to let sit while she saw who was at the door. Her laziness may have saved her life. Who *the fuck* was this guy? Why her? Why tonight? She couldn't even start to process these thoughts. Panic was blooming like a hardy winter rose in her chest and she struggled to choke it back. If she let it spread, she was dead.

Fuck. Decisions.

Okay, breathe.

The master bedroom probably had the best options. Close the stupid hollow door, lock it futilely, and shove the fucking dresser in its way. That ought to buy her about 30 seconds of extra breathing.

Go.

Just as she made the room, slammed and locked the door, and put her shoulder to the surprisingly-stubborn-to-move bureau, she heard him thundering up the stairs and bellowing at the top of his lungs. And why not? The nearest house was about ten acres away, with lots of dense woods between them. They wouldn't hear him if they wanted to. As the bureau grudgingly shifted into place, she rested for a half-second before the man started pounding on the door, screaming in apoplectic rage, none of it coherent beyond the odd "bitch," "kill," "rip," "stab," and "eyes."

No phone, of course. Everyone has cell phones now, so why have landlines? Her cell phone was sitting on the table next to the sofa—where she had been prepared to veg out and watch *Stranger Things* for the umpteenth time. She hadn't even gotten to make the popcorn yet—whole lot of good that phone would do her now. There was an Amazon Alexa in her room, but she didn't think it would hear her over him—and through three walls.

No help coming.

Quick. What's next? Windows? She assessed her situation. Okay, she was trapped on the second floor. No trees. No roof to climb out on, and a not-so-insignificant drop to the ground.

Last resort—bathroom? Adds another barrier between the two of them but puts her in an even more precarious position if he manages to bash that door in, too. There's too small of a window in there to shimmy out of, and no other place to go.

Under the bed? In the closet? Sure, he's literally raving mad, but he's *not* gonna look there, right?

So… Weapon. She needs a weapon. Her father is not the kind to have a stash of guns in his room. In fact, the only guns he owns are locked up tight in the gun safe, ironically for everyone's protection. Good thinking, Dad. Fuck. What else? She rummages through their nightstands, a fuck-ton of perfectly useless shit just piling up on the floors. The closest thing she's found is a two-inch nail file—hang onto that; better than nothing. She vaguely remembers her father used to carry a folding knife, *but where would he put it*? No scissors. Nothing more threatening than a Q-Tip.

Meanwhile, the strange man is still pounding at the door and making threats of bodily harm—but he hasn't realized he can just break through the door—thank God for crazy angry. It was saving her life.

Why did she answer the door? Because it was Halloween—even though she couldn't remember *ever* getting any trick-or-treaters before. He seemed harmless. Clean, polite, and—if she was honest with herself—easy on the eyes with a touch of flirtatiousness. Could have been interesting. Instead, as soon as she opened the door, he was on her. He rocked her jaw with a hard backhand, sending her flying to the kitchen, where she slid just close enough to the dropped knife that saved her life. She had quickly palmed it and rolled over on her back. He had pulled out his own knife and dropped down to his knees in front of her. His intentions were clear: a fuck, and then you're fucked. But fuck that. She was *not* getting raped. *Ever.* She pretended to cower weakly and transferred the knife to her strong arm. If this was her end, she was going to make sure he didn't get away clean. As he reached out with his empty hand to push her flat to the ground, she whipped her arm around as hard as she could and drove the knife deep into his opposite shoulder, burying it home with a satisfying *thud* that erupted screams from him and a fount of blood that sprayed all over her and the floor. And it still would have been bad for her, except he tried to step back instinctively and slipped on his own blood. Fucker. Lucky for her, though. If she'd been just a little bit luckier, he would have cracked his fucking skull on the countertop on his way down, but God, or

Buddha, or whatever only gives so much—the rest you have to take.

She popped up off the ground and started running, zigging instead of zagging, and here she found herself. Wrong way, wrong decision, wrong way to die.

He figured out the only thing between them was two layers of quarter inch thick wood and foam. Now he was raining blows on the door itself, making it tremble in its frame. But, it held. Surprisingly sturdy for your average interior door. She would write the manufacturers a glowing review if she made it through the night. He started pulling back and shouldering into the door, and it wasn't going to be much longer. *Get moving, girlie. Time to fucking kick rocks and move your ass*, she thought.

Her options were as limited as a dollar menu and just as good for her. It would be cold out and she wasn't really dressed for it. Halloween was unusually cold this year; one reason she decided to stay in. In fact, the only reason she was alone tonight was because her parents had taken the younger kids trick-or-treating downtown since they didn't really have any walkable neighbors.

Oh, shit. Another panic flare shot up. Her family. Would they be coming back soon? No clock in the room, and she couldn't remember what time it was when she started getting ready to watch TV. What if they came home while this psycho was still in the house? She had to stop that or stop them. She needed to get out, get to a phone, or get to the road. But what if he followed?

Fuck.

Fuck.

Fuck.

No more time. No more time. Window it is, because he's coming. She ran over to the bathroom, turned the lock from her side of the door and slammed it shut. If he thought she was hiding in the bathroom, maybe he wouldn't notice the window right away—and that might buy her a little more time.

She threw open the window on the side of the house because there were bushes there and maybe that would save her a broken leg or worse. She tried vainly to push up the screen, but her fingers couldn't quite catch the latch because she was shaking. She finally thought, *fuck this noise*, and kicked it out into the yard. The man—boy, really—was almost through the door and wouldn't have to work too hard to get past the dresser and in after her. She could almost see his crazy eyes watching her, but if he saw what she was doing before she could do it, all he would need to do is run outside and wait for her to drop.

Stop dilly-dallying and fucking move.

Now.

She climbed one leg out the window and managed to straddle the windowsill while she pulled the other leg up, over, and through before sliding down so that the bottom half of her body was dangling precariously over the darkened drop to the ground below. There were no lights on this side of the house, and it was dark outside, which meant she could barely make out where she would be landing. She reached up and pulled the window partly shut, slid out until her arms rested on the sill, and pulled the window as far shut as she could from outside. She dangled herself down as far as she could go, fingers straining to maintain purchase on the slick vinyl-encased outer sill. She took a second to breathe deeply, calmed herself as much as she could, and let go.

It seemed an interminable time before she hit the ground, but a second later, she was crashing into the bushes. Rose bushes. With thorns—lots and lots of motherfucking thorns that instantly shredded her legs. Death by a thousand papercuts, or light bleeding anyway. She stifled a scream of pain, tamped it down, swallowed it bitterly, and crawled out of the bushes, cutting her arms and snagging her clothes in a million places on the way out. *Good plan, jackass*, she thought. How had she forgotten the stupid thorns? But she was safe—for now.

Decision time…

Go for the phone and risk him hearing her downstairs? She could hear him up there, screaming and crashing about her parents' bedroom like a raging bull, smashing everything in reach once again and threatening her in some very imaginative ways—and while she was pretty sure her leg wouldn't fit up her cooze sideways, she wasn't going to wait to find out either. The phone seemed like a lifeline in troubled waters, but it also seemed like a major risk.

Next.

Go to a neighbor's house? The nearest house—the only real neighbor in reasonable walking distance—was near impossible to navigate to in the dark through a dense, brambly pine grove. And even if she stumbled through it, she couldn't be sure they were home or that they would open their door to a blood-soaked virtual stranger at night. Plus, they over-decorated for Halloween with loads of inflatable pumpkins, witches, and scarecrows (oh my!). And lights. So many tacky projector lights flashing a gaggle of goblins and ghosts over every square inch of everything. If she went there, if they weren't home, if he followed her, she'd be lit up like a Christmas tree—and more importantly, dead.

So, no.

The only thing she could think to do was to head for the road and walk toward where her parents would be coming from. The stranger didn't seem to have a car—or at least he hadn't parked it in the driveway—and hopefully he wouldn't be able to find her. There were places to hide just off the soft shoulder along the way, and she luckily still had her shoes on—which really *was* lucky, because she almost *never* wore shoes in the house. Luck was on her side so far, but she wasn't sure how far to push it.

It occurred to her that she was just standing there doing nothing and wasting valuable lead time.

Hustle.

Now.

Fucking *go*!

She gingerly started walking away at a very quick pace. She was fighting an instinct to run, but she knew there was still a good ways to go, and she needed to pace herself to not get winded, and she was afraid running would make too much noise. It was a long, tense path across the wide-open expanse of front yard to the road. She thought about going through the woods for cover but decided she would make better time in the open. She cut the diagonal to the road and had started hoofing it down the soft shoulder when she heard him burst through the front door, screaming and running around looking for her in the yard. Another stroke of good fortune—it was the new moon, and a little cloudy, so it was nearly pitch-black outside of the circle of pathway lights that shone on the house. And those lights were between her and him, which meant she could see him, but he couldn't see her— yet. She started double-timing it down the road without another look back.

He was smarter than his rage would presume, though, and figured out what she was doing. Or he had his own brand of luck, because he started toward the road at a brisk jog, and started looking around, shielding his eyes from the light pollution coming from the house. He checked the field across the road and didn't see any movement. He looked to his left and saw nothing in the road as far as he could see, except the dim outline of his car that he had pulled off almost into the woods. He would have missed her entirely—as she was nearing a bend in the road and thirty or so seconds later would have been gone from view entirely—but she forgot about the safety tape on the back of her shoes, and there was just enough light to bounce off them as he whirled in her direction. He saw her. She heard him rapidly pounding the pavement and risked a look back. He was steamrolling down the lane and catching up rapidly—too rapidly.

She rabbited and ducked into the woods on her right and crashed through as gingerly and quietly as a person could into a fall woods—which isn't very quiet at all. The crisp leaves and pine needles crunched incessantly and would have given away her position and direction if the man had cared to pause and listen, but it was like he had her scent anyway, as he bounded into the woods after her mere seconds after she entered.

She tried to picture where she was in the woods. She had played in here most of her life, but never at night, and the woods at night is a different beast altogether. She knew somewhere nearby were the remains of her old fort—which was really a felled tree with some additional limbs draped strategically around it. If she could find that, she may be able to hide safely. He wouldn't be likely to see it in the dark, but then again, neither would she. She was pushing on instinct now, barely thinking beyond that one repeating thought:

run.

Run.

RUN.

Then, like a beacon of hope, a familiar shape caught her eye to the far left. A shadow that cut through the other shadows.

Her fort.

Her hope.

She cut left, leaped another fallen tree at the last second, built speed, and literally slid home, scraping up her side again and fetching up neatly under the cover of the branches adorning her fort. She tried desperately to slow her breathing and quiet her beating heart, which she was sure could be heard for miles. She kept as still as possible to avoid crunching on the dried leaves and carelessly discarded candy wrappers, the ghosts of Halloween past.

She listened intently.

Yes, he was still out there. Moving deliberately. No longer cursing and screaming. Trying to be quiet and stopping frequently to try to get her position. He stopped somewhere nearby. Stood waiting for her to run some more and make some noise, but she was quiet as a sleeping baby, hands cupped around her nose and mouth to dampen any noise and stifle the urge to whimper and cry. There was time for that later—if there was a later.

She slowly and quietly shifted position in the shelter to be able to see out the one large gap she had made for this purpose—she had played War here with her brothers when they were all younger, and you had to keep an eye out for those "darn Nazis." She caught her breath. There he was, panting heavily and looking around wildly for any sign of her flight. Periodically grabbing double fistfuls of his hair and violently yanking it while raging through a clenched mouth. But he couldn't see her, and he didn't recognize the fort as a shelter—yet.

She felt around herself for anything she could use for self-defense, but aside from the candy trash it was pretty clean; even though she had stopped using it years before, apparently her brothers still maintained it and kept it in good shape. She would have to hug them extra hard for that. She was giving up hope of a weapon when her fingers settled on a cold, metallic object about four and a half inches long. She gingerly ran her fingers around it, trying to discern what it was.

Then she suddenly realized fate had once again smiled on her.

Her father had constantly admonished the boys as they grew older about using his things outside and making sure they returned them. But boys being boys, and especially teen and preteen boys, they often left these things outside. And that's why she was now holding her father's folding knife.

She pulled the knife close to her face and slowly opened the blade to its full length. But as it opened, it clicked into place loudly. In the quiet woods, it was like a thunder strike. His head shot in her direction, and although impossible, or at least improbable, she swore his eyes found hers, and he started to smile. Of all the things that had happened this evening, that smile was what she *knew* she would always remember; it sent a cold streak down her spine, and she almost pissed herself in terror. He turned toward her lair and began slowly moving toward her, strolling almost casually, like he had all the time in the world because he thought she was trapped. And she would have been, if not for the comforting weight of the knife's handle growing warm in her hand. She gripped it tightly and spun her body around. She subtly pulled her legs under her but still appeared like a cowering child in her stance. She feigned terror, which wasn't all too hard to do, but felt a cold, hard streak where that fear had once been. She was *pissed* now. Still afraid, but angrier than she had ever been. *Who the fuck did this asshole think he was?* She would not be easy prey for him. She tensed to attack, arms vibrating with fear and surprising anger, waiting for him to close the distance so she could spring at him with the knife. But he stopped and stood, quizzically staring at her.

"There you are," he said, "scared, lonely, waiting to die. I'll bet you never imagined this is the way it would go today." He chuckled to himself and squatted down, staring intently at her. "Honestly, today hasn't gone the way I wanted it to either. See, you were supposed to just be a practice run. In. Out. Rape. Kill. No muss, no fuss—I can't believe you fucking stabbed me. That really hurt, by the way." He shook his head, wincing slightly at the pull in his shoulder wound. "Rookie mistake on my part, and one I will not repeat—so thanks for the lesson. The next girl won't get a chance. At least you can take that with you. I'm just glad your dad had some Percocet in the bathroom cabinet, so now… it's a breeze. Good shit, right?"

He idly twisted the knife in his hand, enjoying the game like a cat toying with its prey, trying to draw out every last drop of the experience. He was lightly drawing the tip through the dirt. "It's almost a shame, you know. I like you. You have… spirit. I bet it would have been something to know you. Oh well… It's getting late, sunshine, and I *really* need to get home and get patched up before this shit wears off—so, let's be at it, shall we?"

He rose to his feet, took a deep breath and almost sighed it out calmly, rolling his neck on his shoulders and lightly stretching. He got down on his knees and reached into the shelter to drag her out into the open. He braced his knife-wielding hand against the top of the shelter and reached in, having to slightly turn his head away to reach her. She was done playing opossum and lunged at him, driving the blade deep into his neck and twisting it before drawing it back out to strike again. He tried to scream, but only a guttural choking noise made it out of his throat. He clutched at his neck futilely and slid backwards to land on his butt, gaping at her almost comically like an audience waiting for the magician to explain the trick.

He was as good as dead—and he knew it.

As the life slipped out of his eyes, he pulled his hand away from his neck, causing a nice arching stream to land inches from her face. He gave her a quick golf clap before losing the ability to sit up any longer. He collapsed onto his back, hitched a breath once, twice, and then was still.

She waited a full five minutes before she crawled out of her shelter, stood up, and regarded his lifeless body. She was shaking, but it wasn't from the cold. It was something else. Some overwhelming rush of emotions: anger, fear, loathing, sorrow, emptiness, and everything in between. She wanted to kick his stupid face. She wanted to run crying back to the house to call the police. That's it—she wanted to cry—and was surprised to discover that she already was. She started sobbing and dropped to her knees, all that energy slipping away, and all that emotion taking its place. How could she ever feel safe again? How could she live with what she just done? No one would ever look at her the same way again. What would her mother and father think?

She sat there, tears tapering off, slowly gathering herself and letting herself regain some semblance of control. Deep breaths. Heartbeat slowing. She still had work to do. She couldn't just fall apart out here in the woods.

He didn't get to do that to her.

She got to her feet and walked home.

The Dark

Jacquelynn Gonzalez

Ever since I can remember, I have been afraid of the dark. You can take me to the top of any mountain, put me on the fastest rollercoaster, or deluge me in an endless pit of spiders and snakes, but it still would not rival to being trapped in the void of evil. Twenty-seven years have passed and my opinion has not changed yet. For my entire life, I have ended my days by turning off the lights, running to bed, and taking cover. However, it was not a vampire in my closet that I was afraid of. In fact, my condolences go out to any vampire who would have tried to cramp themselves up in a closet shared by three children—I cannot even begin to imagine the mounds of shoes and clothes piled up in there. I was not afraid of a demon lurking under my bed, either. All the toys we would push under our beds in an attempt to please our mom would not give any demon a chance. Long story short, any entity that would have tried to take me to the underworld or reign over my soul and body would have given up way long before I heard a scratch on my bedroom walls or a tapping on my window. But if I am not afraid of monsters, what is it that still sends me cowering into my bedroom at night?

I'm older than I was back then and I have my own apartment now. I should be over the tiptoeing to my light switch phase, but I'm not. Just last night, I was cleaning up after my dinner of ramen and crackers when I heard them. The rapping at my door was enough to drive any sensible person insane. I opened my front door and told the children dressed as ghouls and princesses that no, I don't have candy. And no, I'm not sorry. These parents should know better than to let their children run up to a stranger's home, not to mention beg for a piece of sugar they could buy for themselves down the street. Halloween is the holiday for demented people, and everyone knows they come out especially in these late hours. I scribbled "NO CANDY" on a piece of paper and taped it to my door, quickly shutting it and turning each bolt to the right.

It was time for me to go to sleep, which means time to try and outrun the darkness. First, the dining room light goes off. Then I walk faster. Following that is the kitchen, then the living room, and next the hallway. I don't realize it, but with each switch downwards my pace picks up and then I'm sprinting to my room. I slam the door behind me and breathe out a sigh of relief when it finally shuts. I spin around to turn the lock on my door and glance at my monitor, which shows every angle of my apartment. I watch the children peer up at my door, and I scoff at their displeasure. They are so naive of the real world. I lay down, but it is impossible for me to sleep. Not now, not ever, as long as I hear footsteps running up and down my complex. Instead, I try to concentrate on my ceiling fan and listen for the A/C turning off and on instead of the voices. I will never understand what people find so cheerful about Halloween. Nobody knows what is underneath those masks—not even on the ordinary days. I hear my phone ringing, but I do not reach for it. My mother calls to check on me every hour this time of year, despite me telling her that it's useless. A couple sparks on the telephone pole will not save me. Besides, phones are vulnerable—I do not know if my calls are being tapped, and I do not know if the person on the other end is *actually* my mother. I have heard of many cases where people have been cloned, so I have to stay wary.

I do not like telling her so, but I think there is something wrong with my mother. I think there is something wrong with my father, too. A few years ago, I tried explaining their faults to them but it ended making them upset and I have no idea why. If I were crazy like them and then tried criticizing them, then I would be upset too—but I'm the only normal one in our family, so they should be glad I'm even willing to help. They get my words all jumbled up in their crazy minds, though, and they only hear what they want to hear. I said, "You are both very sick" and then they decided to get *me* a therapist, as if *I* am the one who needs it. I gave in, but only because I thought it would make them feel better about themselves. I also do not think my mom is the same woman she was when I was a child—there is something very off about the way she talks to me now, so meticulous and calculated, which further proves that she has been cloned.

The first meeting with my therapist was awful. She sat behind a big desk and had on bright purple lipstick; however, I ignored it and sat in a big, uncomfortable chair. She asked me how my day was, and I said it was "horrible." I was polite to her until she told me I was someone who needed help. I told her that she was the one who needed help, and I pointed out that I wasn't the one wearing makeup to hide who I really am. I asked her about the photos on her desk, and I expressed to her that her husband looked untrustworthy and her kids seemed like they were crazy. She laughed it off as if I were joking, and then handed me a slip of paper which I crumpled up. I thought it was over with, but then my mother told me I had another appointment the following week. Guess what? Just as I had predicted, that therapist was lying to me— their offices had so conveniently "lost power," but I know she just did not like me. In this life, I have realized that everything and everyone is against me. She must have missed me, though, because the week after that, I was driven back. I tried explaining all this to her, but I don't think she will ever understand.

I am not afraid of what's under the bed, and I am not afraid of what is hiding in my closet. I guess if a demon wanted to hide under my bed then he could—it's not like I have dolls piled up anyways. (Apologies for the socks). And if a vampire wants to hide in my closet, then he can knock himself out. Really, I must not even be scared of the dark. If it was the dark that's keeping me from breathing, then I would open up my blinds. Wouldn't I? I would. But I am not going to—my blinds will stay closed, my door will stay shut, and my locks will stay turned. Nighttime is when the real monsters come out.

Over the years my "monsters" have evolved. Their arms and legs aren't elongated to touch the ceiling, their fingers don't resemble boiled spaghetti, they only have two eyes instead of three, and their teeth aren't infinite rows of razors with saliva oozing out between them. Actually, they're pretty normal. Their arms got shorter, their fingers shrank, and their teeth are just like mine—sometimes better, sometimes worse. They all look the same, though, so now I don't know which one I should really watch out for. I try to stay vigilant, but the warning signs on everyone are flashing so intensely that it feels like I'm in Vegas. One has slicked black hair, just like Ted Bundy. The other has aviator glasses, just like Jeffrey Dahmer—but so did Steve Urkel, so maybe I'm being paranoid. But she has long blonde hair just like Aileen, and even the people on TV can be clones of Rodney Alcala. And the manager of my favorite restaurant could be a reincarnation of John Wayne Gacy—after all, he did own a Kentucky Fried Chicken.

The monsters all look identical. That's why I don't wander the sidewalks alone, especially at night. I do not open my front door unless it is something significant like a pizza delivery. Even then, I am sure to only crack the door the tiniest bit just in case the pizza guy is wearing a mask. I wish they didn't smile so much, and I wish they didn't try to force unnecessary conversation. If they think a few chuckles will distract me from the truth, then they are very wrong. If I were braver, and I mean *really* brave, I would retort that "I ordered a pizza—not a friend." I gave up television a long time ago for very obvious reasons. A television is just another way for the people to enter my home. And if not my home, then my mind. The government is constantly trying to put all these ideas in my head, and I, for one, am not taking it. I cannot even listen to music at night. If I do, then I can't hear them walking through my apartment. Because they do, trust me. I have heard it, but I never know what to do when it happens. Sometimes I lay there, complacent and anticipating something to happen. Other times, I pretend I am asleep, because maybe then they will leave me alone. Rarely will I get out of bed and inspect my house, sometimes finding the culprit to be a leaky sink—I know the sink was not leaking when I went to bed, so they must have gotten away before I could incriminate them.

They even speak my language. Usually they're too loud and voluble, but sometimes I can barely hear it. The latter is worse. They do not want me to hear them. They do not want me to know that they are plotting against me, but I do. I can tell by the inflections in their voices. Sometimes the whispers get louder and louder, so loud that I have to touch my ears and make sure they aren't bleeding. Their sentences soak up the air until all I can do is choke on their words, and the only thing left to do is to stare into space and try to concentrate on what the voices are telling me. They are normally adverse. Sometimes I can't focus because they are talking to me, and usually they don't let me get very much sleep. I try not to speak because I do not want them listening to me. I try to ignore them because it gives me peace of mind to think I am alone.

When I *have* to go outside, I try not to look up more than necessary so I can deflect any attention. Even when I'm here at home, I turn all the locks to make sure they know they are not at all welcomed here. In the comfort of my own bedroom, I still feel them watching. I can't even open my blinds anymore because they have gotten so bad. I've grown to realize that they are everywhere. Movie theaters are not safe. Schools are not safe. My neighborhood is not safe. There's even more of them on the other side of the world trying to obliterate me. Not even stupid holidays like Halloween are safe—that's when they all come out.

There is one listening to what I am thinking, and there is one telling me what to put down on this paper. There is one under my bed, in my closet, and several on the street. I will never escape them. There is even one reading this right now.

Trapped

Alice La Roux

I can't breathe. My chest feels tight like someone—or something—is sitting on it. Everything is so dark. I don't know where I am.

Finally, I draw in a ragged breath and gag. The air smells of rot, and I can taste it on my tongue. It's foul. I can barely stretch my arms out in front of myself; I feel like a trapped T. rex with miniature arms. I quickly scold myself, *Now Nina, this is not the time to be flippant or crack jokes. You have no idea where you are.*

Feeling just above me, my fingers make contact with something soft, almost velvety—but it's hard. I can't move my arms to see if the hardness covers my whole body, but a jerk of my foot tells me that it probably does. As much as I don't want to, I take another deep breath because I need to survive. I need to figure out where the hell I am and how I got here. My head aches. In complete blackness, I start scratching at the velvety stuff, trying to pull at it.

What was I doing before this? What's the last thing I remember?

I lay there in the darkness and try to think but everything is so fuzzy.

I remember wine—wine and music. There was dancing too, I think. Was I at a party? I can't think. Something's not right. I'm not right. My skin feels too tight and my head feels like someone is hammering away inside my skull. I can't stay here. I don't even know where *here* is.

I remember him. He's on the periphery of my memory, holding out a hand. Did we dance together? I think it was a Halloween ball. New Orleans. I remember the flicker of candles from inside a twisted pumpkin face. I know him. I *know* I know him.

He was handsome. I feel admiration when I try to think of him. He looked smart in that navy suit of his, with wide shoulders and a strong body. But when I try to recall his face all I see is a blur.

Cinnamon. He smelled like cinnamon—it was a strong scent, masking something else. A chemical fragrance. It lingers here even now—it smells like bleach.

Fear. I felt afraid of something. He drew me in with his looks and his charm—but then I was frightened. I can't think clearly. My head hurts so bad, it feels like my brain has been scrambled with a whisk.

With a tearing noise that fills the small space, I manage to rip away the fabric. I clutch at it for a moment—*what happened to me*? Above me, my hands are touch something smooth and polished. I think it is wood. My fingertips glide over the surface. Why is there wood? I think it's a lid, but I'm not sure. I try and push against it, a feat that proves to be a challenge when I can hardly move. I keep shoving. I need to get out of here—wherever *here* is

Push! Push Nina!

My hands hurt, and I think I've broken a nail or maybe worse as I feel a sharp pain in the tips. A shooting pain spreads down my arms, and I swear I just heard a crunch. I try to ignore it by remembering—remembering what happened next.

We went somewhere quiet; away from the French Quarter. There was no more dancing or music. I did have more wine, but it tasted different. Sweet, with a coppery aftertaste that made my mouth dry. I don't even like wine; I'm definitely a vodka kind of girl. My head was swimming and he placed a hand on my hip to steady me. I giggled as I stumbled into a wall. His touch burned; it gave me butterflies. I remember smiling so much my cheeks ached—then everything started to fade, my head hurt so much. Something was wrong. I couldn't keep my eyes open any longer; the last thing I saw was his grin. Everything was wrong—those white teeth grinning down at me as I fell.

The banging in my head is agonizing; I feel like I could cry but no tears come. I finally manage to push open the lid on my coffin—for I'd realized about five minutes ago that he'd buried me alive—but why? What had I ever done to him? It's like a twisted horror film. Girl goes to a Halloween party and meets a handsome psychopath, ends up buried alive.

What is wrong with my life?

The soil on top of me shifts—he must not have buried me that deep, then. The damp smell of mud and dirt hits me as some of it slides into my coffin. *My* coffin. He tried to kill me. But I have no idea who *he* is.

Think, Nina, think.

I scramble out of the dirt and stretch my aching limbs. Coffins are not comfortable. Then again, they aren't exactly designed for the living. I feel stiff and my gait is slow and wobbly. *My body just needs to wake up*, I tell myself. I need to find him. I look around and I think, *I know where I am. I'm in the woods near my house at the edge of Lakeside.* Why bury me in a box if you're only going to dump me in the woods? Why not just wrap me up and leave me to the beasties? Sloppy psychopath—doesn't he watch TV?

My head hurts.

It's late, the sky is black. I laugh as I realize that I've traded one darkness for another. My laugh sounds strange to my ears, throaty. Maybe I'm dehydrated; after all, I don't know how long I've been buried for. I look back at my underground prison—it's handmade. It's not even a proper coffin. The iron nails are bent and warped where I've fought my way out. Why bother lining a homemade coffin with velvet? Was it guilt?

In the distance, I can hear people laughing, talking, and unaware of my torment. Did anyone even know I was missing? Was my face on a milk carton? Probably not: young girls go missing in New Orleans all the time. Besides, I haven't spoken to my mother in years.

Hush, Nina, now is not the time to get sentimental— you're after answers. Focus.

My head is killing me. I've never had a migraine but this must be what it feels like. My head feels like an egg, cracked open and leaking as the agony spreads.

My feet begin to move of their own volition. I don't know *who* he is, or *where* he is—but my body does. And he's close. Still stiff, I move slowly down the street. I see rotten pumpkins on porches and I know it's not Halloween anymore. Flies linger in the night air as they feast on the pulpy remains. Decorations have been taken down and been packed away, ready for next year. Everything looks so bare, so normal now. My world has been turned upside down but life just continues, mercilessly forgetting about me—one more lost soul in the night.

I lumber towards the old Victorian style house at the end of a cul-de-sac. It stands tall and intimidating. It knows something I do not, I can feel it. I see the faded, peeling blue shutters and I know I'm in the right place. I have never been so sure of anything in all my life.

This is it.

The noise has died down, the streets are empty at this time of night, and I find a certain solace in the loneliness. The parties have ended, no more dancing in the street. Good—I don't want witnesses for what I'm about to do. I'm going to find him, ask him why, and then I'm going to kill him. He needs to pay. I trusted him, this stranger I can't remember, and he tried to murder me.

Why can't I remember his face? My head. The pain. It gets worse the closer I got to the house.

I sneak in through the backdoor, which is unlocked. *Stupid man.* I don't know why, but I head for the basement and wander down the steps. I feel terrified. I felt terrified. I now know that whoever was down there petrified me before he buried me. I remembered the feeling as it struck me to my core. The horror. The terror. It rose up in my throat and choked me. I wanted to be sick—I think I was sick, I don't remember—but the feelings are suffocating me.

At the bottom, I push open a steel door. I blink and blink again as my eyes adjust to the bright light. It looks like a scene from a hospital. White cold tiles cover the walls and there's a small metal drain in the center of the floor. Against the wall to my left I see a stainless-steel table covered with surgical tools and a saw. *Why does he have a saw?* My head hurts. There's a table in the middle of the room, under a light. Everything is spotless. Clean. Pristine.

On shelves, I see jars with things floating in them—a few fingers and an eyeball. I think something moves, but when I look closer it has gone still. *Where am I?* This is worse than anything I could have imagined. *Am I being pranked? Is this one awful joke gone badly? A Halloween trick?*

In the corner of the room I see a giant metal fridge and I can't help myself—I need to know what's inside. I open it to find bags of blood and vials upon vials of this murky-colored stuff labelled "Z Virus." It means nothing to me. I close the door and emptiness fills me.

I hear footsteps and I know he is coming. This man. The one who tried to kill me.

The door slowly opens and there he is—his brown hair is ruffled, he looks tired. He's shocked when he sees me, but then happy. Ecstatic, really. I don't know why—he tried to kill me after all, and he failed.

My head hurts. I try to ask him why, but the words won't come out. They're stuck in my throat and come out like a croak—or a groan. He keeps staring at me; it's like he's trying to memorize every part of my face. What is he looking at? I feel self-conscious and turn to see my reflection in the fridge door.

And now I know why—because he had cut open my skull.

I gently run my fingers over the thick, clumsy stitches he used to put me back together. My hand moves lower, to my neck which is covered in purple bruises. Fingerprint bruises. Next, I examine the gashes and cuts that are all over my body. How had I not noticed them before? I was a bruised mess, like a battered, rotting peach. Dried blood covers me. The smell of rot, the one from the coffin—it had been me. I had been the source of the stench of death that followed me through the night.

I turn to look at him. "Why?! Why?! Why?!" I scream, but only more groans fill the room—no words leave my mouth. I've been silenced by this man, this mad scientist who seduced me with a smile. I remember—it comes back in fragments. I was his experiment. He tortured me, he injected me with his dirty virus, and then he buried me in the woods.

I lunge for him, and this is the first time I see fear on his face. He will pay for trying to kill me. I push him to the ground and smash his skull against the tiles over and over again until something gives. He will pay for killing me. It cracks open like a coconut, with juices running all over the floor—what a mess—the red blood looking stark against the white tiles. *Beautiful really,* I think to myself as it swirls down the drain.

Seeing his mushy brain through the pieces of his shattered skull makes my stomach rumble. When was the last time I ate? I stick two fingers inside that sick, twisted head of his and scoop out the spongy stuff, shoveling it into my hungry mouth.

My head doesn't hurt anymore.

The Residents

Tyson Hanks

Doug Blanchard was not a morning person. He went to bed when his mom told him to, but that didn't mean he went to sleep. Once his mother had tucked him in, and as the sound of her footsteps faded as she went downstairs, Doug would reach under his mattress and pull out his comic books. It wasn't just any comics he kept there—he had plenty of comic books like *Spiderman* and *Star Wars* that he didn't need to hide from his mother. Spiderman and Luke Skywalker were good enough for his desk—but under the mattress? That was a place for something different.

That was a place for horror comics.

Doug would stay up reading about ghosts, witches, and zombies with a flashlight tucked under his chin. Rarely did he actually fall asleep before midnight. Ten-year-olds who stay up that late reading horror comics are not morning people.

Today was different. Doug Blanchard was awake and out of bed at seven-thirty. That's because today was Halloween. What made this Halloween so special was that it was also Saturday, so Doug didn't have to worry about something as frustrating as school.

He was already dressed, and as he trotted downstairs, he ran through the busy schedule he had planned for that day.

He had a few finishing touches to put on his costume—after all, what good was a Harry Potter costume without a wand? While Doug couldn't *exactly* get his hands on an eleven-inch long piece of holly with a core made of phoenix feather; the cherry branch he'd snapped off in the backyard made a good substitute. He just needed to decorate it a bit more to make it look like the famous wizard's.

After he had his wand in order, Doug planned to hang out in front of the TV for a few hours watching *Professor Raven's Monster Marathon*. Next, it was down to the town square for the annual Halloween parade, which should be wrapping up around six-thirty, just in time for trick-or-treating.

Doug had a busy day ahead of him, but before he did anything else, he needed breakfast.

He was splashing some milk on top of a bowl full of Count Chocula when his mom shuffled into the kitchen.

"You're up early, kiddo," Amy Blanchard said. She yawned then, as if she was allergic to the word "kiddo." She also waved a hand in front of her face, hoping to get the yawn out and gone faster.

Doug attempted to respond with a mouthful of cereal. "Howa wacka ma hosoom."

His mother frowned. "Don't be rude, Douglas."

Doug swallowed his Count Chocula. "Sorry, I said I have to work on my costume."

"Oh right," said his mother. "Speaking of that, don't forget that we have to go see Grandpa Frank this afternoon."

Doug *had* forgotten, and now that his mother reminded him, his heart sank.

"Aww, mom!" Doug whined.

"Don't even start. You haven't seen him since his birthday last month and it'll make his day to see you in your costume. You're just going to have to miss out on a few monster movies."

Doug suddenly wanted to throw up, and his anxiety had nothing to do with missing out on *Professor Raven*. It was far more primal than that.

It was simple, raw fear.

Doug was ashamed to admit it, but he was afraid of his grandfather. There was no tangible reason for the fear. Frank Murray had never beaten or cursed at his grandson. He'd never even made Doug rake leaves when he would come to his house to visit—those were the days before Frank Murray moved into WillowWood. Raking leaves for your grandfather is a rite of passage for most families.

Doug Blanchard was afraid of his grandfather because he was old. He had a genuine, crushing fear of old people. After his grandfather had moved into WillowWood, his fear had literally been multiplied exponentially.

WillowWood Estates wasn't the only retirement home in Kane County, but it was the biggest—and according to his mother, the most expensive. The occupancy count would vary month to month—Parkinson's and pancreatic cancer have a way of constantly thinning the herd—but on average, WillowWood housed between 100 and 120 senior citizens at any given time. To Doug, that was a hundred reasons to be scared shitless every time he was forced to visit Grandpa Frank.

Doug thought about his phobia often, and there wasn't any one single thing that drove his fear. The simplest and shallowest reason had to do with how old people looked. To Doug, there was just something horrific about the slightly translucent, liver-spotted flesh of someone in their golden years. Then there was the crazy talk, and to Doug, that was the worst part. When one of the old folks lost it for a bit and got to ranting, Doug would become damn near paralyzed with fear. Even Grandpa Frank got off his rocker now and again. On more than one occasion, Doug would be biting the proverbial bullet and laboring through a visit with his grandfather when the old man would get to calling Doug "Clyde." Clyde Murray was Grandpa Frank's younger brother, and he'd drowned in the Redman Reservoir thirty-seven years before Doug had even been born. His mother always said it was sweet when Grandpa Frank did that, but to Doug, it was terrifying.

At the end of the day, Doug supposed that it was a closeness to death that scared him more than anything. In his mind, no matter how sweet an old person was, they were going to die—because that's what old people did. Somewhere, deep down, Doug felt that death might be contagious. Visiting Grandpa Frank at the "old folks home" meant he'd be around a whole lot of death.

***

Four hours later, sitting in the backseat of his mom's Toyota 4Runner, Doug wasn't feeling any better about his situation. He was dressed in his Harry Potter costume and fiddling with his cherry wood magic wand when his mother pulled into the long driveway that led up to WillowWood Estates. Doug suddenly wished that the wand in his lap was real, and that he was able to conjure up some kind of time-freezing spell, or maybe even a cloning spell, so he could send someone else into WillowWood in his place. By the time his mom put the 4Runner into park, he was actually muttering impromptu incantations and flourishing his wand at himself.

It was to no avail.

"You ready to see Grandpa?" his mother asked as she dropped the keys in her purse.

Not even close, Doug thought. "Sure," he said.

WillowWood was only a single-story facility, but as Doug walked up the pathway to the reception doors, the building was as looming and foreboding as any haunted gothic castle he could have seen on *Professor Raven's Movie Marathon.*

His stomach was churning and his palms were sweaty when he took his first step inside the reception area—that's when Doug realized there was something else that he hated about visiting Grandpa Frank.

The smell.

I don't care how much it costs to keep Grandpa in here, he thought. *It's not enough to cover up the smell of Pine-Sol and piss.*

Outside, a sudden peal of thunder rattled the front doors of WillowWood and it made Doug jump.

Fantastic. Not only do I have to suffer through this visit with Grandpa, but now it looks like it is literally going to rain on my parade.

Doug's mother checked in with the receptionist, who told them that Grandpa Frank was in the common room. To Doug, the large area where his Grandpa and the other residents gathered during the day was less like a "common room" and more like a snake pit.

"Come on, sweetheart," his mother said, "I'm sure Grandpa can't wait to see you."

"Me too," Doug lied.

As they approached the double doors leading to the common room, Doug could feel his breathing increase. Soon after, his heart rate joined the race. By the time his mother pushed open one of the doors and he stepped inside, Doug could feel cold sweat flowing down his sides from his armpits to the waistband of the shorts he wore under his wizard robe.

There were maybe fifty of them in total—senior citizens sitting around various areas of the large space. Some were playing cards, some worked on puzzles, and a large group was working on cutting out pumpkins and witches from construction paper. Another group sat, mesmerized, in front of a large, flat screen TV, watching what little news there was for a Saturday afternoon. Grandpa Frank was sitting by himself, staring out of a large window as the first drops of rain began to pelt its surface.

The room itself had a very institutional feel despite the cheap Halloween decorations that some orderly had hastily hung up. As Doug and his mother started to make their way toward Grandpa Frank, a few of the other residents looked up at Doug and smiled, some making complimentary remarks about his costume. Doug did his best to force a smile and return the cordiality. As they passed a group of seniors sitting around a table with a half-completed puzzle in front of them, a woman looked up and stared directly at Doug.

He gasped.

For just a moment, the woman's eyes were completely black and her mouth was twisted into a sinister smile. Doug blinked rapidly, and when his eyes focused once more, there was no trace of black in the old woman's eyes.

"When are they going to feed us?" an old woman at the other end of the table said. "We're hungry."

Doug looked at the hungry woman and then back to the woman with the strange eyes. *No black.* The woman's left eye was milky and clouded with cataracts, but her right, Doug observed, was actually a very pretty hazel green. Doug also realized that the evil smile he saw wasn't a smile at all, but the lazy droop on one side of her face, the result of a recent stroke.

He gave the woman a quick smile of his own and then turned back to Grandpa Frank at the window. As his grandfather turned and looked at them, Doug was relieved to see that it was apparent that Frank recognized them both.

No sooner had this realization come to him when a bright flash of lightning lit up the landscape outside the window, silhouetting Doug's grandfather against brilliant white. This was followed by a clap of thunder, and Doug and his mother both jumped. Neither of them seemed to notice that none of the other residents in the room so much as flinched.

"Hey, babe!" Grandpa Frank exclaimed. Grandpa had called everyone "babe" for as long as Doug could remember, another good sign that he was in his right mind—at least for now.

"Hi, Daddy." Doug's mother leaned down and kissed the old man on the cheek. Then she gently rubbed the white stubble where she'd kissed him. "Did you forget to shave this morning?"

Grandpa waved a liver-spotted hand, dismissively. "I'm growing a beard. I hear beards are in again."

This made Doug's mother smile. Doug smiled, too. Maybe he could get through this visit without having a panic attack, after all.

What had been a few drops of rain against the window had now progressed to a torrential downpour as Grandpa Frank shifted his crystal-clear gaze—*no cataracts for him*— toward his grandson.

"Hi, Dougie!" the old man said. "Come here and let me take a look at you, babe."

Doug raised his arms and turned so that his grandfather could take in his wizard costume.

"Very nice," his grandpa said. "So, which one are you? Harry Potter or the other one, that Weasley boy?"

Doug stared at Grandpa Frank, shocked. "You know about *Harry Potter*, Grandpa?"

The old man smiled. "Read the whole series. We've got 'em in the library over yonder." He pointed toward a row of books that covered one wall of the common room. "So, which one are you?"

"Oh," Doug said as he reached into his pocket and pulled out a pair of round, costume spectacles and placed them on his face. "I'm Harry."

Grandpa laughed. "Of course. I don't imagine many youngsters would want to dress up as the Weasley fellow."

How about that, Doug thought. *Grandpa likes Harry Potter.*

Grandpa Frank, Doug, and his mother sat for a while chatting. Doug told him all about the parade that was scheduled for that afternoon and how he hoped the weather cleared out before it started. They chatted a little more about the *Harry Potter* books. Doug couldn't believe it, but he was actually enjoying the visit. He could even deal with the smell.

Then his mother's phone rang.

Doug was only slightly aware of the conversation taking place behind him, but when she finally hung up and told him her plans, he was all ears.

"I just have to run to the office real quick," his mother said. "Mr. King is due in court first thing Monday morning and he needs some paperwork to go over this weekend."

"Uh huh," Doug choked out, knowing what was coming next.

"So, why don't you sit here and visit with Grandpa, and I'll be back in about forty-five minutes."

His mother never gave him a chance to object. She just dropped her phone back into her purse, gave Grandpa Frank a kiss on the cheek, and walked out of the common room. The wind and rain lashed against the window harder than ever, as if they were just waiting for Doug to be left alone with the old folks before the elements offered up their best shots.

He watched his mother's back disappear through the double doors on the other side of the room and then turned back to Grandpa Frank. When he saw the look on the old man's face, the old familiar terror wrapped him up like an icy-cold blanket. The look of understanding—that rational glimmer that made it possible to discuss the *Harry Potter* series—was completely gone from his Grandpa's face. In its place was the fleeting and terrifying look of confusion, and now Doug would have to deal with it all by himself.

There was something else in his Grandpa's look, too. It was underneath the confusion. Doug thought it looked like fear, and that drove his own terror even more. When his grandfather spoke again, that terror peaked.

"You gotta help me, Clyde," his Grandpa said. "You gotta get me outta here."

Oh shit! Doug thought. *He thinks I'm his brother.*

"Don't just sit there, asshole!" the old man shouted. "Get me the hell out of here!"

Doug was in full panic mode now. As his friend Mitch would have put it, his grandpa was "losing his shit," and there was no one around to help him deal with it. He scanned the room, searching for a nurse, a janitor—anyone that could help him with Grandpa Frank.

Aside from his Grandpa and the other WillowWood residents, Doug was alone in the common room.

Now his grandpa started pounding the table with his fists, and Doug jumped each time. He had to do something.

Doug swallowed hard. "Wh—what's wrong?"

Thankfully, his grandpa stopped pounding on the table. "It's the people in here, Clyde. There's something wrong with them."

Doug thought of the old woman he'd seen working on the puzzle, and of her black eyes. He turned slowly, needing to see if she was still there.

She was staring directly at him, just as she had when he'd first walked into the room. This time her eyes weren't black, just the one blind, cataract-scorched sphere, and the other a beautiful green. Somehow, however, they were suddenly just as terrifying to Doug. Something else was different this time, too.

The old woman wasn't the only one staring at him.

Doug had thought there were around fifty residents in the room when they had entered, and now they were all looking directly at him.

Oh God, Doug thought. *Where are the nurses?!*

"You see," his grandpa said. "I told you." Doug turned and looked at the old man, who was now starting to stand up. "Come on, Clyde, we're getting out of here."

Doug stood to follow his grandpa—wherever the hell he thought he was going—and when he looked around the room, the other residents were still staring at him. He saw that a few had managed to crawl up onto the long banquet tables where they waited and watched on their hands and knees.

Maybe Grandpa is right, maybe there IS something wrong with them.

A slight scream escaped his throat as a bowl full of candy corn crashed to the floor behind him. Doug turned and saw that another resident had climbed onto a table, knocking the bowl over as he went.

Doug noticed something else, too. The residents were… changing.

At first, it was just slight changes in their faces and their expressions: eyes were changing colors, mouths seemed to grow impossibly wider. What was most frightening was that none of the residents had the usual look of confusion on their faces—now they wore a different look, and it made Doug think of what the other old woman had shouted when he'd first walked in:

"When are they going to feed us?!? We're hungry!"

"Take my hand, Dougie." Grandpa Frank was holding his hand out to Doug, and this helped snap the boy back to reality. Doug barely noticed that his grandpa hadn't called him "Clyde" that time.

He was surprised at the speed at which his grandpa was dragging him along. He was jogging to keep up. His eyes continued to dart around the room. He realized, horrified, that now the other residents seemed to be growing taller as well. At the same time, their wrinkled, translucent arms were stretching so their arthritic fingers now hung nearly to their knees.

Then they started taking their clothes off.

This final act of insanity caused something to break inside Doug. A scream erupted from deep within him. Had puberty been given another couple of years to set in, the scream would have sounded like a guttural war cry, but what came out of Doug was the kind of piercing shriek that rabbits make when being slaughtered.

His grandfather pulled him along—on either side of them, the residents shed their clothing to reveal impossibly long torsos. Their stomachs were sunken and emaciated. Doug instinctively looked between their legs and saw that none of them had any sexual organs that he could see. What terrified the boy most was what was at the ends of those long, slender legs. The residents no longer had feet, they had *hooves*.

The residents began to move as a single entity, closing in on them as they rushed toward the double doors. A cadence of hooves on tile floor rang in Doug's ears. The creatures—there was no other way to describe them now—started to emit sharp clicking noises from what was once their mouths.

CHIT! CHIT! CHIT!

Then, a long, slender arm reached for Doug and fingers with too many knuckles opened to grab him. The fingers missed everything vital but managed to close around the fabric of Doug's wizard robe. He was jerked to a stop.

"GRANDPA!" Doug screamed. "IT'S GOT ME!"

The old man turned, and seeing the creature that had seized his grandson, he took a pen out of his shirt pocket and clicked the tip with his thumb, exposing the sharp ballpoint. Grandpa Frank swung the pen down and buried it in the forearm of the thing that had grabbed Doug's robes.

Dark, greasy blood burst from where the pen had struck home and the creature wailed, releasing its grip on the boy. Now it was Grandpa Frank who grabbed Doug, hauling him, once more, toward the double doors.

They managed to get to the other side of the room without being seized by any more of the creatures, who were all still clattering toward them. The old man slammed his palms into the latch mechanism on the door and it flew open, sending a cartoon skeleton—one of WillowWood's cheap Halloween decorations—flying into the hallway beyond. When they had both burst into the hall, Grandpa Frank slammed the door shut behind them.

Doug started running for the front entrance.

"Wait!" shouted Grandpa Frank. "It's no good—those doors lock automatically to keep the residents from getting out."

Doug stopped, turned, and ran back to his grandpa. Tears were streaming down his face now as he choked out, "What do we do now?"

"We're gonna hunker down in my room," the old man replied. "Come on!"

Grandpa Frank started down the hall, limping noticeably as a result of the efforts of their first escape from the common room. Behind them, Doug heard a loud bang as the creatures slammed into the double doors. He was already at a full sprint by the time the doors actually opened.

CHIT! CHIT! CHIT!

The things were in the hall now, their hooves sliding and clacking after Doug and his grandfather as they ran. The creatures were catching up. Doug stole a glance over his shoulder and saw that the hallway was packed with the things, all scrambling over one another to get to him.

His grandfather finally stopped in front of an open door. The sign next to the door read "Frank Murray." When they were both inside the room, Grandpa Frank slammed the door.

"How do we lock it!?" Doug shouted.

"We can't, but hand me my cane over there—quick!"

Doug turned and grabbed the aluminum walking cane that was propped up against his grandfather's end table. He handed it to the old man, who promptly shoved it under the door handle, just as something on the other side of the door tried to press the handle down.

The door handle was the kind that you pressed down to open as opposed to turning to open, and Doug watched as the cane stopped the handle's downward motion just enough so that the latch wouldn't release. His grandfather took a step back, breathing heavily.

"Little trick we do to keep the nurses out when we want a little extra alone time," the old man said with a smile.

"Grandpa, what are those things?!"

Grandpa Frank shook his head. "I don't have any idea. I started noticing them the first Halloween I was here at WillowWood. Back then, it was just a couple of 'em, but every

Halloween since there's been more and more. Now I guess it's all of 'em."

The idea was insane, and Doug knew it—it was the kind of thing he would have read about in one of the comic books he kept stashed under his mattress—but there was no denying that it was true.

But why hadn't it happened to Grandpa Frank?

Doug didn't have time to ponder the question. The scratching and pounding on the other side of the door grew heavier, and he turned just in time to see the cane get jarred loose and clatter to the floor. Before he realized he was doing it, Doug shot forward and grabbed the door handle, holding it in place with all of his might. The things outside were pressing down on the handle and Doug could feel his grip slipping in his sweaty palms.

"Grandpa!" he yelled. "Help!"

There was no reply from the old man, so Doug closed his eyes, gritted his teeth and put all his weight into holding the door handle in place.

"Grandpa! Please, help me!"

This time, his grandpa *did* reply.

"I can't do that, Clyde."

Doug started to turn around to face his grandfather, but suddenly froze at the sound coming from just over his shoulder.

CHIT! CHIT! CHIT!

Unable to move, Doug stood horrified as long fingers with too many knuckles closed over his shoulder. A slight tug turned him, and he was suddenly facing the thing at the end of those fingers—it was still Grandpa Frank, but it was changing quickly. The Grandpa-thing was already growing taller before his eyes. When Doug looked down, there were hooves where his grandfather's feet were supposed to have been. He sunk to the floor, letting go of the door handle. He slid back on his bottom until his back struck the far wall of the room. As his grandfather completed his transformation, the door opened and the other creatures started slithering into the small room.

As fingers flexed and jaws opened, Doug Blanchard made one last effort at defense and removed the magic wand from his robes. It did him no good. It did him no good because it wasn't a real magic wand, and because it was Halloween.

And because the residents were hungry.

Clutch of Death

Danielle Bailey

I could hear the muffled grunts of the bear while I peered through the old, dingy plate glass window that kept me separated from freedom. Alaska's midnight sun had set about as far as it was going to, leaving a hazy twilight that slept just above the wilderness. There he was, meandering down the heavily used game trail, headed for the river. He shifted his huge weight from shoulder to shoulder while grunting and sniffing, searching for something—possibly the same thing I found myself searching for in that very moment. I loved watching him, waiting up for him. The wildness of it, the untamed feeling it gave me in my isolated captivity, a thrill I have long since forgotten.

My thoughts of far off destinations were ripped back into reality by the sound of his thunderous snore. There was a sudden change in rhythm—its rhetoric often lulled me to sleep, but that was not the case tonight. The dog had smelled the bear and was stirring.

Dear God, please don't let him wake up... I can't do it anymore... I just can't.

Suicide, at this point, sounded like a relief. Reaching the light at the end of the tunnel, so to speak—a light, that at this point, I had lost all hope for. But I couldn't even do that—I couldn't even end it all.

He rolled himself to the edge of the bed, and with a long vehement snort pulled his weight into a sitting position. I knew he would be headed my way, so I slowly inched myself to the window. The heavy weight of the shackles made it impossible to roll completely onto my side, but I mustered up all the strength I had to avoid eye contact. Squirming at the sound of his piss slapping the inside of the yellow bucket, which sat mere feet away from my bed, I recoiled; drawing attention to myself. I could almost hear his cocky grin in the darkness of the cabin, as if my hatred for him was his fuel—his reason for existence.

On cue, his presence was draping over me like smog in a hundred-degree summer. Sticking, clinging to my skin and making me feel as if I hadn't showered in years. His breath bellowed upon my cheeks, hot and reeking like sulfur, as if he had crawled from the bowels of Hell itself. His fingers caressed my forehead, sweeping away the bangs from my eyes so he could get even closer. I knew clenching my eyes shut would only lead to his abhorrent rage, but I didn't care anymore. He could beat me to his delight, but I still wasn't going to look at him. To see into his eyes had become worse than the physical pain itself. His caress turned into a grip on my lower jaw, jerking it back to bring our eyes together.

"Look in my fucking eyes, *bitch*—look!"

His hands followed the length of my body from my shoulders to my ankles like pins being sunken deep into flesh. He gripped just above my left hip, his fingers digging into the bone, and pulled me onto my knees. Of all the positions, this had become my favorite, a conduit to disconnect from all things physical, emotional, and personal.

I thought of my childhood in the short Alaskan autumns; the leaves and branches quickly dying and the sound of our footsteps crunching on the frostbitten grass. Smelling the first wave of bitter cold, and the feeling of the ground freezing into its winter form. Halloween was almost here which gave us an excuse to spend our nights watching old horror movies, my sister and I laughing at the cheesy kills and over-the-top gore while fantasizing about becoming one of those "scream queens" with fake tits and shrill, ear-splitting screams.

Then I saw her—out on that bear trail—ghostly pale and terrified.

I tried to call out to her, but my voice had long since left me. Mute, I only mumbled and moaned. She was looking through the window, looking right through me. This couldn't be real. She *shouldn't* be here. I wanted her to run, to turn back and leave before he saw her—but she wasn't moving. She stood motionless, like I was seeing my own reflection, my own fate—my own end.

Movement in the alders behind her caught my attention. Was it the bear? No, too subtle—his was small and just barely audible at first. In an all too human way, the alders reached out to her, wrapping themselves tightly around her wrists and elevating her up into the massive plants, her silky purple gown lightly brushing the tops of her knees.

She lowered her head, her eyes met mine. I was screaming inside; screaming with every ounce in me when the vines came from underneath, circling themselves around her ankles and inside her gown, leaving a trail of torn flesh where the blood flowed like the river next to us. She was being ripped apart, again and again, right in front of me. I closed my eyes in horror as Morgan turned away from me and headed back for his bed to finish his night sleep.

Soon daylight would break, and the cycle would repeat.

Gasping for air and with my eyes still closed and crying, I clenched the bare, stained and blood-soaked mattress. He left me just enough chain to heave my body forward and bury my face into, and that's where I stayed—frozen and dead until dawn.

A few hours had passed by when I heard Morgan letting the dog out. I turned to peer out the window where the world outside sat normal. The vision of last night infested the furthest corners of my mind, sending waves of grief throughout my chest. I had lost all sense of time—
how long had I been gone? It could have been a month, maybe longer. The leaves were changing, and the wind seemed to be picking up; the river was running faster than before.

Easter had just passed when I found myself being dragged up that gravel beach. The snow had melted away and small budding plants were peaking from the muddy earth. Momma moose were feeding their babies, and the world around me seemed to be waking up and stretching. We were gearing up for the fishing season and the ebbing of summer was sending waves of excitement through us. The beauty of my thoughts had me forgetting where I was when the dog barking outside caught me off guard.

Morgan was off in the woods somewhere, probably scouting out future bear hunting prospects. I'd heard him mention his bear baiting station over the phone a few times and he left for an hour or so each day, leaving his dog tied to a tree outside. The Shepherd was intent on something in the alders at just the spot last night I had seen her last night. Once again, I saw movement—but this time it was different. It was bigger.

Through the brush I could make out human figures, and for a fleeting moment I thought it was the National Guard, maybe someone finally figured out what this cop was up to. Maybe someone finally found out where he was keeping me. Maybe help was right in front of me and I was safe. I tried yelling through the glass, but the intensity of the barking drowned out any noise I could muster at this point. All too soon my hopeful reality deteriorated into horror as a face broke through the thicket.

Filleted flesh fell from its face as the thorns shred through its decay. One eye socket was empty, a hole of nothingness, while the other eye shifted from left to right. It staggered forward and leaned into a somber walk, seemingly untouched by the pain of its physical form. Its trek was a straight line for my window. Gripped by fear, I couldn't make a sound. Before I had time to process what was happening, more of these rotting corpses appeared in an almost militaristic horde headed directly for the cabin. I opened and closed my eyes, rapidly blinking to try and make this nightmare end—but the closer they got the more detail I could see, and the more I knew this was reality.

In the midst of this vast ocean of bodies, one skinny, pale, dark haired figure stood out. Her purple dress hung loosely over her shoulders, shredded and bloody with vines hanging from her body and dragging behind her like tendrils. It was the same woman from last night; her beautiful black hair was tangled and matted, her high cheekbones were gaunt and exposed, and her sea green eyes were murky and lifeless. She leaned forward listing to the left, snarling and grunting with each bare footstep she took.

She pressed her skinless hands up to my window as if she rose up from a watery coral grave. Her face was pallid, blank, and void of all emotion. I reached for her, begging and pleading for her to leave. A tattoo, barely legible in her mangled flesh, read "Violet." Her cold breath frosted the window, and she stared at me as if I was another lifeless body within the group. I could still hear the dog barking but had lost sight of anything outside the mist which encompassed the cabin.

As quickly as she had appeared, Violet and the mob of ghouls behind her dissolved—like they had never existed in the first place.

Morgan came back inside, sweaty from his hike up the mountain. He grabbed a beer from the fridge and began to down it.

"Did you miss me, baby? Yeah… I figured… but hey I'm back now. Your man is home. I wanna hear you speak; I wanna hear you *beg* for me. After all, I'm the only reason you're alive out here and you should be thanking me. Hell, I could drag your ass up to my station and tie you to a tree—I bet you'd bring in a big ol' brownie."

The shock of all I had witnessed left me nauseous, I held onto my shackles with my fingertips while I spat up what small amount of dried fish and water I had in my stomach.

"Ah fuck that's nasty, what the hell is the matter with you. I am trying to be a good person and have a decent conversation, and you just fucking puke everywhere—" He cut himself off mid-sentence and looked at me with his eyebrows raised. It was the first time I had seen any sort of unease come over him.

"When's the last time you had your period?"

I couldn't answer; I clutched my stomach and couldn't remember. I didn't even know how long I had been gone, and I was always bleeding somewhere because of him. I couldn't be honest even if I was, it would be the end for the unborn baby and me. I had to think of something—while my brain was still processing Morgan started in.

"*Fucking answer me right now* before I come over there and—"

"I am on the Depo shot. I don't get periods anymore and I can't get pregnant, Morgan."

"Jesus-fucking-Christ, like I'm supposed to believe that shit—*well fuck*, I enjoyed you while you lasted. I'm gonna go get a test to make sure, but I suggest you get fucking rid of it, or when I get back *I will*. I would prefer a couple more months with you, but if I can't have that—then fuck it."

The sun began to set as Morgan stood up, grabbed his .357 Magnum and holstered it to his side. Taking his dog with him, he slammed the door to the cabin. I heard the engine and propeller of the Cessna 172 roar to life on the gravel beach and taxi down the river. I was alone for the first time in who knows how long—and I was terrified.

I tried to pull my wrists free from the binding cuffs, but I couldn't. I was too weak and he knew it, that's why he felt so comfortable leaving me. Hell, even if I could break free, where would I go? How would I get home? Do I even have a home to go back to? My mind franticly searched for an escape plan. My heart was racing and I felt dizzy over the thought of even attempting to get away when I heard a voice echo in the cabin.

"Willow…"

A soft voice called out my name.

"Willow…"

Terrified, I turned and looked out of the window where a woman stood on the path. Her pale skin reflected the soft glow of the midnight sun. Her wet hair was mingled with seaweed and her lips were a pale blue. Her nude, bloated body was caked with mud and other nameless atrocities.

"Willow…"

She held her hands in front of her and kicked up the earth as she briskly moved towards the cabin. Her eyes were steady and locked on mine, and as they got closer I recognized them. This woman was torture; she brought pain in every step she took. She was almost to the window when I heard the roar of the Cessna circling above me.

I snapped my eyes back to the window expecting to see her face, but there was nothing. Only the same landscape I had been seeing for months now. I heard the plane taxi to a stop outside so I knew we had to be close to a town of some kind. He had been gone for what seemed like an hour. The sun hadn't even set all the way when he opened the door letting in a rush of river air. The dog ran over to his spot by the wood stove and lay down. I saw Morgan set down a grocery bag on the sofa he slept on. A grocery bag—we had to be close to a store. He pulled a small, white box and Dixie cups out of the bag. He grabbed a cup and walked over to me.

"Piss in the cup," he blurted as he started to grab my legs and forced me into a sitting position.

"Morgan, I don't need to—I'm not pregnant."

"I am not going to tell you again Willow, piss in the damn cup *now*."

I couldn't. I froze and my refusal was met with a violent backhand. He grabbed me by the throat and starting squeezing. I couldn't breathe; I was suffocating. fear crippled my ability to fight back and the violence force caused me to empty my bladder. He released his grip and I sunk down onto the mattress, as if my skeleton had left my body.

Morgan took the cup over to where the little white box sat and used the eyedropper to look for an answer that—in my heart—I already knew. This would be the end of my journey; this is where I would finally be released from my torment. A few moments that seemed like an eternity passed by before he dropped the test to the floor and stared at me with nothing but hatred. He said nothing. His silence stretched out before me, and he just shook his head like he was impressed yet disgusted with himself for he had done. He tore his clothes off like he was going to make an example of me before he forced himself onto me. He grabbed my face and held my gaze in his.

"I am gonna fuck you good while I can—but don't worry, I have an idea. I might be able to make this all go away tomorrow. Then I won't have to kill you, and you can be my girl for a little while longer. You do want to stay my girl, don't you? You know we can't raise a child out here, you know they'd catch onto us—you know what we have to do tomorrow. You've only been out here four months, you can't be that far along. Don't worry, baby, I'll make it all disappear."

I couldn't break his gaze to look away, and I couldn't close my eyes. I had to watch as he defiled every ounce of me that was still clinging to life. I could feel every cell in my body being violated. He wrapped his fingers in mine as they hung shackled just above me, and softly kissed my broken and rundown body like he was making amends—like his sexual nature was all an attempt to be gentle, was supposed to make me feel good before he tore the life from within me. His body swept over mine, over and over again, using his fingertips to find the details in my skin. When I thought I couldn't take anymore, he slowed and gasped before pulling away from me, leaving his small beads of sweat to bubble and freeze on what used to be my soft skin.

The sun had almost disappeared behind the mountain, leaving me awake and stagnant, staring out the window watching for that same, big beast to muscle himself down toward the river to bed for the night. I strained my eyes, staring into the last frontier while I felt my insomnia creep into the corners of my mind. *He must be tired tonight*, I thought to myself as I heard his snoring take on that same repetitive and monotonous drone. The bear wasn't coming tonight. Perhaps he had found a better spot, somewhere quieter, away from the sound of the plane and the barking dog. I tried to close my eyes, but I saw myself standing off in the distance, down the path close to the river, naked and holding a bloody knife. I must be dreaming again.

I stared more closely, trying to see what the figure was that lay motionless at my feet. My breathing began to quicken; I could see my chest heaving in and out and my breath fogging through the mist. Blood spattered my bare chest. As I focused my vision to the ground I saw her: Violet. Her mouth lay wide open, her eyes staring up at me and her chest was ripped apart exposing her collarbone and entrails. I stooped down to peer deeper into her, and Violet's head jerked hard to the right and stared directly at me. Panic swept over me before I slipped into a deep sleep.

I woke up to the sound of chairs scraping across the sheets of OSB plywood which made up the floor. It was early, very early for Morgan to be awake. His tall slender body was struggling against the weight of his make shift couch that he was dragging to the end of my bed where my feet lay. He had a Coleman lantern in his right hand and a small gray pouch with a big bottle of rubbing alcohol in his left. He paused briefly while he felt his pockets for his box of matches to light the propane lantern. Once it was lit, I could see his evil dark brown eyes and malevolent smile in the haziness of the musty shack. He set it on the edge of my bed, and started mumbling as he ran his fingers through his oily black hair.

"Morning. You know… I have always wanted to play doctor." He said in a cocky voice, unzipping the small gray pouch and pulling out a scalpel and a speculum. "I should really thank you for this opportunity. Now I don't want to frighten you, but… I would really hold still—Hell, you wouldn't want to knock the lantern over onto yourself. God that'd burn, huh? Almost as bad as rubbing alcohol on broken skin" he said, pouring some of the freezing clear liquid onto my cut-up feet. "Now spread your legs wide so I can get a good look—fuck, it would suck a lot if I missed. Shit, I could just make one big ass hole."

I knew what was coming, but honestly there really isn't any way to brace yourself for something like that. I took a deep breath; at least I would finally be out of this nightmare and hopefully in another realm. No one would ever have to know the truth of what happened here; it would all die with me. He took off his police holster and the belt that lie underneath. He wrapped the belt around my right leg and cinched it down until I could not feel my own blood flow any longer. He pulled the other end of his belt to the wall, where he nailed it in place. It was all for show—I was too weak to even move and had given up even the thought of fighting. I turned my face to stare out that peaceful window for one last time while he began his surgery in this house of dissection.

Something cold was forced inside me. As tears spilled down my cheeks, his scalpel began eviscerating. He didn't know what he was doing, and with every scream that emerged from my small and wilting chest he cut a little deeper, lacerating and leaving torrents of blood. Chunks of flesh dropped from between my legs to the floor for what seemed like hours, and he started soaking my insides with rubbing alcohol. I waited, hoping to pass out, but my shrill screams kept every ounce of my core awake. Without saying a word, or making a noise, Morgan stood up and walked over to the clean towel lying on the other end of his couch. Wiping the bright red blood from his hands, he whispered under his breath and walked out the front door. I lay, facing the ceiling and shaking, unable to peer down at the gruesome scene between my legs. I could feel myself slowly losing my vision and knew it was a matter of time before I joined the life stolen from me in this unforgiving theft.

I jolted up at the sound of the front door being ripped off its hinges; Morgan was in a rage and was kicking and grunting, throwing every object in the cabin around. After fighting the keys and getting my shackles undone, he grabbed me by my hair and dragged me out the front door and up a hill. I was on that bear trail that I had laid awake and watched every night; the trail turned into thick vines and alders making it seem like the forest itself had come to life. Digging into my flesh while I was clawing at the dirt for one last effort to survive, hundreds of feet passed under me before I found myself on my knees, staring into the eye sockets of a rotting corpse.

I hear the noises that surround a corpse before my blurred vision can make out the revolting sight—the sounds of flies buzzing in the fall air, maggots mingling together and plopping off the mangled carcass into the dirt. *It's not a dream this time, it's not a dream* I thought, as it's reeking stench infiltrated my nose and mouth, causing me to cough and gasp, choking back my own vomit. Clumps of hair clung to its skull, skin hanging and peeling away from bone. Then I noticed something through the shirt's scattered remains—blotted ink revealed a name.

Violet.

"Look at her. Phew, she fucking stinks, huh—the bitch I had up here last year. She didn't last as long as you. Too bad too, 'cause she was a good fuck. You two should have met under better circumstances—damn, you two together would have been hot!" Morgan stated, as I heard the sound of his zipper coming undone. Stroking himself, he began visualizing and describing a threesome. "Shit, kinda gross but it's not too late—why don't you lick her pussy, huh? I betcha she'd have liked that. Hell, I'd like that."

Crying, I shook my head back and forth. I wasn't going to do it. I was going to die anyway, so I wasn't going to do it. He would have to kill me first. I could feel him grip the back of my neck before he started shaking me.

"Do it Willow, fucking do it—lick her pussy, you stupid bitch!"

I sat there sobbing, motionless, with a frozen soul—frozen down to my core. Morgan, using every bit of his strength, shoved my face into what use to be her pelvic area. I was suffocating in her decomposing body; maggots began crawling up my nose into my sinus. Every time I gasped for air, I swallowed them; I could feel them making their way into the pit of my stomach. I was becoming one with death itself. My exhausted body couldn't take anymore, and I faded into the darkness.

The sound of teeth scraping bone woke me.

I began blinking rapidly trying to get my bearings and figure out where I was. I could still hear the flies and maggots, though they were muffled by the sound of gnashing teeth. The sun was bright as it began its descent into twilight. All I could make out was a mass of brown fur and the smell of fish intermingled with rotted flesh. Jesus, it was the bear. I lay feet away from the 1200-pound brown bear that was devouring her deteriorated remains. I could hear him pause and pant before he sunk his claws into her collarbone, chewing on what remained of her face. I would be next, I knew it. I needed to get out of here but fear paralyzed me where I lay. I could hear Morgan's dog barking down by the cabin, probably sensing that the bear was back, and only agitating the big beast further.

He stretched out his massive paws, and his nose turned and touched mine. He lifted his beer keg sized head up from the crisp, earthen floor. He rolled his weight forward and pulled himself up into a standing position. He started digging into my back, and turned me so I was facing the sky. I tried to hold back any sound or tears, attempting to play dead, as he possessively sunk his teeth into my left shoulder and began dragging me further up the mountain. Splinters dug themselves into my back, my head catching and tearing on rocks and branches as the massive beast dragged me in between his legs. He slowed in the middle of his matted bed and licked me. Snorting and blowing the stench of rotted fish and flesh into my face, he stood over me, pulling up dirt with huge strength and covering me, burying me to come back to later. I watched him slowly meander back through the alders, headed back for the body.

This was my only chance of escaping. *It was now or never*, I thought as I crawled from my grave. I pulled my naked and bloody body up and began slowly limping down towards the river. I had to get to the creek. I wanted to avoid the bear trail, or any chance the bear had of catching my wind and thankfully the breeze was blowing up the mountain from the river in my favor. I followed the sound of soft rushing water as silently as I could while tiptoeing through the wilderness. The sound of the Cessna starting up and taking off stirred the forest to life, birds took flight and squirrels dashed up trees. He was leaving—I could make it to the cabin and try to get some clothes to cover this mangled mess I had become.

For the first time ever, the small one room cabin brought hope. I collapsed against the outside of the window that for so long had kept me trapped. I was shaking uncontrollably as the biting Alaskan fall pierced my naked skin. I had to get warm, or I would die. Working my way around the cabin, I walked through the open door frame. I grabbed an old t-shirt full of holes and the panties I was wearing when he took me. This would have to work. Something white that I hadn't seen before caught my attention; I walked over and pulled a map from underneath my bunk. It was a map of Alexander Creek leading into the Susitna River; I knew that if I took the Susitna south, it would dump into Cook Inlet. People floated this river in the fall, someone would be out hunting, and someone was bound to see me. I heard the sound of the Cessna circling overhead and realized he hadn't actually left the area, so I grabbed the map and ran out the door into the small creek.

Shaking and terrified I struggled to hold the map up in the howling wind, and rain began to pour down as though Heaven itself was crying for me. I followed the flow of the river south, around a bend before it met an even larger river: the Susitna—this river was flowing too fast for me to walk in, so I crawled up into the embankment.

I crawled through the thicket about 500 feet, stopping ever so often to catch my breath and talk myself into continuing. I finally collapsed, unable to continue, my arm dangling over the sloughing mud, my bleeding fingers caressing the soft freezing flow of the red cold river. I hoped to God that the scent of my incessant blood flow wouldn't lead the bear down to the river. I took in deep breaths of the salty air, letting the cool rain pelt the side of my face and the breeze sway my hair. This wasn't a bad place to let go, I thought. Suddenly, the sound of voices and an engine echoed off in the distance. I pulled my head up and faced south down the river where I saw an airboat, a big wooden cabin and two men, one at the helm and one on the bow. I parted my lips to yell, praying they would see me and not be connected with Morgan somehow, but no sound came out. I held out my hand but as they neared I knew I had to get their attention. Pulling myself through the mud and into the river, I engaged every muscle I had to cling to the hanging roots and pulled myself to my feet.

The man on the bow was huge, well over six-feet with muscles busting through his t-shirt. He made eye contact with me and began yelling to another man in the cabin. He jumped from the bow into the water and treaded upstream to get to me.

"Let go, I'll catch you," the man yelled with his head just above water.

In my weakened state I didn't argue, I let go of the roots, and allowed the river to carry me to him. Once he had a hold of me, we let the water drift us to the bow where the two men joined forces and pulled me up into their boat. They carried me inside, removed my soaking wet clothes, laid me on the deck, and covered me in blankets. The bigger man had short dark hair and a five o'clock shadow with emerald green and gray eyes, and the smaller, thin man had the same dark hair but piercing blue eyes. Nothing had ever felt as good as the warmth of the cabin heating my core and the overwhelming feeling of safety.

"What in the hell happened to you?" The big burly man asked me, as he began changing into warmer clothes himself.

"Morgan…" I exhaled, struggling to tell them the situation, "Morgan this cop took me and had me captive—he is trying to kill me— I am dying. Please help me, please, please, please," I begged through my tears. "He's a cop, and the cops know he has me, don't call them—but please don't let me die. He has a cabin on the bank of the Alexander… don't take me back… please…"

Without hesitation, the smaller man pulled out his satellite phone and began dialing a number; his voice was soft and comforting.

"It's ok sweetie, its ok, my name is Jeremiah, and this big guy is my older brother, Jason. What's your name, hon? How long have you been missing?"

"My name is Willow. I don't know how long I have been gone. He took me sometime after Easter—what day is it?"

"Jesus Christ," Jason blurted, "*It's Halloween*, we are out here looking for next year's hunting prospects—you've been gone damn near six months!"

"He killed someone else," I whispered, "There's another body up there, up at his bait station—I gotta get to a hospital, please…"

Our conversation was cut short by the sound of Jeremiah on the phone with the National Guard. "Roughly 15 minutes? You're bringing a chopper here, right? Yes, like I said she is a missing person. Her name's Willow—what's your last name sweetheart?"

"Williams… Willow Loraine Williams."

"Williams, her full name is Willow Loraine Williams. Yeah, some douche named Morgan—who is apparently a cop—took her back in April. We are headed back up to his cabin now to catch the fucker. I will send you the coordinates, we are on the Alexander now…"

"No please Jeremiah, don't take me back, please! I can't go back there." I yelled through my tears.

"Just breathe," Jason said with an almost irritated voice, "We aren't idiots. We just want to make sure he doesn't have anyone else up there in that cabin—I have been waiting to beat that fucker for years now… hey, Jeremiah, isn't that his place right there?"

"Yeah brother, that's it. Hold on, I'll beach the boat right up in front of his cabin."

The two were hopping out of the boat when I saw Morgan pop his head out of the doorframe. His cocky grin at the guys warned me that he was about to say some stupid shit, but before a single word could come out of his mouth I heard the loud roar of Jason's voice echo in the cabin. Even though I couldn't make out the words, his fingers pointing to the boat led me to believe he was telling him that they had found me. I knew that Jason and Jeremiah didn't entirely comprehend the evil they were dealing with. I crawled into the captain's seat of the boat and saw Morgan take action before the men even had time to react.

Morgan had pulled his .357 and had it pointed directly at Jeremiah's temple. He was a cornered animal and would do anything to protect his secrets. Jeremiah lunged at him, and in the struggle one deafening gunshot pierced the silence. Jeremiah fell limp, brain matter covered Morgan, and in a flash Jason had him.

Jason's hands gripped Morgan's throat, lifting him clear off of the ground. Panic breached Morgan's face as he realized he could no longer breathe.

Throwing him against the side of the cabin, Jason started burying his thumbs into Morgan's eyes, pushing until blood poured down his cheeks. Jason slammed Morgan's head into the building until it hung lethargically, leaving him motionless. He wrapped a spare logging chain around his ankles and dragged him in front of the cabin. Jason wiped his blood-drenched hands on the tip of a metal post, where Morgan had been putting up some type of makeshift fence. After stripping him of his clothes, he sat Morgan on the tip of the post in one heavy motion. Jason pulled his body to dirt and left him impaled, blood gurgling from his mouth and down the backs of his legs, for everyone to see.

The sound of the chopper was loud as it settled itself onto the banks, sending dust and debris in every direction. Men in uniform rushed into the boat with a gurney and began to load me. As IV drips were being started and I was being moved from the boat to the helicopter and away from this poison stream, one man started talking to keep me calm.

"Hi, my name is Sgt. Bradley, but you can call me Victor. We are going to get you out of here and home, all right? I know you have been through a lot but just try and stay calm."

Morgan was off in the distance, his ghastly figure suspended. Jason knelt on his knees holding Jeremiah's lifeless body. I could hear the sound of pain emanating from his chest in each breath he took, it was my fault—he lost his brother and it was my fault. Two other men pulled out body bags, laying two on the beach, and taking a third up the bear trail. I could hear them talking amongst themselves:

"Happy Fucking Halloween, right? I hope my kid sticks with masks and never has to see this shit," he said to his partner while passing Morgan. I looked up the trail and saw Violet standing there, a soft smile spread across her pale face. Her long black curls flowed in the rush of air from the helicopter.

The chopper door slammed shut and lifted us from this graveyard; the trees looked so calm. Nature would continue on as if we had never been there. My thoughts of home, hot tea, warm blankets, and rainy days were cut short as I felt an enormous weight blanket my chest. I could hear my oxygen level alarm sounding in the background; waves of panic engulfed me, and I started losing my hearing and vision. I felt the cool plastic of an oxygen bag on my face and air filling my lungs—once again, my body would have to strain against the cold, unrelenting clutch of death.

bad.dreamer84

Louis Stephenson

Author   b a d . d r e a m e r 8 4
M e s s a g e P o s t e d: Tues Oct 31, 2017 01:04 am
P o s t s u b j e c t: h e l p m e

Haven't visited this place in a while, but I was hoping
someone could please help me with what's been happening
to me over the past couple of weeks.

Lately I've been having these horrible nightmares about this
guy. I know it sounds crazy, but I think I've been dreaming
about a murderer.

The dreams feel so real to me, and I just have this strong
instinct in my gut that won't go away. I can't stop thinking
about it. I have to know if what I'm dreaming is real or not.

Does anyone out there think they can help me???

Author   i n s o m n i a _ g i r l
M e s s a g e P o s t e d: Tues Oct 31, 2017 03:36 am
P o s t s u b j e c t: h e l p m e

I dunno. Maybe…

Would help if you actually told us what's going on in these
dreams that are so bad…

Cute profile pic btw ;-)

A u t h o r   b a d . d r e a m e r 8 4
M e s s a g e P o s t e d: Tues Oct 31, 2017 03:48 am
P o s t s u b j e c t: h e l p m e

Thanks for your response, insomnia_girl.

So far I've been having the same 2 dreams every night.
Always in the same order.

The first one isn't so bad. In the dream it's like I'm looking
through this guy's eyes as he draws this woman's face. The
same woman, over and over. He has hundreds of them.
Whoever she is, I think I'm/he's obsessed with her.

The second dream is much, much worse. I try not to think
about it so I don't dream it, but it never works.

In this dream the first thing I notice is that I'm in a car that's
going really fast, and it's dark outside. And I don't know
why, but all I feel is pure terror. I'm sitting in the passenger
seat and I look over at the driver. He's just as scared as I am.
That's when I see the wire around his neck, and just out the
corner of my eye I can see *him* sitting behind the driver. But
I can't really make him out.

 It's like something doesn't want me to see what he looks like,
as if he's half man, half shadow.

I look away from him, and that's when I realize that I've had
something sitting on my lap the entire time. I pick it up to
see what it is. It's a man's head. Wrapped in a plastic sheet
and held together with wire. But I don't scream. I can't
scream-- I'm too frightened to make a sound. So I just sit
there, staring at this guy's severed head.

Next thing I know, the man in the backseat orders the driver
to pull over, so we come to a stop. That's when he drags me

out of the car and strangles me to death by the side of the road. And that's when I wake up.

I can't help thinking that these dreams aren't just some dumb coincidence.

If you or anyone has heard anything on the news even remotely similar to my story, please let me know one way or the other. Don't think I'll be able to get good night's sleep until I do.

Author	dreamsurfer69
Message Posted:	Tues Oct 31, 2017 04:15 am
Post subject:	help me

whoa! gnarly dream dude! you should pitch that to HBO or something!

Author	insomnia_girl
Message Posted:	Tues Oct 31, 2017 04:17 am
Post subject:	help me

Wow...

So in one dream you're the killer, and in the next one you're the victim?

How trippy is that!

No, I don't think I've ever heard of something like that on the news.

Author   b a d . d r e a m e r 8 4
M e s s a g e P o s t e d: Tues Oct 31, 2017 04:18 am
P o s t s u b j e c t: h e l p m e

Lol. Thanks d r e a m s u r f e r 6 9. I'll take that under advisement.

I thought that would be the case i n s o m n i a _ g i r l.

I still think there's more to it, though.

Author   i n s o m n i a _ g i r l
M e s s a g e P o s t e d: Tues Oct 31, 2017 04:20 am
P o s t s u b j e c t: h e l p m e

Don't take this the wrong the way, but I hope not!!!

Anyways, let me know if you have any more dreams.

My email is *********** @hotmail.com   ;-)

RE: meet up 4 coffee??
From: John Gate (**********@gmail.com)
Sent: 31 October 2017   14:04:23
To: Sarah M (*********** @hotmail.com)

Hey Sarah,

Thank you SO much for the YouTube recommendation. That driving in the rain at night video is really helping me relax. Those sounds of the raindrops hitting the windshield are so soothing.

Which makes this next part even harder for me because I hate to spoil all the fun we've been having, emailing each other and so on, but I finally dreamed something more.

The drawings of the woman I told you about. He does them in her house, in her bedroom at night when she's asleep. She doesn't even know he's there.

And the man's head in the car. I don't know how I know this, but it's the woman's husband. He drowned him somewhere underground and then he decapitated him. I saw it happen. But not through someone else's eyes. I watched the whole thing like it was a snuff movie. It was so horrible.

There was one more dream this time. Whoever this sick man is, I think he owns a store or a shop close by to where the woman lives. It may even be on the same street. But the shop assistant, he knows everything. What he was going to do. How he was going to do it. In fact, I think the night the husband died, he tried to stop him but he was too late.

I'm not sure, but I think I was seeing through the shop assistant's eyes in the dream where I was strangled to death on that roadside.

I don't know what to do. I'm at my wit's end with this. Seriously considering taking you up on your offer to meet up for coffee.

What do you think??

John x

RE: meet up 4 coffee??
From: Sarah M (*********** @hotmail.com)
Sent: 31 October 2017   14:31:45
To: John Gate (**********@gmail.com)

Jeez… been wondering when this was finally gonna happen.

Have you looked any of this up on the web?

I know it's a stretch, but maybe something will pop up.

As for our coffee meet, I did offer, didn't I??? haha

I'm at work now, but I'm free later this afternoon if you feel up to it?

No pressure…

My mobile no. good sir, is ***** *** ***

Hope to hear from ya soon ;-)

Sarah xxxxxxoooooo

Already here. Where r u? Sarah X X X

> Just turning off the motorway. Will be with you in approx. 5 mins. J x x

OK. Will order 4 u. Its a latte 1 sugar–rite??
Sarah X X X

> You know me so well :-) ;-) J x x

That I do. C U Soon, cutie ;-) Sarah X X X

> Soon.

Ur latte's getin cold!! Where r u now??? Sarah X X X

> In parking lot round back. Locked keys in car
> by accident. Sorry for the hold up :-S J xx

On my way 2 the rescue!! Sarah X X X

Author   dreamsurfer69
MessagePosted: Sat Dec 9, 2017 05:55 am
Postsubject: helpme

dude are you a psychic or something? thought you'd wanna
know the police found someone's head cut off on the
motorway this morning. all wrapped in plastic and wire just
like you said. hey but you got one thing wrong though man.
the head didn't come from a guy.

it was a girl.

SELECT: > Postsubject:helpme

The post you are looking for has been deleted by the author.

SELECT: > bad.dreamer84'sProfile

This profile has been deleted by the user.

Author   light.sleeper84
Message Posted: Wed Oct 31, 2018 00:09 am
Post subject: can't sleep

Haven't visited this place in a while, but I was hoping someone could please help me with what's been happening to me over the past couple of weeks.

I know it sounds crazy, but I think I've been dreaming about a murderer.

I have to know if what I'm dreaming is real or not.

Does anyone out there think they can help me???

Author   40-winks-gal
Message Posted: Wed Oct 31, 2018 00:18 am
Post subject: can't sleep

How awful! And on Halloween of all days!

U poor fella...   :-(:-(:-(

What happens in these dreams you've been having?

October Surprise
David Grove

The first scream I heard on October 31, 2018, came from Mr. Lehman's mathematics class. I was in Mr. Rockwell's history class when I heard the scream, which reverberated throughout Port Moody Secondary's upstairs floor.

The upstairs floor quickly became flooded with students and teachers. Mr. Rockwell was the first person to enter Mr. Lehman's classroom, followed by Mr. Jones, a biology teacher, and the school's football coach. They were then joined by the school's lone security guard, a burly man in his late twenties who was unarmed. Two police officers, one man and one woman, entered the classroom approximately fifteen minutes later.

Moody Secondary—which only encompassed grades eleven and twelve when my father was a student there in the late 1980s—was a nine-through-twelve school in 2018. Because of the nine-through-twelve structure, it was difficult for any Moody Secondary student to graduate without spending time in Mr. Lehman's classroom, which was an insufferable experience; he was easily the most boring teacher I'd ever had.

I had Mr. Lehman in the first block of that semester, the opening semester of my senior year, and I was intimately familiar with the layout of the classroom. Lehman's door, which stood directly across from the library in one of the upstairs floor's two long hallways, was situated in the back-left corner of the classroom.

The classroom's two windows, which stood behind Mr. Lehman's desk, one in the top left corner of the room, the other in the top right corner, looked out onto the back of the school, which was surrounded by a thick forest.

In my first-block class, Mr. Lehman focused on geometry, which was the bane of my existence in mathematics. When I saw a pale-faced Mr. Lehman being led out of the classroom by a paramedic, I knew that Mr. Lehman had continued with geometry in the second block. There was a circular, narrow hole in the center of Mr. Lehman's right hand which could only have been created by a geometry compass.

The absence of blood at the scene, both inside and outside Lehman's classroom, indicated that the compass had been withdrawn from Mr. Lehman's right hand as quickly as it had been driven through the flesh and bone.

I concluded that the trajectory of the stabbing motion must have been perfectly vertical, as if the tip of the compass had fallen from the sky. Maybe the wound simply didn't have time to bleed.

The only blood I saw at Moody Secondary that morning was on the compass in question, which the security guard briefly brandished when he popped his head out of the classroom to confer with the Principal. Then the security guard reentered the classroom and quarantined the assailant until the police officers arrived.

It didn't take long for Lehman's second-block students to provide their eyewitness accounts of what had taken place inside the classroom. "Lehman set his hand down on top of Matt's desk, and Matt just grabbed it," recounted Tracey Dodd, who posted several pictures of the episode on her various social media platforms. "Matt pinned Lehman's right hand flat on the desk, and then Matt slowly held up the compass. But there was no expression on Matt's face—he was just *blank*. Then Matt drove the compass through Lehman's hand. It went straight down, right through Lehman's hand. Then Matt ripped it out."

"Matt?" another student asked.

"Matt Johnson," Tracey replied. "He just sat still in his desk afterwards; the rest of us backed away, toward the door. He was mumbling but nothing came out. Then, his mouth dropped open. He let out a low groan, then he fell forward onto his desk."

The police officers entered the classroom with their guns drawn. They removed Matt in handcuffs.

Matt Johnson and I first met at Seaview, our elementary school. Matt and I, along with the various other cast of characters from my childhood, often played ball hockey and touch football after school, and Matt's face appears in several of my baseball and soccer team pictures. After Seaview, Matt followed me to Banting Middle School.

Matt and I were extremely familiar with each other, which isn't the same as actually knowing someone, and is indescribably different than friendship. But you can't go to school with someone for a decade without at least having a deep familiarity with that person, I suppose. I'd certainly spent enough time around Matt for me to be able to state, unequivocally, that the burst of violence he unleashed upon Mr. Lehman was completely out of character for him.

But I probably would have said the same thing about everyone else I'd gone to school with since elementary school. I guess that means it could have happened to anyone. It almost happened to me.

The psychotic impulse that infected Matt's body and mind also visited me in during second block. While I was inside Mr. Rockwell's classroom, a few minutes before Lehman screamed, a voice entered my head.

I felt the impulse.

The voice that entered my head during second block took the form of an otherworldly transmission, which was marred by static and the low whine you hear when you try to access an obscure radio station. The inaudible voice inside my head was ageless and spectral in tone. The lone stream of words I was able to decipher had the cadence of a diabolical suggestion. "Follow the impulse," the voice whispered to me. "Join us."

While Lehman's scream caused the rest of the students in Rockwell's classroom to instantaneously jump, I was strangely unmoved. After the classroom emptied around me, I stayed behind for several minutes, sitting icily still in my desk, blindly staring ahead into the void of the chalkboard.

When the signal evaporated between my ears, I saw that my right hand, which was numb, was clasping a pen. The pen was upside down in my hand. I was holding it like a knife. Horrified, I quickly let go of it. Then I ran outside.

Outside Mr. Rockwell's door, I turned right and walked to the end of a side hallway. Turning left, I stood at the edge of the long hallway that ran past Lehman's classroom and the library. From this position, I watched everything that unfolded around Lehman's classroom. I was standing at the end of the long hallway, staring diagonally toward Lehman's door, when Matt and I made ephemeral eye contact with each other.

The police officers were leading Matt downstairs via the nearest stairwell when I saw Matt's expression, which was catatonic-like and stupefied. His body was pulsating, seething, and his forehead was damp and red. His eyes were fixated in a half-open position that never wavered during the two or three seconds we looked at each other in the hall. Just before Matt disappeared into the stairwell with the police officers, he smiled at me.

After the officers placed Matt in the backseat of a police car, they drove Matt to the Port Moody Police Department, which was located in the heart of downtown Port Moody, between a Dairy Queen and a McDonald's.

My hometown, Port Moody, British Columbia, was a tranquil place to live on October 31, 2018, and the police department had very few serious crimes to deal with. I would be very surprised if any of the police department's approximately forty sworn members had ever fired their guns in the line of duty prior to that date.

The age of maturity in British Columbia was nineteen, which didn't preclude Matt from jail time but almost certainly ruled out the possibility of a serious criminal charge like attempted murder.

What exactly happened to Matt and me at school that day? Why was I able to remain a few millimeters on this side of the line, and why was he not?

Matt was sixteen on October 31, 2018, and I was seventeen. Although I'd like to believe that I was mentally strong enough to fight off the impulse that overwhelmed Matt's senses, I strongly suspect that the one-year advantage I had over Matt was all that saved me. Because Matt was sixteen then, he was eligible to go trick-or-treating in Port Moody. Because I was seventeen, I was not.

In 2015, the Port Moody City Council, for reasons they never fully articulated, passed a Trick or Treating law, which stated that it was illegal for anyone over the age of sixteen to go trick-or-treating anywhere in Port Moody. The "Halloween Law" also included an eight-p.m. curfew. The penalty for breaking the law was a $200 fine.

The last time I'd gone trick-or-treating was in the eighth grade, when I was thirteen. It was socially unacceptable for anyone older than thirteen to wear a costume on

Halloween or to go out begging for candy. Because of this, Halloween really didn't exist at Moody Secondary; there were no Halloween decorations visible inside or outside the school.

After Matt left the school, the rest of that day's class schedule unfolded peacefully. The only lasting evidence that anything sinister had occurred at Port Moody Secondary that day was the jarring sight of Mr. Lehman's darkened, unfilled classroom.

After fifth block, I waited at my locker for Michael Sheehan and Stuart Kent, who were my only two friends at the school and in the world. My friendship with Michael and Stuart, which began at Seaview, also encompassed the three years we spent at Banting Middle School, and I was extremely hopeful that it would survive Moody Secondary and university. I used to dream that our kids would play sports together and our wives would be best friends. Michael and Stuart were fairly popular at Moody Secondary—I think that they could have been even more popular if they hadn't been shackled with the responsibility of shepherding me from elementary school to senior high. I depended on them for my survival.

Michael and Stuart played on the Moody Secondary Blues basketball team between grades nine and eleven, and during the summer of 2018, which took me from six-feet tall to being just under six-three, I was determined to make the team in our senior year. Although I hadn't played organized basketball between Seaview and Moody Secondary, I played basketball almost every day in the Moody gym between grades nine and eleven, and I gained a reputation for being an excellent shooter—as long as no one was in my face. My small hands made it difficult for me to dribble the ball with authority, and my feet were slow, which made me a defensive liability, but I made the team—which isn't the same as being a player. When Mr. Rockwell, who coached the boys' team, informed me of his decision to put me on the roster, he warned me that it was very unlikely that I would see playing time in any game that was competitive. That left me with garbage time.

By October 31, 2018, our team had played in a handful of games, and I'd perfected the role of benchwarmer, which was like being a glorified water-boy. I didn't feel like I was part of anything. I also thought that being a member of the basketball team would help me with girls—but as of October 31, 2018, I'd never been on a date or kissed a girl.

My name is Don Black, and my existence, up until this fateful point in time, had been every bit as innocuous as such a nondescript name would suggest: Don Black.

"Did you sense anything strange going on in the school during second block?" I asked Michael and Stuart in front of my locker.

"Other than Lehman being stabbed?" Michael chuckled. "I was downstairs, just outside the cafeteria, and I could hear it clear as a bell."

"I think everyone who's ever been in his class has thought about doing something like that," Stuart chimed. "Of course, I don't mean killing him."

"Not just that," I said. "There was something going on, which I can't describe."

"What if you asked a girl out?" Michael said. "That would be really strange, wouldn't it?"

"Did you see Tracey Williams today?" Stuart asked me.

Tracey Williams, whom I first saw in my grade eleven English literature class, was the girl whom I regarded as being the love of my life. She had doe eyes, silky blonde hair, and a warm skin tone. I had never even spoken to her.

"You know I don't have any classes with her this semester," I said. "What happened?"

"It's that time of the month you always talked about when you had that class with her last year," replied Stuart, who shared a third-block Chemistry class with Tracey. "Her hair was pulled back, and she had a lethargic expression on her face. She wasn't wearing any makeup. She walked very gingerly, and when her legs moved, I could almost hear all of that crimson period blood sloshing around."

"I bet it tastes like Dr. Pepper," I whispered.

"You're a psycho, man," Michael said to me. "It's sick how you continue to obsess over that girl—when are you going to ask her out?"

"I heard a voice," I said, changing the subject after I closed my locker door. "It was in my head. "Follow the impulse. Join us." That's what I heard. What do you make of that?"

Michael and Stuart broke into laughter, which I think had as much to do with the deadpan tone of my voice as the words themselves.

"Get the fuck out of here," said Stuart. "What are you talking about?"

"Are you hearing voices now?" Michael asked me. He leaned into me until his mouth was less than six inches away from my right ear. "Don! Can you hear me? You need to get laid."

"I didn't hear it again after second block," I said.

After leaving the school, we headed for Michael's car, a black-and-yellow, muscle-bound Ford Mustang. The car was parked at the far end of the school's upper parking lot, which was shaded by overhanging brush from the surrounding forest. The shade created a disarming contrast between darkness and light, which made it difficult to see anything clearly in the upper parking lot.

As Michael, Stuart, and I were approaching Michael's car, there was another scream.

This scream originated from the petite body of Carmen Reid, and while the scream never left her body, it entered my mind. I heard it. I knew a scream was bubbling inside Carmen when I saw her bulging eyes. If not for the large, strong hands clasped around Carmen's throat, I'm convinced that she would have unleashed a meaty, powerful, throaty scream. The hands belonged to Sean O'Leary, Carmen's longtime boyfriend. Carmen and Sean started dating at Banting, and they were one of Moody Secondary's most recognizable couples. Their potent chemistry was evident every time they were together. It was obvious to anyone who saw them together that their relationship contained a strong sexual component.

What wasn't nearly as evident was the fact that Carmen was a year older than Sean, who had hair on his chest and a moustache by the time he was sixteen.

When I turned to my right and saw Carmen, she was on the hood of Sean's truck, lying on her back, legs twitching. Any thought I might have had that I was witnessing some kind of sexual act between Carmen and Sean was erased from my mind when I saw Sean's eyes. He had the same docile, vacant look that I'd found earlier in Matt Johnson's stare.

Michael, Stuart, and I must have stood in place for at least five seconds, watching in disbelief. Then I stepped forward and pushed Sean away from Carmen, who immediately exhaled. "Are you okay?" I asked Carmen, who nodded.

Sean's eyes fluttered. He stumbled backward, shaking his head. "Are you okay?" I asked him.

"I'm fine," he said, turning to face me. "Why did you push me like that?"

"It looked like you were strangling her," I said, pointing at Carmen, who was standing halfway between Michael's car and Sean's truck.

Sean looked at me like I was crazy. He started to laugh until he saw tears in Carmen's eyes. "What are you talking about?" he asked me.

The reunion between Carmen and Sean began with her slapping him across the face when he tried to move in for a hug. "Why did you do that?" she asked him. "You were hurting me."   "I'm sorry," he said. His hands slowly reached out to her until they clasped her waist. Then she let him wrap his arms around her. "I don't know what happened."

Then they started kissing. Sean's right hand was inside Carmen's blouse when Michael's car exited the parking lot.

From the upper parking lot entrance, which sat at the top of a hill, Michael's car headed down Albert Street, where Port Moody Secondary was tucked away, shielded from the rest of Port Moody by a forest of green trees.

The straight road ended in front of a three-way intersection, facing the Barnet Highway, which offered the most direct route to downtown Vancouver. To the right of Michael's car was St. John's Street, which was Port Moody's main artery.

When the traffic light turned green, Michael turned left and ascended Port Moody's snake hill. The steep hill, which made for a torturous walk, extended from the bottom of Port Moody to its highest point.

On the way to my house, which sat near the top of Port Moody, Michael's car drove past Woodland Park, the disheveled townhouse rental community he lived in for as long as I knew him.

Although Woodland Park, which consisted of a dozen or so townhome buildings, spread over seven acres and was infested with cockroaches and rats, it was one of the few affordable places to live in Port Moody, which was one of the hottest real estate markets in all of British Columbia in 2018.

After leaving the Woodlands behind, we drove past another townhouse complex, the Evergreens, which was where Stuart lived. The Evergreens and Woodlands both bordered Seaview, and there was a childhood memory attached to every blade of grass and sidewalk within that contained universe. Until we left Seaview, this was our entire world.

After leaving the Evergreens behind, Michael made a right turn and entered College Park, the residential neighborhood I grew up in. Compared to the Evergreens and the Woodlands, College Park was a pristine utopia.

Because College Park, which was only accessible via two long, winding roads, felt so insulated from the rest of Port Moody and the world, I felt completely safe and sheltered inside College Park's invisible borders. Although College Park's borders were completely unguarded, no intruder went undetected. Everyone who lived outside of College Park was a stranger. I do not remember a single crime being committed inside College Park prior to October 31, 2018.

When my father, who lived in College Park his entire life, told me that he remembered a time when College Park was a bloody, shadowy badlands, I assumed that he was joking. But he wasn't—he was trying to scare me, to illustrate the contrast between new and old College Park, my father pointed toward a lot of shiny houses in the heart of College Park. According to my father, in the early to mid-1980s, when my father was at Seaview, the lot was occupied by a strip plaza whose chief tenant—after several other businesses fled the location—was a seedy Mac's convenience store. "The store was a festering cancer," my father told me. "I went there to play the arcade games, which were a magnet for delinquents. They were faceless, regenerating monsters. They were always buzzing around the store and the unpatrolled lot when my friends and I were there. They melted into the patch of long weeds and yellow grass behind the store whenever there were too many adults around."

Adjacent to the lot, there was an affordable housing square, which was the only monument that remained from the College Park of the 1980s. "A lot of Seaview kids lived there," my father said. "It was a shithole back then, almost a slum, much worse than the Woodlands. There were several rapes and stabbings in the area."

"I don't believe you," I told him.

"Believe me," my father insisted. "College Park was once a place where children weren't allowed to walk the streets alone at night."

Michael's car had just reached the apex of a hill when he braked hard. Sitting alone in the backseat, which was my regular position, I immediately fell forward. When I leaned over the divide, between Michael and Stuart, I saw three boys standing in front of Michael's car.

The boys were standing alongside one another, evenly separated by a distance of no more than eighteen inches. They were wearing costumes. This made me think that they were returning home from Seaview, which had always held a Halloween costume assembly when Michael, Stuart, and I were there. The three boys looked like they were eight or nine years old, which would have put them in the second or third grade. They were clearly primary kids.

The boy on the far left was wearing a Spider-Man costume, and the boy on the far right looked like Dracula. The boy in the center was wearing a silver skull mask with cut-out eyeholes, the rest of his body was covered in a charcoal-colored jumpsuit.

Although Skull Boy's eyes were visible, along with the flesh around his eyelids, the mask's mesh-covered mouth did an effective job of cloaking his identity. It was immediately apparent to me that Skull Boy was the leader.

Watching Skull Boy exercise his wordless command over Dracula and Spider-Man was like watching an orchestral conductor marshalling their instruments. With his palms facing Michael's windshield, Skull Boy raised his hands in the air until they were parallel with his chin. Then Skull Boy slowly closed his hands and turned them into fists. In unison, the trio stepped forward until they were no more than a foot away from the Mustang's grille.

After they came to a stop, Skull Boy pulled out a sword, which his right hand drew from a sheath attached to his back.

It was a scimitar, which I recognized from the legion of fantasy role-playing and video game campaigns I'd engaged in over the years. Although Skull Boy's sword was clearly a reproduction, the glint of its curved blade left me with no doubt that it would function very satisfactorily as a killing weapon.

"What the fuck are these dickheads doing?" Michael asked. He honked his horn, which produced no reaction from the trick-or-treaters. "Get off the road!"

"I'll take care of this," Stuart vowed. Stuart was just about to open the passenger door and leap out of the car when I grabbed his left shoulder with my right hand, which stopped him.

"No," I said. "That's a real sword. He could kill you."

The impasse continued for another seven or eight seconds. Then, Skull Boy stepped forward another few inches, holding the sword out in front of him, turning the blade until it was perfectly vertical with the car.

Then Skull Boy slowly lowered the blade until the tip caressed the hood of Michael's car, and the three boys stepped out of the way of Michael's car.

When Michael launched the car forward, the three boys were standing in front of a bus stop. From the backseat, I turned and followed Skull Boy's face until the growing distance between us turned the white of his eyes into black, sunken orbs.

It was just before three thirty when Michael's car stopped alongside my spacious driveway. My blunt, functional, pre-owned 2013 Toyota Corolla was alone in the driveway. Climbing out of the backseat of Michael's car, I looked around the neighborhood, which was almost entirely devoid of Halloween markings.

Since the eighth grade, Michael, Stuart, and I spent every Halloween shooting off fireworks. Since 2015, we made a point of doing this after eight o'clock.

"You've got the fireworks, right?" Michael asked me, just before he drove away.

"They're in my closet," I assured him.

Instead of immediately turning to face the front of my house, I stood in place and watched Michael's car descend the hill that ran back and forth in front of my driveway.

From the front edge of my driveway, the bottom of the hill in front of my house curved to the right. After Michael's car made the right turn and disappeared, I continued to look down the hill, staring diagonally to my left, until I could no longer hear the flutter of the Mustang's chrome rims, the grinding of the turbine wheels. "Be careful," I whispered.

I was waiting for the next scream.

When I stepped through the front door of my house, I had no idea that my younger brother, Chad, was home.

He was completely silent and didn't make a sound when I entered the house, which was very unusual for him. I almost shrieked when I wandered into the living room and found him sitting on one of the living room's two couches. He was staring ahead at the television, which was off.

I waved my right hand in front of his eyes until Chad, who was in the seventh grade at Banting, silently acknowledged me. Without moving his arms and legs, he turned his head to the left and upward. Then he nodded.

"Are you going trick-or-treating tonight?" I asked.

"Of course," he said. "I'm twelve."

Then he rose from the couch and went downstairs to the basement. I plodded upstairs to my bedroom.

The fireworks that Michael, Stuart, and I intended to deploy that night were stored in my bedroom closet. Standing in front of the open closet, I looked down and surveyed the cache of fireworks, which included black cats, boomers, ground spinners, roman candles, smoke bombs, and sparklers. Mingled with the fireworks were several bottles of white-out correction fluid, which worked very well in conjunction with the boomers. When a boomer was inserted into the narrow mouth of a bottle, the gooey, thick substance allowed the it to sit upright, while the wick just barely teetered over the rim. When a boomer was ignited inside a white-out bottle, the explosion created an abstract, unfocused white tableau, which was most clearly appreciated when a bottle was exploded while sitting upright on top of a level, smooth surface. Three-ring binders were perfect for this. We thought we were making art.

I was listening to the radio while sitting upright on my bed with my back leaning against the headboard when the impulse entered my body and mind for the second time. When I reached out with my left hand and turned down the volume on the radio, the static that cluttered the earlier transmission faded away. I could hear the voice clearly.

"Join us," the voice said.

When I turned the volume back up, the transmission withered and then disappeared.

At just after four thirty, I went back downstairs and waited in the living room for my father, a financial planner, who usually arrived home approximately twenty minutes past five o'clock.

My mother, who was one of the top-producing real estate agents in the Tri-Cities, the region that encompassed Coquitlam, Port Moody, and Port Coquitlam, arrived home around quarter to six. After quickly changing her clothes, she entered the kitchen and hastily assembled that night's dinner, which consisted of barbecued chicken, salad, and wild rice.

After dinner, Chad walked upstairs to his room. When he came back downstairs, he was dressed as a pirate. I stepped out of the living room and met him in the hallway as he was putting on his shoes.

"Are you feeling okay?" I asked him.

"I'm fine," he said.

"You seemed upset about something when I came home."

"I just had a rough day at school," he said, flashing an apologetic smile. "Hey, are you going out tonight?"

I nodded and pointed upstairs. "I've got the fireworks," I said.

"Have fun," he said, reaching for the front door. "I'll see you later."

Then he was gone.

I returned to the living room and waited for the opening wave of trick-or-treaters. It was just after six o'clock. As usual, my parents had bought enough candy to accommodate ten Halloweens in College Park. The opening half hour brought twenty or so trick-or-treaters, and the interactions I had with them were fleeting and uneventful; I was quietly ecstatic about this.

This peace lasted until around quarter to seven. My parents and I were in the living room when we heard a fist slam against the front door with unreasonable force.

"Is the overhead light on?" my father asked me.

"It's not dark enough to turn on the overhead light," I said. "The doorbell is plainly visible."

Then, several fists pounded on the door in unison and someone kicked the door.

"I'll deal with this," my father vowed.

I formed a blockade in front of my father with my chest and hands, shaking my head. "I'll take care of it," I said.

After nudging my father backward toward the living room, I turned and raced toward the front door. When I ripped open the front door, I saw Skull Boy. "Trick-or-treat," he said. Dracula and Spider-Man were standing behind him.

With my right hand, I reached out and grabbed onto Skull Boy's mask. He grunted and shrieked, furiously twisting his body to free himself from my grip. Then he started raking, scratching my right hand with his long, sharpened fingernails. When I attempted to yank the mask off of Skull Boy's face, which was my primary objective, the latex mask became quite sticky, which stalled my progress. Skull Boy's nostrils were just barely visible to me when he broke free of my grip. After pulling the mask back down around his head, he unsheathed his scimitar, which wasn't nearly as realistic-looking as the one I'd seen earlier. This one was made of sturdy plastic.

I seized Skull Boy's right wrist with my left hand, and then I curled my right arm around his right elbow, which I then flexed. Dracula and Spider-Man stood in place, breathing heavily, glaring at me. I heard a growl of pain from within the skull mask. When I gave Skull Boy's right arm another slight twist, I felt his grip on the sword loosen. When it fell to the ground, I kicked him in the stomach. Then, I calmly reached down and picked up the toy sword.

"If I see any of you around here again, I'll kill you— you hear me?" I said, extending the sword. "Get out of here now!"

They ran away. With my toes extended over the edge of the doorsill, looking diagonally to my left, I saw them move downhill until they were out of sight.

Before I locked the front door and turned off all of the lights in the house, I met identical twin girls, both dressed as matching witches. They looked like they were five or six years old. Before I gave them candy, I looked around for their parents, who were nowhere in sight. "Where are your parents?" I asked the twins in a concerned tone. Standing at the front door, I didn't see anyone in the neighborhood who looked to be older than sixteen.

I reached into my left pocket and pulled out my outdated flip cell phone, which was the only portable electronic device I owned in 2018. "You're too small to be out alone," I said to the girls, holding out the phone. "Do your parents know where you are? Are you lost? Do you want me to call someone?"

"We're not alone," one of the girls said, pointing uphill, toward a huddle of trick-or-treaters. I gave them each two pieces of candy, which I dropped, from high over their heads, straight down into their gaping bags. "Thank you," they said simultaneously. Then they turned their backs to me and walked away. It was nearly quarter to eight.

When I looked up and down the hill, I saw an unusually large number of trick-or-treaters roaming the streets—but none of them were trick-or-treating. None of them were holding bags anymore; they were congregating.

They were clustered according to age. There were three or four of them, more or less, in every group I spotted. There had to be at least thirty trick-or-treaters in all, which meant that there could have been at least forty or fifty more of them throughout the rest of College Park. I imagined hundreds and thousands of them.

They sauntered through the byzantine maze of cul-de-sacs and side streets that coursed through College Park's veins. Then they merged into a single group. When they did this, they looked like disparate puddles of blood or oil being sucked together by a ghostly force to form a central mass.

After I closed the door and turned off the lights, I dumped the remaining candy into the refrigerator and then joined my parents in the living room. "Are you going out with Michael and Stuart tonight?" my father asked me, just as he rose from his chair.

I'd almost forgotten about Michael, Stuart, and the fireworks that were stashed in my bedroom closet. "Maybe I should stay home tonight," I said.

"You're not worried about the curfew, are you?" my mother asked me.

"I'll pay the fine," my father assured me before he headed upstairs to bed. "It would be worth it just to expose what a stupid law that is. I can't believe someone hasn't challenged it in court already."

I followed my father upstairs and entered my bedroom, where I retrieved the fireworks, which I deposited into a gym bag. When the eight o'clock hour arrived, when the curfew went into effect, I was standing in the kitchen, facing the front of the house and watching the streets, which were clogged with trick-or-treaters.

They overran College Park. But this uprising wasn't limited to College Park or the other residential neighborhoods in Port Moody—this was happening all over the world. The sounds of anarchy erupted throughout College Park. I heard car alarms, glass breaking, police sirens…

And screaming.

There were too many screams to count. They blended into a bizarre symphony of mayhem. The only interruption in the screaming was that created by gunfire.

I saw one of the trick-or-treaters, a teenage girl, holding a Glock semi-automatic pistol, which was the standard-issue sidearm for Port Moody's police officers. I watched as the trick-or-treaters swarmed and murdered a police officer and then commandeered that officer's car. As I'd feared, Port Moody's police department proved to be completely ineffectual against the trick-or-treaters. None of the police officers or residents could bring themselves to hurt the children, much less kill them. This is the main reason why the trick-or-treaters won.

I felt the impulse again. "Nothing can stop us," the wraithlike voice whispered to me. "There's nowhere to hide. We know where you are."

I looked all around me. I was still in the kitchen, facing the front of the house. Light rain was falling outside. It was just after eight o'clock, and College Park was dark and still. The gym bag containing the fireworks had fallen out of my right hand, which was now clutching a knife.

I heard my father walk downstairs. As he glanced in my direction, on his way into the kitchen, it was obvious that nothing I'd experienced had registered with him.

He poured a glass of milk and then walked upstairs, where I heard my parents watching television in the master bedroom. A few minutes later, Michael's car pulled into the driveway.

I couldn't hear or see any trick-or-treaters as I exited the house and walked toward Michael's car. It felt, and looked, like there had been a power outage in College Park. All of the houses looked like tombstones—I couldn't even detect the presence of any candles or lanterns—the streets were black and desolate.

I thought about Matt Johnson.

When Michael's car reached the bottom of College Park, he made a left turn and drove past the main entrance to the Evergreens, following a gradually-sloping hill to the edge of Seaview Elementary School. He turned right and entered the school's parking lot, which sat adjacent to a lumpy, uneven lawn.

Although the lawn, which was too choppy and small to be called a field, couldn't have been more than twelve yards long, it was home to many thrilling recess and lunch-hour football and soccer games during our primary years, between kindergarten and the third grade. I opened the gym bag and deposited the fireworks onto the center of the lawn. Then Michael, Stuart, and I formed a circle around the pile, surrounded by the Evergreens and the Woodlands, the parking lot and the school's frontmost buildings.

As we started igniting the fireworks, I slowly began to relax. I recalled the joy I'd previously derived from being scared. I started laughing. I grabbed a lit roman candle with both of my hands and gleefully aimed the blazing balls toward the sky. It took us approximately forty minutes to work our way through all of the fireworks. The only time we paused was when we heard a police siren, which quickly faded away. We were watching a ground spinner change colors on the grass when a shuttle bus rushed past the school entrance, headed toward College Park.

After setting off the fireworks, we drove across the street to the Woodlands. We stealthily crept into Michael's basement, where we munched on candy and watched a horror film.

As the film neared its conclusion, Stuart gave me a nudge. "I heard a voice earlier," he said, staring directly at me.

"Very funny," I said.

"No," he blurted. "It happened after I got home. It felt and sounded like someone was inside my head. Do you remember those horrible migraines I had when I was younger?"

"Of course," I said. "You missed at least five days of school every year because of them."

"This was like one of those multiplied by ten," Stuart said. "It almost knocked me out. I had to go upstairs to my room."

Michael's eyes moved back and forth between us, like he was watching Stuart and I play tennis.

"Did it command you to do anything?" I asked Stuart.

"Join us," he said. "Kill."

"Kill?" I asked Stuart, who laughed before he weakly nodded.

"Then it went away," said Stuart. "I feel fine now."

"You're both fucking joking, *right*?" Michael asked us.

"That's what happened to me at school in second block," I said. "That's what happened to Matt Johnson."

"I didn't talk back to him," Stuart said, giggling slightly. "There's nothing wrong with hearing voices, as long as you don't talk back to them, right?"

"Him," I whispered.

It was just past eleven thirty when we left Michael's basement. On the way back to Michael's car, Michael and I said goodbye to Stuart, who was only about two blocks away from his home in the Evergreens.

Then Michael drove me home. When I stepped through the front door of 333 Princeton Avenue, I was greeted by total silence. I'd just removed my shoes when the impulse reentered me.

"I'm upstairs," the voice said. "I've been waiting for you."

I ran upstairs. I paused at the top of the stairs, facing the darkened bathroom, listening to the maddening drip of the leaky shower faucet. A streak of blood slithered across the bathroom doorway. The blood trail began inside the master bedroom and ended at the opposite end of the hall, in front of Chad's room.

I slowly turned to my left and stared at the master bedroom door, which had been left ajar. When I entered the master bedroom, I almost stepped over my mother's back. She was lying face down on the carpet, positioned between the front left corner of the bed and the television. Her back and chest were riddled with stab wounds and her throat had been slashed from ear to ear.

My father was on the bed, lying flat on his back, facing the ceiling. I barely noticed his multiple stab wounds. His eyes had been carved out of the sockets.

I heard movement down the hall.

When I ran out of the bedroom, I saw Chad, who stepped out of his room. His pirate costume, which was covered with blood and viscera, was hanging off of him. He was chewing on one of our father's eyeballs. "This is the best Halloween candy," he said after swallowing.

Then he held up the other eyeball, which was inside a homemade candy wrapper, and he flung it at me. It bounced off of my chest and fell to the floor. "Join me," he said.

Masks

David Garrote and Jean Cleaver

ANDREW:

Halloween is more Irish than St. Patrick's Day: the holiday evolved from the Celtic festival of Samhain, when, according to popular beliefs, ghosts wandered the land and humans left treats out to appease them, lest an irate, or at least ravenous, spirit visit their abodes. I'm a 20-something, third-generation Irish-American, which means that while my grandparents appreciated Saint Patrick for his fourth-century holy crusade against our pagan ancestors' polytheistic ways, I view March 17th as an excuse to wear green while knocking back more than my share of Tullamore Dew.

Halloween, however—*that* is a holiday for which I show reverence, because it's the one evening on earth when I feel normal. Sure, there are the horror conventions and comic-cons, where people—*my* people—gather and display their best cosplay and FX makeup, but no matter how flawless my design and execution, I always feel slightly self-conscious wandering about an indoor stadium, weaving past the vendor booths and for-fee photo-ops, the fluorescent lights glaring down on my wig and melting my face paint and liquid adhesive. There are festivals in almost every culture that embrace the custom of wearing costumes. For the Jews, there's Purim. For the Brazilians, it's Festa Junina. At the Cheung Chau Bun Festival in Hong Kong, participants dress up as divine beings and scale towers. If I were independently wealthy and could do anything for the rest of my life, I'd roam the earth, visiting each nook and cranny of the world as the day of its costume celebration was held. I could be someone else, some*thing* else, every twenty-four hours. Until that opportunity materializes, however, I will savor each and every October 31ˢᵗ.

I thought I was alone in my obsession until I stumbled upon Cybil in a horror chat room at the end of September. It all began in a group thread on independent horror films. Truth be told, I had just come home after a few drinks with my office mates and I was feeling particularly emboldened with liquid courage, and besides, horror flicks happen to be a subject area about which I am an expert. Monday morning quarterbacking, my commentary bordered on the obnoxious level at some points, but it never deterred Cybil: I would come to learn that she could give it back with twice the intensity that I did, and more than anything, that quality was what drew me to her.

Dr.Decker'sZipperMask: Found footage screenplays are crap. Show me one that doesn't make me wonder why the fuck a person feels the need to turn on a camera before they turn on a light or maybe even put on a piece of clothing, and I'll eat my words

KissMyAshleyWilliams: *Blair Witch* was a novel idea for its time. Anything that is completed half-assed is of course not going to measure up. Plus, the trick's been over-performed. That's why it seems tired to you.

Cloverfield888: Wha??! You're dissing my jam, dude

HorrorSlut95: Sometimes it's done well, sometimes it's not. It doesn't mean the whole screenplay is crap. You gotta suspend your disbelief to think that someone is going to turn on their camera, <u>then</u> turn on their bedroom light in order to buy into *Hell House, LLC*, but that doesn't mean it wasn't awesome.

TravisThe Man: *The Poughkeepsie Tapes*. Classic.

Dr.Decker'sZipperMask: It's the lazy-man's screenplay cheat. You don't have to give any exposition to lead into the scare.

HorrorSlut95: I get it. Not a very Cronenberg-y thing to do. LOL— I like your screen name ;) Don't force me to interrogate you or I'll wrap a string of Christmas lights around your arms bahaha

Dr.Decker'sZipperMask: "Say it! Say it! ...Then, don't say it." Haha

TravisThe Man: Cronenberg's the man. *Rabid*! Gotta respect making Marilyn Chambers a blood-thirsty zombie.

KissMyAshleyWilliams: *The Dead Zone* is my favorite Cronenberg. Classic Walken.

HorrorSlut95: "The ice is gonna break!"
Dr.Decker's ZipperMask likes this.

TravisThe Man: Don't even get me started on *The Fly*.

Cloverfield888: I thought we were talking about found footage films?

CYBIL:

It was *my* fantasy world that *no on*e knew about. My online persona that I only slipped into after ten at night, when the housework was done, the kids were sleeping, and the husband was snoring. I pulled out my laptop, opened my secret page and logged into the horror chat boards. It was nice to have a secret and little something of my own, when in my daily life I couldn't even take a crap or shower without a child asking me questions or wanting to just hang out; I needed my own time. While I never did anything wrong, besides use foul language and vague sexual suggestions now and then, I never felt guilty as no one really knew who I was, and I never took anything I did outside of my laptop… at first.

Four glasses of wine and being turned down for sex by husband one night resulted in my screen name, *HorrorSlut95.* I felt unwanted, unloved, and under-appreciated in my real world, so online, I wanted to be a sexy vixen that everyone wanted and feared. Not someone you yelled for when you wanted another drink or couldn't find the remote. The chat room allowed me to make "friends" and vent in ways I couldn't in my real life. I say friends in quotes because I'm not a fool: I know the people online are doing the same thing as me. Travis The Man is probably some overweight unemployed twenty-year-old living with his mom; Cloverfield888 is likely a lonely, plain-looking girl in Idaho who has an eating disorder. The point is, I didn't care who or what they were in real life: I just cared about what we talked about and who we were in our chats, because they gave me something to look forward to every day.

Horror was a love of mine from an early age. My father, who was a stupid drunk but the most lovable guy you ever knew, took me to see *The Fly* with Jeff Goldblum when I was eight years old, in the theater. I don't know if he was an idiot and thought it was a kid's movie or if he just thought I was mature enough for my age. Regardless, I was petrified, but fascinated. The rest of my youth and teen years, I watched every horror movie I could, but I was smarter than my father. I knew that a "girl" who liked horror was frowned upon, at least back then, so I watched most alone. God, I wish I were a teen now: horror is so much more accepted. In the eighties, girls only went to see a scary flick to hold onto their boyfriends who pretended not to be scared themselves. Now, with conventions and countless television shows, it's a whole new ballgame. I'm a bit open now that I *like* horror movies, but I'm the only one in the house that does; my husband thinks they are stupid and mindless and the kids are too little to attempt showing them one.

In my real life, I'm simply alone in my love.

It was around four or five months of logging on almost every night when I started to notice that Dr.Decker'sZipperMask's posts intrigued me more than the others. We started to talk directly to each other and ignore the rest of the chatters on the boards. It wasn't long before we started direct messaging each other and having full out conversations: always, always about horror. I was relieved and disappointed that he never once asked me about my personal life. I knew I would desperately keep my life secret, but at the same time, I wanted him to know me and I wanted to know the real him. However, I was smart enough to not be delusional—the person on the other end of the screenname could be anyone and anything—but part of me didn't care.

It wasn't until we started talking about our shared obsession with Halloween that things started to get... personal. I never heard a single person talk so beautifully and passionately about the season and it simply melted my bored, neglected heart. The night of our first "Halloween Roundtable" as we called it, we stayed up messaging each other until almost four in the morning and when I went to bed, knowing the kids would be jumping on me in less than two hours, I knew, without a doubt, that something would happen with Dr.Decker'sZipperMask that would change my life forever. What scared me, or more so excited me, was that I didn't know if it would be good or bad.

ANDREW:

Halloween used to be called Cabbage Night, at least in New England. The name stems from an old Scottish tradition of young maids reading the stumps of cabbages like tea leaves in an attempt to predict what life with their husbands would be like. Somehow, this tradition morphed into tossing raw and rotten vegetables, including cabbage, at their neighbor's abodes. Now Cabbage Night is the evening before Halloween. I never partook in the whole vegetable vandalism thing: for me, the holiday is less about the tricks or treats and more about celebrating the dark side present in all of us. That, and the freedom either to become someone else for an evening— or to reveal one's true face.

Dr.Decker'sZipperMask: *Session 9* was filmed in my hometown. I'm just north of Boston, on the shore. They used a real abandoned mental hospital for the shoot. I was pretty young when they shot it, so I don't remember, but my older brother tells me he skulked around the outskirts of the set for a few days.

HorrorSlut95: Well, Brad Anderson is from my state... coincidence?! ((Ominous music plays)) LOL He's from the south shore, though: I'm closer to the Massachusetts border, near Springfield. If my eerily accurate knowledge of horror movies is correct, *Home Before Dark* was shot at that same hospital. Old flick. Creepy but good.

Dr.Decker'sZipperMask: Really? That means we're only a few hours away.

And yes, that spontaneous knowledge of such a tangential film IS eerie. Haha

HorrorSlut95: You love it!

Dr.Decker'sZipperMask: yeah, true

HorrorSlut95: So, tell me about the origins of this handle. I know *Nightbreed*, I know Clive Barker. Why the Decker character?

Dr.Decker'sZipperMask: Well, like I've said in the past, it's David Cronenberg, first and foremost. But more than that, that character—he's such a sociopath. His whole quest to kill monsters when he himself is a monster is delicious irony. Plus, we all wear masks metaphorically, don't we? It just happens that the real him is revealed when he puts ON a physical mask. I like that twist.

HorrorSlut95: Yeah, I can see that. I'm more of a *Hellraiser* fan myself.

Dr.Decker'sZipperMask: There's this ongoing theme of being an outcast and the outcast finding his tribe... everyone wants to be part of something, to feel like they're not alone, don't they? I mean, we joined a chat room to be with people just like ourselves. It's not so different.

HorrorSlut95: I wonder if there's a chat room for serial killers. What they would chat about? Like, "Man, I had this chick tied up in my basement the other day, and I ran out of magazines to cut letters out of for my manifesto to the cops, so I made a quick run to the Circle K to buy a few, and wouldn't you know it? She freed herself and escaped!" "Been there: sucks to be you, dude" LMAO

Dr.Decker'sZipperMask: Wait a minute—this *isn't* the subreddit for serial killers? Uh… whoops! Hahaha

I didn't know Cybil's name in the beginning. In the beginning, she was simply a screen name. Then, I found myself thinking of her in my daily life. Something would happen and I'd think to myself, I gotta tell *her* about that. Or, *she* would get such a kick out of that. I had no idea what she looked like; I had no idea what her life was like when she wasn't online with me. Did she have a boyfriend? Was she my age or even a woman? I had to admit, I was developing a weird crush on her—at least, on the persona she wore when she chatted with me each night—and began to neglect real-life, flesh and blood dating opportunities.

I grew up in Danvers, Mass, and although I work in Boston, I moved into a cozy one-bedroom apartment five blocks from my parents' house. Back in the 1700s, Danvers was part of what is now known as Salem—yes, *THAT* Salem. The closer the calendar ticks to Halloween, the crazier it gets around this neck of the woods. People say that the population doubles in Salem on Halloween, and that only counts the living attendees. The museums, the shops, the restaurants: they are mobbed on that night, and the cobblestone streets of downtown are jammed with tourists like Bourbon Street on Fat Tuesday. That gave me an idea. One evening, as October ground slowly to a close, I logged in early, eager to ask HorrorSlut95 my question before I lost my nerve completely. I stalled, and it wasn't until we were rounding the time when traditionally, both of us had to sign off and get some shut eye that I forced myself to make the leap.

Dr.Decker'sZipperMask: So, any plans for the big night?

HorrorSlut95: Meh. I usually have a costume party to go to, but this year, nothing seems to be going on. I'm bummed. What about you?

Dr.Decker'sZipperMask: Well, Salem is one big Mardi Gras come Halloween: it seems like a billion people are here. A lot of revelers like us. Ever been?

HorrorSlut95: I've been to Salem—I mean, I've been to the museums and stuff, during the day in the summer. My family stopped there once on our way up to New Hampshire for vacation. But no, I've never been on the big night. It must be amazing!

Dr.Decker'sZipperMask: Why don't you come up this year?

There was an awkward pause from her end of the screen. I convinced myself that her cat had just fallen off the bed, or maybe her phone rang and she got distracted—but I knew it was likely hesitation at the possibility of meeting in person.

But then, she responded.

HorrorSlut95: What time were you thinking?

Dr.Decker'sZipperMask: hmm... IDK, maybe 8, 7 o'clock? I know that's early, but if you have to drive all this way—

HorrorSlut95: 7 it is then.

CYBIL:

At first it was an escape. Then it became a routine. Then a need. The chats with Dr. Decker became something I had to have each night. The few, very rare, times he was not on or I couldn't log in because of a child puking, I felt like I missed a meal. I was starving for the attention and the next night I would have to pretend to not be too eager, but I'd always stay on longer than normal. What was a need became an obsession, and what became an obsession was about to become a reality after Dr. Decker revealed to me his real name: Andrew. We still stayed away from last names and we both refused to discuss ages or share pictures, but having names to call each other, real names—or at least we thought—changed my little night time game into something… personal.

When I found out that Andrew lived only a few hours away, my heart skipped a beat so hard I had to take a breath and pause. I had never felt such a literal "skipped a beat" feeling like that. Not even when my husband asked me to marry him. I spent two solid says thinking about why that was. Why was it that some stranger, who I really knew nothing about, could make my heart sink and flutter more than the man I longed to marry for three solid years of our courtship? It bothered me for a while, but then I allowed myself to enjoy the feeling and to realize that maybe my entire life was a sham. The house, the husband, the kids, and my pointless job that I did simply to get out of the house—all of it was for show for the rest of the world to see, so they would *not* see the real me. It was a performance that, unbeknownst to me, I was acting in my entire life.

HorrorSlut95 was the real me—what I wanted to do with Andrew, those were my real desires. Not that bullshit book club I ran or the PTA meetings I took minutes for: those were all part of the act. The real Cybil, she wanted to be dark and dirty, mean and cruel, wild and scary. Andrew was going to let that side out of me. While I had never been too much of a sexual person—which resulted in countless complaints from my husband—the thought of Andrew suddenly awakened my body. I felt more aware and aroused at everything in the world. When I made "love" to my husband (on Tuesday nights only at 9:45 for seven minutes), I actually enjoyed it as I thought of Andrew. My husband even noticed and got so excited at my found interested in sex that he actually tried to have unscheduled sex with me, which I turned down.

If he only knew what I was really thinking about…

Asking to meet Andrew never occurred to me, mostly because I didn't want to ruin the fun I was having by having some awkward meeting at Starbucks with a fat, badly complexioned twenty-five-year-old who couldn't talk to me the same way in person. I didn't want to lose what I had online; the fantasy life I was living was enough to appease the dark side of me—for a while. But when Andrew asked to meet me, that "skipped a beat" feeling was ten-fold and my entire body felt electric tingles through every inch, so much so I couldn't even respond until my body eased out of its adrenaline high. While it would be hard to make an excuse to disappear a full night from the family, especially on a holiday where I was in charge of the costumes and trick-or-treating routes, I didn't care. I instantly said yes and started to make some plans. The only question was, what was I going to do with Andrew—and could I get away with it?

ANDREW:

Although Valentine's Day is the holiday people most closely associate with romance, Halloween was once the night pagan Celts would play fortune-telling games, believing that the evening's magic could reveal future mates and potential spouses. Even the tradition of bobbing for apples stems from a nuptial prophesy: it was thought that the first person to bite an apple would be the next in line at the chapel to wed.

HorrorSlut95: So... where shall we meet? And how will we know each other?

Dr.Decker'sZipperMask: Let's say outside of the Witch Dungeon Museum. There are stocks in front of the building—how about there?

I paused. I had been torn about what cosplay to display this year. My initial instinct was to go with my tried and true standby: Jigsaw from the *Saw* movies, but that would require wearing the Styrofoam head I'd created, and I wanted to meet Cybil face-to-face, not face-to-two inches of plastic. Then I realized: the answer was right in front of me.

Dr.Decker'sZipperMask: ...and I'll be wearing a costume that expresses the very essence of my soul. You'll have to try to figure out what that means, but after six months on this site, I suspect that you know me well enough to pick me and my costume out of a crowd. What about you? Will you be in costume, or will you be Cybil? Or HorrorSlut95?

HorrorSlut95: Hmmm. If you know ME as well as you think you do, or know my persona at least, you'll spot me right away, no matter how I'm dressed. But yeah, I'll be attired for the occasion. ;)

Dr.Decker'sZipperMask: Okay. Four days away. It's a date, or, a meeting, or, a face-to-face... or, a?

HorrorSlut95: ... a culmination of a long anticipation?

Dr.Decker'sZipperMask: I like that. Very poetic. "A culmination of a long anticipation."

We signed off for the evening, my heart still racing long after my phone was attached to the charging station and my mind racing circles around my head. What would happen when we met? Would it be awkward? Would she want to sit and talk in person? I hoped not. I was always a quicker thinker, a smoother talker, online than I was face-to-face. Would she mind walking, seeing the sights? I considered the layout of Salem in my memory; from the museum, we could walk up Federal Street and up St. Peter, maybe hit the Bit Bar for a few drinks, or maybe... even better, we could sneak into Howard Street Cemetery, maybe scare up a spirit or two. They say that Howard Street was where Giles Corey, killed during the Salem Witch Hysteria, died. He refused to answer *yea* or *nay* to the charges of witchcraft leveled against him, and so he suffered a death worse than hanging: he was pressed—crushed by heavier and heavier weight—until his body collapsed. I always thought that was tough as shit, refusing to respond to an accusation even as one's internal organs forcefully fused together like clay in a Play-Doh Fun Factory machine.

Yeah... that sounded like just the excursion to pursue with a Horror Slut.

I dragged the long storage boxes out from under my bed and rifled through the one I knew held the mask I was looking for. When my hands grazed its rough, burlap surface, I pulled it slowly from its resting spot, held it in front of me, and slid it over my head, aligning the tiny eye-holes to my field of vision. It still fit like a glove: I had gotten to be a top-notch sewing champ over the years. The grey woolen gloves and my

347

Old Hickory seven-inch butcher knife lay neatly on the left side of the storage box, and I grabbed them and stood for a moment, trying to remember where I had hung my black trench coat.

It was nearly one in the morning. I had to get up for work in five hours, but I knew I'd be too excited to sleep. Cybil was right: Halloween would be the culmination of a long time of anticipation. I could hardly wait.

CYBIL:

What does one choose to wear for a first impression and really... for their coming out? Its more than nerve-racking. Part of me wants to dress as one of my favorite killers, but at the same time, I think it's important to... be myself, for the first time ever. It was only four days away, not only did I have to decide on the costume, I also had to make it. This anxiety almost took over the constant wash of excitement I was feeling. The excitement was so evident, even the kids noticed that "Mommy was nice." I pushed aside the fact that their statement meant I was normally a bitch.

Three days before the big meet I was going grocery shopping alone—which in itself was a treat to not have to deal with the kids grabbing various items and causing trouble—when inspiration hit me in the cleaning aisle. It was something about the yellow rubber gloves that made all the gears click together. That night, after spending two hundred dollars and running to seven different stores to find all the stuff I needed, I started to put together my costume. It wasn't from a movie, it was an original idea—it was the *true* me.

That night, after getting the kids to bed and the husband was snoring, I logged on and told Andrew that I couldn't talk that night, that I had to prepare for our meeting.

He found this intriguing, but begged me to stay online with him, I did for another hour, but then abruptly told him if he wanted the best night of his life, then he had to let me go and get my costume ready. He was stern and no matter how many hints he asked for, I told him nothing, wished him a good night and then logged off.

A few minutes later I was our garage attic, it was the most private place I could find in our house. On the computer, I could hide my actions by pulling up another screen, but getting into a full costume, one that would horrify the kids and confuse the fuck out of the husband, I had to be sure no one would walk in one me. It took three trips to bring all my items up with me and to spread out a sheet on the floor so I wouldn't get splinters and set up folding chair to sit on. Thankfully, my Mother's old dressing mirror was in storage up there, so I had something to model my ideas in front of.

Over the next four hours, I cut, sewed and tried things on, over and over again, until I was happy with what I had made. It was bizarre, sexy and most importantly—scary. The concept was to confuse a man, to make him think, *oh shit*, look at her, but then to take in the entire thing and say, "…shit, that's fucked up." I've never considered myself sexy and only once in my life had I worn anything as revealing, and that was in the privacy of my own bedroom. I've always been overly conservative in the dressing department. This costume was not me—or to be more correct, this costume, really *was* me.

Standing in the mirror, I felt a sense of joy and excitement that I had never felt before rush through my body. I started to move differently, I started to talk in a voice I didn't recognize. As I caught a glimpse of my green eye through the mask in the mirror, I froze. All the rules and morals I had so carefully followed my whole life jumped out and screamed at me to *cut it out*, to *stop what I was doing*, to *put this away* and *go back to bed with your husband.* I took off the mask and looked at my face—I wanted to throw up.

I was instantly ashamed and thought I wouldn't go through with this night, I couldn't.

As I dropped my head in shame, I caught a glimpse of how sexy my legs looked, I had never thought of them as sexy. I looked in the mirror and saw the skin of my tits—of course I had seen them my whole life, but I had never seen them pushed up and standing for their own attention like this, I got slightly aroused—at myself. Then, then I saw the knife in my hand, it was shiny and so goddamn beautiful…

The real me came back out again.

I took two steps towards the mirror, slid the mask back on my face and screamed, "*Fuck You!*" into the mirror. Without even thinking, the knife went up and shattered the glass. As the shards fell to the floor, I didn't even worry about waking anyone up—Mommy was dead. Oh, she might play the part to keep up appearances, but she was no longer in charge. The real me was here now, and it was going to use Halloween as its coming out party.

And Andrew… he was the oblation who was going to set me free.

ANDREW:

There is an ancient Irish folktale that goes like this:

Jack was a frugal man, even when he was out having a few pints with his mates. One evening, he took to the drink with the Devil himself. Ever the spendthrift, Jack talked his new drinking buddy into turning himself into a coin: that way, the two could pay for their rounds at the pub without Jack having to dig into his own wallet. However, once the Devil transformed himself, Jack scooped him up and placed the coin in his pocket alongside a silver cross that would prohibit the demon from changing back into his real form. Realizing he was trapped, the Devil agreed not to seek revenge for at least a year if Jack freed him from his imprisonment. Jack agreed, with the additional stipulation that the Devil could never claim his soul after he died.

When Jack finally passed away, even God didn't want such a devious spirit in heaven, and since the Devil had renounced any claim to him in hell, Jack was forced to wander the earth for eternity. He had only a piece of burning coal to light his way, so to make carriage easier, he snatched a turnip from a neighbor's garden, hollowed it out, and placed the lump inside to form a makeshift lantern. From that day forward, he was known as Jack of the Lantern, or Jack-o'-lantern, and local residents made a habit of carving frightening countenances into their root vegetables to scare away his cursed soul during harvest.

My grandfather told me that story when I was a kid, and it always stuck with me. Some say the moral of the story is that stinginess—monetary as well as emotional—leads to loneliness; in my opinion, it's that you should never box yourself into situations you can't wiggle out from.

I arrived at the Dungeon Museum a half hour early to stake out my vantage point. I didn't place my mask over my head until I was around the corner—although the burlap was relatively porous and easier to see through than cotton or latex, I still lost quite a bit of peripheral vision when wearing it, so I thought it safest to wait. I planted myself on a bench two building up, across the street. Crowds swarmed the attraction: soccer moms draped hands and heads in the wooden stocks for photo opportunities with their spouses; college kids puffed on vape pens and scratched the unkempt beards that peered out from under plastic masks and face

351

paint. Although I hadn't seen her approach, something in me knew it was Cybil when a striking young woman appeared suddenly from the side of the brick building.

She was wearing a fifties' baby doll mask that covered only the top half of her face, sort of like the one the girls wear in this slasher movie I saw in 2008 or 2009, which left her mouth in plain view. Strawberry blonde waves spilled out behind it and draped around her shoulders, which were bare save for the thin straps of apron that read *Killer Mother* in classic and elegant needle point style. Behind the apron, she only wore black panties with fishnet stockings, making her long, alabaster legs seem to glow in the twilight. Her combat boots seemed out of place but made a statement about how she could kick ass. The best part was the yellow rubber gloves that made her look like a mom about to do dishes—but on a darker side, a woman about to kill you and not leave prints. Slid gently behind the tight strap of her apron was a realistic-looking kitchen knife, shining in the soft street light.

I stood to get a better view. She was pretty—much more attractive than I could have hoped—and seemed younger than I had anticipated. Not taking my eyes from her, I walked soundlessly along the sidewalk and closer to the stocks. When we were less than ten feet from one another, she stopped and looked at me long and hard. Then, a sideways grin bloomed. She slowed her gait and seemed to slither as she approached me.

"Andrew," she said, more as a statement than a question. "The anticipation was worth it." She grabbed my hand, not to shake it, but to hold it in hers. "Where shall we go?" She entwined her fingers with mine.

Her body was so tiny, so fragile compared to mine. Her skin was smooth, like she had rolled naked on a silk sheet and had absorbed it like a sponge, and I had to steady my breath so that I didn't appear too anxious to get her alone. I had known I would be excited to meet her; I hadn't realized that my fantasy would begin to leak into my reality. There were so many people around us. I would have to wait until we were truly alone to do what I had planned.

"Cybil," I answered. "I'm so glad to meet you *at last*." I stroked the outside of her palm with my thumb. "Follow my lead."

We walked in silence for several minutes until we turned onto Federal Street. The sun was winking its last bit of brightness on the horizon, leaving our surroundings covered in dusky mood lighting. "Want to get a drink?" I asked finally. The Bit Bar was only a few blocks up, and I was torn. On one hand, a few drinks might loosen Cybil up a bit, make her more pliable. On the other, it would be loud in the bar, and likely jammed with people. I was unsure in which direction to push, but Cybil made the decision for me.

"Nah," she said. "I'm much more interested in seeing where Giles Corey died. You said you knew the way?"

I squeezed her hand and we quickened our pace. The Howard Street Cemetery was a tourist attraction, but eventually, it would empty, and its wide expanse and innumerable headstones meant enough sheltered open space to perform a number of covert activities. We passed the parking lot on the right and cut through an alleyway; in a matter of minutes, we were standing at the edge of the graveyard. Cybil squeezed my hand once and let go, and when she turned to look at me, I watched her mouth change.

CYBIL:

Standing at the entrance to the graveyard, I couldn't believe I was there: that I had tricked my family to thinking I was at an all-night horror movie marathon, that I actually got the nerve to go out in public dressed like this. Mostly though, I couldn't believe the moment—the moment I had unknowingly waited for my entire life—was here. Letting go of Andrew's hand, which was so warm and comforting, I spun around and looked him up and down before pursing my lips and blowing him a kiss. "We talked for six months. No more talking. Now, unzip your... zipper..." I said as seductively as I could and turned and ran away from him.

There were hordes of people, dressed in countless different costumes walking through the graveyard with lanterns, flashlights and glow sticks. Everyone was a bit scared and most, respectful of the dead. It was glorious, beautiful, and a sight that every true lover of the macabre should see. I had researched the graveyard online beforehand and had arrived early to scoped it out: I knew exactly where I was leading Andrew, the place where we would consummate our relationship. I ran at just enough speed to make him have jog behind me, but playfully enough to make him know it was a game and that he shouldn't catch me until I stopped.

In the furthest corner, behind two tall old oak trees, I pretended to trip and fall like a pathetic victim in a slasher film. Rolling me over onto my back, Andrew stood over me in full costume, breathing heavy with his mask still on. He pulled out a knife and showed it to me: he understood the game. The site of the zipper-faced man standing above me, the moonlight behind him, the sounds of children laughing and the setting of the gravestones, it was almost too much for my body to handle. I felt spasms of joy and anticipation fire through me so hard I could barely breathe and my hands trembled.

Andrew walked over me, but then nervously looked around the graveyard. "There are a lot of people here, we—we might get caught. If we do, you know it's counted as a lewd act; we could become registered sex offenders." His statement infuriated me. It was ruining my fantasy, but I needed him to play along, so I was going to have to be dirty. I licked my lips then reached down and started to hike up my apron. "Doctor—shut the fuck up and don't ruin this, or I will walk away, and you will never know, see, or hear from me again. Now get on your knees and come to me." Amazingly, it worked. He didn't even look around—he simply dropped to his knees and started to shuffle over to me. I spread my legs wide and he moved between them as he reached up to take off his mask. "Stop! The mask stays on," I said. He seemed disappointed by this, but then nodded and reached for his belt buckle, just as I reached for something else.

I've never met a woman who said losing their virginity was wonderful—it's almost always awkward, painful, and embarrassing to say the least. With Andrew, my first time, it was far from any of those things: it was pure, unadulterated ecstasy. The way my knife plunged into his throat so softly and smoothly, the confused panicky motions his arms made— I'm not ashamed to say I orgasmed--the first real, hard, full-body orgasm of my life--the second his hot blood spilled onto my thighs. As I pulled the knife out and stood up, I wanted to take his mask off to see his face writhing in pain, but I knew it would ruin my plan. I could do that with the *next* victim. The second, third, and fourth stabs—the chest, stomach and ribs— were just as good as the first: pure bliss, pure joy. It's hard to explain, but it was the first time in my entire damn life I felt like I truly existed.

The only hard part that night was moving him so he was propped against the tree. With the mask on, people thought he was a Halloween Prank all night. In truth, it wasn't until five the next night that the cops were called after the caretaker tried to move the "dummy." I stayed with Andrew's body for a solid fifteen minutes after he died. Two groups of kids walked by and I played up the scene, pretending to stab the body some more. I even said stupid lines like, "You're next!" Kids screamed and laughed and ran away. After I made certain he was completely dead, I cut off his right thumb, took his phone and wallet, and walked away. I spent the next three hours walking around Salem, enjoying the festivities and scaring people with my "realistic" looking blood. It was hands-down the best night of my life.

On the way home, I was still on a high, but mostly because I knew this was the first of many, many more kills to come. I pulled over at a rest stop on the Massachusetts turnpike, used Andrew's thumb to open his phone and delete all evidence of his contact with me—including his entire account for the chat rooms. I tossed his thumb in the woods for the animals and smashed his phone before cleaning up in the bathroom and getting out of my costume. I was home by three in the morning.

The next day, my family didn't even ask me how the movies were.

The following evening, I was back in the chat room; this time, with a new screen name: *KillerMommy7.* In less than ten minutes, I had started conversations with ten new men. I couldn't wait until I could add one of the men's licenses to Andrew's. It resides, safe and sound, in a small box in the attic above the garage—along with my rubber gloves, my apron, and of course, my mask.

About the Authors

JR Pepper is a photographer, lecturer, and writer. Her photography, most notably her recreational spirit photography, and lectures have been featured on Vice.com, and in *The Village Voice* and *Kotaku* as well as various volumes of the Chilean fanzine *Estrellita Mia*, *Haunted America FAQ*, and *Jack the Ripper FAQ*. She remains incredibly proud of her image restoration work with The Burns Archive and Morbid Anatomy Library. This is her first published story. She currently lives in New York near a cemetery with her lovely dog, a nervous guinea pig, and an evil rabbit named HP Buncraft. Her work can be seen at www.girlduality.com.

George Plank is the first and last in a series of failed cloning attempts and is the first person in his family to escape from the facility with an English degree. George is a comedian, author, and actor with an IMDB entry he's ashamed of. George's works have been heard on local radio and will be used as Exhibit C in his upcoming court trial. If you see a George in the wild, approach with caution: he is more scared of you than you are of him.

Jon Steffens is a Valuation Specialist of music and entertainment collectibles from Mesquite, Texas. He was a regular contributor to *Rue Morgue* magazine from 2014-2018 and has contributed to *The Overstreet Guide to Collecting Horror* and the Czech-American newspaper *Czech Slavnosti*. He enjoys collecting punk and hardcore CDs like it's still 1998 and getting wrecked at Brazilian Jiu-Jitsu class a couple times a week.

Neil May is a full-time Master Electrician with a flair for writing after hours. He is in the process of completing his first self-published novel, *Edin within the Woods*. Currently living in Alberta, Canada, he splits his spare time between family and writing his next novel. He enjoys music, reading, and playing guitar.

Nick Manzolillo's writing has appeared in over forty publications including *Wicked Haunted: An Anthology of the New England Horror Writers*, *Grievous Angel*, *Red Room* magazine, and the *Tales to Terrify* podcast. He has an MFA in Creative and Professional Writing from Western Connecticut State University. By day he works as a content specialist for TopBuzz, a news app. A native Rhode Islander, he currently lives in Manhattan where he spends what little free time he has growing a beard. You can follow his publications at: nickmanzolillo.com

Ian McDowell is the author of the novels *Mordred's Curse* and *Merlin's Gift*. His fiction has appeared in *Asimov's Science Fiction*, *Fantasy & Science Fiction*, *Weird Tales*, *Cemetery Dance* and the anthologies *Love in Vein, the Year's Best Horror* and the Science Fiction Book Club's *Best Short Novels 2005*. He grew up in Fayetteville, NC, where future actor and make-up artist Tom Savini was his neighbor. Ian currently lives in Greensboro, NC, where his journalism about the region's real Civil War history as a hotbed of resistance to the Confederacy has earned him threats from militant proponents of "Southern Heritage."

Michael Gore is a New England mortician by day and secretive writer by night. The author of two twisted short story collections, *Tales from a Mortician* and *Skeletons in the Attic: More Tales from a Mortician.*

Lewis Crane is an English student and radio show host at the University of Aberdeen in Scotland. "Home" is Lewis's first published piece and the first horror piece written by him. He has a passion for writing and literature and hosts a radio show called *By the Lamplight* on the Aberdeen Student Radio which looks at and analyzes the poetry and prose of the past and present. Literary inspirations include the works of H.G. Wells, Stephen King, and Carson McCullers as well as the poetry of Robert Frost.

Ken Stephenson is full-time Commissioning Engineer that travels all over the country and a part time writer who lives in Clearfield, PA with his wife of 26 years and two beautiful daughters. He posts regularly to Reddit/nosleep. He enjoys golf, video games (XBOX), and all things horror. This is his first published work but not his last.

Rebecca Rowland is a former torture artist of adolescents (high school English teacher) turned-librarian-slash-copy-editor-slash-freelance-writer who has lived in just about every northern suburb of Boston but would really love to settle down in Savannah, Georgia to absorb Flannery O'Connor's soul. As a follow-up to her ghostwritten memoir of a former victims' rights advocate for another publishing house, her first collection of short stories, *The Horrors Hiding in Plain Sight*, will be released by AMInk in the fall of 2018. This is her first assignment as a collection editor but she hopes it will not be her last.

J. Tonzelli is a novelist, storyist, and film critic who currently resides in the woods of rural South Jersey. He has previously written the anthology *The End of Summer: Thirteen Tales of Halloween* and co-writes the kid-friendly horror series "Fright Friends Adventures," which includes *The House on Creep Street* and *Beware the Monstrous Manther*! He likes goats, Halloween, abandoned buildings, and horror films—especially '80s slashers—anything involving ghosts, and everything by John Carpenter. You can read his cinema musings on CutPrintFilm.com and DailyGrindhouse.com or get updates and free fiction at JTonzelli.com.

Daniel Loubier lives on the Connecticut shore. He is responsible for *Dead Summit*, *Dead Summit: Containment*, *Those Among Us*, *Exorcising My Demons: An Actress' Journey to The Exorcist and Beyond*, many short stories, and two small children. His wife is also responsible for the children (but not the writing). Daniel's favorite time of year is Halloween season, and he is very proud to be included in this anthology. You can find out more about him on Amazon, www.danloubier.com, and by following @writerdad on Instagram. He also dabbles with Facebook but is trying to quit.

Michel Sabourin has previously written for *Scream* magazine and HorrorTalk.com. He lives in Richmond, Virginia with his wife and four children. He is a featured photographer, author, and a lover of the macabre.

Jacquelynn Gonzalez is a 16-year-old student who resides in Texas. She enjoys horror movies, writing, baking, and reading crime stories.

Alice La Roux is a Welsh author from a small town who is still trying to find her genre while dabbling in erotica, fantasy, and horror. She graduated from university with an MA in English Literature and a passion for telling tales. She owes her husband, best friend, and sister everything—without them, she wouldn't be writing.

Tyson Hanks is the author of multiple short stories that have been published in numerous collections, including the World War I horror anthology *Kneeling in the Silver Light* and *The Dark and Stormy Night*. His debut novel, *Greetings from Barker Marsh,* was published in 2016. Tyson is an Army veteran and currently lives in Florida, where he works as a freelance writer. You can follow Tyson at www.tysonhanks.com; Facebook: Author Tyson Hanks; and on Twitter: @TysonAuthor.

Danielle Bailey is an accomplished poet and author who was first published in grade school and is currently pursuing her career writing horror and suspense short stories. A former charter boat deckhand, she is influenced by heavy metal music and horror films. Her hobbies include photography, and being outside and on the ocean. She is a mother of two boys and lives with her husband in the beautiful Kenai, Alaska. You can find more about her on her website https://dray5032.wixsite.com/website.

Louis Stephenson is a writer and horror fanatic who resides in Liverpool, England. The first horror movie he ever saw was *A Nightmare on Elm Street*. His writing hero is Richard Laymon and his favorite book is *Endless Night*. He graduated from university with a degree in Film & TV Screenwriting and in his spare time, he likes to compose music, eat cheeseburgers and has volunteered his unprofessional opinion on the state of today's horror movies to one or two film review websites over the past few years. He is currently in the finishing stages of his first novella.

David Grove is the author of the books *Making Friday the 13th*, *Fantastic 4: The Making of the Movie*, *Jamie Lee Curtis: Scream Queen*, *On Location in Blairstown: The Making of Friday the 13th* and *Jan-Michael Vincent: Edge of Greatness*. His first novel, *The Yearbook*, was published in 2017. He's currently writing a book on the career and life of actor Bill Bixby.

David Garrote and Jean Cleaver are the pen names of a male-female writing team based in Massachusetts who, while happily attached to other people, bicker like an old married couple. Until *The Purge* becomes the law of the land, they will have to be content writing stories where one of them murders the other in a bizarre yet excruciatingly painful way. Both like cats and enjoy horror movies, pizza, and cheese.

For more books to kill for, visit

www.DarkInkBooks.com

Made in the USA
Columbia, SC
27 July 2018